ELLERY QUEEN

AMERICA'S MASTER STORYTELLER OF SUSPENSE AND MYSTERY

CAT OF MANY TAILS

By Ellery Queen
Published by Ballantine Books:

THE FOURTH SIDE OF THE TRIANGLE

DOUBLE, DOUBLE

THE PLAYER ON THE OTHER SIDE

AND ON THE EIGHTH DAY

CAT OF MANY TAILS

THE AMERICAN GUN MYSTERY

Cat of Many Tails

By Ellery Queen

BALLANTINE BOOKS • NEW YORK

ISBN 0-345-28292-2

Manufactured in the United States of America

First Edition: October 1975
Fourth Printing: November 1979

First Canadian Printing: November 1975

1

The strangling of Archibald Dudley Abernethy was the first scene in a nine-act tragedy whose locale was the City of New York.

Which misbehaved.

Seven and one-half persons inhabiting an area of over three hundred square miles lost their multiple heads all at once. The storm center of the phenomenon was Manhattan, that "Gotham" which, as the *New York Times* pointed out during the worst of it, had been inspired by a legendary English village whose inhabitants were noted for their foolishness. It was a not entirely happy allusion, for there was nothing jocular in the reality. The panic seizure caused far more fatalities than the Cat; there were numerous injured; and what traumata were suffered by the children of the City, infected by the bogey fears of their elders, will not be comprehended until the psychiatrists can pry into the neuroses of the next generation.

In the small area of agreement in which the scientists met afterward, several specific indictments were drawn. One charged the newspapers. Certainly the New York press cannot disclaim some responsibility for what happened. The defense that "we give John Public the news as it happens, how it happens, and for as long as it happens," as the editor of the *New York Extra* put it, is plausible but fails to explain why John Public had to be given the news of the Cat's activities in such necrotic detail, embellished by such a riches of cartoonical crape and obituary embroidery. The object of this elaborate treatment was, of course, to sell more newspapers—an object which succeeded so admirably that, as one circulation manager privately admitted, "We really panicked 'em."

Radio was named codefendant. Those same networks which uttered approving sounds in the direction of every obsessionist who inveighed against radio mystery and crime programs as being the First Cause of hysteria, delinquency, seclusive behavior, *idée fixe,* sexual precocity, nailbiting, nightmare, enuresis, profanity, and other antisocial ills of juvenile America saw nothing wrong in thoroughly airing the depredations of the Cat, with sound effects . . . as if the sensational were rendered harmless by the mere fact of its being not fiction. It was later charged, not without justice, that a single five-minute newscast devoted to the latest horror of the strangler did more to shatter the nerves of the listening population than all the mystery programs of all the networks percussively put together. But by that time the mischief was done.

Others fished deeper. There were certain elements in the Cat's crimes, they said, which plucked universal chords of horror. One was the means employed. Breath being life and its denial death, their argument ran, the pattern of strangulation was bound to arouse the most basic fears. Another was the haphazard choice of victims—"selection by caprice," they termed it. Man, they stated, faces death most equably when he thinks he is to die for some purpose. But the Cat, they said, picked his victims at random. It reduced the living to the level of the sub-human and gave the individual's extinction no more importance or dignity than the chance crushing of an ant. This made defenses, especially moral defenses, impossible; there was nowhere to hide; therefore panic. And still a third factor, they went on, was the total lack of recognition. No one lived who saw the terrorizer at his chill and motiveless work; he left no clues to his age, sex, height, weight, coloration, habits, speech, origin, even to his species. For all the data available, he might well have been a cat—or an incubus. Where nothing was to be perceived, the agitated imagination went berserk. The result was a Thing come true.

And the philosophers took the world view, opening casements to the great panorama of current events. *Weltanschauung!* they cried. The old oblate spheroid was wobbling on its axis, trying to resist stresses, cracking along faults of strain. A generation which had lived through two global conflicts; which had buried millions of the mangled, the starved, the tortured, the murdered; which rose to the bait of world peace through the bloody waters of the age and found itself, hooked by the cynical barb, of nationalism; which cowered under the inexplicable fungus of the atomic bomb, not understanding, not wishing to understand; which helplessly watched the strategists of diplomacy plot the tactics of an Armageddon that never came; which was hauled this way and that, solicited, exhorted, suspected, flattered, accused, driven, unseated, inflamed, abandoned, never at peace, never at rest, the object of pressures and contrary forces by the night and the day and the hour—the real victims of the universal War of Nerves . . . it was no wonder, the philosophers said, that such a generation should bolt screaming at the first squeak of the unknown. In a world that was desensitized, irresponsible, threatened and threatening, hysteria was not to be marveled at. It had attacked New York City; had it struck anywhere in the world, the people of that place would have given way. What had to be understood, they said, was that the people had welcomed panic, not surrendered to it. In a planet shaking to pieces underfoot it was too agonizing to remain sane. Fantasy was a refuge and a relief.

But it remained for an ordinary New Yorker, a 20-year-old law student, to state the case in language most people could understand. "I've just been reading up on Danny Webster," he said. "In one case he was mixed up in, trial of a fellow named Joseph White, Webster tossed this one over the plate: *Every unpunished murder takes away something from the security of every man's life.* I figure when you live in our cockeyed kind of world, when some boogyman they call the Cat starts sloughing folks right and left

3

and nobody can get to first base on it, and as far as Joe Schmo can see this Cat's going to keep right on strangling the population till there's not enough customers left to fill the left field bleachers at Ebbets Field—or am I boring you and by the way whatever happened to Durocher?" The law student's name was Gerald Ellis Kollodny and he made the statement to a Hearst reporter on sidewalk-interview assignment; the statement was reprinted in the *New Yorker,* the *Saturday Review of Literature,* and *Reader's Digest; M-G-M News* invited Mr. Kollodny to repeat himself before its cameras; and New Yorkers nodded and said that was just about how it had stacked up.

• 2

August 25 brought one of those simmering subtropical nights in which summer New York specializes. Ellery was in his study stripped to his shorts, trying to write. But his fingers kept sliding off the keys and finally he turned off his desk light and padded to a window.

The City was blackly quiet, flattened by the pressures of the night. Eastward thousands would be drifting into Central Park to throw themselves to the steamy grass. To the northeast, in Harlem and the Bronx, Little Italy, Yorkville; to the southeast, on the Lower East Side and across the river in Queens and Brooklyn; to the south, in Chelsea, Greenwich Village, Chinatown—wherever there were tenements—fire escapes would be crowded nests in the smother, houses emptied, streets full of lackadaisical people. The parkways would be bug trails. Cars would swarm over the bridges—Brooklyn, Manhattan, Williamsburg, Queensborough, George Washington, Triborough— hunting a breeze. At Coney Island, Brighton, Manhattan Beach, the Rockaways, Jones Beach, the sands would be seeded by millions of the sleepless turned restlessly to the sea. The excursion boats would be scuttling up and down the Hudson and the ferries staggering like overloaded old women to Weehawken and Staten Island.

Heat lightning ripped the sky, disclosing the tower of the Empire State Building. A huge photographic process; for the shutterflash of a citysized camera taking a picture of the night.

A little to the south hung a bright spume. But it was a mirage. Times Square would be sweltering under it; the people would be in Radio City Music Hall, the Roxy, the Capitol, the Strand, the Paramount, the State—wherever there was a promise of lower temperatures.

Some would seek the subways. The coupled cars kept their connecting doors open and when the trains rushed along between stations there was a violent displacement of the tunnel air, hellish but a wind. The choice position was in the front doorway of the head car beside the motorman's cubicle. Here the masses would be thickest, swaying in a grateful catalepsy.

In Washington Square, along Fifth Avenue, 57th Street, upper Broadway, Riverside Drive, Central Park West, 110th Street, Lexington Avenue, Madison, the busses would accept the few and spurn the many and they would rush up and down, north and south, east and west, chasing their tails like . . .

Ellery blundered back to his desk, lit a cigaret.

No matter where I start, he thought, I wind up in the same damned place.

That Cat's getting to be a problem.

He tilted, embracing his neck. His fingers slithered in the universal ooze and he tightened them, thinking that he could stand an over-all tightening. Nonskid thoughts. A new lining job on the will.

The Cat.

Ellery smoked, crookedly.

A great temptation.

In the Wrightsville Van Horn case Ellery had run into stunning treachery. He had found himself betrayed by his own logic. The old blade had turned suddenly in his hand; he had aimed at the guilty with it and it had run through the innocent. So he had put it away and taken up his typewriter. As Inspector Queen said, ivory tower stuff.

Unhappily, he had to share his turret with an old knight who josted daily with the wicked. Inspector Richard Queen of the New York Police Department being also the unhorsed champion's sire, it was a perilous proximity.

"I don't want to hear about a case," Ellery would say. "Just let me be."

"What's the matter?" his father would jeer. "Afraid you might be tempted?"

"I've given all that up. I'm not interested any longer."

But that was before the Cat strangled Archibald Dudley Abernethy.

He had tried to ignore the murder of Abernethy. And for some time he had succeeded in doing so. But the creature's round little face with its round little eyes had an annoying way of staring out at him from his morning newspaper.

In the end he had brought himself up to date.

It was interesting, an interesting case.

He had never seen a less meaningful face. It was not vicious, or kind, or sly, or stupid; it was not even enigmatic. It was nothing, a rotundity, a 44-year-old fetus-face; one of nature's undeveloped experiments.

Yes, an interesting homicide.

And then the second strangling.

And the third.

And . . .

The apartment door *blupped!*

"Dad?"

Ellery jumped, banging his shin. He limped hurriedly to the living room.

"Hi there." Inspector Queen already had his jacket

6

and necktie off; he was removing his shoes. "You look cool, son."

The Inspector looked gray.

"Tough day?" It was not the heat. The old man was as weatherproof as a desert rat.

"Anything on the ice, Ellery?"

"Lemonade. Quarts of it."

The Inspector shuffled into the kitchen. Ellery heard the icebox open and close. "By the way, congratulate me."

"Congratulate you on what?"

"On being handed today," said his father, reappearing with a frosty glass, "the biggest pig in the poke of my alleged—I say alleged—career." He threw his head back and drank. Throat showing, he looked even grayer.

"Fired?"

"Worse."

"Promoted."

"Well," said the Inspector, seating himself, "I'm now top dog in the Cat chase."

"The Cat."

"You know, the Cat?"

Ellery leaned against the study jamb.

"The Commissioner called me in," said the Inspector, folding his hands about the glass, "and he told me he'd had the move under consideration for some time. He's creating a special Cat squad. I'm in full charge. As I said, top dog."

"Caninized." Ellery laughed.

"Maybe you find this situation full of yuks," said his father, "but as for me, give me liberty and lots of it." He drained what was left in the glass. "Ellery, I damn near told the Commissioner to his face today that Dick Queen's too old a bird to be handed a deal like this. I've given the P.D. a pretty full lifetime of faithful service. I deserve better."

"But you took it."

"Yes, I took it," said the Inspector, "and God help me, I even said, 'Thanks, Commissioner.' And then I got the feeling," he went on in a worried way, "that he had some angle he wasn't putting on the line and son, I wanted to duck out even more. I can still do it."

"You talking about quitting?"

"Well, I'm just talking. Anyway, you can't say you don't come by it honestly."

"Ourrrrch." Ellery went to one of the living room windows. "But it's not my brawl," he complained to New York. "I played around a little, that's all. For a long time I was lucky. But when I found out I was using loaded dice—"

"I see your point. Yes. And this crap game's for keeps."

Ellery turned around. "Aren't you exaggerating?"

"Ellery, this is an emergency."

"Oh, come."

"I said," said the old man, "an emergency."

"A few murders. Granted they're puzzling. That's hardly a new twist. What's the percentage of unsolved homicides? I don't understand you, Dad. I had a reason for quitting; I'd taken on something and I flubbed it, causing a death or two by the way. But you're a pro. This is an assignment. The responsibility for failure, if you fail, is the Commissioner's. And suppose these stranglings aren't solved—"

"My dear philosopher," said the Inspector, rolling the empty glass between his palms, "if these stranglings aren't solved, and damned quickly, something's going to pop in this man's town."

"Pop? In New York? How do you mean?"

"It hasn't really got going yet. Just signs. The number of phone calls to Headquarters asking for information, instructions, reassurance, anything. The increase in false alarm police calls, especially at night. The jitters of the men on duty. A little more all-around tension than there ought to be. A . . ." the Inspector groped with his glass . . . "a sort of concentration of interest on the part of the public. They're too interested. It isn't natural."

"Just because an overheated cartoonist—"

"Just because! Who cares a hoot in Hell Gate what's

8

caused it? It's on its way, Ellery. Why is the only smash hit on Broadway this summer that ridiculous murder farce, *The Cat*? Every critic in town panned it as the smelliest piece of rat cheese to hit New York in five years, and it's the only show doing business. Winchell's latest is 'Cat-Astrophes.' Berle turned down a cat joke, said he didn't think the subject was funny. The pet shops report they haven't sold a kitten in a month. They're beginning to see the Cat in Riverdale, Canarsie, Greenpoint, the East Bronx, Park Row, Park Avenue, Park Plaza. We're starting to find alley cats strangled with cords all over the city. Forsythe Street. Pitkin Avenue. Lenox. Second. Tenth. Bruckner Boulevard—"

"Kids."

"Sure, we've even caught some of them at it. But it's a symptom, Ellery. A symptom of something that scares the stiffener out of me, and I'm man enough to admit it."

"Have you eaten anything today?"

"Five murders and the biggest city in the world gets the shakes! Why? How do you explain it?"

Ellery was silent.

"Come on," said the Inspector sarcastically. "You won't endanger your amateur standing."

But Ellery was only thinking. "Maybe," he said, "maybe it's the strange feel of it. New York will take fifty polio cases a day in its stride, but let two cases of Asiatic cholera break out and under the right conditions you might have mass hysteria. There's something alien about these stranglings. They make indifference impossible. When a man like Abernethy can get it, anyone can get it." He stopped. The Inspector was staring at him.

"You seem to know a lot about it."

"Just what I've happened to catch in the papers."

"Like to know more? Worm's eye view?"

"Well . . ."

"Sit down, son."

"Dad—"

"Sit down!"

Ellery sat down. After all, the man was his father.

"Five murders so far," said the Inspector. "All in Manhattan. All stranglings. Same kind of cord used in each."

"That tussah silk number? Indian silk?"

"Oh, you know that."

"The papers say you've got nowhere trying to trace them."

"The papers are correct. It's a strong, coarse-fibered silk of—so help me—Indian jungle origin, and it's the only clue we have."

"What?"

"I repeat: not a single cursed other clue. Nothing! Nothing, Ellery. No prints. No witnesses. No suspects. No motives. There isn't a thing to work on. The killer comes and goes like a breeze, leaving only two things behind, a corpse and a cord. The first victim was—"

"Abernethy, Archibald Dudley. Aged 44. Three-room apartment on East 19th Street near Gramercy Park. A bachelor left alone by the death of his invalid mother a few years ago. His father, a clergyman, died in 1922. Abernethy never worked a lick in his life. Took care of mama and afterward of himself. 4-F in the war. Did his own cooking, housekeeping. No apparent interests. No entangling alliances. No anything. A colorless, juiceless nonentity. Has the time of Abernethy's death been fixed more accurately?"

"Doc Prouty is pretty well satisfied he was strangled around midnight of June 3. We have reason to believe Abernethy knew the killer; the whole setup smacked of an appointment. We've eliminated relatives; they're scattered to hell and gone and none of them could have done it. Friends? Abernethy didn't have any, not one. He was the original lone wolf."

"Or sheep."

"As far as I can see, we didn't miss a trick," said the Inspector morosely. "We checked the super of the building. We checked a drunk janitor. Every tenant in the house. Even the renting agent."

10

"I understand Abernethy lived off the income from a trust—"

"Handled by a bank for umpty years. He had no lawyer. He had no business—how he occupied his time since his mother's death God only knows; we don't. Just vegetated, I guess."

"Tradesmen?"

"All checked off."

"Barber, too?"

"You mean from the killer's getting behind his sweet petit point chair?" The Inspector did not smile. "He shaved himself. Once a month he got a haircut in a shop off Union Square. He'd gone there for over twenty years and they didn't even know his name. Just the same we checked the three barbers. And no dice."

"You're convinced there was no woman in Abernethy's life?"

"Positive."

"And no man?"

"No evidence that he was even a homo. He was a small fat skunk egg. No hits, no runs, no errors."

"One error. At least one." Inspector Queen started, but then his lips tightened. Ellery sloshed a little in his chair. "No man can be the total blank the facts make out Abernethy to have been. It's just not possible. And the proof that it's not is that he was murdered. He had a feeble life of *some* sort. He did *something*. All five of them did. What about Violette Smith?"

"Violette Smith," said the Inspector, closing his eyes. "Number 2 on the Cat's hit parade. Strangled just nineteen days after Abernethy—date, June 22, sometime between 6 P.M. and midnight. Unmarried. 42. Lived alone in a two-room apartment on the top floor of a bug trap on West 44th, over a *pizzeria*. Side entrance, walkup. Three other tenants in the building besides the restaurant downstairs. Had lived at that address six years. Before that on 73rd and West End Avenue. Before that on Cherry Street in the Village, where she'd been born.

11

"Violette Smith," said the Inspector without opening his eyes, "was the opposite of Archie Abernethy in just about every conceivable way. He was a hermit, she knew everybody around Times Square. He was a babe in the woods, she was a she-wolf. He'd been protected by mama all his life, the only protection she knew was the kind she had to pay. Abernethy had no vices, Violette had no virtues. She was a dipso, a reefer addict, and she'd just graduated to the hard stuff when she got hers. He never earned a penny in his life, she made her living the hard way."

"Sixth Avenue mostly, I gather," said Ellery.

"Not true. Violotte never worked the pavements. Her hustling was on call; she had a mighty busy phone.

"Whereas in Abernethy's case," the Inspector droned on, "we had nothing to work on, in Violette's we hit the jackpot. Normally, when a woman like her gets knocked off, you check the agent, the girl friends, the clients, the dope peddler, the mobster who's always in the background somewhere—and somewhere along the line you hit the answer. Well, this setup was normal enough; Vi had a record of nine arrests, she'd done some time, she was tied up with Frank Pompo, all the rest of it. Only nothing got anywhere."

"Are you sure—"

"—it was a Cat job? As a matter of fact, at first we weren't. If not for the use of the cord—"

"Same Indian silk."

"The color was different. Pinkish, a salmony kind of color. But the silk was that tussah stuff, all right, same as in Abernethy's case, only his was blue. Of course, when the third one came along, and the fourth and fifth, the pattern was clear and we're sure now the Smith woman was one of the series. The more we dig in the surer we get. The picture, atmosphere, are the same. A killer who came and went and didn't even leave a shadow on a windowshade."

"Still—"

But the old man was shaking his head. "We've

12

worked the vine overtime. If Violette was slated to go we'd get some hint of it. But the stools don't know a thing. It's not that they've clammed up; they just don't know.

"She wasn't in any trouble. This definitely wasn't a crackdown for holding out, or anything like that. Vi was in the racket for a living and she was smart enough to play ball without a squawk. She took shake-downs as part of the hazards of the business. She was well-liked, one of the old reliables."

"Over 40," said Ellery. "In a wearing profession. I don't suppose—"

"Suicide? Impossible."

Ellery scratched his nose. "Tell me more."

"She wasn't found for over thirty-six hours. On the morning of June 24 a girl friend of hers who'd been trying to reach her by phone a whole day and night climbed the stairs, found Violette's door shut but not locked, went in—"

"Abernethy's body was found seated in an easy-chair," said Ellery. "Exactly how was the Smith woman found?"

"Her flat was a bedroom and sitting room—kitchenette was one of those wall-unit jobs. She was found on the floor in the doorway between the two rooms."

"Facing which way?" asked Ellery quickly.

"I know, I know, but there was no way of telling. She was all bunched up. Might have fallen from any position."

"Attacked from which direction?"

"From behind, same as Abernethy. And the cord knotted."

"Oh, yes, there's that."

"What?"

"The cord was knotted in Abernethy's case, too. It's bothered me."

"Why?" The Inspector sat up.

"Well . . . there's a sort of finality about it."

"A what?"

"Decorative, but was it necessary? You'd hardly

let go till your victim was dead, would you? Then why the knot? In fact, it would be pretty hard to tie a knot while the victim was strangling. It suggests that the knots were tied after they were dead."

His father was staring.

"It's like putting a bow on a package that's quite adequately wrapped. The extra—I almost said the artistic—touch. Neat, satisfying. Satisfying a . . . what would you say? a passion for completeness? finality? Yes, so damned final."

"What in the world are you talking about?"

"I'm not sure," said Ellery mournfully. "Tell me—was there a sign of forcible entry?"

"No. The general opinion is that she expected her killer. Like Abernethy."

"Posing as a client?"

"Could be. If he was, it was only to get in. The bedroom wasn't disturbed and while she was found wearing a wrapper, she had a slip and panties on underneath. The testimony is she nearly always wore a negligee when she was home. But it could have been anybody, Ellery. Someone she knew well or someone she didn't know so well or even someone she didn't know at all. It wasn't hard," said the Inspector, "to make Miss Smith's acquaintance."

"The other tenants—"

"Nobody heard a thing. The restaurant people didn't even know she existed. You know how it is in New York."

"Ask no questions and mind your own business."

"While the lady upstairs is getting herself dead."

The Inspector got up and fussed to a window. But immediately he returned to his chair, scowling. "In other words," he said, "we drew a blank in the Smith case, too. Then—"

"Question. Did you find any connection between Abernethy and Violette Smith? Any at all?"

"No."

"Go on."

"Cometh Number 3," said the Inspector in a sort of liturgical mutter. "Rian O'Reilly, 40-year-old shoe

14

salesman, living with his wife and four kids in a Chelsea tenement. Date, July 18; twenty-six days after the Smith murder.

"O'Reilly's kill," the Inspector said, "was so damn . . . so damn discouraging. He was a hardworking fellow, good husband, crazy father, struggling to keep his head above water and having a tough time of it. To keep his family going O'Reilly held down two jobs, a full-timer in a lower Broadway shoe store, a night relief job in a shop on Fulton and Flatbush across the river in Brooklyn. He'd have managed to scrape along if he hadn't run into such hard luck. One of his children got polio two years ago. Another got pneumonia. Then his wife splashed herself with hot paraffin putting up grape jelly and he paid a skin specialist for a year trying to heal her burn. On top of that another kid was run over by a hit-and-run driver who was never identified and spent three months in a hospital. O'Reilly's borrowed the limit against his $1000 insurance policy. His wife had hocked her measly engagement ring. They'd had a '39 Chevvy—O'Reilly sold it to pay doctors' bills.

"O'Reilly liked his nip now and then, but he gave up drinking. Even beer. He held himself down to ten cigarettes a day, and he'd been a heavy smoker. His wife put up box lunches and he didn't eat supper till he got home, usually after midnight. In the past year he'd suffered a lot from toothache, but he wouldn't go to a dentist, said he didn't have time for such foolishness. But he'd toss around some at night, his wife said."

The heat flowed through their windows. Inspector Queen wiped his face with a ball of handkerchief.

"O'Reilly was no Saturday night Irishman. He was a little guy, thin and ugly, with heavy eyebrows that made him look worried even when he was dead. He used to tell his wife he was a physical coward, but she thought he'd had plenty of guts. I guess he did, at that. He was born in Hell's Kitchen and his life was one long battle. With his drunk of a father and with the street hoodlums when he was a boy, and

15

after that with poverty and sickness. Remembering his old man, who used to beat up his mother, O'Reilly tried to make up for it to his own wife and children. His whole life was his family.

"He was wild about classical music. He couldn't read a note and he'd never had a lesson, but he could hum snatches of a lot of operas and symphonies and during the summer he tried to take in as many of the free Sunday concerts in Central Park as he could. He was always after his kids to tune in WQXR, used to say he thought Beethoven would do them a lot more good than *The Shadow*. One of his boys has a talent for the violin; O'Reilly finally had to stop his lessons. The night that happened, Mrs. O'Reilly said, he cried like a baby all night.

"This was the man," said Inspector Queen, watching his curling toes, "whose strangled body was found early in the morning of July 19 by the janitor of the building. The janitor was mopping the entrance hall down when he noticed a heap of clothes in the dark space behind the stairway. It was O'Reilly, dead.

"Prouty fixed the time of death as between midnight and 1 A.M. of the 18th-19th. Obviously, O'Reilly was just coming home from his night job in Brooklyn. We checked with the store and the time he left jibed, sure enough, with his movements if he'd gone directly home and been attacked as he entered the house on the way upstairs. There was a lump on the side of his head—"

"The result of a blow, or from a fall," asked Ellery.

"We're not sure. A blow seems more likely, because he was dragged—there are rubberheel scrapes on the marble—from just inside the front door to the spot under the stairs where the janitor found him. No struggle, and nobody heard anything." The Inspector pinched his nose so hard the tip remained whitish for a few seconds. "Mrs. O'Reilly had been up all night waiting for her husband, afraid to leave the kids alone in the apartment. She was just going to phone the police—they held on to their phone, she

16

said, because O'Reilly always said suppose one of the kids got sick in the middle of the night?—when the cop the janitor'd called came up to give her the bad news.

"She told me she'd been scared and nervous ever since the Abernethy murder. 'Rian had to come home from Brooklyn so late,' she said. 'I kept at him to quit the night job, and then when that woman on West 44th Street was choked to death too I nearly went out of my mind. But Rian only laughed. He said nobody'd bother to kill *him,* he wasn't worth killing."

Ellery planted his elbows on his naked knees and his face secretively between his hands.

The Inspector said, "Seems like it's getting hotter," and Ellery mumbled something. "It's against nature," complained the Inspector. He took off his shirt and undershirt and he plastered them with a smack against the back of his chair. "Leaving a widow and four children, with what was left of his insurance going to pay for his burial. I understand his priest is trying to do something, but it's a poor parish and O'Reilly's heirs are now enjoying City relief."

"And now his kids will be listening to *The Shadow* if they can hang on to their radio." Ellery rubbed his neck. "No clues."

"No clues."

"The cord."

"Same silk, blue."

"Knotted at the back?"

"Plenty of rhyme," muttered Ellery. "But where's the reason?"

"You tell O'Reilly's widow."

And Ellery was quiet. But after a while he said, "It was about that time that the cartoonist was inspired. I remember the unveiling of the Cat. He jumped out at you from the editorial page of the *Extra* . . . such as it was and is. One of the great monsters of cartoonical time. The man should get the Pulitzer prize for Satanism. A diabolical economy of line; the imagination fills in what the artist leaves out. Guaranteed to share your bed. *How Many Tails Has the Cat?*

asks the caption. And we count three distinct appendages, curling at the ends back upon themselves. Not thick true tails, you understand. More like cords. Ending in nooselike openings just right for necks . . . which aren't there. And one cord bears the number *1,* and the second cord bears the number *2* and the third cord the number *3.* No *Abernethy, Smith,* or *O'Reilly.* He was so right. The Cat is quantitative. It's numbers that equalize all men, the Founding Fathers and Abe Lincoln to the contrary notwithstanding. The Cat is the great leveler of humanity. It's no accident that his claws are shaped like sickles."

"Sweet talk, but the point is the day after August 9 there was the Cat again," said the Inspector, "and he'd grown a fourth tail."

"And I remember that, too," nodded Ellery.

"Monica McKell. August 9. Twenty-two days after O'Reilly."

"The perennial debutante. A mere 37 and going strong."

"Park and 53rd. Café society. A table jumper they got to call Leaping Lena."

"Or in a more refined phrase of Lucius Beebe—Madcap Monica."

"That's the one," said the Inspector. "Also known as McKell's Folly, McKell being her old man, the oil millionaire, who told me Monica was the only wildcat he'd never brought in. But you could see he was proud of her. She was wild, all right—cut her teeth on a gin bottle, came out during Prohibition, and her favorite trick when she was tight was to get behind the bar and outmix the bartender. They say she mixed the best Martini in New York, drunk or sober. She was born in a penthouse and died in the subway. Downhill all the way.

"Monica never married. She once said that the only unrelated male she'd ever known that she could stand having around for any length of time was a horse named Leibowitz, and the only reason she didn't marry him, she said, was that she doubted she could housebreak him. She was engaged a dozen times, but at the last minute she'd take a walk. Her father would yell, and her ma, who's a handkerchief-twister, would get hysterics, but it was no deal. They had high hopes about Monica's last engagement—it looked as if she was really going to marry this Hungarian count—but the Cat put a crimp in that."

"In the subway," said Ellery.

"Sure, how did she get there. Well, it was this way. Monica McKell was the biggest booster the New York subway system ever had. She'd ride it every chance she got. She told Elsa Maxwell it was the only place a girl could get the feel of the people. She took a particular delight in dragging her escorts there, especially when they were in tails.

"Funny," said the Inspector, "that it should have been the subway that did her in. Monica was out clubbing that night with Snooky—her count—and a bunch of their friends. They wound up in some Village dive, and around a quarter of four in the morning Monica got tired tending bar and they decided to call it a night. They began piling into cabs—all except Monica, who stood her ground and argued that if they really believed in the American way they'd all go home in the subway. The others were game, but the count got his Hungarian up—he was also tanked on vodka-and-Cokes—and said something like if he wanted to smell peasants he'd have stayed in Hungary and he'd be damned if he'd lower himself, into the ground or any other way, and she could bloody well go home in the subway herself if she wanted to so bad. And she did.

"And she did," said the Inspector, licking his lips, "and she was found a little after 6 A.M. lying on a bench near the tailpiece of the platform of the Sheridan Square station. A trackwalker found her. He called a cop and the cop took one look and went green. There was the salmon-colored silk cord around her neck."

The Inspector got up and went into the kitchen and came back with the pitcher of lemonade. They drank in silence and then the Inspector put the pitcher back in the icebox.

When he returned, Ellery said with a frown, "Was there time for—?"

"No," said the Inspector. "She'd been dead about two hours. That would place the murder attack at around 4 A.M. or a little later, just about time for her to have walked over to Sheridan Square from the night club and maybe wait around a few minutes—you know how the trains run at that hour of the morning. But Count Szebo was with the others until at least 5:30. They all stopped in at an allnight hamburger place on Madison and 48th on their way uptown. Every minute of his time is accounted for well past the murder period. Anyway, what would the point have been? Old man McKell had contracted to settle a hot million on Szebo when the knot was tied—excuse me, that was a bad figure of speech. I mean the count would have strangled himself before he'd lay a finger to that valuable throat. He doesn't have a Hungarian pretzel.

"In Monica McKell's case," said the Inspector, shaking his head, "we were able to trace her movements right up the entrance of the Sheridan Square station. A nighthawk cab spotted her about halfway to the station from the club, pulled up alongside. She was on foot, alone. But she laughed and said to the hack, 'You've got me wrong, my friend. I'm a poor working girl and I've just got a dime to get home on," and she opened her gold mesh bag and showed him; there was nothing in it but a lipstick, a compact, and a dime, he said. And she marched off down the street, the hack said, the diamond bracelet on her arm sparkling under the street lights. Squinting along like a movie star, was the way he put it. Actually, she was wearing a gold lamé creation designed like a Hindu sari, with a jacket of white mink thrown over it.

"And another cab driver parked near the station saw her cross the Square and disappear down the steps. She was still on foot, still alone.

"There was no one on duty at the change booth

20

at that hour. Presumably she put her dime in the turnstile and walked down the platform to the end bench. A few minutes later she was dead.

"Her jewelry, her bag, her jacket weren't touched.

"We've found no evidence that anybody else was on the platform with her. The second cab driver picked up a fare right after he saw Monica go down the subway steps, and apparently he was the only one around. The Cat may have been waiting on the platform; the Cat may have followed Monica down from the street after ducking into doorways to avoid being seen by the two cab drivers; or the Cat may have got off at Sheridan Square from an uptown train and found her there—there's nothing to tell. If she put up a battle, there's no sign of it. If she screamed, no one heard it. And that was the end of Monica McKell—born in New York, died in New York. From penthouse to subway. Downhill all the way."

After a long time Ellery said, "A girl like that must have been mixed up in a thousand pulp story plots. I've heard a lot of scandal . . ."

"I am now," sighed his father, "the world's foremost authority on the Mysteries of Monica. I can tell you, for instance, that she had a burn scar just under the left breast that she didn't get from falling on a hot stove. I know just where she was, and with whom, in February of 1946 when she disappeared and her father had us and the FBI chasing our tails looking for her, and despite what the papers said at the time her kid brother Jimmy had nothing to do with it—he'd just got out of the Service and he was having his own troubles readjusting to civilian life. I know how Monica came to get the autographed photo of Legs Diamond that's still hanging on her bedroom wall, and it's not for the reason you'd think. I know why she was asked to leave Nassau the year Sir Harry Oakes was murdered, and who asked her. I even know something J. Parnell Thomas never found out—that she was a card-carrying member of the Communist Party between 1938 and 1941, when she quit to become a Christian Fronter for four months, and then jumped that to take a course in Yoga Breathing Exercises under a Hollywood swami named Lal Dhyana Jackson.

"Yes, sir, I know everything there is to know about Leaping Lena, or Madcap Monica," said the Inspector, "except how she came to be strangled by the Cat . . . I can tell you this, Ellery. If when the Cat walked up to her on that subway platform he said, 'Excuse me, Miss McKell, I'm the Cat and I'm going to strangle you,' she probably moved over on the bench and said, 'How perfectly thrilling. Sit down and tell me more.' "

Ellery jumped up. He took a turn around the living room, busily, like a runner limbering up. Inspector Queen watched the sweat roll down his back.

"And that," said the Inspector, "is where we're hung up."

"Nothing—?"

"Not a bastardly thing. I suppose," the old man said angrily, "I can't blame McKell Senior for offering $100,000 reward, but all it's done is give the papers another angle to play up and flood us with a barrage of happy gas from ten thousand crackpots. And it hasn't been any help having McKell's high-priced prima donna dicks underfoot, either!"

"What about the current mouse?"

"Number 5?" The Inspector cracked his knuckles, clicking off integers in a bitter arithmetic. "Simone Phillips, 35, lived with a younger sister in a coldwater flat on East 102nd Street." He grimaced. "This mouse couldn't even rustle her own cheese. Simone'd had something wrong with her spine since childhood and she was paralyzed from the waist down. Spent most of her life in bed. What you might call a pushover."

"Yes." Ellery was sucking a piece of lemon and making a face. "Doesn't seem cricket, somehow. Even from the Cat."

"It happened last Friday night. August 19. Ten days after the McKell woman. Celeste—the younger sister—fixed Simone up, turned on the radio for her,

22

and left for a neighborhood movie. Around 9 o'clock."

"Pretty late?"

"She went for just the main feature. Celeste said Simone hated being left alone, but she simply had to get out once a week—"

"Oh, this was routine?"

"Yes. The sister went every Friday night—her only recreation, by the way. Simone was helpless and Celeste was the only one she had. Anyway, Celeste got back a little after 11. She found the paralytic strangled. Salmon-colored silk cord tied around her neck."

"The crippled woman could hardly have let anyone in. Weren't there any signs—?"

"Celeste never locked the apartment door when she had to leave Simone. Simone was deathly afraid of gas leaks and fires, afraid she'd be caught helpless in bed sometime when her sister wasn't there. Leaving the door unlocked eased her mind. For the same reason they had a phone, which they certainly couldn't afford."

"Last Friday night. Almost as hot as tonight," mused Ellery. "In that district the people would all be congregated on the stoop, hanging out the windows. Do you mean to tell me no one saw anything?"

"There's so much testimony to the effect that no stranger entered the building through the front entrance between 9 and 11 that I'm convinced the Cat got in through the rear. There's a back door leading out to a court, and the court is accessible, from one of a half-dozen different directions, the backs of the other houses and the two side streets; it runs right through. The Phillips flat is on the ground floor, rear. The hall is dark, has only a 25-watt light. That's the way he got in, all right, and out again. But we've been over the square block a dozen times, inside the buildings and out, and we haven't turned up a thing."

"No screams."

"If she did yell, nobody paid any attention to it. You know what a tenement district's like on a hot night—kids out on the street till all hours and screams a dime a dozen. But my hunch is she didn't make a sound. I've never seen such fright on a human face. Paralysis on top of paralysis. She didn't put up the scrawniest kind of scrap. Wouldn't surprise me if she just sat there with her mouth open, pop-eyed, while the Cat took his cord out and tied it around her neck and pulled it tight. Yes, sir, this was his easiest strike."

The Inspector pulled himself to his feet. "Simone was very fat, from the waist up. The kind of fat that gives you the feeling that if you poked it you'd go clear through to the other side. As if she had no bones, no muscle."

"Musculus," said Ellery, sucking the lemon. "Little mouse. The shrunken little mice to the mouse. Little atrophies."

"Well, she'd been parked in that bed over twenty-five years." The old man trudged to one of the windows. "Sure is a scorcher."

"Simone, Celeste."

"What?" said the Inspector.

"Their names. So Gallic. Maternal poetry? And if not, how come 'Phillips'?"

"Their father was French. The family name was originally Phillippe, but he Anglicized it when he came to America."

"Mother French, too?"

"I think so, but they were married in New York. Phillips was in the import-export business and he made a fortune during the First World War. He dropped it all in the '29 crash and blew his brains out, leaving Mrs. Phillips penniless."

"With a paralyzed child. Tough."

"Mrs. Phillips managed by taking in sewing. They made out fine, Celeste says—in fact, she was enrolled as a freshman in N.Y.U. downtown when Mrs. Phillips died of pleurisy-pneumonia. That was five years ago."

"Must have been even tougher. For Celeste."

"It couldn't have been a peach parfait. Simone

needed constant attention. Celeste had to quit school."

"How'd she manage?"

"Celeste has a modeling job in a dress shop her mother did business with. Afternoons and all day Saturday. She has a beautiful figure, dark coloring—pretty goodlooking number. She could make a lot more somewhere else, she told me, but the store isn't far from their home and she couldn't leave Simone alone too long. I got the impression Celeste was pretty much dominated by Simone and this was confirmed by the neighbors. They told me Simone nagged at Celeste all the time, whining and complaining and making the younger sister, who they all think is a saint, run her legs off. Probably accounts for her beat-up look; she really was dragging her chin when I saw her."

"Tell me," said Ellery. "On Friday night last did this saintly young character go to the movies alone?"

"Yes."

"Does she usually?"

The Inspector looked surprised. "I don't know."

"Might pay to find out." Ellery leaned far forward to smooth out a wrinkle in the rug. "Doesn't she have a boy friend?"

"I don't think so. I gather she hasn't had much opportunity to meet men."

"How old is this Celeste?"

"23."

"Ripe young age. —The cord *was* tussah silk?"

"Yes."

The rug was now smooth.

"And that's all you have to tell me?"

"Oh, there's lots more, especially about Abernethy, Violette Smith, and Monica McKell."

"What?"

"I'll be happy to open the files to you."

Ellery was silent.

"Want to go over them?" asked his father.

"You found no connection among any of the five victims."

"Not a particle."

"None of them knew any of the others."

"As far as we can tell."

"They had no common friends, acquaintances, relatives?"

"So far we haven't hit any."

"Religious affiliation?" asked Ellery suddenly.

"Abernethy was a communicant of the Episcopal Church—in fact, at one time, before his father died, he was studying for the ministry. But he gave that up to take care of his mother on a regular basis. Certainly there's no record that he ever went after his mother died.

"Violette Smith's family are Lutherans. As far as we know, she herself went to no church. Her family threw her out years ago.

"Monica McKell—all the McKells—Presbyterian. Mr. and Mrs. McKell are very active in church affairs and Monica—it sort of surprised me—was quite religious.

"Rian O'Reilly was a devout Roman Catholic.

"Simone Phillips came of French Protestants on both sides, but she herself was interested in Christian Science."

"Likes, dislikes, habits, hobbies . . ."

The Inspector turned from the window. "What?"

"I'm fishing for a common denominator. The victims form a highly conglomerate group. Yet there must be some quality, some experience, some function they shared . . ."

"There's not a single indication that the poor mutts were tied up any way at all."

"As far as you know."

The Inspector laughed. "Ellery, I've been on this merry-go-round since the first ride and I tell you there's as much sense in these killings as there was in a Nazi crematorium.

"The murders haven't followed any time pattern or recognizable sequence. The intervals between the various crimes have been nineteen days, twenty-six, twenty-two, ten. It's true that they all occurred at night, but that's when cats walk, isn't it?

"The victims came from all over the City. East 19th near Gramercy Park. West 44th between Broadway and Sixth. West 20th near Ninth. Park and 53rd, in this case the victim actually getting it under Sheridan Square in Greenwich Village. And East 102nd.

"Economically? Upper crust, middle class, the poor. Socially? You find a pattern that includes an Abernethy, a Violette Smith, a Rian O'Reilly, a Monica McKell, and a Simone Phillips.

"Motive? Not gain. Not jealousy. Not anything *personal*.

"There's nothing to indicate that these have been sex crimes, or that a sex drive is even behind it.

"Ellery, this is killing for the sake of killing. The Cat's enemies are the human race. Anybody on two legs, will do. If you ask me, that's what's really cooking in New York. And unless we clamp the lid on this—this *homicide*, it's going to boil over."

"And yet," said Ellery, "for an undiscriminating, unselective, blood-lusting and mankind-hating brute, I must say the Cat shows a nice appreciation of certain values."

"Values?"

"Well, take time. The Cat uses time the way Thoreau did, as a stream, to go fishing in. To catch Abernethy in his bachelor apartment he'd have to run the risk of being seen or heard entering or leaving, because Abernethy was an early-to-bed man. What's more, Abernethy rarely had a visitor, so that going to his door at a normal hour might have aroused a neighbor's curiosity. So what does the Cat do? He contrives to get Abernethy to agree to an appointment at an hour when the building's settled down for the night. To accomplish this called for the considerable feat of making an ossified bachelor change a habit of years' standing. In other words, the Cat weighed the difficulties against the time and he chose in favor of the time.

"In Violette Smith's case, whether it was done by appointment or as a result of careful study of her business practices, you can't deny that the Cat

27

did pick a *time* when a very busy lady was in her flat alone.

"O'Reilly? Most vulnerable when he came home from his Brooklyn night job. And there was the Cat lying in wait in the downstairs hall. Nicely timed, wouldn't you say?"

The Inspector listened without comment.

"Monica McKell? A woman obviously running away from herself. And that kind of woman—from that kind of background—loses herself in crowds. She was always surrounded by people. It's no accident that she adored the subway. Monica must have presented a problem. Still—the Cat caught her alone, in a place and at a time which were most favorable for his project. How many nights did he trail her, I wonder, watching for just the right *moment?*

"And Simone, the paralytic. Easy pickings once he got to her. But how to get to her without being seen? Crowded tenement, the summer—daytime was out of the question, even when Celeste was away at work. But at night her sister is always with her. Always? Well, not exactly. On Friday nights the annoying Celeste goes to the movies. And Simone is strangled when? On a Friday night."

"You finished?"

"Yes."

Inspector Queen was remote. "Very plausible," he said. "Very convincing. But you're arguing from the premise that the Cat picks people in advance. Suppose I argue from the premise that he does nothing of the sort?—a premise, incidentally, that's borne out by the total lack of connection among the victims.

"Then the Cat happened to be prowling on West 44th Street one night, picked a likely-looking building at random, chose the top floor apartment because it was closer to a roof getaway, pretended to be a salesman for nylons or French perfume—anything to get in—and that was the end of somebody whose name happened to be Violette Smith, call girl.

"On the night of July 18 he was feeling the urge again and chance took him to the Chelsea district.

It was around midnight, his favorite hunting hour. He follows a tired-looking little guy into a hall and that's the end of a hard-working Irishman named O'Reilly. It might just as well have turned out to be William Miller, a shipping clerk who came home from a date with a Bronx girl around 2 A.M. and walked up the stairs under which O'Reilly's body was lying, still warm.

"In the early morning hours of August 9 the Cat was on the loose in the Village. He spotted an unescorted woman, walking. He followed her to the Sheridan Square subway and that was the end of Well-Known New York Socialite, who should have stuck to her twelve-cylinder job.

"And on the night of August 19 he was up around 102nd Street hankering after another neck, and he got into a nice dark court and pussyfooted around till he saw through a ground floor window a fat young woman lying in a bed, alone. And that was the end of Simone Phillips.

"Now tell me something—anything—that says it didn't happen that way."

"Abernethy?"

"You left Abernethy out," said Ellery. "Abernethy the Vague. Admittedly not a hard thing to do. But he is dead, he *was* strangled with one of those silk cords, and didn't you yourself say it was by appointment?"

"I said the whole setup smacked of an appointment. But we don't *know* it. Something could have made him sit up past his usual bedtime that night, maybe a radio program, or he fell asleep in the easychair. The Cat could have been in the building on the loose and seen the light under Abernethy's door and knocked—"

"At which Abernethy let him in?"

"All he'd have to have done was unlock the door."

"An Abernethy? At midnight?"

"Or maybe he'd forgotten to check his spring latch and the Cat just walked in, releasing it on his way out."

"Then why didn't Archibald use his lungs? Or run? How is it he permitted the Cat to get behind him while he sat in his chair?"

"He might have been—like Simone Phillips—scared stiff."

"Yes," said Ellery, "I suppose that's possible."

"I know," muttered the Inspector. "The Abernethy thing doesn't conform. Nothing conforms." He shrugged. "I'm not saying you're not right, Ellery. But you see what we're up against. And the whole blasted thing's in my lap now. It would be bad enough if that's all I had to worry about. But he's not through; you know that. There's going to be another one, and another one after that, until we catch him or he drops dead from overexercise. How can we prevent it? There aren't enough cops in the U.S. to make every nook and cranny of a city like New York murderproof. We can't even be sure he'll keep restricting his activities to Manhattan. And the other boroughs know it. They're getting identical reactions from the public in the Bronx, Brooklyn, Queens, Richmond. Hell, it's being felt on Long Island, in Westchester, Connecticut, New Jersey, all the commuter places. Sometimes I think it's a bad dream. Ellery—"

Ellery's lips parted.

"Don't answer till I'm finished. You feel that you failed in the Van Horn case and that because you failed two people went to their deaths. Lord knows I've tried to help you get it out of your system. But I guess nobody can talk away another man's conscience . . . I've had to sit by and watch you crawl into a hole while you kept swearing by the beards of all the Prophets that you'd never mix into another case.

"But son," said the old man, "this is a special kind of deal. This one is tough. It's tough not only on its own merits—which are tough enough—but because of the atmosphere it's creating. This isn't just a matter of clearing up a few murders, Ellery. It's a race against—against citywide collapse. And don't make with the eyebrow: I tell you it's coming. It's only a question of time. Just one murder in the wrong place . . . Nobody downtown's out to rob me of the glory: not in this one. They're all feeling sorry for the old duck. Let me tell you something." The Inspector stared down at 87th Street, bracing himself against the window frame. "I mentioned earlier that I thought the Commissioner had an angle in putting me at the head of this special Cat squad. The boss thinks you're a screwball, but he's often asked me when you're going to snap out of the sulks and get back to using the crazy talents God gave you. Well, my opinion, Ellery, is that he's put me on the spot deliberately."

"For what reason?"

"To force you into the case."

"You're not serious!"

His father looked at him.

"But he wouldn't do a thing like that." Ellery's face was dark. "Not to you. That's the dirtiest kind of slap in the face."

"To stop these stranglings, son, I'd do a lot worse. Anyway, what's the odds? You're no superman. Nobody expects miracles. It's even a sort of insult to you. In an emergency people will try anything, even tough old eggs like the Commissioner."

"Thanks," mumbled Ellery. "That sets me up. It really does."

"Kidding aside. It would hit me pretty hard to think that when I needed you most you let me down. Ellery, how about getting into this?"

"You," said the son, "are an extremely clever old man."

The Inspector grinned.

"Naturally if I thought I could help out in a thing as serious as this I'd . . . But, damn it, Dad, I feel virginal. I want to and I don't want to. Let me sleep on it. I'd be no use to you or anybody in my present state."

"Fair enough," said his father briskly. "Good grief, I've been making speeches. How do these politicians do it? How about some more lemonade, son, with a shot of gin in it to take the bite off?"

31

"In my case, it'll take more than a shot."

"Motion seconded."

But neither meant it.

The Inspector sat down at the kitchen table with a groan, thinking that with Ellery the usual psychology was a waste of breath. The Cat and Ellery seemed two twinges of the same pain.

He leaned back against the tiled wall, tipping his chair.

The blasted heat . . .

He opened his eyes to find the Police Commissioner of the City of New York leaning over him.

"Dick, Dick," the Commissioner was saying. "Wake up."

Ellery was in the kitchen doorway, still in his shorts.

The Commissioner was hatless and the gabardine around his armpits was soaked.

Inspector Queen blinked up at him.

"I told them I'd notify you in person."

"Notify me about what, Commissioner?"

"The Cat's got another tail."

"When?" The old man licked his lips.

"Tonight. Between 10:30 and midnight."

"Where?" He brushed past them, darted into the living room, grabbed at his shoes.

"Central Park, not far from the 110th Street entrance. In some bushes behind a rock."

"Who?"

"Beatrice Willikins, 32, single, sole support of an aged father. She'd taken him to the Park for some air and left him on a bench to go looking for water. She never came back and finally he called a Park patrolman. The patrolman found her a couple of hundred feet away, strangled. Salmon-colored silk cord. Purse not touched. Hit over the head from behind and signs of dragging into the bushes. The strangulation took place there, probably while she was unconscious. No superficial indication of rape."

"No, Dad," said Ellery. "Those are wet. Here's a fresh shirt and undershirt."

"Bushes, Park," said the Inspector rapidly. "That's a break. Or is it? Prints on the ground?"

"So far, nothing. But Dick," said the Commissioner, "something new's been added."

The Inspector looked at him. He was trying to button his shirt. Ellery did it for him.

"Beatrice Willikins lived at West 128th Street."

"West," said the Inspector mechanically, sticking an arm into the jacket Ellery was holding up. Ellery was staring at the Commissioner.

"Near Lenox."

"Harlem?"

The Commissioner swabbed his neck. "This one might do it, Dick. If someone lost his head."

Inspector Queen ran to the door. He was very pale. "This means all night, Ellery. You go to bed."

But Ellery was saying, "This one might do what if someone lost his head, Commissioner?"

"Push the button that blows New York higher than Hiroshima."

"Come on, Commissioner," said the Inspector impatiently from the foyer.

"Wait." Ellery was looking politely at the Commissioner, and the Commissioner was looking just as politely at him. "If you'll give me three minutes, I'll go with you."

● 3 ·

The sixth tail of the Cat, which went on display on the morning of August 26, offered a delicate departure from the mode. Where its five fellows were hairlines enclosing white space, this tail was solidly inked in. Thus New York City was informed that the Cat had crossed the color line. By the glowing encirclement of one black throat, to the seven million pale necks already within the orbit of the noose were joined five hundred thousand others.

It was notable that, while Inspector Queen occupied himself in Harlem with Beatrice Willikins's demise, the Mayor called a dawn press conference at City Hall which was attended by the Police Commissioner and other officials.

"We are convinced, gentlemen," said the Mayor, "that there is no race angle to Beatric Willikins's murder. The one thing we've got to avoid is a repetition of the kind of tension that brought on the so-called Black Ides of March in 1935. A trivial incident and false rumor resulted in three deaths, thirty-odd people hospitalized for bullet wounds, and over two hundred others treated for injuries, cuts, and abrasions. Not to mention property damage amounting to more than $2,000,000."

"I was under the impression, Mr. Mayor," remarked a reporter for one of the Harlem newspapers, "that—to quote from the report of the bi-racial commission appointed by Mayor La Guardia to investigate the riot—it was caused by 'resentments against radical discrimination and poverty in the midst of plenty.'"

"Of course," replied the Mayor quickly. "There are always underlying social and economic causes. Frankly, that's what we're a little apprehensive about. New York is a melting pot of every race, national origin, and creed under the sun. One out of every fifteen of our fellow New Yorkers is Negro. Three out of every ten are Jewish. There are more Italians in New York City than in Genoa. More Germans than in Bremen. More Irish than in Dublin. We've got Poles, Greeks, Russians, Spaniards, Turks, Portuguese, Chinese, Scandinavians, Filipinos, Persians —everything. That's what makes us the greatest city on earth. But it also keeps us on the lid of a volcano. Postwar tensions haven't helped. These stranglings have made the whole City nervous and we don't want anything foolish to touch off public disorders. Naturally, that last remark is off the record.

"Gentlemen, our most sensible course is to treat these murders, uh, as routine. Non-sensationally. They're a bit off the beaten path and they present some rather tough problems, but we have the finest crime-investigating agency in the world, we're working on the murders night and day, and the break may be expected at any time."

"Beatrice Willikins," said the Commissioner, "was strangled by the Cat. She was Negro. The five other victims have all been white. That's the thing for you boys to emphasize."

"Our angle might be, Commissioner," said the reporter for the Harlem paper, "that the Cat is a firm democratic believer in civil rights."

In the shout that followed, an atmosphere was created which enabled the Mayor to close the conference without disclosing that the latest murder was giving the head of the new Cat squad a very bad time.

They were sitting around in the squad room of the main Harlem precinct weighing reports on Beatrice Willikins. The investigation on the scene, in the Park, had yielded nothing. The ground behind the boulder was rocky and if the Cat had left the print of his pads on it the first confusion following the discovery of the young woman's body had scuffed it out. An inch-by-inch examination of the grass, soil, and paths in the vicinity of the boulder produced only two hairpins, both identified as coming from the victim's head. Laboratory analysis of certain particles scraped from under the victim's fingernails, at first thought to be coagulated blood or bloody tissue, proved that they consisted principally of lip rouge, of a shade popular with Negro women and which matched exactly the rouge still on the dead girl's lips. There was no trace of the weapon with which the Cat had struck her head and the bruise gave no clue to its nature: it could only be described by that most inconclusive of terms, "blunt instrument."

As for the catch of the police dragnet, thrown around the area within minutes of the body's discovery, it consisted of a great many citizens of both colors and sexes and all ages, uniformly overheated, excited, frightened, and guilty-looking; none, however, gave off precisely the whiff for which Ellery's nostrils were sniffing. It took the entire night to screen them. At the end with echoes of bedlam still in their ears, the police had only two likely fish, a white and a black, the white an unemployed jazz trumpet player 27 years old found lying on the grass smoking a marijuana cigaret, the black a skinny, undersized runner for a Lenox Avenue drop. The Negro, a middleaged man, was caught in the act of peddling the numbers. Each was stripped to the skin and thoroughly examined without result. The policy employee was released when Negro detectives rounded up witnesses who accounted for his whereabouts for an hour preceding the general crime period, and for some time after that; at which everyone, remembering the Black Ides, looked happy. The white musician was taken to Headquarters for further questioning. But, as Inspector Queen remarked, it didn't look promising: if he was the Cat, he had been in New York on June 3, June 22, July 18, August 9, and August 19; whereas the trumpet player claimed to have left New York in May and returned only five days before. He said he had been employed during that period on a round-the-world luxury boat. He had described the boat, the captain, the purser, and other members of the ship's orchestra; and, in some detail, several feminine passengers.

So they tackled it from the other end and hoisted the victim to the scales. Which tipped depressingly on the side of rectitude and good works.

Beatrice Willikins had been a responsible member of the Negro community, belonging to the Abyssinian Baptist Church and active in many of its groups. Born and raised in Harlem, and educated at Howard

University, she had been employed by a child welfare agency and her work had been exclusively with the underprivileged and delinquent children of Harlem.

She had contributed sociological articles to *Journal of Negro Education* and poetry to *Phylon*. Occasional freelance pieces under her byline had appeared in the *Amsterdam-Star News, Pittsburgh Courier,* and the Atlanta *Daily World*.

Beatrice Willikins's associations had been impeccable. Her friends were Negro educators, social workers, writers, and professional people. Her work had taken her from Black Bohemia to San Juan Hill; she had come in frequent contact with dope peddlers, pimps, the streetwalkers of "The Market Place"; Puerto Ricans, Negro Moslems, French Africans, Black Jews, darkskinned Mexicans and Cubans, Negroid Chinese and Japanese. But she had gone among them as a friend and healer, unresented and unmolested. The police of Harlem had known her as a quietly determined defender of juvenile delinquents.

"She was a fighter," the precinct captain told Inspector Queen, "but she wasn't any fanatic. I don't know of anybody in Harlem, white or black, who didn't respect her."

In 1942 she had been engaged to a young Negro physician named Lawrence Caton. Dr. Caton had gone into the Army and he had been killed in Italy. Her fiancé's death had apparently sealed off the girl's emotional life; there was no record that she had ever gone out with another man.

The Inspector took a Negro lieutenant aside, and the detective nodded and went over to the bench on which the girl's father was seated, beside Ellery.

"Pap, who do you figure did the girl in?"

The aged man mumbled something.

"What?"

"He says," said Ellery, "that his name is Frederick Willikins and his father was a slave in Georgia."

"That's fine, that's okay, Pap, but what man was she messing around with? White man?"

The old man stiffened. They could see him struggle with something. Finally he drew back his brown skull, like a snake, and struck.

The Negro detective stooped and wiped the old man's spittle from his shoe.

"I guess old Pappy here figures I insulted him. On two counts."

"It's important." The Inspector moved toward the bench.

"Better let me, Inspector," said the detective. "He's got a spitting eye." He stooped over the old man again. "Okay, Pap, your daughter was a gal in a million. Now you want to bring down the wrath on the one who give it to her, don't you?"

He mumbled again.

"I think he said, Lieutenant," said Ellery, "something about the Lord providing."

"Not in Harlem," said the detective. "Pap, you keep your mind on this. All we want to know is, did your girl Bea know some white?"

The old man did not answer.

"It's all this pale hide around here," said the Negro lieutenant apologetically. "Pap, who is he? What did he look like? Bea ever tell a white skin off?"

The brown skull drew back again.

"Better save that juice," growled the lieutenant. "Come on, Pappy, all I want is one answer to one question. Bea had a phone. Did a white man keep calling her up?"

The withered lips drew back in a tormented grin. "She has truck with a white, I kill her with my own two hands." Then he shrank into the corner of the bench.

"Say."

But the Inspector was shaking his head. "He's 80 if he's a day, Lieutenant. And look at his hands. All crippled up with arthritis. He couldn't strangle a sick kitten."

Ellery got up. "There's nothing here. I need a few hours' sleep, Dad. And so do you."

"You go along home, Ellery. If I get a chance I'll stretch out on a cot upstairs. Where will you be tonight?"

"At Headquarters," said Ellery. "With those files."

On the morning of August 27 the Cat was at his old stand on the editorial page of the *New York Extra* doing a brisk business in fear. But business can be brisker, and during the day the circulation manager of the *Extra* earned a bonus, the reason for which became evident on the morning of the 28th. In that issue the Cat moved over to Page 1, cartoonically speaking, on a longterm lease; a new tenancy so successful that by midmorning not a copy was to be found on any newsstand in the City.

And, as if to celebrate his leasehold, he waved a new tail.

It was ingenious. At first glance—there was no caption—the picture advertised a new horror: There were the six numbered tails and the giant-sized seventh, a scratchline arrogance. The reader seized the paper and hunted in vain among the headlines. Puzzled, he returned to the drawing; whereupon he saw it as it was, the noose shaped by the great tail numbered 7 being no noose at all but a question mark.

In the places of authority there was sharp disagreement as to precisely which question the question mark marked. The *Extra's* editor, in an interesting telephone conversation with the Mayor on the afternoon of the 28th, protested in a wide-eyed tone of voice that the question was, obviously, *Is the Cat going to claim a seventh victim?*— a logical, ethical, public-service, newsworthy query, the editor said, arising smack from the facts of record. The Mayor replied carbolically that it seemed to him, and to a great many other New Yorkers who had seen the cartoon and who were even now harrying the City Hall and Police Headquarters telephone operators, that the question it posed was, crudely and brutally, *Who's going to be the's Cat's seventh victim?*—executed, moreover, in a drooling-whiskered, chop-licking style which was

39

distinctly not in the public service, quite the contrary, and which he, the Mayor, might have expected from an opposition newspaper which was incapable of subordinating dirty politics to the public interest. The editor retorted that he, the Mayor, ought to know, as he was lugging around a rather large bundle of soiled laundry himself, and the Mayor shouted, "What do you mean by that slanderous remark?", at which the editor replied that he yielded to no man in his admiration for the rank and file of New York's Finest but everybody who knew the score knew that the Mayor's appointee, the present Commissioner, was an old party fire-horse who couldn't catch a pop fly let alone a desperate criminal, and if the Mayor was so deletedly concerned about the public interest why didn't he appoint somebody sharp to the top police post?—then maybe the people of the City of New York could go back to sleeping nights. What was more, this was a suggestion the *Extra* intended to toss off in its lead editorial tomorrow—"in the public interest, Mr. Mayor, you understand." With which the editor of the *Extra* hung up to receive a circulation report that left him glowing.

He glowed too soon.

As the Mayor angrily sniffed the green carnation in his lapel, the Commissioner said, "Jack, if you want my resignation—"

"Don't pay any attention to that rag, Barney."

"It has a lot of readers. Why not cross it up before that editorial hits the streets tomorrow?"

"By firing you? I'll be damned if I will." And the Mayor added thoughtfully, "And I'll be damned if I won't, too."

"Exactly," said the Commissioner, lighting a cigar. "I've given the whole situation a lot of thought. Jack, what New York needs in this crisis is a hero, a Moses, somebody who'll capture their imaginations and—"

"Distract their attention?"

"Well . . ."

"Come on, Barney, what's on your mind?"

"Well, you appoint this fellow something like . . . well, like Special Cat Catcher for the Mayor."

"Pied Piper of Gotham, hm?" muttered His Honor. "No, that was rats. We've got plenty of those, too."

"No connection with the P.D. A roving assignment. Sort of advisory. And you could break the story just too late for the *Extra* to yank that editorial."

"Don't you mean, Barney," murmured the Mayor, "that you want me to appoint a fall guy who'll absorb the heat and take all the raps, while you and the Department get off the spot and back to everyday operations?"

"Well, it's a fact," said the Commissioner, looking critically at his cigar, "that the men, from the brass down, have been thinking more of headlines than results—"

"Suppose this fellow," asked the Mayor, "beats you to the Cat?"

The Commissioner laughed.

Rather abruptly, the Mayor said, "Barney, whom did you have in mind?"

"A real glamor boy, Jack. Native New Yorker, no political ax to grind, nationally known as a crime investigator, yet he's a civilian. He can't refuse, because I softened him up first by dropping the whole hot potato in his old man's lap."

The Mayor slowly brought his swivel chair back to the vertical.

The Commissioner nodded.

The Mayor reached for his private line. "Barney," he said, "this time I think you've outfoxed yourself. Oh, Birdy. Get me Ellery Queen."

"I'm overcome, Mr. Mayor," said Ellery. "But certainly my qualifications—"

"I can't think of a better man to become Special Investigator for the Mayor. Should have thought of it long ago. I'll be frank with you, Mr. Queen—"

"Yes," said Ellery.

"Sometimes a case comes along," said the Mayor, one eye on his Police Commissioner, "that's so off the trail, so eccentric, it licks even the finest cop. I think this Cat business needs the kind of special talents you've demonstrated so brilliantly in the past. A fresh and unorthodox approach."

"Those are kind words, Mr. Mayor, but wouldn't a thing like this create hard feeling on Centre Street?"

"I think I can promise you, Mr. Queen," said His Honor dryly, "the full co-operation of the Department."

"I see," said Ellery. "I suppose my father—"

"The only one I've discussed this with is the Commissioner. Will you accept?"

"May I take a few minutes to think it over?"

"I'll be waiting here at my office for your call."

Ellery hung up.

"Special Investigator to the Mayor," said the Inspector, who had been listening on the extension. "They're really getting fussed."

"Not about the Cat," Ellery laughed. "The case is getting too torrid to touch and somebody's looking for a potential burnt sacrifice to stand up and take the heat."

"The Commissioner . . ."

"He's really played that angle, hasn't he?"

The Inspector scowled. "Not the Mayor, Ellery. The Mayor's a politician, but he's also an honest man. If he fell for this, it's for the reason he gave you. Why not do it?"

Ellery was silent.

"All this would do would make it official . . ."

"And tougher."

"What you're afraid of," said his father deliberately, "is being committed."

"Well, I'd have to see it through."

"I hate to get personal, but doesn't that make two of us? Ellery, the move might be important in another way."

"How?"

"Just the act of your taking this job might scare the Cat off. Thought of that?"

"No."

"The publicity alone—"

"I meant no, it won't."

"You underestimate your rep."

"You underestimate our kitty. I have the feeling," said Ellery, "that nothing can scare him off."

His voice conveyed such a burdensome knowledge that the Inspector started. "For a second there you had me thinking . . ." But then he said slowly, *"Ellery, you've spotted something."*

Between them lay the archaeology of murder. Detail photographs of the victims, full and side views. General views of the scenes of the crimes, interiors, exteriors, closeups, from various angles. Cross-sketchings, neatly compass-directed and drawn to specified scale. The file of appurtenant fingerprints. A whole library of reports, records, assignments, details of work complete with notations of time, place, names, addresses, findings, questions and answers and statements and technical information. And, on a separate table, *res gestae* evidence, the originals.

Nowhere in this classified heterogeneity had a recognizable clue been discovered.

In a sharper tone the Inspector said, "Have you?"

Ellery said, *"Maybe."*

The Inspector opened his mouth.

"Don't ask me any more. Dad. It's something, but where it may lead . . ." Ellery looked unhappy. "I've spent forty-eight hours on this. But I want to go over it again."

Inspector Queen said into his phone, "Get the Mayor. Tell him Ellery Queen."

He sounded at peace for the first time in twelve weeks.

The news burst upon the City with a roar that soothed even the Police Commissioner. The noise was largely jubilant. The Mayor's mail increased fivefold and the City Hall switchboard was unable to handle the volume of telephone calls. Commentators and columnists approved. It was noted that within twenty-four hours the gross number of false alarm police calls had been reduced by half and the strangulation of alley cats all but stopped. A small section of the press scoffed, but its collective voice was too feeble to register against the applause. As for the *New York Extra,* Ellery's appointment caught it with the issue containing its editorial blast all but run off; and although in a followup edition the paper excoriated the Mayor for "undermining the morale of the finest police force in the world," the Mayor's announcement took the sting out of the charge.

"Mr. Queen's appointment," the Mayor's handout had said in part, "in no way conflicts with, weakens, or is an expression of lack of confidence in, the regular police authority. The homicide record of the New York Police Department speaks for itself. But in view of the rather peculiar nature of this particular series of homicides, I have felt it advisable to enlist the aid of an expert who has specialized in unusual crimes. The suggestion that Ellery Queen be appointed Special Investigator came from the Police Commissioner himself, with whom Mr. Queen will work in the closest co-operation."

The Mayor repeated his statement over the air the same night.

At City Hall, after the swearing-in ceremony, punctuated by flashlight shots of the Mayor and Ellery Queen, of Ellery Queen and the Police Commissioner, of the Police Commissioner and the Mayor, and of the Mayor, the Police Commissioner, and Ellery Queen, Ellery read a prepared statement.

"The Cat has been at large in Manhattan for almost three months. In that period he has murdered six people. The file on six homicides weighs just about as much as the responsibilities I have accepted in taking this post. But while I have a great deal of catching up to do, I am sufficiently familiar with the facts to feel justified in stating even at this time that the case can and will be solved and the killer caught. Whether he will be caught before he commits another murder remains, of course, to be seen. But if the Cat should claim another victim tonight, I ask everyone to bear in mind that more New Yorkers are killed by automobiles in one day on our streets than the Cat has killed in three months."

Immediately he finished reading the statement, Ellery was asked by the reporter for the *Extra* if he was not already "withholding information": "Did you mean by saying 'I am sufficiently familiar with the facts to feel justified in stating that the case will be solved' that you've got a hot lead?"

Ellery smiled faintly and said: "I'll stand on my statement as read."

In the next few days his course was puzzling. He did not act like a man who has found something. He did not act at all. He retired to the Queen apartment and remained invisible to the public eye. As for the public ear, he took his telephone off the cradle, leaving Inspector Queen's direct line to Headquarters as his sole contact with the City. The Queen front door he kept locked.

It was not quite what the Commissioner had planned, and Inspector Queen heard rumblings of his discontent. But the old man merely continued to lay reports before Ellery as they came in, without comment or question. One of these concerned the marijuana-smoking trumpet player detained in the Beatrice Willikins investigation: the musician's story had been substantiated and he had been released. Ellery scarcely glanced at the report. He balanced on his coccyx chainsmoking as he studied the lunar topography of his study ceiling, that epic issue between the Queens and their wily landlord. But the Inspector knew that Ellery was not thinking of the unattainable calcimine.

During the evening of August 31, however, Ellery was back at the reports. Inspector Queen was about to leave his office after another day which had contrived to be both full and empty when his private line came to life and he picked up the phone to hear his son's voice.

"I've been going over the reports on the cords again—"

"Yes, Ellery."

"I was thinking of a possible way to determine the Cat's manual preference."

"What do you have in mind?"

"The technique worked out years ago on the Continent by the Belgian, Goddefroy, and others."

"With rope?"

"Yes. The surface fibers will lie in the direction opposite to that of the pulling or other motions involving friction."

"Well, sure. We've settled a few hanging cases that way where the question was suicide or murder. What of it?"

"The Cat loops the silk cord around his victim's neck from behind. Before he can start pulling and tightening the noose, he's got to cross the ends over each other. Theoretically, therefore, there ought to be a point of friction where the noose crosses itself at the nape of the neck.

"In two of these cases, O'Reilly and Violette Smith, the neck photos show that during the stranglings—before knots were tied—the two ends of the cord did make contact in crossing."

"Yes."

"All right. He's pulling with both hands, one to each end of the cord, in opposite directions. But unless he's ambidextrous, he's not pulling with equal force. One hand will tend to hold, while the other—his favored hand—will tend to pull. In other words, if he's righthanded the end of the cord held by his left hand ought to show a point of friction, and the end of the cord held by his right hand ought to show a line of friction. Vice versa if he's lefthanded. Tussah silk is coarsefibered. There may be observable effects."

"It's a thought," muttered the Inspector.

"Call me back when you find out, Dad."

"I don't know how long it'll take. The lab's been overworked and it's late. You'd better not wait up. I'll stick around here till I find out."

The Inspector made several telephone calls, leaving word that he was to be notified the moment a finding was made. Then, because he had a couch hauled into his office several weeks before, he stretched out on it thinking he would close his eyes for just a few minutes.

When he opened them, the September 1 sun was pouring in speckled splendor through his dusty windows.

One of his phones was ringing.

He tottered over to his desk.

"What happened to you?" asked Ellery.

"I lay down for a cat nap last night and the next thing I knew the phone was ringing."

"I was about to call a policeman. What about those cord findings?"

"I haven't . . . Wait, the report's on my desk. Damn it, why didn't they wake me?" After a moment, the Inspector said: "Inconclusive."

"Oh."

"Their opinion is that O'Reilly and the Smith woman thrashed about from side to side during the attacks just enough to make the Cat alternate his pull from one hand to the other and back. In a sort of seesaw movement. Maybe O'Reilly was only stunned and fought back. Anyway, there's no point of friction determinable. What slight friction areas are detectable in the silk are about equally divided between right and left."

"And there you are." But then Ellery said in an altogether different tone, "Dad, come right home."

"Home? I'm just starting my day, Ellery."

"Come home."

The Inspector dropped the phone and ran.

"What's up?" Inspector Queen was breathing hard from his sprint up the stairs.

"Read these. They came in this morning's mail."

The Inspector sat down slowly in the leather armchair. One envelope bore the brash imprint of the *New York Extra,* the address typewritten; the other was small, pinkish, and secretive-looking and it had been addressed by hand.

47

From the *Extra* envelope he took a slip of yellow scratch-pad paper.

DEAR E.Q.—What did you do, rip out your phone? Or are you looking for the Cat in Bechuanaland? I've been up to your place six times in the past couple of days and no answer.

I've got to see you.

JAMES GUYMER MCKELL

P.S. Known to the trade as "Jimmy Leggitt." Leg-It, get it? Call me at the *Extra*.

J.G.M.

"Monica McKell's kid brother!"

"Read the other one."

The notepaper of the second letter matched the envelope. This was elegance unaccustomed, a yearning after effect. The hand was hurried and a bit wretched.

DEAR MR. QUEEN,

I have been trying to reach you by telephone ever since the radio announced your appointment as Special Investigator of the Cat murders.

Can you possibly see me? This is *not* an attempt to get your autograph.

Please.

Sincerely,
CELESTE PHILLIPS

"Simone Phillip's sister." The Inspector laid the two letters down on an endtable, carefully. "Going to see them?"

"Yes. I phoned the Phillips girl at her home and I reached McKell at his paper. They both sound pretty young. I've seen some of McKell's stuff on the Cat cases under the name of Leggitt, but nothing that connected him personally with any of them. Did you know Leggitt and McKell were the same man?"

48

"No." The Inspector seemed disturbed by his ignorance. "I've seen him, of course, but in the McKell home on Park Avenue. I suppose being a legman is the thing to do just now in his set. Did they say what they wanted?"

"Celeste Phillips said she'd rather tell me in person. I told McKell if it was an interview he was after for that ragbag he works for I'd heave him out on his ear, but he assured me it was personal."

"Both in the same morning," muttered the Inspector. "Did either mention the other?"

"No."

"When are they due?"

"I violated a cardinal rule of the Manual. I'm seeing them at the same time. 11 o'clock."

"Five of! I've got to shower, shave, and get into clean clothes." The old man, hurrying to his bedroom, added over his shoulder, "Hold them here. By force, if you have to."

When the refurbished man emerged, his son was gallantly applying the flame of a lighter to a cigaret held by two slim gloved fingers to two female lips of distinction. She was sleekly modish from her hairdo to her shoetips, but young—the New York woman as she would like to be, but not quite grown up to it. The Inspector had seen girls like her on Fifth Avenue in the late afternoons, alone and unapproachable, the healthy raw material of youth covered by a patina of chic. But she was never upper crust; there was no boredom in her. *Vogue* just graduated from *Seventeen,* and very beautiful.

The Inspector was confused. It was Celeste Phillips. But what had happened to her?

"Hello, Miss Phillips." They shook hands; her grip was quick, withdrawing. She wasn't expecting me, he thought; Ellery didn't say I was home. "I almost didn't recognize you." It was incredible; less than two weeks. "Please sit down."

Over her shoulder as she turned he glimpsed Ellery being quizzical. The Inspector recalled his description of Simone Phillip's sister and he shrugged in reply. It was impossible to see this spick-and-span girl against the smeary background of the flat on 102nd Street. Yet she still lived there; Ellery had reached her there. Inspector Queen decided that it was the clothes. Probably borrowed for the occasion from that dress shop she models in, he thought. The rest was makeup. When she got home and returned the finery and washed her face she would be again the Cinderella he remembered. Or would she? He was really not so sure. The sunny shallows under her bright black eyes, which had replaced the purple deeps he remembered, would not blot off with a towel. And certain planes then in her face had . . . been buried with her sister?

By the pricking of my thumbs . . .

"Don't let me interrupt anything," said the Inspector with a smile.

"Oh, I was just telling Mr. Queen how impossible the apartment situation still is." Her fingers were unclasping and reclasping the catch on her bag with a life of their own.

"You're intending to move?" At the Inspector's glance the fingers flew to a stop.

"As soon as I can find another place."

"Yes, you'll be starting a new life," the Inspector nodded. "Most people do. In cases like this." Then he said, "Did you get rid of the bed?"

"Oh, no. I sleep in it." She said very quickly, "I've been sleeping on a cot for years. Simone's bed is so comfortable. She'd want me to. And then . . . I'm not afraid of my sister, you see."

"Well," said Ellery. "That's a good healthy attitude. Dad, I'd just about got round to the point of asking Miss Phillips why she wanted to see me."

"I want to help, Mr. Queen." She had a *Vogue* voice this morning, too. So careful.

"Help? In what way?"

"I don't know. I don't even know . . ." She covered her distress with a *Vogue* smile. "I don't understand it myself. Sometimes you feel you just have to do something. You don't know why."

"Why did you come, Miss Phillips?"

She twisted in the chair. But then she snapped forward and she was no longer a figure in a magazine but a very young woman stripped all but bare. "I pitied my sister terribly. She was a cripple in more ways than one. Anybody would be, chained to a bed so long. Absolutely helpless. I hated myself for not being a cripple, too. I always felt so *guilty*.

"How can I explain it?" she cried. "Simone wanted to live. She was, oh, greedy about it. She was interested in everything. I had to tell her how people in the streets looked, what the sky was like on a cloudy day, the garbage men, the lines of wash across the court. She kept the radio going from morning to night. She had to know all about the movie stars and the society people, who was getting married, who was getting divorced, who was having a baby. When I went out with some man, which wasn't too often, I had to tell her what he said, how he said it—what his line was, the passes he made, how I felt about the icky phase of going out.

"And she hated me. She was jealous. When I came home from work I used to wipe the makeup off before I stepped into the house. I never . . . dressed or undressed in front of her if I could help it. Only—she'd make me. She seemed to like being jealous; she'd get a kick out of it.

"And then there were other times when she'd cry and I knew she loved me very much."

"She was right," Celeste Phillips said in a hard voice. "There was no justice in her being a cripple. It was a punishment she didn't deserve and she was determined not to give up. She wanted to live much more than I do. Much more.

"Killing her wasn't—wasn't *fair*.

"I want to help find the one who killed her. I don't understand it and I can't believe yet that it really happened to us—to her . . . I've got to be part of his punishment. I can't just stand around doing nothing. I'm not afraid or kittenish or silly. Let me help, Mr. Queen. I'll carry your briefcase, run errands, type letters, answer your phone—anything. Whatever you say. Whatever you think I can do."

She looked down at her white doeskins, blinking angrily.

The Queens kept looking at her.

"I'm really awfully, terribly sorry," said a voice, "but I rang and rang—"

Celeste jumped up and ran to the window. A long wrinkle ran like a crack from one shoulder to the opposite hip and the young man in the doorway seemed spellbound by it. As if he half-expected a shell to fall off.

He said again, "I can't tell you how sorry," not taking his eyes from her back, "but I lost a sister by that route myself. I'll come back later."

Celeste said, "Oh!" and she turned around quickly.

They stared at each other across the room.

Ellery said, "Miss Phillips and—I gather—Mr. McKell."

"Ever see New York the way it's going to look the day after God Almighty strikes us all dead because He's sick and tired of us?—I mean, Wall Street on Sunday morning?" Jimmy McKell was saying to Celeste Phillips ten minutes later. As far as he was concerned, the Almighty had already begun, with the Queens. "Or Big Liz coming up the bay? Or the mid-Hudson from the Yonkers ferry in June? Or Central Park from a Central Park South penthouse looking north any old time? Ever taste a *bagel*? *Halvah*? Chopped liver with chicken fat and a slice of black radish? *Shish kebab*? Anchovy *pizza*?"

"No," said Celeste primly.

"This is ridiculous." He waved his absurd arms. He looks like young Abe Lincoln, thought Ellery. All length and enthusiasm, awkward and lovely. An ugly, humorous mouth and eyes not so frank as his voice. His brown suit was positively disreputable. 25 or 26. "And you call yourself a New Yorker, Celeste?"

Celeste stiffened. "Maybe, *Mister* McKell, being

poor all my life has something to do with it." She has the French heritage of middleclass propriety, Ellery thought.

"You sound like my saintly father in reverse," said James Guymer McKell. "He never ate a *bagel*, either. Are you anti-Semitic?"

"I'm not anti-anything," gasped Celeste.

"Some of my father's best friends are anti-Semitic," said young McKell. "Listen, Celeste, if we're going to be friends you've got to understand that my father and I—"

"I've got my own tender heart to thank for this," said Celeste coldly. "That and the fact that my sister—"

"And mine."

She said, flushing, "I'm sorry."

Jimmy McKell flung a grasshopper leg up and over. "I live on a legman's stipend, my girl, and not because I like it, either. It's that or go into oil with my father. I wouldn't go into oil if I was—if I was a Portuguese sardine."

Celeste looked suspicious but interested.

"I thought, McKell," remarked the Inspector, "that you lived with your people in that Park Avenue museum."

"Yes," smiled Celeste. "How much board do you pay?"

"Eighteen bucks a week," said Jimmy, "just about enough to buy the butler's cigars. And I don't know that I'm getting my money's worth. For my silken flop, with running hot toddies, I have to take long sermons on class distinction, a Communist in every garage, how we must rebuild Germany, what this country needs is a Big Businessman in the White House, my-boy-marry-into-Steel, and that grand old favorite, The Unions Be Damned. The only reason I stay to take it is that I'm kind of sentimental about my mother. And now that Monica . . ."

"Yes?" said Ellery.

Jimmy McKell looked around. "What? Say, I've kind of forgotten what I came for, haven't I? It's that old debbil sex again. Pin-up GI McKell, they used to call me."

"Tell me about your sister," said Celeste suddenly, pinching her skirt forward.

"Monica?" He pulled a cigaret with the texture of a prune from his pocket, and a large match. Celeste covertly watched him light up and lean forward in a jackknife, one eye cocked against the smoke, his elbows on his shanks and an overgrown hand tossing the match stump up and down. Jimmy Stewart and Gregory Peck, Celeste thought. And—yes—the teeniest dash of Raymond Massey around the mouth. Young-wise and boy-old. Homely and sweet. Probably had every woman in New York running after him. "A good joe. Everything they said about Monica was true, yet they never got to know her. Least of all father or mother. It was her own fault; she was misery-misery-misery inside, and she put up a front to cover it that was tougher to get through than a tank trap. Monica could be mean, and cruel, and toward the end she was getting worse."

He tossed the match into an ashtray. "Father had always spoiled her rotten. He taught her what power was and he gave her his own contempt for people. His attitude toward me's always been different; he made me toe the line from the start. We used to have some pretty rough times. Monica was a grown woman when I was still in knee pants, and it was Monica who slugged it out with father in my defense. He never could stand up to Monica.

"Mother was always afraid of her."

Jimmy hooked a garter-revealing leg over the arm of the chair. "My sister grew up—as long as you're asking—without a slum kid's chance to find out what she really wanted out of life. Whatever it was, it wasn't what she had, and that's what made my father into an even meaner old man than he'd ordinarily have been, because in his view she had everything. I found out by spending three years in the Army as a dough-foot, two of them crawling around the Pacific mosquito parks on my belly. Monica never did find out.

The only outlet she had was kicking the rules in the pants. And all the time, underneath, she was scared and mixed up . . . It's a funny deal, Celeste," said Jimmy suddenly, staring at her.

"Yes . . . Jimmy?"

"I know a lot about you." She was startled at that. "I've been covering the Cat cases since the Abernethy murder—I get special privileges at the Bastille because they find me useful for dirt-digging purposes in the upper crust. I actually talked to you after your sister was murdered."

"You did? I didn't . . ."

"Naturally, I was just one of the vultures, and you were pretty numb. But I remember thinking at the time that you and I had a lot in common. We were both way out of our class and we both had sisters who were cripples and whom we loved and understood and who got the same nasty, sickening deal."

"Yes."

"I've been meaning to look you up when you'd had a chance to unpack the bags under your eyes and get your defenses up a little. I was thinking about you when I walked up those stairs."

Celeste looked at him.

"Cross my heart and hope to die in the oil business." Jimmy grinned, but only for an instant. He turned abruptly to Ellery. "I run off at the mouth, Queen, but only when I'm with fellow-workers. I'm a great lover of humanity and it comes out here. But I also know how and when to button up. I was interested—as a reporter—when Abernethy, Violette, and O'Reilly were knocked off; when my own sister got it, it got personal. I've got to be on the inside in this cat race. I'm no boy genius, but I've learned to toddle around this town and I think you can use me. If my newspaper connection rules me out, I'll quit today. Myself, I think it's an advantage; gives me entree I wouldn't have otherwise. But that's strictly up to you. Maybe before you say no I ought to go on record before witnesses that I wouldn't write anything for that lousy

55

bedsheet I work for that you nixed. Do I get the job?"

Ellery went to the mantelpiece for a pipe. He took a long time filling it.

"That makes two questions, Mr. Queen," said Celeste in a tense voice, "you haven't answered."

Inspector Queen said, "Excuse us a minute. Ellery, I'd like to talk to you."

Ellery followed his father into the study and the Inspector shut the door. "You're not considering it."

"Yes."

"Ellery, for God's sake. Send them home!"

Ellery lit his pipe.

"Are you out of your mind? A couple of hopped-up kids. And they're both connected with the case!"

Ellery puffed.

"Look here, son. If it's help you want, you've got the entire Department on call. We've got a flock of ex-GIs who'd give you everything this youngster could and a lot more—they're trained men. If you want a pretty girl, there's at least three I can think of right now in the Policewomen's Bureau who'd give the Phillips number a run for her money. And they're trained, too."

"But they're not," said Ellery thoughtfully, "connected with the case."

The Inspector blinked. Ellery grinned and went back to the living room.

"Very unorthodox," he said. "I'm inclined to go for it."

"Oh, Mr. Queen."

"What did I tell you, Celeste?"

The Inspector snarled from the doorway, "Ellery, I've got to phone my office," and he slammed the door.

"But it might be dangerous."

"I know some judo," said Jimmy helpfully.

"It's not funny, McKell, Maybe very dangerous."

"Listen, son." Jimmy was growling. "The little folks we kids played tag with in New Guinea didn't wrap a cord around your neck. They cut it. But you'll notice mine is still in one piece. Of course, Celeste

56

here—that's different. Inside work, I'd say. Something exciting, useful, and safe."

"How about Celeste's speaking for herself, Jimmy?"

"Go on, Miss Alden."

"I'm scared," said Celeste.

"Sure you are! That's what I—"

"I was scared when I walked in and I'll be scared when I walk out. But being scared won't stop me from doing anything I can to help catch Simone's murderer."

"Well, now," began Jimmy.

"No," she said. Distinctly.

Jimmy reddened. He mumbled, "My mistake," and dug another refugee cigaret from his pocket.

"And we've got to have something else understood," said Ellery, as if nothing had happened. "This is no fraternity of rollicking companions, like the Three Musketeers. I'm Big Chief Plotto and I take nobody into my confidence. I give unexplained orders. I expect them to be carried out without protest, without questions, in confidence . . . and without consultation even between yourselves."

They looked up at that.

"Perhaps I should have made that part of it clear first. You're not coworkers in this little QBI. Nothing as cosy as that. You're accountable always and solely to me, what I give you to do is your personal assignment not to be communicated to each other or anyone else; and for the support of this declaration I expect you to pledge your lives, your fortunes, and your sacred honor if any. If you feel you can't join me under these conditions, say so now and we'll write this session off as a pleasantly wasted hour."

They were silent.

"Celeste?"

She clutched her bag. "I said I'd do anything. I accept."

But Ellery persisted. "You won't question your instructions?"

"No."

"No matter what they happen to be?"

"No."

"No matter how unpleasant or incomprehensible?"

"No," said Celeste.

"And you agree not to disclose your instructions to anyone?"

"I agree, Mr. Queen."

"Even to Jimmy?"

"To anybody."

"Jimmy?"

"You're a tougher boss than the human oak knot who holds down the city desk at the *Extra*."

"Amusing," smiled Ellery, "but it doesn't answer my question."

"I'm in."

"On those precise terms?"

"Yes, sir."

Ellery looked at them for a moment.

"Wait here."

He went quickly into his study, shutting the door.

As Ellery began to write on a tablet, his father came in from his bedroom. The old man stood at the desk watching, his lips pushed out.

"Anything new downtown, Dad?" murmured Ellery, writing.

"Just a call from the Commissioner asking—"

"Asking what?"

"Just asking."

Ellery tore the sheet off the pad, put it into a plain envelope, sealed the envelope, and wrote on its face, "J."

He began to write on another sheet.

"Nothing at all, hm?"

"Oh, it's not all Cat," said the Inspector, watching. "Murder on West 75th and Amsterdam. Double header. Betrayed wife trails hubby to apartment and lets both sinners have it. With a pearl-handled job, .22."

"Anybody I know?" Ellery cheerfully tore the second sheet off the pad.

"Dead woman was a nightclub dancer, Oriental numbers a specialty. Dead man was a wealthy lobbyist. Wife's a society woman prominent in church affairs."

"Sex, politics, society, and religion," said Ellery as he sealed the second envelope. "What more could anyone ask?" He wrote on the envelope, "C."

"It'll take the heat off for a few days, anyway." As Ellery got up his father demanded, "What's that you just wrote?"

"Instructions to my 87th Street Irregulars."

"You're really going through with this Hollywood dam-foolery?"

Ellery went back to the living room.

The Inspector paused in the doorway again, bitterly.

To Celeste Ellery handed the sealed envelope marked "C," to Jimmy the sealed envelope marked "J."

"No, don't open them now. Read, destroy, and report back to me here when you're ready."

Celeste was a little pale as she tucked her envelope into her bag. Jimmy crammed his into his outside pocket, but he kept his hand there.

"Going my way, Celeste?"

"No," said Ellery. "Leave separately. You first, Jimmy.

Jimmy jammed his hat on and loped out.

To Celeste the room seemed empty.

"When do I go, Mr. Queen?"

"I'll tell you."

Ellery went to one of the windows. Celeste settled back again, opened her bag, took out a compact. The envelope she did not touch. After a while she replaced the compact and shut her bag. She sat looking at the dark fireplace. Inspector Queen, in the study doorway, said nothing at all.

"All right, Celeste."

About five minutes had passed. Celeste left without a word.

"Now," exploded the Inspector, "will you tell me what you wrote in those damned notes?"

"Sure." Ellery was watching the street. "As soon as she comes out of the house."

They waited.

"She stopped to read the note," said the Inspector.

"And there she goes." Ellery strolled over to the armchair. "Why, Dad," he said, "in Celeste's note I instructed her to find out all she can about Jimmy McKell. In Jimmy's note I instructed him to find out all he can about Celeste Phillips."

Ellery relit his pipe, puffing placidly.

"You conniver," breathed his father. "The one thing I didn't think of, and the only thing that makes sense."

"If Heaven drops a date, the wise man opens his mouth. Chinese proverb."

The Inspector launched himself from the jamb, steaming around the room like Scuffy the Tugboat.

"Beautiful," he chortled. "They'll have to head for each other like two—" He stopped.

"Cats?" Ellery took the pipe from his mouth. "That's just it, Dad. I don't know. This could be brutal. But we can't take chances. We simply mustn't."

"Oh, it's ridiculous," snapped the old man. "A couple of romantic kids."

"I thought I detected the inspectorial nose twitch once or twice during Celeste's true confession."

"Well, in this business you suspect everybody at least once. But when you stop to think about it, you—"

"You what? We don't know a thing about the Cat. The Cat may be male, female, 16, 60, white, black, brown, or purple."

"I thought you told me a few days ago that you'd spotted something. What was it, a mirage?"

"Irony really isn't your long suit, Dad. I didn't mean something about the Cat himself."

The Inspector shrugged. He started for the door.

"I meant something about the Cat's operations."

The old man pulled up, turned around.

"What did you say?"

"The six murders have certain elements in common."

"Elements in *common?*"

Ellery nodded.

"How many?" The Inspector sounded choked.

"At least three. I can think of a fourth, too."

His father ran back. "What, son? What are they?"

But Ellery did not answer.

After a moment the Inspector hitched his trousers up and, very pale, marched out of the room.

"Dad?"

"What?" His angry voice shot in from the foyer.

"I need more time."

"For what? So he can wring a few more necks?"

"That was below the belt. You ought to know these things can't be rushed sometimes."

Ellery sprang to his feet. And he was pale, too. "Dad, they mean something. They must! But what?"

● 4

Ellery was nervy that weekend. For hours he occupied himself with compass, ruler, pencil, graph paper. Plotting the curves of statistical mysteries. Finally he hurled his co-ordinates into the fireplace and sent them up in smoke. Inspector Queen, coming upon him that broiling Sunday apparently warming himself at a fire, made the feeble remark that if he had to live in purgatory he was going to do something about lowering the temperature.

Ellery laughed disagreeably. "There are no fans in hell."

And he went into his study and made a point of closing the door.

But his father followed.

"Son."

Ellery was standing at his desk. Glaring down at the case. He had not shaved for three days; under the rank stubble his skin was green and mortal.

Looks more like a vegetable gone to seed than a man, thought his father. And he said again, "Son."

"Dad, I'd better give up."

The Inspector chuckled. "You know you won't. Feel like talking?"

"If you can suggest a cheerful topic of conversation."

The Inspector turned on the fan. "Well, there's always the weather. By the way, heard from your—what did you call those two—Irregulars?"

Ellery shook his head.

"How about a walk in the Park? Or a bus ride?"

"Nothing new?" muttered Ellery.

"Don't bother shaving. You won't meet anybody you know; the City's half-empty. What do you say, son?"

"That's another thing." Ellery looked out. There was a crimson hem on the sky. It brushed the buildings. "This damned weekend."

"Now look," said his father. "The Cat's operated strictly on working days. No Saturday, no Sunday, and he bypassed the only holiday since he got going, Fourth of July. So we don't have to get the jitters about the Labor Day weekend."

"You know what New York's like on Labor Day night." The buildings bloodied. Twenty-four hours from now, he thought. "Bottlenecks at every road, bridge, tunnel, terminal. Everybody cramming back into town at the same time."

"Come on, Ellery! Let's take in a movie. Or, I'll tell you what. We'll rustle up a revue. I wouldn't mind seeing a leg show tonight."

Ellery failed to smile. "I'd only take the Cat with me. You go on and enjoy yourself, Dad. I'd be no fun at all."

The Inspector, a sensible man, went.

But he did not go to a leg show.

With the assistance of a busman, he went downtown to Police Headquarters instead.

The dark turned cherry-colored in the heat as the French blades swished toward his neck. He held himself ready. He was calm, even happy. The tumbril below was jammed with cats knitting solemnly with silk cords of blue and salmon-pink and nodding their approval. A small cat, no larger than an ant, sat just under his nose looking up at him. This cat had black eyes. As he all but felt the flick of the knife and the clean and total pain across his neck it seemed to him the night lifted and a great light flew over everything.

Ellery opened his eyes.

His cheek throbbed where something on the desk had corrupted it and he was wondering that the screeching agony of the dream persisted past its borders when it occurred to him that the telephone in his father's bedroom was ringing in a nasty monotone.

He got up and went into the bedroom and turned on the light.

1:45.

"Hello." His neck ached.

"Ellery." The Inspector's voice stung him awake. "I've been ringing for ten minutes."

"I fell asleep at my desk. What's up, Dad? Where are you?"

"Where would I be on this line? I've been hanging around all evening. Still dressed?"

"Yes."

"Meet me right away at the Park-Lester apartment house. It's on East 84th between Fifth and Madison."

1:45 A.M. It is therefore Labor Day. The 25th of August to the 5th of September. Eleven days. Eleven is one more than ten. Between Phillips, Simone, and Willikins, Beatrice, it was ten days. One more than ten makes . . .

"Ellery, you there?"

"Who is it?" His head ached abominably.

"Ever hear of Dr. Edward Cazalis?"

"Cazalis?"

"Never mind—"

"The psychiatrist?"

"Yes."

"Impossible!"

You crept along the catwalk of a rationale while the night split into a billion tinsel fragments.

"What did you say, Ellery?"

He felt hung up in far space. Lost.

"It couldn't be Dr. Cazalis." He mustered his forces.

The Inspector's voice said craftily, "Now what would make you say a thing like that, son?"

"Because of his age. Cazalis can't be the seventh victim. It's out of the question. There's a mistake somewhere."

"Age?" The old man floundered. "What the devil has Cazalis's age got to do with anything?"

"He must be in his mid-60s. It can't be Cazalis. It's not in the scheme."

"What scheme?" His father was shouting.

"It's not Dr. Cazalis, is it? If it's Dr. Cazalis . . ."

"It just happens it isn't!"

Ellery sighed.

"It's Cazalis's wife's niece," said the Inspector peevishly. "She's Lenore Richardson. The Park-Lester is where the Richardsons live. The girl, her father and mother."

"Do you know how old she was?"

"Late or middle 20s, I think."

"Not married?"

"I don't think so. I have very little information. I've got to hang up now, Ellery. Get a move on."

"I'll be right there."

"Wait. How do you know Cazalis wasn't—?"

Just across the Park, Ellery was thinking, staring at the phone on the cradle. He had already forgotten having put it there.

The phone book.

He ran back to the study, grabbed the Manhattan directory.

Richardson.

Richardson Lenore 12 ½ E. 84.

There was also a *Richardson Zachary 12 ½ E. 84* listed at the same number.

Ellery went about shaving and changing his clothes in a blissful nirvana.

Later, it was possible to synthesize his night-long impressions into one complex. The night itself was a jumble. Faces flowed and crossed and hung apart; fragments of things said, voices broken, tears shed, looks passed, men coming, telephones ringing, pencils writing; doors, a chaise, a photograph, photographers, measurements, sketches, a small bluish fist, the dangle of a silk cord, a gold Louis XVI clock on an Italian marble fireplace, an oils nude, a torn book jacket . . .

But Ellery's mind was a machine. The unselective evidence of his senses stoked it, and after a while out came a product.

Tonight's production, by a squirrel instinct, Ellery stored away, sensing a future need.

The girl herself told him nothing. He could see what she might have been, but only from a photograph; the flesh, hardened at the supreme moment of the struggle not to die, was the usual meaningless petrifaction. She had been small and cuddlesome, with soft brown curly hair. Her nose was saucy and her mouth—from the photograph—had been pettish. She was manicured and pedicured and her hair had been recently set. The lingerie under her pongee negligee was expensive. The book she had been reading at the pounce of the Cat was a tattered reprint of *Forever Amber*. The remains of an orange and a few cherry pits lay on the inlaid occasional table beside the chaise. On the table also were a bowl of fruit, a silver cigaret box, an ashtray with fourteen lipstick-tipped butts in it, and a silver table lighter in the shape of an armored knight.

In the withering lividity of death the girl looked

50; in the photograph, a recent one, untouched 18. She had been 25 and an only child.

Ellery dismissed Lenore Richardson as a regrettable intrusion.

The living told no more.

They were four: the father and mother of the murdered girl; the girl's aunt—Mrs. Richardson's sister—Mrs. Cazalis; and the eminent Dr. Cazalis.

There was no family fellowship in their grief. This Ellery found stimulating, and he studied them carefully one by one.

The mother passed what was left of the night in uncurbed hysterics. Mrs. Richardson was a superb woman of middle age, rather too fashionably gowned, and overjeweled. Ellery thought he discovered in her a chronic anxiety, unrelated to her sorrow; like the frown of a colicky infant. She was apparently the kind of woman who hoards life like a miser. The gold of her youth having tarnished, what little remained she kept gilding and packaging in extravagant self-delusion. Now she writhed and shrieked as if, in losing her daughter, she had found something long mislaid.

The father, a gray little rigid man of 60, looked like a jeweler, or a librarian. Actually, he was the head of Richardson, Leeper & Company, one of the oldest wholesale drygoods houses in New York. Ellery had passed the Richardson, Leeper & Company building often in his prowls about the City. It stood nine stories high on half a square block on Broadway and 17th Street. The firm was known for its old-fashioned merchant virtues: sternly nonunionized, run on the benevolent-patron system, with employees who tottered comfortably along in the traces until they dropped. Richardson would be unswervingly honest, unalterably stubborn, and as narrow as a straight line. This was all quite beyond him. He could only sit by himself in a corner glancing bewilderedly from the tormented woman in the evening gown to the tumbled little mountain range under the blanket.

66

Richardson's sister-in-law was much younger than his wife; Ellery judged Mrs. Cazalis to be early-fortyish. She was pallid, slender, tall, and self-contained. Unlike her older sister, she had found her orbit; her eyes went often to her husband. She had a submissive quality Ellery had found frequently in the wives of brilliant men. This was a woman whose marriage was the sum of existence to her, in a pitifully arithmetic way. In a society composed largely of Mrs. Richardsons, Mrs. Cazalis would tend to have few friends and few social interests. She comforted her middleaged sister as a mother might soothe a child in a tantrum; it was only during Mrs. Richardson's wilder vocalisms that the younger woman's ministrations took on an edge of rebuke and resentment. It was as if she felt herself cheapened and cheated. There was a virginal, unthawed sensitivity in her, a chill delicacy of feeling, which recoiled from her sister's exhibitionism.

It was during one of these moments that an amused male voice said in Ellery's ear, "I see you've noticed it."

Ellery turned quickly. It was Dr. Cazalis, big and stoop-shouldered and powerful, with cold milky eyes and masses of icegray hair; a glacier of a man. His voice was deliberate and carried a musical undertone of cynicism. Ellery had heard somewhere that Dr. Cazalis had an unusual history for a psychiatrist; meeting the man for the first time, he was disposed to acceptance of the report. He must be 65, Ellery thought, possibly older; in semi-retirement, taking only a few cases, chiefly women, and those on a selective basis—it all added up to failing health, the declining phase of a medical career, the coronary age; and yet Dr. Cazalis seemed, aside from a certain restlessness of his large thick surgeon's hands, a vigorous and functioning personality; certainly not a man to spare himself. It was a puzzle, not the less interesting for its irrelevance. His rather encyclopedic eyes were unavoidable. He sees everything, thought Ellery, and he tells exactly nothing; or what he tells is automatically conditioned by what he thinks his hearer ought to know.

"Noticed what, Dr. Cazalis?"

"The difference between my wife and her sister. Where Lenore was concerned, my sister-in-law was criminally inadequate. She was afraid of the child, jealous and overindulgent. Alternated between pampering and screaming at her. And in the sulks ignored Lenore entirely. Now Della's in a panic overwhelmed by feelings of guilt. Clinically speaking, mothers like Della wish for the death of their young and when it happens they set up a terrified howl for forgiveness. Her grief is for herself."

"It seems to me Mrs. Cazalis is as aware of that as you are, Doctor."

The psychiatrist shrugged. "My wife's done what she could. We lost two babies in the delivery room within four years of our marriage and Mrs. Cazalis was never able to have another. She transferred her affections to Della's child and it compensated each of them—I mean my wife and Lenore—for her own lack. It couldn't be complete, of course; for one thing, the biological but otherwise inadequate mama is always a problem. Essentially," said the doctor dryly, glancing over at the sisters, "essentially unsatisfactory even in mourning. The mother beats her breast and the aunt suffers in silence. I was rather fond of the little chicken," said Dr. Cazalis suddenly, "myself." He walked away.

By 5 A.M. they had the facts orderly. Such as there were.

The girl had been home alone. She was to have accompanied her father and mother to a party in Westchester at the home of one of Mrs. Richardson's friends, but Lenore had begged off. ("She was due for her mensis," Mrs. Cazalis told Inspector Queen. "Lenore always had a hard time. She told me in the morning over the phone that she wouldn't be able to go. And Della was cross with her.") Mr. and Mrs. Richardson had left for Westchester shortly after 6

68

o'clock; it was a dinner party. One of the two domestics, the cook, was away for the holiday, having left Saturday afternoon to visit her family in Pennyslvania. The other, a maid, had been given the night off by Lenore herself; since she did not sleep in, she was not expected until morning.

The Cazalises, who lived eight blocks away, at Park Avenue and 78th Street, had been worried about Lenore all evening. At 8:30 Mrs. Cazalis had telephoned. Lenore had said she was "in the usual crampy dumps" but otherwise all right and that her aunt and uncle were not to "throw fits" about her. But when Mrs. Cazalis learned that Lenore had characteristically failed to eat anything, she had gone over to the Richardson apartment, prepared a warm meal, forced Lenore to eat it, made the girl comfortable on the chaise in the living room, and had spent perhaps an hour with her niece afterward, talking.

Lenore had been depressed. Her mother, she had told her aunt, had been hounding her to "get married and stop running from one man to another like a stupid high school girl." Lenore had been deeply in love with a boy who was killed at St.-Lô, a poor boy of Jewish origin of whom Mrs. Richardson had violently disapproved; "Mother doesn't understand and she won't let him alone even when he's dead." Mrs. Cazalis had let the girl pour out her troubles and then had tried to get her to bed. But Lenore said "with all this pain" she would stay up reading; the heat was bothering her, too. Mrs. Cazalis had urged her not to stay up too late, had kissed her good night, and left. It was about 10 P.M. She had last seen her niece reclining on the chaise, reaching for a book, and smiling.

At home, Mrs. Cazalis had wept, her husband had soothed her, and he had sent her to bed. Dr. Cazalis was staying up over an involved case history and he had promised his wife he would call Lenore before turning in, "as the chances are Della and Zach won't be rolling in till 3 or 4 in the morning." At a few minutes past midnight the doctor phoned the Richardson apartment. There was no answer. Five minutes later he tried again. There was an extension in Lenore's bedroom so that even if she had gone to sleep the repeated rings of the phone should have aroused her. Disturbed, Dr. Cazalis had decided to investigate. Without awakening his wife, he had walked over to the Park-Lester and found Lenore Richardson on the chaise with the salmon-colored silk cord imbedded in her flesh, dead of strangulation.

His in-laws had still not returned. Except for the dead girl, the apartment was empty. Dr. Cazalis had notified the police and, finding the telephone number of Mrs. Richardson's Westchester friends on the foyer table—"I left it for Lenore in case she felt sick and wanted me to come home," sobbed Mrs. Richardson—he had notified them that something had "happened" to Lenore. He had then phoned his wife to come at once, as she was, in a taxi. Mrs. Cazalis had hurried over with a long coat thrown over her nightgown to find the police already there. She collapsed, but by the time the Richardsons arrived she had recovered sufficiently to take charge of her sister—"for which," muttered Inspector Queen, "she ought to get the Nobel peace award."

The usual variation on the theme, thought Ellery. Chips of incident and accident, the death-colored core remaining. The non-crackable nut.

("I took one look at the silk cord around her neck," said Dr. Cazalis, "and I recall only one coherent thought. 'The Cat.'")

Pending daylight examination of the terrace and roof—the living room French doors had stood open all evening—they were inclined to the belief that the Cat had gained entrance boldly through the front door by way of the self-service penthouse elevator. Mrs. Cazalis recalled having tried the front door from the foyer on her way out at 10 o'clock and, at that time, the door was locked; but on her husband's arrival about 12:30 A.M. the door was wide open, held ajar by a doorstop. Since the doorstop revealed the dead girl's fingerprints, it was evident that Lenore had

70

propped the apartment door open after her aunt's departure, probably to encourage some slight circulation of air; it was a stifling night. The night doorman remembered Mrs. Cazalis's arrival and departure and Dr. Cazalis's arrival after midnight; but he admitted that he had slipped out several times in the course of the evening to get a cold bottle of beer at the delicatessen at 86th Street and Madison Avenue and that, even while he was on duty in the lobby, a prowler could have got past him unnoticed: "It's been a hot night, half the tenants are out of town, and I snoozed on the lobby settee on and off the whole evening." He had seen and heard nothing out of the ordinary.

Neighbors had heard no screams.

The fingerprint men turned up nothing of interest.

Dr. Prouty of the Medical Examiner's office was unable to fix the time of death more accurately than the limits defined by Mrs. Cazalis's departure and her husband's arrival.

The strangling cord was of tussah silk.

"Henry James would have called it," said Dr. Cazalis, "the fatal futility of facts."

They were sitting around at dawn in the wreckage of the night over cold ginger ale and beer. Mrs. Cazalis had prepared a platter of cold chicken sandwiches to which no one applied but Inspector Queen, and he only under Ellery's bullying. The body had been removed on the official order; the sinister blanket was gone; a breeze blew from the penthouse terrace. Mrs. Richardson was asleep in her bedroom under sedation.

"With all respect to the Great Casuist," replied Ellery, "it's not the futility of facts that's fatal, Doctor, but their scarcity."

"In seven murders?" cried the doctor's wife.

"Seven multiplied by zero, Mrs. Cazalis. Well, perhaps not quite, but it's very difficult."

Inspector Queen's jaws were going mechanically. He seemed not to be listening.

"What can I do!"

They were startled. Lenore's father had been still so long.

"I've got to do something. I can't just sit here. I have a great deal of money . . ."

"I'm afraid money won't do it, Mr. Richardson," said Ellery. "Monica McKell's father had the same idea. His offer of $100,000 reward on August 10 hasn't even been threatened. It's simply increased the work of the police."

"How about turning in, Zach?" suggested Dr. Cazalis.

"She didn't have an enemy in the world. Ed, you know that. Everyone was mad about her. Why did this . . . why did he pick Lenore? She was all I had. Why my daughter?"

"Why anybody's daughter, Mr. Richardson?"

"I don't care about the others. What do we pay our police for!"

Richardson was on his feet, his cheeks cerise.

"Zach."

He sagged, and after a moment he mumbled something and went out very quietly.

"No, dear, let him go," said the psychiatrist quickly to his wife. "Zach has that sturdy Scotch sense of the fitness of things and life is very precious to him. But I've got to worry about you. Your eyes are drooping out of your head. Come on, darling, I'll take you home."

"No, Edward."

"Della's asleep—"

"I won't go without you. And you're needed here." Mrs. Cazalis took her husband's paw. "Edward, you are. You can't stay out of this now. Tell me you'll do something."

"Certainly. I'll take you home."

"I'm not a child!"

The big man sprang to his feet. "But what can I do? These people are trained to this sort of thing. I wouldn't expect them to walk into my office and tell me how to treat a patient!"

"Don't make me seem stupid, Edward." Her voice

had sharpened. "You can tell these gentlemen what you've told me so many times. Your theories—"

"Unfortunately, that's all they are. Now let's be sensible. You're going home this—"

"Della needs me." The taut voice was stretching.

"Darling." He seemed startled.

"You know what Lenore meant to me." Mrs. Cazalis broke. "You know, you know!"

"Of course." His glance warned Ellery and Inspector Queen off. "Lenore meant a great deal to me, too. Now stop, you'll make yourself very ill."

"Edward, you know what you said to me!"

"I'll do what I can. You've got to cut this out, dearest. Stop it." Gradually, in his arms, her sobs subsided.

"But you haven't promised."

"You needn't go home. I think you're right. Della will need you. Use the guest room, dear. I'll give you something to make you sleep."

"Edward, promise!"

"I promise. Now I'm putting you to bed."

When Dr. Cazalis returned, he looked apologetic. "I should have seen those hysterics coming on."

"I'd welcome a good old-fashioned emotional binge myself right now," murmured Ellery. "By the way, Doctor, which theories was Mrs. Cazalis referring to?"

"Theories?" Inspector Queen looked around. "Who's got theories?"

"Why, I suppose I have," said Dr. Cazalis, seating himself and reaching for a sandwich. "Say, what are those fellows doing out there, anyway?"

"Examining the terrace and roof. Tell me about these theories of yours, Doctor." The Inspector took one of Ellery's cigarets; he never smoked cigarets.

"I suppose everybody in New York has one or two," smiled the psychiatrist. "The Cat murders would naturally not pass a psychiatrist by. And even though

73

I don't have the inside information at your disposal—"

"It wouldn't add much to what you've read."

Cazalis grunted. "I was about to say, Inspector, that I'm sure it wouldn't make any material difference. Where it seems to me you people have gone off is in applying to these murders the normal investigatory technique. You've concentrated on the victims—admittedly the sensible methodology in ordinary cases, but in this one exactly wrong. In this case you stand a better chance concentrating on the murderer."

"How do you mean?"

"Isn't it true that the victims have had nothing in common?"

"Yes?"

"Their lives crossed nowhere?"

"As far as we can tell."

"Take my word for it, you'll never find a significant point of contact. The seven seem unrelated because they are unrelated. At no time did they stand a greater chance of interrelationship than if the murderer had shut his eyes and opened the telephone directory, let's say, to seven different pages at random, determined to kill the forty-ninth person listed in the second column of each page."

Ellery stirred.

"We have, then," continued Dr. Cazalis, swallowing the last of his sandwich, "seven persons dying by the same hand who have no interidentity or contiguity. What does this mean in practical terms? A series of apparently *indiscriminate* acts of violence. To the trained mind, this spells psychosis. I say 'apparently' indiscriminate, by the way, because the conduct of the psychotic appears unmotivated only when judged in the perspective of reality—that is, by more or less healthy minds viewing the world as it is. The psychotic has his motivations, but they proceed from distorted views of reality and falsification of facts.

"My opinion, based on an analysis of the data available to me, is that the Cat—damn that cartoonist! an infamous libel on a very well-balanced beast!

74

—suffers from what we call a systematized delusional state, a paranoid psychosis."

"Well, naturally," said the Inspector, who seemed disappointed, "one of our first theories was that the killer's insane."

"Insanity is the popular and legal term," said Dr. Cazalis with a shrug. "There are any number of individuals who, though not insane in a legal sense, are nevertheless subjects of a psychosis. I suggest we stick to the medical terminology."

"Psychotic, then. We've checked the mental hospitals time and again without result."

"Not all psychotics are institutionalized, Inspector Queen," said the psychiatrist dryly. "That's exactly my point. If, for example, the Cat is a paranoid psychotic of the schizophrenic type, he may well be as normal in appearance and behavior—to the untrained eye—as any of us. He might remain unsuspected for a long time, during which he could do plenty of damage."

"I never yet talked to one of you birds," said the Inspector wearily, "that I didn't come away with my chin dragging."

"I gather, Dad," said Ellery, "that Dr. Cazalis has more to disseminate than gloom. Go on, Doctor."

"I was merely going to suggest the alternative, which is that he may be undergoing treatment, or may have been recently under treatment, by a private doctor. It would seem to me whoever's committing these crimes is a local product, all seven murders having taken place in Manhattan, so a good place to start checking would be right in the borough here. It would mean, obviously, getting the co-operation of every man in the field. Each one, being briefed on what to look for, could comb his own records for patients, either current or discharged, who might be possibilities; and those possibilities would have to be questioned by trained people for clinical clues as well as investigated by you people in the routine way. It might be a total frost, of course, and there'd be a dickens of a lot of work—"

"It's not the work," muttered Inspector Queen. "It's the trained personnel that's bothering me."

"Well, I'd be glad to do what I could to help. You heard my wife! I don't have many patients these days—" the psychiatrist made a face—"I'm tapering off to retirement—so it wouldn't work any special hardship on me."

"Handsome offer, Dr. Cazalis." The Inspector rubbed his mustache. "I'll admit this has opened up a field we haven't scratched. Ellery, what do you think?"

"By all means," said Ellery promptly. "It's a constructive suggestion and might well lead straight to our man."

"Do I detect the faintest note of doubt?" smiled Dr. Cazalis. His powerful fingers were drumming on the table.

"Perhaps."

"You don't agree with my analysis."

"Not entirely, Doctor."

The psychiatrist stopped drumming.

"I'm not convinced that the crimes are indiscriminate."

"Then you have information I haven't."

"No. I base my opinion on the same data, I'm sure. But, you see, there's a pattern in these crimes."

"Pattern?" Cazalis stared.

"The murders have a number of elements in common."

"Including this one?" rasped the Inspector.

"Yes, Dad."

Dr. Cazalis began to drum again. "I take it you don't mean consistency of methods—the cords, strangling—"

"No. I mean elements common to the seven victims. I'm convinced they signify a plan of some sort, but what it arises from, what its nature is, where it's going . . ." Ellery's eyes clouded.

"Sounds interesting." Dr. Cazalis was studying

Ellery surgically. "If you're right, Mr. Queen, I'm wrong."

"We may both be right. I have the feeling we are. 'Though this be madness, yet there is method in 't.'" They laughed together. "Dad, I'd emphatically recommend that Dr. Cazalis's suggestion be followed up, and right away."

"We're breaking every rule in the book," groaned his father. "Doctor, would you consider taking full charge?"

"I? Of the psychiatric end?"

"That's right."

Dr. Cazalis's fingers stopped exercising. But they remained, as it were, available.

"This is going to be as big a selling as a medical job. It won't work unless every doctor in the field co-operates. With you heading that phase of the investigation—with your reputation and professional connections, Doctor—it's a guarantee of thorough coverage I don't think we'd get another way. As a matter of fact," said the Inspector thoughtfully, "it wouldn't be a bad arrangement for other reasons. The Mayor's already appointed my son special investigator. We're covering the official end. With you in charge of a medical inquiry, it would give us a three-pronged offensive. Maybe," said the Inspector, exhibiting his denture, "maybe we'd even turn up a little something."

He said abruptly, "I'd have too get confirmation of this downtown, Dr. Cazalis, but something tells me the Mayor and the Commissioner will be very happy about the whole thing. Pending an okay, can I tell them you're available?"

The psychiatrist threw up his hands. "What was that line from a movie I once saw? 'Bilked by my own chicanery!' All right, Inspector, I'm hooked. What's the procedure?"

"Where are you going to be later today?"

"Depends on how Della and Zach behave themselves. Either here or at home, Inspector. This morning I'm going to try to get a few hours' sleep."

77

"Try?" Ellery stretched, rising. "In my case it won't be the least problem."

"Sleeping is always a problem with me. I'm a chronic insomniac—a symptom which is generally part of the clinical picture," said the psychiatrist with a smile, "of dementia, general paresis, and so on, but don't tell my patients. I keep well supplied with sleeping pills."

"I'll phone you this afternoon, Dr. Cazalis."

Cazalis nodded to the Inspector and strolled out.

The Queens were silent. The men working on the terrace were beginning to drift away. Sergeant Velie was crossing the terrace in the sun.

"What do you think?" asked the Inspector suddenly.

"Think? About what, Dad?"

"Cazalis."

"Oh.—Very solid citizen."

"Yes, isn't he."

"Nothing doing," said Sergeant Velie. "No sign of a damn thing, Inspector. He got in by that penthouse elevator, all right."

"The only thing is," mumbled the Inspector, "I wish he'd stop those figure exercise of his. Makes me nervous.—Oh, Velie. Knock off and get some shuteye."

"What about those newspaper guys?"

"They've probably ganged up on Dr. Cazalis. Run interference for him and tell them I'll be right there. With my own pet line of double talk."

The sergeant nodded and clumped off, yawning.

"How about you, Dad?"

"I'll have to go downtown first. You going home now?"

"If I can get away in one piece."

"Wait in the hall closet. I'll decoy 'em into the livng room here and then you can make the break."

They parted rather awkwardly.

When Ellery woke up he found his father perched on the edge of the bed, looking at him.

78

"Dad. What time is it?"

"Past 5."

Ellery stretched. "Just pull in?"

"Uh-huh."

"Anything new in crime?"

"P.m. shows nothing so far. The cord's a washout. It's the other six continued."

"How's the atmosphere? Safe?"

"I wouldn't say so." Inspector Queen hugged himself as if he were cold. "They're really laying into this one. Every line into Headquarters and City Hall jammed. The papers have taken the gloves off and they're yelping for blood. Whatever good the announcement of your appointment did has gone up the flue with the murder of the Richardson girl. When I walked into the Mayor's office with the Commissioner this morning to confer on the Cazalis thing His Honor practically kissed me. Phoned Cazalis then and there. First thing he said over the phone was, 'Dr. Cazalis, when can you hold a press conference?' "

"Cazalis going to do it?"

"He's doing it right this minute. And going on the air tonight."

"I must be a great disappointment to His Honor." Ellery laughed. "Now hit the sack or you'll be a candidate for a medical conference yourself."

The Inspector failed to move.

"There's something else?"

"Ellery." The old man pulled up his left leg and began slowly to untie his shoelace. "There's been some nasty talk downtown. I wouldn't ask you this except that if I'm to keep taking it on the chin I've got to know what round it is."

"Ask me what?"

"I want you to tell me what you've spotted. He began on the other shoe. "For my own information, you understand," he explained to the shoe. "Or let me put it another way. If I'm to keep singeing my pants I want to know what the hell I'm sitting on."

It was a kind of declaration of independence, conceived in grievance and delivered for just cause.

Ellery looked unhappy.

He reached for a cigaret and an ashtray and lay back with the tray balanced on his chest.

"All right," he said. "From your standpoint I'm a disloyal dispenser of nothing and from your standpoint I suppose I am. Now let's see whether what I've been holding out on you could prove of the slightest utility to you, me, the Mayor, the Commissioner, or the shade of Poe.

"One: Archibald Dudley Abernethy was 44 years old. Violette Smith was 42 years old. Rian O'Reilly was 40 years old. Monica McKell was 37 years old. Simone Phillips was 35 years old. Beatrice Willikins was 32 years old. Lenore Richardson was 25 years old. 44, 42, 40, 37, 35, 32, 25."

The Inspector was staring.

"Each victim's been younger than the victim preceding. That's why I was so positive Dr. Cazalis couldn't have been Number 7; he's older than any of them. To have been seventh on the list he'd have to have been under 32, the sixth victim's age . . . that is, if there was a descending-age pattern. And it turned out that Number 7, the Richardson girl, was 25, and I was right. There *is* a descending-age pattern. Mathematically irregular differences, but they're always younger, younger."

The old man gripped his right shoe. "We didn't see that. Nobody saw it."

"Well, it's one of those exasperating little fragments of sense in a jumble. Like the hidden-face puzzles. You look and look, and suddenly there it is. But what does it mean? It's sense, all right, but what sense? It springs from a cause, but what cause? It can't conceivably be the result of coincidence; not seven! And yet the longer you examine it, the less it seems to signify. Can you think of a single satisfactory reason why anyone should go to the trouble of killing successively younger people—who haven't the faintest connection with one another? I can't."

"I's a poser, all right," his father muttered.

"It's true I might announce tonight that no New York 25 years old or older had anything to worry about because the Cat's going down the actuarial tables and he's passed Age 25 . . ."

"Very funny," said the Inspector feebly. "It sounds like—like something out of Gilbert and Sullivan. They'd all think you were crazy and if they thought you were sane it would only pack all the anxiety down into the—the lower brackets."

"Something like that," nodded Ellery. "So I kept it to myself.

"Two." He crushed the cigaret out and cradled his head, staring at the ceiling. "Of the seven victims, two have been male, five female. Until this last one, the victims have been 32 years old or older. Well past the minimum age of consent, wouldn't you say?"

"The what?"

"I mean, we live in a connubial society. All the roads of our culture lead to the American Home, which is not conceived as the citadel of celibacy; if the point requires any proof, we have only to consider, gentlemen, the delicious sense of naughtiness we get out of the mere phrase 'bachelor apartment.' Our women spend their maidenhood catching a husband and the rest of their lives trying to hold on to him; our men spend their entire boyhood envying their father and consequently can't wait when they grow up to marry the next best thing to their mother. Why do you suppose the American male is obsessed with the mammae? What I'm trying to say—"

"Well, for heaven's sake, say it!"

"—is that if you picked seven American adults at random, all of them over 25 years of age, six of them over 32, what are the odds that all but one of them will be unmarried?"

"O'Reilly," said the Inspector in an awed voice. "By God, O'Reilly was the only one."

"Or you could put it another way. Of the two men,

81

Abernethy was a bachelor and O'Reilly was married. That seemed to cancel out the men. But of the five women, all have been single! When you stop to think of it, that's really remarkable. Five women between the ages of 42 and 25 and not one of them succeeded in the great American rat race. As in the case of the descending ages, coincidence is unthinkable. Then the Cat deliberately chooses—among his female victims, at least—only unmarried ones. Why? Inform me."

Inspector Queen gnawed his nails. "The only thing I can think of is that he dangles the marriage bait in order to get in close. But—"

"But that just isn't the explanation, right. No such Lothario's turned up, or the slightest trace of one.

"Of course, I could have cried the glad tidings to Mrs. New York that the only females who need fear the embrace of the Cat are virgins, misogamists, and Lesbians, but—"

"Go on," snarled his father.

"Three: Abernethy was strangled with a blue silk cord, Violette Smith with a salmon-colored one, O'Reilly blue, Monica McKell salmon, Simone Phillips salmon, Beatrice Willikins salmon, Lenore Richardson salmon. There's even a report on that."

Mumbled the Inspector: "I'd forgotten that."

"One color for the males, another for the females. Consistently. Why?"

After a time the Inspector said, rather timidly: "The other day, son, you mentioned a fourth point . . ."

"Oh. Yes. They *all* had phones."

His father rubbed an eye.

"In a way, the very prosiness of the point makes it the most provocative. To me, anyway. Seven victims, seven phones. Even Simone, the poor cripple. They all had phones or, where the subscriber was someone else—as in the cases of Lenore Richardson, Simone Phillips, and Monica McKell—they had separate listings in the directory; I checked.

"I don't know the figures, but I should imagine

there's a ratio of some twenty-five phones in the United States per hundred population. One out of four. In the big urban centers, like New York, the percentage may be greater. Let's say in New York one out of three. Yet of the seven victims tagged by the Cat, not one, not two, not four, but all seven had phones.

"The first explanation to suggest itself is that the Cat picks his dainties out of the phone book. Pure lottery. But in a lottery the odds against picking seven victims successively each of whoms turns out to be younger than the last would be literally incalculable. Then the Cat makes his selections on some other basis.

"Still, all his victims are listed in the Manhattan directory. Those phones are a point, a point."

Ellery set the ashtray on his night table and swung his legs off the bed to squat, mourner-fashion. "It's damnable," he moaned. "If there were one break in the sequence—one victim older than the last, one woman strangled who was married or who'd ever been married, one man found necktied in salmon—or heliotrope!—one who didn't have a phone . . . Those points in common exist for *reasons*. Or maybe," said Ellery, sitting up suddenly, "or maybe the points in common exist for the *same* reason. A sort of great common denominator. The Rosetta stone. One key to all the doors. Do you know, that would be nice."

But Inspector Queen was mumbling as he stripped. "That getting-younger business. When you think of it . . . Two years' difference in age between Abernethy and Violette. Two years between Vi and O'Reilly. Three years between O'Reilly and McKell's sister. Two years between her and Celeste's sister. Three years between her and Beatrice Willikins. Two and three. Never more than three. In six cases. And then—"

"Yes," said Ellery, "and then Lenore Richardson and we find a jump in the age differential from a previous maximal three to seven . . . That haunted me all last night."

And now the Inspector was denuded, his little sexagenarian hide impaled on the point of a needle.

"What's haunting me," he mumbled, "is who's next?"

Ellery turned away.

"And that's all you had, son?"

"That's all I *have*."

"I'm going to bed." The little naked man shuffled out.

● 5

Inspector Queen overslept. He came galloping out at 9:45 Tuesday morning like a late starter under the whip, but when he saw who was having coffee with Ellery he slowed to a walk which neatly ended at the breakfast table.

"Well, look who's among us," beamed the Inspector. "Good morning, McKell."

"Morning, Inspector." said Jimmy McKell. "On your way to the abattoir?"

"Mmmmmmmmch," inhaled the Inspector. "I think I'll have a slup or two of the life-giving mocha myself." He pulled out a chair and sat down. "Morning son."

"Morning, morning," said Ellery absently, reaching for the coffeepot. "Jimmy came up with the papers."

"Do people still read?"

"Cazalis's interview."

"Oh."

"Goodnaturedly but firmly neutral. The calm voice of organized knowledge. We promise nothing. But one has the feeling that an Osirian hand directed by a radiant eye has taken over. The Mayor must be in the eleventh heaven."

"I thought it was seven," said Jimmy McKell.

"Not in the Egyptian cosmography, Jimmy. And there is something Pharaonic about Cazalis. 'Soldiers, from these pyramids forty centuries look down upon you.'"

"Napoleon."

"In Egypt. Cazalis is soothing syrup to the general. Simply wonderful for morale."

"Don't mind him," grinned the Inspector, reading the paper. "You'll never win . . . Say, this is pretty good medicine at that. You given up journalism, McKell? I didn't spot you among the rest of the scavengers yesterday."

"The Richardson deal?" Jimmy looked secretive. "Yesterday was Labor Day. My day. I'm a working stiff."

"Took off, eh?"

"Who labors best and so on," said Ellery. "Or was it in line of duty, Jimmy?"

"Something like that."

"You had a date with Celeste Phillips."

Jimmy laughed. "And not just yesterday. It's been one sweet journey through time. You give the most interesting assignments, dearie. You should have been a city editor."

"I take it you two have been getting along."

"We manage," replied Jimmy, "to tolerate each other."

"Nice girl," nodded the Inspector. "Son, that tasted like a refill."

"Ready to talk about it, Jimmy?"

"Say, it's getting to be my favorite subject."

"Let's have another all around." Ellery poured, amiably.

"I don't know what you two witch doctors are up to," said Jimmy, "but I'm happy to report that this is a wench of exceptional merit, and in my circles I'm known as Iconoclast McKell, Female Images a Specialty." He fingered his cup. "All kidding aside, I feel like a heel."

"Heeling is a hard profession," said Ellery. "Would

85

you mind itemizing the assignment's virtues, as you found them?"

"Well, the gal has looks, brains, personality, guts, ambition—"

"Ambition?"

"Celeste wants to go back to college. You know she had to quit in her freshman year to take care of Simone. When Simone's mother died back in—"

"Simone's mother?" Ellery frowned. "You make it sound as if Simone's mother wasn't Celeste's mother."

"Didn't you know that?"

"Know what?"

"That Celeste wasn't the daughter of Mrs. Phillips?"

"You mean those two weren't sisters?" The Inspector's cup rattled.

Jimmy McKell looked from Queen to Queen. He pushed his chair back. "I don't know that I'm fond of this," he said. "In fact, I know damn well I'm not."

"Why, what's the matter, Jimmy?"

"You tell me!"

"But there's nothing to tell," said Ellery. "I asked you to find out what you could about Celeste. If we now have something new on her—"

"On her?"

"I mean about her, something we didn't know, why, you've only justified my confidence in you."

"May we dispense with the horse droppings, sleuth?"

"Jimmy, sit down."

"I want to know what cooks!"

"Why all the heat?" growled Inspector Queen. "You'll have me thinking in a minute . . ."

"Right." Jimmy sat down suddenly. "There's nothing to think. Simone was Celeste's third cousin or something. Celeste's parents were killed in a gas stove explosion when she was a baby. Mrs. Phillips was her only relative in New York and took her in. That's all there is to it. When Mrs. Phillips died, Celeste naturally took care of Simone; they always considered each other sisters. I know a hell of a lot of real sisters who wouldn't have done what Celeste did!"

"Even speaking not Delphically," said Ellery, "so do I."

"What?"

"Go on, Jimmy."

"She's crazy to get a college education—it half-killed her when she had to give it up at Mrs. Phillips's death. The books that kid's read! Deep stuff—philosophy, psychology—why, Celeste knows more right now than I do, and I've got a Princeton sheepskin acquired by sweat, toil, and grand larceny. Now that Simone's gone, the kid's free to live her own life again, go back to school and make something of herself. She's going to enroll this week in Washington Square College for the fall semester. She wants a B.A., majoring in English and philosophy, and then she'll go on to graduate work. Maybe teach."

"She must want it a great deal to cut out a program like that for herself on a night school basis."

"Night school? Who said anything about night school?"

"We still live in a competitive economy, Jimmy. Or," said Ellery cheerfully, "were you thinking of taking that problem off her hands?"

"Maybe," said the Inspector with a wink, "maybe that question is irrelevant, immaterial, and none of our business."

Jimmy gripped the table. "Are you crumbums suggesting—?"

"No, no, Jimmy. With benefit of clergy, of course."

"Oh. Well . . . let's leave me out of it." His homely face was angry and watchful.

"She can't work as a model daytimes and go to day college too, Jimmy," said Ellery.

"She's giving up that job."

"Really?" said the Inspector.

"Oh," said Ellery, "she's got herself a night job."

"No job at all!"

"I'm afraid," said Ellery mournfully, "I lost you

somewhere back in the third canto. No job at all? How is she going to support herself?"

"With Simone's nestegg!" Jimmy was shouting now.

"Nestegg?"

"What er . . . what nestegg would that be, Jimmy?" asked the Inspector.

"Look." Jimmy inflated his chest. "You asked me to do a dirty chore and I've done it. I don't understand this, any of it. But assuming you're a big wheel in the gray cell department, Queen, and I'm just a little screw rattling around, will you tell me what the devil difference any of this makes?"

"No more difference than the truth ever makes."

"Sounds profound, but I suspect a gimmick."

"McKell." Inspector Queen was grim. "I've had a lot of men working on this case and I've been in it myself up to my Adam's apple. This is the first I've heard about Simone Phillip's leaving anybody anything but a lower back ache. Why didn't Celeste tell us?"

"Because she only found it last week! Because it's got nothing to do with the murder!"

"Found it?" murmured Ellery. "Where?"

"She was cleaning out Simone's junk. There was an old wooden table clock, a French deal that was a family heirloom or something—it hadn't run for ten years and Simone would never let Celeste have it fixed, kept it on a shelf over her bed. Well, when Celeste took it down last week it slipped out of her hands and cracked open like an egg on the floor. There was a big roll of bills inside, bound with a rubber band."

"Money? I thought Simone—"

"So did Celeste. The money had been left by Simone's father. There was a note in his handwriting bound in with the bills. According to the note, written just before he committed suicide, from the date on it, he managed to save $10,000 out of the wreckage when he dropped his fortune in the '29 market crash. He had left the ten grand to his wife."

"And Celeste knew nothing about it?"

"Mrs. Phillips and Simone never mentioned it to her. Most of the dough is there, about $8600. Celeste thinks the missing $1400 went toward Simone's doctors' bills in the early days, when Mrs. Phillips still had hopes she could be cured. Certainly Simone knew all about it, because she had fits if Celeste went anywhere near the clock. Well, now the money is Celeste's and it's going to make life tolerable for her for a while. And that's the great big mysterious story," said Jimmy with outthrust jaw, "the moral of which—if you ask me—is that, invalid or no invalid, Simone was a firstclass drip. Imagine letting that poor kid nurse her in the Black Hole of Calcutta and shag her legs off trying to support both of them when all the time Simone had almost nine grand stashed away! What was she keeping it for, the junior prom? . . . What's the matter? Why the steely looks?"

"What do you think, Dad?"

"Any way you slice it, Ellery, it's a motive."

"*Motive?*" said Jimmy.

"The first one we've found." The Inspector went to a window, looking unhappy.

Jimmy McKell began to laugh. But then he stopped laughing.

"I wondered last week if there might be a motive," said Ellery, thoughtfully. "When she came here."

"*Celeste?*"

Ellery did not reply.

"I know," said Jimmy. "This is something out of H. G. Wells. An unknown gas drifts into the earth's atmosphere out of interstellar space and everybody in the world goes fay. Including the great Ellery Queen. Why, Queen," he snarled, "she came here to help you *find* the killer of Simone!"

"Who, it develops, wasn't her sister and had deliberately held her in peonage for years."

"Give me air. Sweet, sane air."

"I'm not saying it's so, Jimmy. But by the same token can you say it isn't?"

"Damned right I can! That kid is as pure as I was till I stumbled into this Siberian Casbah this morning and got polluted! Besides, I thought you were looking for the Cat—seven-times strangler!"

"Ellery." Inspector Queen came back to the table. He had apparently fought an engagement with himself and won it. Or lost it. "It's out of the question. Not that girl."

"Now there's a man," shouted Jimmy, "who's still got one toenail on the ground!"

Ellery stared into his cooling coffee. "Jimmy, have you ever heard of the ABC theory of multiple murder?"

"The *what?*"

"X wants to kill D. X's motive isn't apparent, but if he killed D in the ordinary way the police investigation would disclose eventually that the only person, or most likely person, with motive to kill D was X. X's problem is, How can he kill D and gain his object without having his motive stand out? X sees that one way to accomplish this is by surrounding D's murder with a smokescreen of other murders, deliberately committed with the same technique in order to tie them up as a series of interrelated crimes. Consequently, X first murders A, B, and C . . . wholly innocent people, you understand, with whom he's not in the least involved. Only then does he murder D.

"The effect of this is to make the murder of D appear merely a single link in a chain of crimes. The police will not be looking for someone with motive against D, they will look for someone with motive against A, B, C, *and* D. But since X had no motive whatever for murdering A, B, and C, his motive against D is either overlooked or ignored. At least, that's the theory."

"How to become a detective in one easy lesson," said Jimmy McKell. "In a series of murders, last one with motive is It and leave my fee in the hypodermic needle, please."

"Not quite," said Ellery, without rancor. "X is smarter than that. To stop at the one murder which incriminates him, he realizes, is to bring it into exactly the prominence he has been trying to avoid by making it one of a series. Therefore, X follows the relevant murder of D with the irrelevant murders of E, F, and G—and H and I and J, if necessary. He kills as many nonsignificant persons as he feels will successfully obfuscate his motive against the significant one."

"Pushing my way through the thicket of scholarly language," grinned Jimmy, "I now get it. This 23-year-old she-gorilla with the detachable chassis, this fiend in human form, strangles Abernethy, the Smith babe, O'Reilly, Monica, Beatrice Willikins, and little Lenore Richardson just so she can sandwich in the bumpoff of her crippled cousin Simone. Queen, have you seen a good doctor lately?"

"Celeste gave up five years of her life to Simone," said Ellery patiently. "She faced the prospect of giving up—how many more? Ten? Twenty? Simone might have lived on and on. Evidently Celeste had given her excellent care; the medical report indicates no bedsores, for example, the prevention of which in such cases requires constant attention.

"But Celeste wants desperately to make something of herself. Celeste would like to get away from the cheerless and limiting environment to which Simone's existence condemns her. Celeste is also young, pretty, and hot-blooded, and her life with Simone is frustrating emotionally. On top of all this, Celeste finds one night—not last week, but last May, let's say—a young fortune, which Simone has kept a secret from her all these years and possession of which would enable Celeste to satisfy her needs and wants for a considerable period. Only one thing stands in the way of possessing it—and putting it to use—and that's her cousin Simone. She can't bring herself to leave a helpless invalid—"

"So she kills her," chuckled Jimmy. "Along with six other folks."

"We've obviously hypothesized a person of confused motivations and personality—"

"I take it back. You don't need a checkup, Queen. You need a checkdown. From the scalp."

"Jimmy, I haven't said Celeste killed Simone and the others. I haven't even indicated an opinion as to its likelihood. I'm putting the known facts together in one possible way. In a shambles that's already seen seven people slaughtered and for all we know may eventually include a great many more, would you have me ignore Celeste simply because she's young and attractive?"

"Attractive. If what you're 'hypothesizing' about Celeste is true, she's a maniac."

"Read yesterday's interview with Dr. Edward Cazalis, Noted Psychiatrist. A maniac—of a very deceptive type—is exactly what Noted Psychiatrist is looking for, and I must say he makes out a convincing case."

"*I* am the type maniac," said Jimmy through his large teeth, "who can take just so much sanity. Watch out below!" And he went over the breakfast table as if it were the edge of a pool.

But Ellery was on his feet and to one side rather more quickly, and Jimmy McKell landed on his nose in a splash of tepid coffee.

"I must say that was silly, Jimmy. Are you all right?"

"Leggo, you character assassin!" yelled Jimmy, swinging.

"Here, sonny-boy." The Inspector caught Jimmy's arm. "You've been reading too many of Ellery's books."

Jimmy shook off the Inspector's hand. He was livid. "Queen, you get somebody else to do your stooling. I'm through. And what's more, I'm going to tell Celeste what she's up against. Yes, and how you suckered me into collecting your garbage for you! And if she upchucks at the mere proximity of McKell, it'll be no more than the yokel deserves!"

"Please don't do that, Jimmy."

"Why not?"

"Our agreement."

"Produce it in writing. What did you buy, Mephisto—my soul?"

"No one forced you into this, Jimmy. You came

to me, offered your services, I accepted them on explicit conditions. Remember that, Jimmy?"

Jimmy glowered.

"Granted it's a quadrillion-to-one shot. Just on that remote possibility, will you keep your mouth shut?"

"Do you know what you're asking me to do?"

"Keep your promise."

"I'm in love with her."

"Oh," said Ellery. "That's really too bad."

The Inspector exclaimed: "So soon?"

Jimmy laughed. "Did they clock it in your day, Inspector?"

"Jimmy. You haven't answered my question."

When the doorbell rang.

The Queens looked at each other quickly.

"Who is it?" called the Inspector.

"Celeste Phillips."

But it was James Guymer McKell who reached the door first, swooping down like a stork.

"Jimmy. You didn't tell me you were—"

His long arms dropped around her.

"Jimmy." She struggled, laughing.

"I want you to be the last to know," snarled Jimmy McKell. "I love you."

"Jimmy, what . . . !"

He kissed her angrily on the lips and took off, sailing down the stairs.

"Come in, Celeste," said Ellery.

Celeste went crimson. She came in fumbling for her compact. Her lipstick was smeared and she kept looking at it in her mirror.

"I don't know what to say. Is Jimmy plastered? This early in the morning?" She laughed, but she was embarrassed and, Ellery thought, a little scared.

"Looked to me," said the Inspector, "as if he knew just what he was doing. Hey, Ellery?"

"Looked to *me* like the basis for a nuisance charge."

"*All* right," laughed Celeste, eying the repairs. "But I really don't know what to say." She was dressed less modishly this morning, but it was a new dress. Her own, thought Ellery. Bought with Simone's money.

"It's a situation not covered by Miss Post. I imagine James will go into it in detail at the first opportunity."

"Sit down, Miss Phillips, sit down," said the Inspector.

"Thank you. But what's the matter with him? He seemed upset. Is anything wrong?"

"First time I told a girl I loved her, I found myself making pleats in her father's best derby. Ellery, were you expecting Miss Phillips this morning?"

"No."

"You told me to come when I had something to report, Mr. Queen." Her black eyes were troubled. "Why did you ask me to find out everything I could about Jimmy McKell?"

"Remember our compact, Celeste?"

She looked down at her manicured nails.

"Now, Ellery, don't be a fuddy-duddy before your time," said the Inspector genially. "A kiss cancels all contracts. Why, Miss Phillips, there's no mystery about it. Jimmy McKell is a newspaperman. This might have been a dodge for him to get in on the inside of the Cat case, beat other reporters to news breaks. We had to be sure Jimmy's interest was personal, as he claimed. Do you find him a straight-shooter?"

"He's simply drearily honest. If that's what you're worried about . . ."

"Well, that's that, isn't it?" beamed the Inspector.

"But as long as you're here, Celeste," said Ellery, "you may as well tell us the rest."

"I really can't add anything to what Jimmy told you about himself last week. He's never got along with his father and, since he got out of the Service, they hardly speak to each other because Jimmy insists on living his own life. He really does pay his father $18 a week for board." Celeste giggled. "Jimmy says he's going to make it $75 as soon as the lawyers unwind all the red tape."

"Lawyers?"

"Oh, that business of his grandfather's estate."

"His grandfather," said the Inspector. "Now, let's see. That would be . . ."

"Mrs. McKell's father, Inspector. He was a very rich man who died when Jimmy was 13. Jimmy and his sister were their mother's father's grandchildren and he left a big estate for them in trust. The income from the estate was to start being paid when each grandchild reached the age of 30. Monica'd been collecting her share for seven years, but Jimmy wasn't due to start for five years more, or whenever it is. The only thing is, now Jimmy will get the whole thing, because under his grandfather's will if one of the two grandchildren died the entire estate—principal and income—was to go to the survivor at once. There's millions in the estate and Jimmy's sick about the whole thing, I mean the way it's coming to him. Through Monica's death and all . . . what's the matter?"

Ellery was looking at his father. "How was that missed?"

"I don't know. None of the McKells said a word about an existing trust from an outside source. Of course, we'd have found out eventually."

"Found out *what?*" asked Celeste fretfully.

Neither man answered.

After a moment she got up. "Do you mean . . ."

"The fact is," said Ellery, "the death of Monica McKell means a fortune to her brother, who lives on a reporter's salary. It's what's known in our depressing profession, Celeste, as a motive."

"*Motive.*"

Rage reshaped her. It was an alteration that began deep inside, like the first tiny release of energy in the heart of an explosive. Then it burst, and Celeste sprang.

Even as he felt the rip of her fingernails, Ellery thought absurdly: Like a cat.

"To use me to trap him!"

She kept screaming as Ellery seized the clawing hand and his father came up fast from behind.

"To think Jimmy'd do a thing like that! To *think* it! I'm going to tell him!"

Sobbing, she wrenched away and ran.

They saw Jimmy McKell step out of the basement areaway as the front door burst open and Celeste Phillips flew out. He must have said something, because the girl whirled, looking down. Then she ran down the brownstone steps and hurled herself at him. She was crying and talking wildly. When she stopped, he said something to her very quietly and she put her hand to her mouth.

Then a cab veered inquiringly toward the curb and Jimmy held the door open and Celeste crept in. He got in after her and the cab raced off.

"End of an experiment," sighed Ellery. "Or the beginning of one."

Inspector Queen grunted. "Do you believe that baloney you sliced for McKell about ABC, D, X, and what have you?"

"It's possible."

"That somebody connected with only one of the seven murders is behind all of them as a coverup?"

"It's possible."

"I know it's possible! I asked you if you believe it."

"Can you be certain someone connected with only one of the seven murders isn't behind all of them?"

The Inspector shrugged.

Ellery tossed the stained handkerchief on the sofa. "As far as Celeste and Jimmy are concerned, the way they came to me logically admitted of suspicion. The fact that each one has just disclosed information damaging to the other, viewed without sentiment and on its own merits, only enlarges the suspicion area. Still, I'm willing to go on belief—I don't believe either is the Cat, no. There's a factor that goes beyond logic.

Or maybe," said Ellery, "maybe I'm rusty. Do you suppose that could be it?"

"You're not convinced."

"Are you?"

"You'll be questioning me next!"

"Or myself."

The Inspector reached for his hat, scowling. "I'm going downtown."

• 6

The Cazalis phase of the investigation ran into shoal water immediately.

As originally charted by Dr. Cazalis, the psychiatric inquiry was to be a fishing expedition of all the specializing physicians in the local field, a sort of grand fleet sailing under a unified command. But it became evident that the expedition would have to be remapped. Each specialist, it appeared, was his own captain, guarding his nets and lines and the secrets of his fishing grounds with Japanese zeal. He regarded his catch as his exceptional property and no other fisher should have them.

To the credit of most, their scruples were largely ethical. The sanctity of the physician-patient confessional could not, *in propria persona,* be invaded even by other physicians. Dr. Cazalis surmounted the first obstacle by proposing the adoption of a published-case history technique. Each psychiatrist was to go through his files, select his possiblities on the broadest base, and make transcripts in which all identifying allusions were to be altered, leaving only the initials of the patient for reference. This suggestion was approved. When the case histories came in a five-doctor central board, headed by Dr. Cazalis, was to go work. The board was to consider each history, rejecting those which in the consultative view were unlikely. By this method many persons would be screened out while being spared the violation of their privacy.

Here, however, agreement went aground.

How were the remaining cases to be treated? Anonymity could be preserved only so far. Then names must be disclosed.

The inquiry almost foundered on this reef.

For therapeutic reasons the type and class of suspect Dr. Cazalis's plan involved could not be handled as the police handled the daily haul of the dragnet, even assuming that the problem of protecting the confidences of the consulting room could be solved. Inspector Queen was directing and co-ordinating the activities of over three hundred detectives under orders to stop at nothing. Since early June each morning's lineup had been crowded not merely with dope addicts, alcoholics, old sex offenders, and criminal psychopaths with penal or institutional records but also with vagrants, prowlers, "suspicious characters" of all descriptions—a category which in three months had swollen alarmingly from the internal pressures of the case. In the high prevailing temperature, civil rights had tended to shrink as official frustration expanded. There had been typhoons of protest from all quarters. The courts had been showered with writs. Citizens had howled, politicians had roared, judges had thundered. But the investigation was plunging ahead in the teeth of all this. Dr. Cazalis's colleagues would have been reluctant to submit their patients to normal police procedures; how, they demanded, could they be expected to turn their patients over to the authorities in this stormy, overheated atmosphere? To many of their charges even an ordinary questioning session would raise dangers. These people were under treatment for mental and emotional disorders. The work of months or years might be undone in an hour by detectives callously intent only on finding a connection between the suspect and the Cat.

There were other difficulties. The patients originated for the most part in the prominences of the cultural geography. Many were socially well-known or came from well-known families. The arts and sciences were heavily represented, the theatrical world, business, finance, even politics. Democracy or no democracy, said the psychiatrists, such people could not be thrown into the lineup as if they were poolroom loiterers or park prowlers. How were they to be questioned? How far might the questions go? Which questions should be avoided and who was to decide? And who was to do the questioning, and when, and where?

The whole thing, they said, was impossible.

It took the better part of the week to work out a plan satisfactory to the majority. The solution took shape when it was recognized that no single *modus operandi* was practicable. There would have to be a separate plan, as it were, for each patient.

Accordingly a list of key questions, carefully composed so as to conceal their origin and objective, was drawn up by Dr. Cazalis and his board in collaboration with Inspector Queen. Each doctor co-operating received a confidential copy of this list. The individual physician was to do his own questioning, in his own office, of those patients on his suspect roll whom he considered it therapeutically risky to turn over to others. He agreed to file reports of these sessions with the board. Patients who in the judgment of their doctors could be safely interviewed by others were to be handled directly by the board at any one of their several offices. The police were not to come into contact with any patient except in the final stage of the medical inquiry, and then only where the findings compelled it. Even at this point the procedure was to emphasize the protection of the patient rather than the overriding hunt for damaging facts. Wherever possible in these cases the investigation was to proceed around the suspect instead of through him.

To the police it was a clumsy and irritating plan; but as Dr. Cazalis, who had begun to look haggard, pointed out to the Police Commissioner and Inspector Queen, the alternative was no investigation at all. The Inspector threw up his hands and his superior said politely that he had been looking forward to a rather more alluring prospect.

So, it appeared, had the Mayor. At an unhappy meeting in City Hall, Dr. Cazalis was inflexible: there were to be no further interviews with the press on his part or on the part of anyone associated with him in the psychiatric phase of the investigation. "I gave my professional word on that, Mr. Mayor. Let one patient's name leak to the newpapers and the whole thing will blow up in my face."

The Mayor replied with a plaintive, "Yes, yes, Dr. Cazalis, I hadn't thought it through, I'm sure. Good luck, and keep right on it, won't you?"

But when the psychiatrist had left, the Mayor remarked bitterly to his private secretary, "It's that damned Ellery Queen business all over again. By the way, Birdy, whatever happened to that fellow?"

What had happened was that the Mayor's Special Investigator had taken to the streets. Ellery might have been seen these days—and he was seen, by various Headquarters men—at eccentric hours lounging on the sidewalk across from the building on East 19th Street where Archibald Dudley Abernethy had come to an end, or standing in the hall outside the ex-Abernethy apartment, which was now occupied by a Guatemalan member of the United Nations secretariat and his wife, or wandering about Gramercy Park and Union Square; silently consuming pizza in the Italian restaurant on West 44th Street over which Violette Smith had flirted successfully with death, or leaning against the banister of the top floor hall listening to a piano stammer along behind the apartment door to which was thumbtacked a large sign:

This Is IT—Yes!!!!
All Squares, Visiting
Firemen, Ear Benders,
Pearl Divers, and
Peeping Toms
KEEP OUT!!

SONG WRITER AT WORK!!

poking about beneath the staircase in the lobby of
a Chelsea tenement at the spot where the body of
Rian O'Reilly had been found; sitting on a bench
at the end of the Sheridan Square subway-station
platform, uptown side, with the shade of Madcap
Monica McKell; prowling beneath the washlines in
a certain rear court on East 102nd Street and never
once catching a glimpse of the emancipated cousin
of fat little Simone Phillips; standing before the
brassrailed stoop of a house on West 128th Street
in a swarm of dark children, or strolling down Lenox
Avenue among brown and saffron people to the 110th
Street entrance to Central Park, or sitting on a park
bench not far from the entrance or on the nearby
boulder which had been the rock, if not the salvation,
of Beatrice Willikins; or trudging along East 84th
Street from Fifth Avenue to Madison past the canopied
entrance of the Park-Lester and up Madison and
back again to circumambulate the block, or taking the
private elevator in the Park-Lester's neighbor to a
boarded-up penthouse whose occupants were away
for the summer to stare frankly across the parapet
at the terrace beyond which Lenore Richardson had
gripped *Forever Amber* in the convulsion of strangulation.

Ellery rarely spoke to anyone on these excursions.
They took place by day as well as by night, as if
he wished to view the sites in both perspectives.

He returned to the seven localities again and again.
Once he was picked up by a detective who did not
know him and spent several hours as a suspicious

character in the nearest precinct house before Inspector Queen hurried in to identify him.

Had he been asked what he was about, the Mayor's Special Investigator would have been at a loss for a communicable reply. It was difficult to put into words. How materialize a terror, much more see him whole? This was one whose feet had whispered over pavements, displacing nothing larger than molecules. You followed his trackless path, sniffing upwind, hopefully.

All that week the eighth tail of the Cat, the now familiar question mark, hooked and held the eye of New York.

Ellery was walking up Park Avenue. It was the Saturday night after Lenore Richardson's murder and he was drifting in a vacuum.

He had left the night life of the City behind. In the 70s only piles of articulated stone kept him company, and an occasional goldbraided doorman.

At 78th Street Ellery paused before the royal blue-awninged house where the Cazalises lived. The ground-floor Cazalis apartment, with its private office entrance directly off the street, showed lights, but the vanes of the Venetian blinds were closed and Ellery wondered if Dr. Cazalis and his fellow-psychiatrists were at work behind them. Brewing the potion, stirring the caldron; wrapping truth in darkness. They would never find the Cat in their co-wizard's notes. He did not know how he knew this, but he knew it.

He walked on and some time later found himself turning into 84th Street.

But he passed the Park-Lester without breaking the rhythm of his torpor.

At the corner of 84th and Fifth, Ellery stopped. It was still early, the evening was warm, but the Avenue was a nervous emptiness. Where were the Saturday night arm-in-arm strollers? Even the automobile traffic seemed lighter. And the busses whined by carrying remarkably few passengers.

Facing him across Fifth Avenue was the Metropolitan Museum of Art, a broadbeamed old lady sitting patiently in darkness.

He crossed over on the green light and began to walk uptown along the old lady's flank. Beyond her lay the black and silent Park.

They're beginning to stick to the well-lighted areas, he thought. *O comfort-killing night, image of Hell.* No friendly darkness now. Especially here. In this part of the jungle the beast had pounced twice.

He almost cried out at the touch on his arm.

"Sergeant."

"I tailed you for two blocks before I recognized you," said Sergeant Velie, falling into step.

"On duty tonight?"

"Naw."

"Then what are you doing around here?"

"Oh . . . just walking around." The big fellow said carelessly, "I'm baching it these days."

"Why, where's your family, Velie?"

"Sent the wife and kid to my mother-in-law's for a month."

"To Cincinnati? Is Barbara-Ann—?"

"No, Barbsy's okay. And as far as school is concerned," said Sergeant Velie argumentatively, "she can catch up any time. She's got her ma's brains."

"Oh," said Ellery; and they ambled on in silence.

After a long time the Sergeant said, "I'm not intruding on anything, I trust?"

"No."

"I mean, I thought you might be on the prowl." The Sergeant laughed.

"Just going over the Cat's route. For the umpteenth time. Backwards, Sergeant. Richardson, Lenore, to Willikins, Beatrice. Number 7 to Number 6. East 84th to Harlem. The Lord's anointed to His unshorn lamb. One mile or so between and the Cat jumps it by way of the moon. Do you have a light?"

They stopped under a street lamp and the Sergeant struck a match.

"Talking about the Cat's route," he said. "You

know, Maestro, I've been giving this case a lot of thought."

"Thanks, Velie."

They crossed 96th Street.

"I long ago gave up," the Sergeant was saying—"I'm speaking only for Thomas Velie, you understand—gave up trying to get anywhere on this carrousel. My personal opinion is when the Cat's knocked off it will be by dumb-bunny luck. Some rookie cop'll walk up to a drunk bent over like he's regretting the whole thing and bingo, it'll be the Cat tying a bow in the latest neck. But just the same," said the Sergeant, "you can't help figuring the angles."

"No," said Ellery, "you certainly can't."

"Now I don't know what your impression is, and of course this is all off the record, but I got busy the other night with a map of Manhattan and environs that I traced off my kid's geography book and I started spotting in the locations of the seven homicides. Just for the hell of it." The Sergeant's voice lowered. "Well, sir, I think I got something."

"What?" asked Ellery. A couple were passing, the man arguing and pointing to the Park and the woman shaking her head, walking very fast. The Sergeant stopped abruptly; but Ellery said, "It's all right, Velie. That's only a Saturday night date with ideas."

"Yeah," said the Sergeant sagely, "sex suckers all men."

But they did not move until they saw the man and woman climb into a southbound bus.

"You'd got something, Velie."

"Oh! Yeah. I put a heavy dot on each location on the map, see. The first one—Abernethy's, East 19th—I marked that one *1*. The second one—Violette Smith's on West 44th off Times Square—I mark *2*. And so forth."

"You," said Ellery, "and that *Extra* cartoonist."

"Then when I've got all seven spotted and numbered, I begin drawing lines. A line from *1* to *2*. A line from *2* to *3*. Et cetera. And what do you think?"

"What?"

"It's got a kind of a design."

"Really? No, wait, Sergeant. The Park gives me nothing tonight. Let's strike crosstown." They crossed 99th and began to make their way east through the dark and quiet street. "Design?"

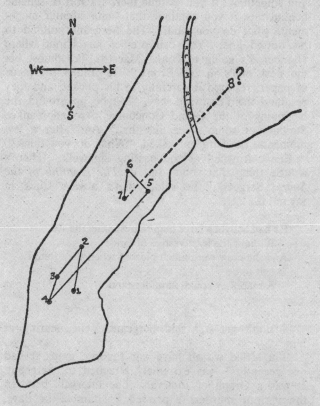

"Look." Sergeant Velie pulled a wad of tracing paper from his pocket and unfolded it on the corner of 99th and Madison. "It's a kind of double-circular movement, Maestro. Straight up from *1* to *2*, sharp down again but westerly from *2* to *3*, keeps going southwest to *4*, then what? Sharp up again. A long one this time, crossing the 1–2 line. Up, down, over and up again. Now look! Now it starts all over again! Oh, not at exactly the same angles, of course, but close enough to be interesting, hmmm? Again it's up and over from 5 to 6—northwesterly—then sharp down to 7 . . ." The Sergeant paused. "Let me show you something. If you assume there's a sort of scheme behind this, if you continue that same circular movement, what do you find?" The Sergeant pointed to his dotted line. "You can predict just about where Number 8's going to come! Maestro, I'd almost bet the next one's in the Bronx." He folded his piece of paper, restored it carefully to his pocket, and they resumed their eastward way. "Maybe up around the beginning of the Grand Concourse. Around Yankee Stadium or some place like that." And after a few moments, the Sergeant asked, "What do you think?"

Ellery frowned at the passing sidewalk. "There's a little thing that comes out of *The Hunting of the Snark,* Sergeant," he said, "that's always stuck in my mind.

> "He had bought a large map representing the sea,
>   Without the least vestige of land:
> And the crew were much pleased when they found
>   it to be
> A map they could all understand."

"I don't get it," said Sergeant Velie, staring at him.

"I'm afraid we all have our favorite maps. I had one recently I was extremely attached to, Sergeant. It was a Graph of Intervals. The intervals between the various murders expressed in number of days. The result was something that looked like a large question mark lying flat on its face. It was a lesson in humility. I burned it, and I advise you to do the same with yours."

After that, the Sergeant just strode along, muttering occasionally.

"Why, look where we are," said Ellery.

The Sergeant, who had been acting dignified, started as he glanced up at the street sign.

"So you see, Sergeant, it's the detective who returns to the scene of the crime. Drawn by a sort of horizontal gravity."

"Drawn by my garter belt. You knew just where you were going."

"Unconsciously, maybe. Shall we press our luck?"

"Last one in is a dirty name," said the Sergeant, unbending; and they plunged into the noisy breakers of 102nd Street.

"I wonder how my female ex-Irregular is getting along."

"Say, I heard about that. That was a pretty smart trick."

"Not so smart. The shortest collaboration on record.—Hold it, Velie."

Ellery stopped to fish for a cigaret. The Sergeant dutifully struck a match, saying, "Where?"

"In that doorway behind me. Almost missed him."

The flame snuffed out and Sergeant Velie said in a loud voice, "Darn it all, old man, let's get on over here," and they moved around a frantic hopscotch game toward the building line. The big man grinned. "Hell, it's Piggott." He struck another match near the doorway and Ellery bent over.

"Evening, evening," said the detective from somewhere. "I saw you two amateurs coming a block away."

"Is there a law against it?" demanded Sergeant Velie. "What are you working tonight, Piggo? Yeah, I'll have one." He took a cigaret from Ellery.

"Watch it! Here he comes."

Ellery and the Sergeant jumped into the doorway beside the Headquarters man. A tall fellow had come out of an unlighted vestibule halfway up the street, on their side. He began pushing his way through the children.

107

"I've been tailing him all night," said the detective.

"On whose orders, Piggott?"

"Your old man's."

"How long has this been going on?"

"All week. Hesse and I are divvying him."

"Didn't the Inspector tell you?" asked Sergeant Velie.

"I've hardly seen him this week."

"It's nothing exciting," said the detective. "Just satisfying the taxpayers, the Inspector said."

"How's he been spending his time?"

"Walking and standing still."

"Up here much?"

"Till last night."

"What's he been up to in that vestibule tonight?"

"Watching the entrance of the girl's house across the street."

Ellery nodded. Then he said, "Is she home?"

"We all pulled in here about a half hour ago. She spent the evening in the 42nd Street Library. Reference Room. So that's where we were, too. Then he tailed her here, and I tailed him, and here we are."

"Has he gone in there?"

"No, sir."

"He hasn't approached her, spoken to her?"

"Hell, she didn't know he was following her. It's been kind of like a Humphrey Bogart movie, at that. Johnson's been tailing *her*. He's been in the back court across the street since we pulled in here."

"Sounds like a Canarsie clambake." Then the Sergeant said swiftly, "Piggo, get *lost*."

The tall man was coming directly toward their doorway.

"Well, well," said Ellery, stepping out. "Hi."

"I thought I'd save you some wear and tear." Jimmy McKell stood innerbraced, looking from Ellery to Sergeant Velie and back again. Behind them, the doorway was empty. "What's the significant idea?"

"Idea?" said Ellery, considering it.

"I saw you two rubberheels sneak into this doorway. What are you doing, watching Celeste Phillips?"

"Not me," said Ellery. "Were you, Sergeant?"

"I wouldn't do a thing like that," said the Sergeant.

"Very funny." Jimmy McKell kept looking at them. "Why don't you ask me what I'm doing here?"

"All right, Jimmy. What are you doing here?"

"The same thing you are." Jimmy excavated a cigaret, brushed off the linty detritus, and stuck it like a flag between his lips. His tone was amiable, however. "Only my angle is maybe different. I'm told there's somebody doing the town collecting necks. Now that woman has one of the prettiest head supports in Christendom." He lit the cigaret.

"Protecting her, huh?" said the Sergeant. "You play long shots, reporter."

"Two-Million-to-One McKell, they call me." Jimmy tossed the match; it glanced off Velie's ear. "Well, I'll be seeing you. If that's my kismet." He began to walk away.

"Jimmy, wait."

"For what?"

"What do you say we drop in on her?"

Jimmy sauntered back. "For what?"

"I've been meaning to have a talk with you two."

"For what?"

"You're both entitled to an explanation, Jimmy."

"You don't have to explain anything to me. My nose knows."

"No kidding."

"I'm not. It really does."

"I don't blame you for being griped—"

"Hell, who's griped? What's a little thing like being suspected of seven murders? I mean between pals?" He stepped close all at once and Sergeant Velie stirred. Jimmy's lips were out. "Queen, that was the most two-faced, poisonous deal since the days of the Medicis. To sick me onto Celeste and Celeste onto me. I ought to boff you for that."

The Sergeant said, "Here."

"Take that ham hock off me."

"It's all right, Sergeant." Ellery was preoccupied and morose. "But Jimmy, I had to make some test."

"Some test is right."

"Yes, it was on the silly side. But you both came to me at such a convenient moment. I couldn't close my eyes to the possibility that one of you—"

"Is the Cat." Jimmy laughed.

"We're not dealing with normality."

"Do I look abnormal? Does Celeste?"

"Not to my eyes, no. But then I don't have psychiatric vision." Ellery grinned. "And dementia, for example, is a youthful disease."

"Praecox McKell. Well, they called me a lot worse in the late Hot War."

"Jimmy, I never really believed it. I don't believe it now."

"But there's always the mathematical chance."

"Come on, let's drop in on Celeste."

"I take it if I refuse," said Jimmy, not budging, "Charley the Anthropoid here will pinch me?"

"I'll pinch you," said Sergeant Velie. "Where it hurts."

"See what I mean?" said Jimmy bitterly. "We're just not compatible." And he strode away, breaking up the hopscotch game and pursued by the curses of little children.

"Let him go, Velie."

After a few moments Detective Piggott's voice said, "There goes my bread and butter. Night, Brother Elks." When they looked around, Piggott was gone.

"So he's been watching Celeste to save her from the Cat," said Ellery as they began to cross the street.

"In a swine's eyeball."

"Oh, Jimmy means it, Sergeant. At least he thinks he does."

"What is he, feebleminded?"

"Hardly." Ellery laughed. "But he's suffering from a severe attack of what our friend Cazalis might call—though I doubt it—confusional inanity. Otherwise known as the love psychosis."

The Sergeant grunted. They stopped before the

tenement and he looked around casually. "You know what I think, Maestro?"

"After that double wingback map of Manhattan of yours I wouldn't even attempt a guess."

"Go ahead and horse," said the Sergeant. "But I think you put a bee in his buzzer."

"Explain."

"I think maybe McKell thinks maybe Celeste *is* the Cat."

Ellery glanced up at the behemoth as if he had never really seen him before.

"You know what I think, Velie?"

"What?"

"I think you're right." And, looking slightly ill, he said, "Let's go in."

The hall was cheaply dim and pungent. A boy and a girl jumped apart as Ellery and Velie walked in; they had been clutching each other in the shadows beside the staircase. "Oh, *thank* you, I had such a lovely time," said the girl, running up the stairs. The boy smirked. "I ain't complaining, Carole." He slouched out, winking at the two men.

A door at the rear stood open, a line of wash clipping its upper corner to the dark sky.

"Piggott said Johnson was out there, Maestro."

"Not any more Johnson isn't," said a voice from under the stairs. "I got an old camp chair in here, Sarge."

"'Lo, Johnson," said the Sergeant, not turning. "How's the trick?"

"With those two juvenile delinquents that were just here it was colossal. You calling on C.P.?"

"Is she still up?" Ellery asked the darkness.

"There's the light under her door, Mr. Queen."

"That door there," said the Sergeant.

"Alone, Johnson?"

"Uh-huh." There was a yawn.

Ellery went over and knocked on the door. Sergeant Velie moved to one side, out of range.

After a moment, Ellery knocked again.

"Who is it?" She sounded frightened.

"Ellery Queen. Please open, Celeste."

They heard her undo the latch chain very slowly.

"What do you want?"

In the box of light she stood bristling. One hand clutched a large book to her breast. It looked like an old book, one fingered with respect.

Survey of English Literature—First Year.

Saturday night on East 102nd Street. A voom with the Venerable Bede. Bebop with *Beowulf*. Holding hands with Hakluyt's *Divers Voyages*. Jive print in double columns, kneedeep in footnotes.

She blocked his view of the room. He had never seen this room, only photographs.

She was dressed in a full black pleated skirt and a tailored white blouse and her hair was disordered, as if she had had her fists in it as she read. There was blue ink on one finger. What he could make out of her face was a little shocking. The violet stains had spread and her skin was blotchy, cupped to bitter heads.

"May I come in?" asked Ellery with a smile.

"No. What do you want?"

"In this neighborhood, Maestro," said Sergeant Velie, "you couldn't run for your life."

Celeste took a quick look out. She immediately withdrew her head. "I remember *him*."

Sergeant Velie stiffened.

"Haven't you done enough damage?"

"Celeste—"

"Or did you come to arrest me? Not that I'd put it past you. I suppose Jimmy McKell and I were accomplices. We strangled all those people together. Each of us pulling on one end of the silk cords."

"Celeste, if you'll let me—"

"You've spoiled everything. *Everything.*"

The door slammed in his face. They heard the furious turn of the key, the lash of the latch chain.

"Each on one end," mused Sergeant Velie. "Think that's such a crosseyed idea? Did anybody take that into consideration? Two of them?"

Ellery muttered, "They've had a blowup."

"Sure, last night. It was just terrible," said Johnson's voice cheerfully. "He says she suspected him of being the Cat and she says nonono it's him who suspected *her* of being the Cat. Then they both deny it like mad. Going at it hot and heavy—I was out in the court there and I was afraid they'd collect a crowd and I'd have to fade. Well, sir, she starts bawling like she means it and what does he do but say a naughty word and damn near bust the hinges off the door blasting his way out."

"Love's sweet young stuff," said the Sergeant. "Do you suppose it could have been an act? Maybe they're wise to you, Johnson. Hey, Maestro. Where you going?"

Ellery sounded miserable. "Home."

All during the week following Ellery had a sense of marking time. Nothing occurred of the least interest. He saw the reports on Jimmy McKell and Celeste Phillips; they had made up, they had quarreled again, they had made up again. Other reports had all but stopped coming in. One morning Ellery dropped in to view the lineup performance. As entertainment it was depressing, and it told nothing, but he experienced the satisfaction of a man who has performed a duty. He did not go again. He cleverly refrained from venturing below Centre Street and the good Magistrate at City Hall seemed to have forgotten his existence, for which Ellery was abysmally grateful. He saw little of his father and he purposely avoided asking questions about the progress of Dr. Cazalis's investigation . . . And the Cat's eighth tail remained a question mark on the front page of the *Extra*.

Even the newspapers were marking time.

It was curious. The *status quo ante* in American journalism is not a standing still; it is a going backward. A Page 1 story remains there only so long as it grows. Let it stop growing and it finds itself on Page 6, and it will continue this oblivious process until it backs

113

right out of the paper. But the Cat story blandly bucked the rule. If it got nowhere, neither did it lose headway. It rode anchor on the front page. It was news even when it was not.

In a way, it was more news when it was not than when it was, when the Cat lay napping in his den than when he padded out to hunt another neck. His inactivity exerted a special attraction, horrid and hypnotic: the magnetism of suspense. It was like a smolder between bursts of flame. If, as Jefferson said, newspapers "serve to carry off noxious vapors and smoke." the New York press could only obey the physics of the times.

It was during these intervals that the public nervousness was most remarkable. The waiting was worse than the event. When the Cat killed, people were actually relieved for a few days, in a semi-hysterical way; they and theirs were safe once more. But their dread was not destroyed; it was merely becalmed. Relief soon wore off, suspense surfaced again, the night anxieties, the counting of the days, the pitching wonder as to who would be next.

It was no use pitting the mathematical improbabilities against the individual's fears. The psychological laws of lottery ruled, the only difference being that in this policy game the prize was not money but extinction. Tickets were free to all New Yorkers, and each holder knew in his heart he would win at the next drawing.

So the week wore on.

Ellery was thankful to see the week end; by Saturday it had become insupportable. His absurd Graph of Intervals persisted in haunting him. Between Victims 1 and 2, nineteen days; between Victims 2 and 3, twenty-six days; between Victims 3 and 4, twenty-two days; between Victims 4 and 5—Monica McKell to Simone Phillips—the teasing, inexplicable drop to six days; and then the reascending curve of eleven days between Victims 6 and 7. Was this the beginning of a new upward spiral? Were the intervals leveling off? It was now the twelfth day after the strangling of Mrs. Cazalis's niece.

In the uncertainty, each moment excreted fear.

Ellery spent that Saturday chasing police calls. It was the first time he had used any of the vague powers conferred on him by the Mayor's appointment. He was not even sure it would work. But when he commandeered a car with a police radio, a black seven-passenger limousine with no identifying insignia occupied by a plainclothes chauffeur and his plainclothes companion showed up promptly. Most of the time Ellery slumped low in the tonneau listening to interminable accounts of "real baffling cases." Each detective was the size of Sergeant Velie and each was equipped with inexhaustible lungs.

Ellery kept wondering on and off through the long tiresome day what had happened to his father. No one seemed to know where Inspector Queen was; he had left the apartment before Ellery rose, he had not been to Headquarters, he had not called in.

They roared with open siren from the Battery to the Harlem River, from Riverside Drive to First Avenue. They were in on the breakup of a teenage street fight in San Juan Hill and the arrest of a cocaine addict caught trying to slip a forged prescription by an alert Yorkville pharmacist. They visited the scenes of holdups, traffic accidents, minor assaults; on the agenda in order were a queue-pulling match off Chatham Square, an attempted rape in a Hell's Kitchen hallway, the case of a getaway car in a Third Avenue pawnshop robbery. They witnessed the bloodless capture of a meek gangster in Little Italy wanted for questioning in an old homicide, the escape of a Lithuanian cook from a Little Hungary restaurant where he had suddenly gone berserk. There were four suicides—above the average for such a short period, the detectives explained, but it had been a bad summer, one in the Bowling Green subway station, an elderly Brooklynite who had thrown himself in the path of an incoming IRT express; another a Herald Square window-jumping case, a girl registered in a hotel from

Chicopee Falls, Mass., identified as an eloper; another a gas range job in a Rivington Street tenement, a woman and a baby; the fourth an alcoholic case in the West 130s who had slashed his wrists. There were two homicide calls: the first, shortly before noon, a knifing in a Harlem poolroom; the second, at 6:30, a woman beaten to death with a Stillson wrench in the East 50s by her husband, an advertising agency executive. This last aroused some interest in the detectives since it involved another man, a Broadway character, and they were disposed to linger; but Ellery waved them on.

There were no strangulations, with or without cords.

"Just another day," said the detective at the wheel as he slid the squad car into 87th Street. He sounded apologetic.

"Why not keep going tonight?" suggested the other detective as Ellery got out. "Saturday night's always lively, Mr. Queen, and maybe it's the Cat's night out."

"By the twitching of my left ventricle," said Ellery, "I can tell it isn't. Doesn't matter, anyway—I can always read about it in the papers. Will you boys join me in a friendly glass?"

"Well, now," said the driver.

But the other detective said, "Give your old woman a break for once, Frank. And I've got a long haul, Mr. Queen. Out to Rockville Center. Thanks just the same."

Upstairs, Ellery found a note from his father.

It was a scribble marked *7 P.M.*

EL—Been phoning since 5. Dashed home to leave this note. Meet me at Cazalis's the minute you get in. Big powwow set for 7:30.

7:35.
Ellery ran.

When the uniformed maid ushered him into the Cazalis living room, the first person he saw was the Mayor of the City of New York. That harrowed servant of the people was lying back in an easychair, hands clasped about a tall glass, glaring at a bust of Sigmund Freud above Ellery's head.

The Police Commissioner, seated beside the Mayor, was studying the fume of his cigar.

Dr. Cazalis sat on a Turkish divan, bolstered by silk pillows. His wife held on to his hand.

At a window stood Inspector Queen, cocooned in silence.

The air was chill.

"Don't tell me, please," said Ellery. "It's a wash-out."

No one replied. Mrs. Cazalis rose and prepared a Scotch-and-soda, which Ellery accepted with genuine gratitude.

"Ellery, where have you been today?" But the Inspector failed to sound as if he cared.

"Out chasing radio calls. Don't be misled, Mr. Mayor," said Ellery. "It's the first time since I took over. Hereafter I'll do my special investigating from an armchair—that is, if there *is* a hereafter?"

The Mayor's glance touched him briefly, almost with loathing. "Sit down, Queen, sit down."

"Nobody's answered my question."

"It wasn't a question, it was a statement," said Dr. Cazalis from the pillows. "And as a statement it exactly states the case."

"Sit down, Queen," snapped the Mayor again.

"Thank you, Mr. Mayor. I'll keep my father company." Ellery was startled by Dr. Cazalis's appearance. His pale eyes were inflamed and his skin was plowed so raw that Ellery thought of floodwater soil eroded into gullies; the glacier had given way. And he recalled Cazalis's remark about his insomnia. "Doctor, you look depreciated."

"There's been considerable wear and tear."

"He's worn out," said Mrs. Cazalis shrilly. "He

drives himself so. No more sense than an infant. He's been at this day and night since . . ."

Her husband squeezed her hand. "The whole psychiatric attack, Mr. Queen, is a fizzle. We've got exactly nowhere."

Inspector Queen said curtly: "This week I've been working close to Dr. Cazalis, Ellery. We wound up today. There were a number of possibilities. We ran every one of them down."

"Quietly, you understand," said the Mayor bitterly. "No toes stepped on. Not a word in the papers."

"Well," said Dr. Cazalis, "it was a long chance at best. My fault entirely. It seemed a notion at the time."

"At the time, Edward? Isn't it still?" Mrs. Cazalis was regarding her husband in a puzzled way.

"Humpty Dumpty, dear."

"I don't understand."

"I take it, Queen," said the Mayor, "you haven't got to first base?"

"I never took the bat off my shoulder, Mr. Mayor."

"I see." Here goes a Special Investigator, thought Ellery. "Inspector Queen, what's your feeling?"

"We have a very touchy case, Mr. Mayor. In the usual murder investigation, the range of suspicion is limited. The husband, the 'friend,' the handyman, the rival, the enemy, and so on. Motive begins to stick out. The field narrows. Opportunity narrows it even further. We've got human material to work on. Sooner or later in even the most complicated case we make a rap stick. But in this one . . . How are you going to narrow the field? Where do you start? No connection among the victims anywhere. No suspects. No clues. Every murder a dead end. The Cat could be anybody in New York."

"You can still say that, Inspector?" cried the Mayor. "After all these weeks?"

The Inspector's lips thinned. "I'm ready to hand in my shield right now."

"No, no, Inspector, I was just thinking aloud."

The Mayor glanced at his Police Commissioner. "Well, Barney, where do we go from here?"

The Commissioner tapped a long ash very carefully into a tray. "When you get right down to it, there's no place we can go. We've done, and we're doing, everything humanly possible. I could suggest a new Police Commissioner, Jack, but I doubt if that would satisfy anybody except the *Extra* and the other crowd, and I'm Irish enough to believe it wouldn't necessarily bag your Cat, either."

The Mayor waved, impatiently. "The question is, *are* we doing everything possible? It seems to me where we may have gone off is in assuming that the Cat is a New Yorker. Suppose he comes from Bayonne? Stamford? Yonkers? He may be a commuter—"

"Or a Californian," said Ellery.

"What? What was that?" exclaimed the Mayor.

"A Californian, or an Illinoisan, or a Hawaiian."

The Mayor said irritably, "Queen, I can't see that that sort of talk gets us anywhere. The point is, Barney, have we done anything outside the City?"

"Everything we can."

"We've had every community within a radius of fifty miles of the City alerted for at least six weeks," said the Inspector. "From the start they've been requested to keep their eyes peeled for psychos. But so far—"

"Jack, until we get a concrete reason for believing otherwise, nobody can crucify us for concentrating on Manhattan."

"My personal opinion," added the Inspector, "has been all along that he's a Manhattanite. To me this Cat smells local."

"Besides, Jack," said the Commissioner with a certain dryness, "our jurisdiction ends at the City limits. After that we've got a tin cup in our hands and take what the saints provide."

The Mayor set his glass down with a little bang and went over to the fireplace. Ellery was nuzzling his Scotch with a faraway look, the Commissioner was back at his cigar examination, Dr. Cazalis and

119

Inspector Queen were blinking at each other across the room to keep awake, and Mrs. Cazalis sat like a grenadier.

The Mayor turned suddenly. "Dr. Cazalis, what are the chances of extending your psychiatric investigation to include the entire metropolitan area?"

"Manhattan is the concentration point."

"But there are other psychiatrists outside?"

"Oh, yes."

"What about them?"

"Well . . . it would take months, and then you wouldn't get anything like satisfactory coverage. Even here, in the heart of things, where I exert a pretty direct professional influence, I haven't been able to get better than 65 to 70 per cent of the men in the field to co-operate. If the survey were extended to Westchester, Long Island, Connecticut, New Jersey . . ." Dr. Cazalis shook his head. "As far as I personally am concerned, Mr. Mayor, it would be pretty much out of the question. I haven't either the strength or the time to tackle such a project."

Mrs. Cazalis's lips parted.

"Won't you at least continue covering Manhattan, then, Dr. Cazalis? The answer may well lie in the files of one of the 30 or 35 per cent you say refused to play along. Won't you keep after those people?"

Dr. Cazalis's fingers pumped rapidly. "Well, I've been hoping . . ."

"Edward, you're not giving up. You're not!"

"*Et tu,* darling? I thought I had no more sense than an infant."

"I mean for going at it the way you have. Ed, how can you stop altogether? Now?"

"Why, dear, simply by doing so. I was paranoid to attempt it."

She said something in such a low tone that Dr. Cazalis said, "What, dear?"

"I said what about Lenore!"

She was on her feet.

"Darling." Dr. Cazalis scrambled off the divan. "All this tonight's upset you—"

"Tonight? Did you think I wasn't upset yesterday? And the day before?" She sobbed into her hands. "If Lenore had been your sister's child . . . had meant as much to you as she did to me . . ."

"I think, gentlemen," said the Mayor quickly, "we've imposed on Mrs. Cazalis's hospitality long enough."

"I'm sorry!" She was really trying to stop. "I'm so sorry. Edward, let me go. Please. I want to . . . get something."

"Tell you what, darling. Give me twenty-four hours' sleep, a two-inch T-bone when I wake up, and I'll tackle it where I left off. Good enough?"

She kissed him suddenly. Then, murmuring something, she hurried out.

"I submit, gentlemen," said the Mayor, "that we owe Mrs. Cazalis a few dozen roses."

"My only weakness," laughed the psychiatrist. "I never could resist the diffusion of the female lachrymal glands."

"Then, Doctor," said Ellery, "you may be in for a bad time."

"How's that, Mr. Queen?"

"If you'll run over the ages of the seven victims, you'll find that each victim had been younger than the one preceding."

The Commissioner's cigar almost fell out of his mouth.

The Mayor went brick-red.

"The seventh victim, Doctor—your wife's niece— was 25 years old. If any prediction is possible in this case, it's that Victim Number 8 will be under 25. Unless you're successful, or we are, we may soon be investigating the strangulation of children." Ellery set his glass down. "Would you say good night to Mrs. Cazalis for me?"

• 7

The so-called "Cat Riots" of September 22-23 marked the dread appearance in New York City of *mobile vulgus* for the first time since the Harlem disorders of almost fifteen years before. But in this case the mob was predominantly white; as a wry vindication of the Mayor's dawn press conference of the previous month, there was no "race angle." The only racial fears involved were the primitive ones of all mankind.

Students of mob psychology found the Cat Riots interesting. If in one sense the woman whose hysterical outburst set off the panic in Metropol Hall exerted the function of the inevitable *meneur*—the leader each mob tends to throw up, who starts the cheering or the running away—if the hysterical woman represented the fuse which sparked the explosion, she in her turn had been ignited by the inflammatory Citizens' Action Teams which had sprung up all over the Greater City during the immediately preceding Four Days and whose activities were responsible for her presence in the Hall. And no one could say with certainty who originally inspired those groups; at least no individual responsibility was ever determined.

The shortlived movement which came to be known as the Four Days (although from inception to culminating riot it spanned six days) was first publicly taken note of early on Monday, September 19, in the late morning editions of the newspapers.

An "association of neighbors" had been formed over the past weekend on the Lower East Side under the name of "The Division Street Vigilantes." At an organizing meeting held Saturday night a series of resolutions had been drawn up in the form of a

122

"Declaration" which was ratified "in full convention assembled" on the following afternoon. Its "Preamble" asserted "the rights of lawabiding American citizens, in the failure of regular law enforcement," to band together "for common security." Anyone in the prescribed neighborhood was eligible to join. World War II veterans were especially solicited. Various partrols were to be set up: a Streets Patrol, a Roofs Patrol, an Alleys Patrol. There was a separate Unit Patrol for each dwelling or other building in the area. The function of the patrols was "to stand guard against the marauder who has been terrorizing the City of New York." (There was some intra-organizational protest against the use of "fancy language," but the language stood when the Resolutions Committee pointed out that "on Division Street and around here we're supposed to be a bunch of pigs.") Discipline was to be military. Patrolmen were to be equipped with flashlights, armbands, "and available weapons of defense." A 9 P.M. curfew for children was to be enforced. Street level lighting was to be maintained until daybreak; special arrangements were being made with landlords of dwellings and stores.

In the same news story was noted the simultaneous formation of three similar organizations, apparently unconnected with one another or with the Division Street Vigilantes. One was in the Murray Hill section and called itself "The Murray Hill Committee of Safety." Another took in the area between West 72nd Street and West 79th Street and was named "The West End Minutemen." The third centered in Washington Square, "The Village Home Guard."

Considering the differences among the three groups culturally, socially, and economically, their avowed purposes and operating methods were astonishingly similar to those of the Division Street Vigilantes.

Editorials that morning commented on "the coincidence of four widely separated communities getting the same idea over the same weekend" and wondered "if it is so much of a coincidence as it appears."

The anti-Administration papers blamed the Mayor and the Police Commissioner and used phrases like "the traditional American way" and "the right to defend the American home." The more responsible journals deplored the movement and one of them was "confident that the traditional good humor of New York will laugh these well-meaning but overexcited people back to their senses." Max Stone, editorial writer of the leading liberal paper, wrote: "This is fascism on the sidewalks of New York."

By 6 P.M. Monday the newscasters were reporting to their audiences that "at least three dozen action committees have sprung up in scattered neighborhoods of the five boroughs since the announcement this morning of the organization of the Division Street, Murray Hill, West End Avenue, and Greenwich Village groups."

The late evening editions of the newspapers were able to say that "the idea is spreading like an old-fashioned prairie fire. By press time the number of action committees was over a hundred."

By Tuesday morning the count was reported as "hundreds."

The term "Citizens' Action Teams" seems to have first appeared in a Tuesday *Extra* story on the amazing citywide phenomenon. The story was bylined "Jimmy Leggitt." The phrase took hold when Winchell, Lyons, Wilson, and Sullivan noted in their columns that its initials spelled "cat." And CATs they remained.

At an emergency meeting in the Mayor's office Monday night, the Police Commissioner expressed himself as being in favor of "taking tough police measures to stop this thing dead in its tracks. We can't have every Joe, Moe, and Schmo in town a selfappointed cop. It's anarchy, Jack!" But the Mayor shook his head. "You're not going to put out a fire by passing a law against it, Barney. We can't stop this movement by force; it's out of the question. What we've got to do is try to control it."

At his press conference Tuesday morning the Mayor said with a smile, "I repeat that this Cat thing has been exaggerated far out of proportion and there is absolutely no basis for public alarm with the Police Department working on it twenty-four hours a day. These groups will function much more in the public interest with the advice and assistance of the authorities. The Police Commissioner and his various heads of department will be on hand all day today to receive delegations of these groups with the end in view of systematizing and co-ordinating their activities, in much the way that the splendid ARP groups operated during the War."

Disturbingly, the groups did not appear to be received.

On Tuesday night the Mayor went on the air. He did not in the slightest impugn the integrity and good intentions of the people forming home defense groups, but he felt sure all reasonable people would agree that the police power of the greatest city in the world could not be permitted to be usurped by individual citizens, no matter how honest or well-intentioned, in defiance of legal authority. "Let it not be said that the City of New York in the fifth decade of the twentieth century resorted to frontier town vigilante law." The dangers implicit in this sort of thing were recognized by all, he was certain, as far exceeding any possible threat of one homicidally inclined psychotic. "In the old days, before the establishment of official police systems, night patrols of citizens were undoubtedly necessary to protect communities from the robberies and murders of the criminal element; but in the face of the record of New York's Finest. what justifications is there for such patrols today?" He would regret, the Mayor stated, having to resort to countermeasures in the allover public interest. He knew such a step would prove unnecessary. "I urge all already functioning groups of this nature, and groups in the process of organizing, to get in touch immediately with their police precincts for instructions."

By Wednesday morning the failure of the Mayor's radio appeal was apparent. The most irresponsible rumors circulated in the City: that the National Guard had been called out, that the Mayor had made an emergency-flight personal appeal to President Truman in the White House, that the Police Commissioner had resigned, that in a clash between a Washington Heights CAT patrol and police two persons had been killed and nine injured. The Mayor canceled all appointments for the day and remained in continuous conference. Top officials of the Police Department were unanimous in favor of presenting ultimatums to the CAT groups: Disband at once or face arrest. The Mayor refused to sanction such action. No disorders had been reported, he pointed out; apparently the groups were maintaining internal discipline and restricting themselves to their avowed activities. Besides, the movement by now embraced too many people for such measures. "They might lead to open clashes and we'd have riots all over the City. That might mean calling for troops. I'll exhaust every peaceful means before I lay New York open to that."

By midafternoon Wednesday word came that "the central committee" of "the combined Citizens' Action Teams of New York City" had engaged the vast and windy Metropol Hall on Eighth Avenue for "a monster mass meeting" Thursday night. Immediately after, the Mayor's secretary announced a delegation of this committee.

They filed in, a little nervous but with stubborn looks on their faces. The Mayor and his conferees regarded the deputation with curiosity. They seemed a cross-section of the City's people. There were no sharp or shady faces among them. The spokesman, a tall man in his 30s with the look of a mechanic, identified himself as "Jerome K. Frankburner, veteran."

"We've come here, Mr. Mayor, to invite you to talk at our mass meeting tomorrow night. Metropol Hall seats twenty thousand people, we'll have a radio and television setup, and everybody in the City will be sitting in. It's democracy, it's American. What we'd like you to tell us, Mr. Mayor, is what you've done to stop the Cat and what plans you and your subordinates have for the future. And if it's straight talk that makes sense we guarantee that by Friday morning there won't be a C.A.T. in business. Will you come?"

The Mayor said, "Would you gentlemen wait here?" and he took his people into a private office next door.

"Jack, don't do it!"

"Why not, Barney?"

"What can we tell them that we haven't told them a hundred times already? Let's ban the meeting. If there's trouble, crack down on their leaders."

"I don't know, Barney," said one of the Mayor's advisers, a power in the Party. "They're no hoodlums. These people represent a lot of good votes. We'd better go easy."

There were other expressions of opinion, some siding with the Police Commissioner, some with the Party man.

"You haven't said anything, Inspector Queen," said the Mayor suddenly. "What's your opinion?"

"The way I see it," replied Inspector Queen, "it's going to be mighty tough for the Cat to stay away from the meeting."

"Or to put it another way," said the Mayor—"although that's a very valuable thought, Inspector—I was elected on a people's platform and I'm going to stay on it."

He opened the door and said, "I'll be there, gentlemen."

The events of the night of September 22 began in an atmosphere of seriousness and responsibility. Metropol Hall was filled by 7 P.M. and an overflow crowd gathered which soon numbered thousands. But there was exemplary order and the heavy concentration of police had little to do. The inevitable enterprising notions distributor had sent hawkers out to peddle ticklers with a cat's head on the end and oversized C.A.T. lapel buttons of cardboard, and others were peddling orange-and-black cats' heads with grisly expressions which were recognizably advance stocks of Hallowe'en gimcrackery, but there were few buyers in the crowd and the police hustled the vendors along. There were noticeably few children and an almost total absence of horseplay. Inside the Hall people were either quiet or spoke in whispers. In the streets around the Hall the crowds were patient and well-behaved; too patient and too well-behaved, according to old hands of the Traffic Division, who would have welcomed, it appeared, a few dozen drunks, a rousing fistfight or two, or a picket line of Communist demonstrators. But no drunks were visible, the people were strangely passive, and if Communists were among them it was as individuals.

The Traffic brass, testing the wind, put in a call for more mounted police and radio-patrol çars.

A noose dropped quietly around the entire area at 8 P.M. Between 51st and 57th Streets south to north, and between Seventh and Ninth Avenues east to west, solid lines of police appeared to screen off each intersection. Automobile traffic was detoured. Pedestrians were permitted to penetrate the police lines entering the area, but none were allowed to leave before identifying themselves and answering certain questions.

Throughout the district hundreds of plainclothesmen circulated.

Inside the Hall there were hundreds of others.

Among them was one Ellery Queen.

On the platform sat the central committee of the combined Citizens' Action Teams of New York. They were a polyglot group in which no single face stood out; they might have been a jury in a courtroom, and they all wore the intent but self-conscious expressions of jurymen. The Mayor and his official party occupied the seats of honor—"which means," as the Mayor remarked behind his hand to Dr. Edward Cazalis, "where they can keep an eye on us." The speaker's rostrum was flanked with massed American flags. Radio and public address microphones clustered before it. The television people were set up and waiting.

The meeting was opened at 9 P.M. by Jerome K. Frankburner, acting chairman of the evening. Frankburner wore a GI uniform. On the breast of his tunic glittered several decorations, and his sleeve carried an impressive weight of overseas stripes. Above the military figure hung a grim face. He spoke without notes, quietly.

"This is the voice of a New Yorker," Frankburner began. "It doesn't matter what my name is or where I live. I'm speaking for hundreds of New York neighborhood groups who have organized to protect our families and our neighbors' families from a citywide menace. Lots of us fought in the last war and we're all lawabiding Americans. We represent no self-seeking group. We have no axes to grind. You won't find any chiselers, racketeers, or Commies among us. We're Democrats, Republicans, Independents, Liberals, Socialists. We're Protestants, Catholics, Jews. We're whites and we're Negroes. We're business people, white collar people, laboring people, professional people. We're second-generation Americans and we're fourth-generation Americans. We're New York.

"I'm not going to make a speech. We're not here to listen to me. All I want to do is ask a few questions.

"Mr. Mayor, people are being murdered right and left by some lunatic. It's almost four months since the Cat got going and he's still on the prowl. All right, you can't catch him or you haven't been able to yet. Meanwhile what protection do we have? I'm not saying anything against our police. They're a hardworking bunch like the rest of us. But the people of New York ask you: What have our police done about it?"

A sound went through the Hall and met another from outdoors. It was very little, a distant flutter of thunder, but in the Hall and throughout the surrounding streets police nervously fingered their clubs and tightened ranks and on the platform beside the speaker the Mayor and his Police Commissioner were seen to go a little pale.

"To the last man and woman," said Frankburner, a ring coming into his voice, "we're against vigilante law. But we're asking you, Mr. Mayor, what other recourse we have. My wife or my mother might be feeling that silk cord around her throat tonight, and the police wouldn't be in on it till it was all over but the funeral arrangements.

"Mr. Mayor, we've invited you here tonight to tell is what plans you and the law-enforcement authority have for giving us the protection we feel we haven't got.

"Ladies and gentlemen. His Honor, the Mayor of New York."

The Mayor spoke for a long time. He spoke in a sober, neighborly way, exercising his considerable charm and knowledge of the City's people. He traced the history of the New York Police Department, its growth, its gigantic organization, its complexity. He cited the record of its eighteen thousand men and women in guarding law and maintaining order. He gave some reassuring statistics on homicide arrests and convictions. He went into the legal and social aspects of vigilantism and its threats to democratic institutions, its tendency to degenerate from original high purposes to mob rule and the satisfaction of the worst passions of the lowest elements. He pointed to the dangers—violence begetting violence, leading to military intervention, to martial law, and to the suppression of civil liberties, "the first step on the road to fascism and totalitarianism."

"And all this," the Mayor said goodhumoredly, "because temporarily we have failed to locate a single homicidal maniac in the haystack of a city of over seven and one-half millions of people."

But the Mayor's speech, for all its ease and sanity and persuasiveness, was not eliciting those little signs and responses by which veteran public speakers gauge the success or failure of their exertions. This audience gave no signs and responses whatever. It simply sat, or stood, listening. A multibreathing, unstirred entity waiting for something . . . a loosening word.

The Mayor knew it; his voice took on an edge.

His party knew it; they whispered to one another on the platform with exaggerated ease, conscious of the eyes, the television cameras.

Rather abruptly, the Mayor asked the Police Commissioner to give an accounting of the specific measures already taken and "being planned" for the apprehension of the Cat.

As the Commissioner approached the rostrum, Ellery rose in the audience and began to walk down the central aisle toward the press section, scanning the ranks of human heads.

He spotted Jimmy McKell shortly after the Commissioner began to speak.

McKell was twisted about in his seat, glaring at a girl three rows behind him. The girl, pink, was looking at the Commissioner.

Celeste Phillips.

Ellery could not have said what thought, feeling, intuition kept him in the vicinity. Perhaps it was merely the sight of familiar faces.

He dropped to his heels in the aisle at the end of Celeste's row.

He was uneasy. There was something in the air of Metropol Hall that affected him unpleasantly. He saw that others were in the grip of the same disquiet. A sort of mass auto-intoxication. The crowd breathing its own poisons.

And then he knew what it was.

Fear.

The crowd breathing its own fear. It came out of people in invisible droplets, loaded down the air.

What had seemed patience, passivity, expectancy . . . nothing but fear.

They were not listening to the voice of the man on the platform.

They were listening to the inner voice of fear.

"THE CAT!"

It came as the Commissioner turned a page of his notes in the silence.

He looked up very quickly.

The Mayor, Dr. Cazalis, half-rose.

Twenty thousand heads turned.

It had been a woman's scream, pitched to a rare level and held there. It raised the flesh.

A group of men were pushing their way with flailing arms through the standees at the rear of the Hall.

The Commissioner began to say: "Get that woman qui—"

"THE CAT!"

A little eddy of noise began to spin; another; another. A man rose from his seat, a woman, a couple, a group. Craning.

"Ladies and gentlemen, please be seated. Just a hyster—"

"THE CAT!"

"Please!" The Mayor, on the rostrum beside the Commissioner. "Please! Please!"

People were running along the side aisles.

At the rear, a fight was going on.

"THE CAT!"

Somewhere upstairs a man's voice bellowed. It was choked off, as if he were being throttled.

"Take your seats! Officers!"

Bluecoats materialized all over the auditorium.

The disturbance at the rear was now a yeasty corruption, eating into the main aisle, nibbling at the seats.

"THE CAT!"

A dozen women began to scream.

"HE'S HERE!"

Like a stone, it smashed against the great mirror of the audience and the audience shivered and broke. Little cracks widened magically. Where masses had sat or stood, gaps appeared, grew rapidly, splintered in crazy directions. Men began climbing seats, using their fists. People went down. The police vanished. Trickles of shrieks ran together. Metropol Hall became a great cataract obliterating human sound.

On the platform the Mayor, Frankburner, the Commissioner, were shouting into the public address microphones, jostling one another. Their voices mingled; a faint blend, lost in the uproar.

The aisles were logjammed, people punching, twisting, falling toward the exists.

Overhead a balcony rail snapped; a man fell into the orchestra. People were carried down the balcony staircases. Some slipped, disappeared. At the upstairs fire exits hordes struggled over a living, shrieking carpet.

Suddenly the whole contained mass found vents and shot out into the streets, into the frozen thousands, in a moment boiling them to frenzy, turning the area about Metropol Hall into a giant frying pan. Its ingredients sizzled over the police lines, melting men, horses, machines, overflowing the intersections and pouring uptown and down, toward Broadway and toward Ninth Avenue—a smoking liquid that burned everything in its path.

Ellery remembered shouting Jimmy McKell's name as the stampede began, remembered pointing to a petrified Celeste Phillips, trying himself to buck the wall of flesh which pushed him back. He managed to struggle on to a seat, keep his footing there. He saw Jimmy fight his way slowly over three rows, reach the terrified girl, seize her waist. Then they were sucked into the mass and Ellery lost them.

He devoted himself thereafter to keeping off the floor.

A long time afterward he found his father helping the Mayor and the Commissioner direct rescue operations. They had no time for more than a few words. Both were hatless, bleeding, in tatters; all that was left of the Inspector's jacket was the right sleeve. No, he had not seen McKell or the Phillips girl. Or Dr. Cazalis. His eye kept stealing toward the neat and lengthening line of the dead. Then the Inspector was called away and Ellery plodded back into Metropol Hall to help with the casualties. He was one of an impromptu army: police, firemen, ambulance doctors, Red Cross workers, volunteers from the streets. Sirens kept up their outcry, silencing the moans of the injured.

Other horrors took shape as reports kept pouring in. The mob in fleeing had accidentally broken some shop windows in the side streets between Eighth Avenue and Broadway. Looting had begun, led by hoodlums, loiterers, kid gangs. Bystanders who had tried to interfere had been beaten; shopkeepers had been assaulted and in some instances knifed. For a long time the looting had threatened to get out of hand; there was a furious hour as theaters emptying into Broadway had fed the chaos. Hotels had locked their doors. But the police drove patrol cars into the mobs, mounted patrolmen charged concentrations of rioters, and gradually they were dispersed. Hundreds of stores had sustained broken windows and rifled stocks as far south as 42nd Street. Polyclinic Hospital was bedding the injured in corridors; Red Cross emergency first-aid stations had been set up throughout the Times Square area. Ambulances were speeding into the district from as far north as Fordham Hospital. Lindy's, Toots Shor's, Jack Dempsey's, other restaurants in the vicinity were sending coffee and sandwiches to the relief workers.

At 4:45 A.M. one Evarts Jones, an attorney, handed the following statement to the press:

I am authorized by Jerome K. Frankburner, chairman of tonight's disastrous meeting, and by the central committee of the so-called CATs of Greater New York City, to announce that all units will be immediately disbanded and organized patrol activities will cease.

Mr. Frankburner and the committee speak for all citizens who joined in this well-meant but ill-advised popular movement when they express their great sorrow and profound regret over what occurred in Metropol Hall last night.

Pressed by reporters for a personal statement, Frankburner shook his head. "I'm too punchy to say anything. What can anybody say? We were dead wrong. The Mayor was dead right."

At dawn the Cat Riots were quelled and the Four Days were a bloody paragraph in the unwritten almanacs.

Later, the Mayor in silence distributed the statistics of the night's disorders to the press.

The Dead

Women	19
Men	14
Children	6
TOTAL	39

Seriously Injured

Women	68
Men	34
Children	13
TOTAL	115

Minor Injuries, Fractures, Abrasions, etc.

Women	189
Men	152
Children	10
TOTAL	351

Arrested on Charges of Looting, Unlawful Assemblage, Inciting to Violence, etc.

127 persons (including minors)

Property Damage (estimated)

$4,500,000

The woman whose screams touched off the panic and the rioting that followed, said the Mayor, was trampled to death. Her name was Mrs. Maybelle Legontz, 48, a widow, childless. Her body was identi-

135

fied at 2:38 A.M. by a brother, Stephen Chorumkowski, steamfitter, of 421 West 65th Street. Persons in the audience in the immediate vicinity of Mrs. Legontz had testified that to the best of their recollection she had not been attacked or molested by anyone; but the standees had been packed together and an accidental nudge by some bystander may have exploded her nervous fears.

Mrs. Legontz had a medical history of neurasthenia, a condition which first appeared following the death of her husband, a sand-hog, of the "bends."

There was no possibility that she had been the Cat.

It had been, the Mayor agreed with the reporters, one of the worst outbreaks in New York's history, perhaps the worst since the draft riots of 1863.

Ellery found himself in the milky darkness seated on one of the benches of Rockefeller Plaza. There was no one else in the Plaza but Prometheus. Ellery's head was dancy and the chill of the New York morning against the torn places on his hands and face was deliciously personal, keeping him in a rare consciousness.

Prometheus spoke from his watery niche in the sunken court and Ellery took a certain comfort in his company.

"You're wondering how it all came about," began the golden giant, "that this beast in human form you call the Cat has been able, through the mere bawling of his name, to drive thousands of men out of their heads and send them like frightened animals to an animal death.

"I'm so old I don't recall where I originally came from, except that it's supposed to have been without women—which I find very unconvincing—but I seem to remember that I found it necessary to bring to men the gift of fire. If I really did that, I'm the founder of civilization, so I feel qualified to make certain extended remarks on the late unpleasantness.

"The truth is, what happened last night had nothing to do with the Cat at all.

136

"The world today reminds me of the very old days, when religions were being born. I mean, modern society resembles primitive society to an amusing degree. There's the same concentration on democratic government, for example, while certain of your number who claim to be in touch with higher powers push to the top to rule. You make the same virtue out of common names and common bloods, investing both with mystic mumbo jumbo. In sexual affairs, your women are equally overrespected and kept inside a convenient cage of sanctity, while important affairs are arrogated to themselves by your males. You've even reverted to food taboos in your worship of diets and vitamins.

"But I find the most interesting similarity," continued Prometheus, apparently impervious to the cold dawn which was making Ellery rattle like an old gourd, "in the way you react to your environment. The crowd, not the individual, is the thinking unit. And the thinking power of a crowd, as last night's unfortunate events demonstrated, is of an extremely low order. You're bursting with ignorance, and ignorance breeds panicky fears. You're afraid of nearly everything, but most of all you're afraid of personal contact with the problems of your time. So you're only too happy to huddle together inside the high magic wall of tradition and let your leaders manipulate the mysteries. They stand between you and the terrors of the unknown.

"But once in a while your priests of power fail you and suddenly you're left to face the unknown in person. Those on whom you relied to bring you salvation and luck, to shield you from the mysteries of life and of death, no longer stand between you and the dreadful darkness. All over your world the magic wall has crumbled, leaving your people paralyzed on the edge of the Pit.

"In such a state of affairs," said Prometheus, "is it to be wondered at that a single hysterical voice, screaming a single silly taboo, can frighten thousands into running away?"

Ellery awoke on the bench to pain and an early sun burnishing his tutor. There were people in the Plaza and automobiles were rushing by. It seemed to him that someone was making an awful lot of noise and he got up angrily.

The cries were coming from the west, hoarse and exultant.

Boys voices, booming in the canyons.

Ellery limped up the steps, crossed the street, and made his way stiffly toward Sixth Avenue.

There's no hurry, he thought. They're peddling the obituary of the C.A.T. So many dead, so many injured, so many dollars' worth of wreckage. Read all about it.

No, thank you. Hot coffee will do nicely instead.

Ellery limped along trying not to think at all.

But bubbles kept bobbing up.

Obituary of C.A.T. Obituary of *Cat* . . . now that would be something. Obituary of Cat. Come seven.

Our wishes lengthen as our sun declines.

Ellery laughed.

Or as another immortal put it, I should of stood in bed.

Brother Q, you're through. Only you had to rise from the dead. To chase a Cat.

What next?

What do you do?

Where do you look?

How do you look?

In the fresh shadow of the Music Hall marquee the boy's mouth was going through an acrobatic exercise under his popping eyes.

Never an ill wind, thought Ellery as he watched the pile of papers dwindle.

And he began to pass, to cross Sixth Avenue for his coffee, when a shouted syllable made sense and something on top of the heap flew up and lodged in his brain.

Ellery fumbled for a coin. The coin felt cold.

"Extra."

He stood there being elbowed right and left.

There was the familiar Cat, but he had an eighth tail and it was not a question mark.

• 8

Her name was Stella Petrucchi. She lived with her family on Thompson Street, less than a half a mile below Washington Square. She was 22 years of age; of Italian parentage; of the Roman Catholic faith.

For almost five years Stella Petrucchi had been employed as a stenographer in the same law office on Madison Avenue and 40th Street.

Her father had been in the United States for forty-five years. He was a wholesale fish merchant in Fulton Market. He came from Livorno. Stella's mother was also from the province of Toscana.

Stella was the sixth of seven children. Of her three brothers, one was a priest and the two others were in business with George Petrucchi. Of her three sisters, the eldest was a nun of the Carmelite order, one was married to an Italian cheese and olive oil importer, the third was a student at Hunter College. All the Petrucchi children but the priest, who was the eldest, had been born in New York City.

They had thought at first that Stella was part of the immortal debris littering the vicinity of Metropol Hall, overlooked in the streetcleaning. But the silk cord around the girl's neck gave her the special distinction conferred by the Cat and they found that when they pulled her head back by the tumbled black hair and exposed her throat.

A pair of patrolmen had run across her body a block and a half from Metropol Hall at just about

139

the time the Mayor was giving reporters the statistics of the carnage. It was lying on the cement of an alley between two stores, ten feet from the Eighth Avenue sidewalk.

She had been strangled, said the Medical Examiner's man, some time before midnight.

The identification was made by Father Petrucchi and the married sister, Mrs. Teresa Bascalone. Mr. and Mrs. George Petrucchi collapsed on being informed of the tragedy.

A man, Howard Whithacker, 32, who gave a West 4th Street rooming house address, was closely questioned.

Whithacker was a very tall, lean, blackhaired man with closely set diamond black eyes, a horny skin, and Gothic cheekbones. He looked considerably older than the age he gave.

His occupation, he stated, was "unsuccessful poet." On being pressed, he grudgingly admitted that he "kept body and soul together" by working as a counterman in a Greenwich Avenue cafeteria.

Whithacker said that he had known Stella Petrucchi for sixteen months. They had met in the cafeteria late one night the previous spring. She had been out on a date and had stopped in with her escort at two in the morning. The escort, "a deep Bronx troglodyte with handpainted mermaids on his tie," had jeered at Whithacker's midwestern speech. Whithacker had picked up a baked apple from the counter between them, leaned over, and crammed the apple into the offending mouth. "After that, Stella used to drop in almost every night and we became kind of friendly."

He denied angrily having had an affair with the girl. When this line of questioning persisted, he became quite violent and had to be subdued. "She was a pure, sweet soul," he yelled. "Sex with her was out of the question!"

Whithacker talked reluctantly about his background. He hailed from Beatrice, Nebraska. His people were farmers; the original stock had been Scotch—a great-grandfather had come up out of Kentucky in

140

1829 in a group of Campbellites. There was Pawnee blood in the family and a splatter of Bohemian and Danish. "I'm one of the percentage Americans," said Howard Whithacker. "All decimal points. You know?" At home, he said, he attended the Disciples of Christ church.

He was a graduate of the University of Nebraska.

At the beginning of the war he had enlisted in the Navy, "winding up in the Pacific. I was blown into the water by a kamikaze who darn near made it. My ears still ring sometimes. It had a remarkable effect on my poetry."

After the war, finding Beatrice confining, he went to New York—"financed by my brother Duggin, who thinks I'm peotry's gift to Gage County, Nebraska."

His sole published work since his arrival two years before consisted of a verse entitled "Corn in the Coral." It had appeared in Greenwich Village's newspaper, the *Villager,* in the spring of 1947; Whithacker produced a greasy clipping to prove it. "My brother Duggin is now convinced I'm not another John Neihardt. However," he said, "I have received considerable encouragement from fellow-poets in the Village, and of course Stella adored me. We have regular 3 A.M. poetry-reading sessions in the cafeteria. I live Spartanly but adequately. The death of Stella Petrucchi leaves an empty pigeonhole in my heart; she was a dear child without a brain cell in her head."

He denied indignantly having taken money from her.

As to the events of the night of September 22, Whithacker stated that Thursday night being his night off, he had met Stella outside her office building to take her to the Metropol Hall mass meeting. "A cat poem had been taking shape in my mind for some time," he explained. "It was important that I attend. Stella, of course, always looked forward to our Thursday nights together."

They had walked crosstown, stopping in at an Eighth Avenue spaghetti house "owned by a cousin of Stella's father. I discussed the Citizens' Action Teams movement with Mr. Ferriquancchi and we were both surprised to find that the subject made Stella extremely nervous. Ignazio said we oughtn't to go if Stella felt that way and I offered to go alone, but Stella said no, she wanted to go, at last somebody was doing something about the murders. She said she asked the Virgin Mother every night to keep everyone she knew safe."

They had managed to get into Metropol Hall and had found downstairs seats well to the front of the auditorium.

"When the stampede started, Stella and I tried to hold on to each other, but the damn cattle tore us apart. The last I saw of her she was being carried off in a crowd of lunatics, screaming something at me. But I couldn't hear. I never saw her alive again."

Whithacker had been lucky, suffering no more than a torn pocket and some pummeling.

"I crowded with a few other people in a doorway across from the Hall to keep out of harm's way. When the worst was over I started searching for Stella. I couldn't find her among the dead or injured at the Hall so I began looking along Eighth Avenue, the side streets, Broadway. I wandered around all night."

Whithacker was asked why he had not telephoned to the Petrucchis; the family had been up all night frantic over Stella's failure to come home. They had not known about her appointment with him.

"That's the reason. They didn't know about me. Stella said it was better that way. She said they were strict Catholics and it would only cause a ruckus if they found out she was going around with a non-Catholic. She didn't mind her father's cousin Ignazio knowing about us, she said, because Mr. Ferriquancchi is anti-Papist and nobody in the Petrucchi family has anything to do with him anyway."

At 7:30 A.M. Whithacker had returned to Metropol Hall for another checkup, intending to telephone the Petrucchis "despite their religious scruples" if this last effort to locate Stella failed.

At his first question he was seized by the police.

"I must have passed the entrance to that alley a dozen times during the night," Howard Whithacker said. "But it was dark, and how was I to know Stella was laid out in there?"

Whithacker was held "for further questioning."

"No," Inspector Richard Queen told reporters, "we have absolutely nothing on him. But we want to check his story, and so on." The "and so on" was taken by the press—correctly—to refer both to related matters in the recent past and to a certain interesting wildness of eye, manner, and speech in Stella Petrucchi's friend.

There was no medical evidence of rape or attempted rape.

The girl's purse was missing; but it was found later, its contents intact, in the debris of the Hall. A gold religious medal on a fine chain about her neck had not been touched.

The strangling cord was of the familiar tussah silk, dyed salmon-pink. It had been knotted at the nape exactly as in the previous cases. Laboratory examination of the cord turned up nothing of significance.

It seemed clear that Stella Petrucchi had taken refuge in the alley after being hurled into the street with the rest of the Metropol audience. But whether the Cat had been waiting for her in the alley, or had entered with her, or had followed her in, there was no way of telling.

The probability was that she had suspected nothing until the clutch of the silk. She might well have entered the alley at the Cat's invitation, assuming he caught up with her and offered to "protect" her from harm at the hands of the mob.

As usual, he had left no trail.

It was past noon when Ellery pulled himself up the stairs to find the door of the Queen apartment unlocked. Wondering, he went in; and the first thing he saw on entering his bedroom was a torn nylon stocking dangling from the seat of his ladder-back chair. Over one of the chair posts was hooked a white brassiere.

He bent over his bed and shook her.

Her eyes popped open.

"You're all right."

Celeste shuddered. "Don't *ever* do that again! For a split century I thought it was the Cat."

"Is Jimmy . . .?"

"Jimmy's all right, too."

Ellery found himself sitting on the edge of his bed; the back of his neck throbbed again. "I've often dreamed about this situation," he said, rubbing it.

"What situation?" She stretched her long legs stiff under the sheet, moaning, "Oh, I ache."

"I know," said Ellery. "This all happened in a Peter Arno drawing."

"What?" said Celeste sleepily. "Is it still today?"

Her black hair coursed over his pillow in sweet poetic streams. "But exhaustion," Ellery explained, "is the enemy of poetry."

"What? You look kind of dilapidated. Are *you* all right?"

"I will be once I get the hang of sleeping again."

"I am sorry!" Celeste clutched the sheet to her and sat up quickly. "I wasn't really awake. Er, I'm not . . . I mean, I didn't want to poke around in your bureau . . ."

"You cad," said a stern voice. "Would you boot out an unclothed maiden?"

"Jimmy!" said Celeste happily.

Jimmy McKell was in the bedroom doorway, one arm about a large, mysterious-looking paper sack.

"Well," said Ellery. "The McKell. Indestructible, I see."

"I see you made it, too, Ellery."

They grinned at each other. Jimmy was wearing one of Ellery's most cherished sports jackets, which was too small for him, and Ellery's newest tie.

"Mine were torn clean off me," explained Jimmy. "How you feeling, woman?"

"Like September Morn at an American Legion

144

convention. *Would* you two step into the next room?"

In the living room Jimmy scowled. "You look beat, old-timer. What's with the Petrucchi girl?"

"Oh, you know about that."

"Heard it on your radio this morning." Jimmy set the sack down.

"What's in that bag?"

"Some hardtack and pemmican. Your larder'd run dry. Have you eaten anything, bud?"

"No."

"Neither have we. Hey, Celeste!" Jimmy shouted. "Never mind making with the clothes. Rustle us some breakfast!"

Celeste laughed from Ellery's bathroom.

"You two seem awfully gay," remarked Ellery, feeling for the armchair.

"Funny how it hits you." Jimmy laughed, too. "You get mixed up in something like last night's fandango and all of a sudden everything drops into the slot. Even stupidity. I thought I'd seen everything in the Pacific, but I hadn't. The war was murder, all right, but organized. You wear a uniform and you carry a gun and you take great big orders and somebody cooks your chow and you kill or get killed, all according to the book. But last night . . . tooth and claw. Man stripped to the bloody bones. Disintegration of the tribe. Every fellow-cannibal your enemy. It's good to be alive, that's all."

"Hello, Celeste," said Ellery.

Her clothes were macerated and although she had evidently brushed them and applied pins to secret parts, they looked like hardening lava. Her legs were rowdy: she carried her stockings.

"I don't suppose you'd have an old pair of nylons around, Mr. Queen?"

"No," said Ellery gravely. "My father, you know."

"Oh, dear. Well! I'll fix you men something in a jiffy," and Celeste went into the kitchen with the sack.

"Superior, hey?" Jimmy stared at the swinging

145

door. "You'll note, Brother Queen, that the lady made no apology for her appearance. Definitely superior."

"How'd you two manage to keep together last night?" asked Ellery, closing his eyes.

"Now don't cork off on us, Ellery." Jimmy began setting the dropleaf table. "Why, the fact is we didn't."

"Oh?" said Ellery, opening one eye.

"We lost each other right after I got to her. She doesn't remember how she got out, and neither do I. We kept hunting for each other all night. I found her around 5 A.M. sitting on the steps of Polyclinic Hospital, bawling."

Ellery closed the eye.

"How do you like your bacon, Mr. Queen?" called Celeste.

Jimmy said, "Are you there?" and Ellery mumbled something. "Curly and wet, he says!—What, Ellery?"

"The last word," said Ellery, "was 'bawling.'"

"Her eyes out. I tell you, I was touched. Anyway, we had some coffee at an allnight joint and then we went looking for you. But you'd disappeared. We thought you'd probably got out all right and gone home, so we came up here. Nobody home, so I said to Celeste, 'He won't mind,' and I climbed up the fire escape. For an eye, Ellery, you're very careless about your windows."

"Go on," said Ellery, when Jimmy stopped.

"I don't know if I can explain it. Why we came, I mean. I don't think Celeste and I said two dozen words to each other after we clutched this morning. I think we both realized your position for the first time and we wanted to tell you we've been a couple of firstclass *schlemihls* and didn't quite know how to do it." Jimmy straightened a spoon. "This thing is awfully gross," he said to the spoon. "The war all over again. In another form. The individual doesn't mean a damn. Human dignity gets flushed down the drain. You have to get up to your elbow in muck to hold on to it. I didn't see that till last night, Ellery."

146

"Neither did I." Celeste was in the kitchen doorway with a piece of toast in one hand and a buttery knife in the other. Ellery thought, Piggott and Johnson lost them last night; they must have. "You were right, Mr. Queen. After what we saw last night you were right."

"About what, Celeste?"

"About suspecting Jimmy and me. Jimmy and me or anybody."

"I guess what we wanted to hear you say was 'Come back, all is forgiven,'" grinned Jimmy. But then he began on the cutlery again.

"So you waited here for me."

"When we heard the news we knew what was keeping you. I made Celeste get into your bed—she was dead on her feet—and I parked on the sofa in here. Anything to connect the Petrucchi girl with the others?"

"No."

"What about this cornhusker-poet character? What's his name?"

"Whithacker?" Ellery shrugged. "Dr. Cazalis seems interested in him and they're going to examine him carefully."

"I'm one hell of a newspaperman." Jimmy banged a spoon down. "All right, I'll say it. Do you want us back?"

"I don't have anything for you to do, Jimmy."

"For me!" cried Celeste.

"Or for you."

"You don't want us back."

"I do. But I have no work for you." Ellery got up, groping for a cigaret. But his hands dropped. "I don't know where to turn. That's the truth. I'm absolutely hung up."

Jimmy and Celeste looked swiftly at each other. Then Jimmy said, "You're also absolutely pooped. What you need is to slice a herring with Morpheus. Hey, Celeste! *The coffee!*"

Ellery awoke to the sound of a loud voice.
He switched on the night light.
8:12

The voice was driving. Ellery crawled out of bed, pulled on his robe and slippers, and hurried to the living room.

The voice was the radio's. His father was lying back in the armchair. Jimmy and Celeste crouched on the sofa in a nest of newspapers.

"You two still here?"

Jimmy grunted. His long chin was nuzzling his chest and Celeste kept rubbing her drawnup bare leg in a reassuring way.

The Inspector was all bones and gray wilt.

"Dad—"

"Listen."

"—reported tonight," said the voice. "A third-rail short circuit on the BMT subway at Canal Street caused a panic and forty-six persons were treated for injuries. Trains out of Grand Central Terminal and Pennsylvania Station are running from ninety minutes to two hours behind schedule. The parkways out of the City are a solid double line of cars as far north as Greenwich and White Plains. Traffic is clogged for a large area around the Manhattan approaches to the Holland and Lincoln Tunnels and the George Washington Bridge. Nassau County authorities report that traffic conditions on the major Long Island parkways are out of control. New Jersey, Connecticut, and upstate New York police report—"

Ellery snapped the radio off.

"What is it?" he asked wildly. "War?" His glance flew to the windows, as if he expected to see a flaming sky.

"New York's turned Malay," said Jimmy with a laugh.

"The *amok*. They'll have to rewrite the psychology books." He began to get up, but Celeste pulled him back.

"Fighting? Panic?"

"That Metropol Hall business last night was just the beginning, Ellery." The Inspector was fighting something, nausea or rage. "It snapped a vital part. Started a sort of chain reaction. Or maybe it was

148

the Petrucchi murder on top of the panic and riot—that was bad timing. Anyway, it's all over the City. Been spreading all day."

"They're running," said Celeste. "Everybody's running."

"Running where?"

"Nobody seems to know. Just running."

"It's the Black Death all over again," said Jimmy McKell. "Didn't you know? We're back in the Middle Ages. New York is now the pesthole of the Western Hemisphere, Ellery. In two weeks you'll be able to shoot hyenas in Macy's basement."

"Shut up, McKell." The old man's head rolled on the back of his chair. "There's a lot of disorder, son, a lot. Looting, holdups . . . It's been particularly bad on Fifth Avenue, 86th around Lexington, 125th, upper Broadway, and around Maiden Lane downtown. And traffic accidents, hundreds of traffic accidents. I've never seen anything like it. Not in New York."

Ellery went to one of the windows. The street was empty. A fire engine screamed somewhere. The sky glowed to the southwest.

"And they say," began Celeste.

"Who says?" Jimmy laughed again. "Well, that's the point, my friends, whereupon today I'm proud to be one of the capillaries in the circulation system of organized opinion. We've really swung it this time, comrades." He kicked a drooping newspaper. "Responsible journalism! And the blessed radio—"

"Jimmy," said Celeste.

"Well, old Rip's got to hear the news, hasn't he? He's slept through history, Miss Phillips. Did you know, sir, that there's a citywide quarantine? It's a fact. Or is it? That all schools will be shut down indefinitely—O happy day? That Father Knickerbocker's chickens are to be evacuated to camps outside the metropolitan area? That all flights from La Guardia, Newark, and Idlewild have been nixed? That the Cat's made of extremely green cheese?"

Ellery was silent.

"Also," said Jimmy McKell, "Beldame Rumor hath it that the Mayor's been attacked by the Cat, that the FBI's taken over Police Headquarters, that the Stock Exchange positively will not open its doors tomorrow—and that's a fact, seeing that tomorrow's Saturday." Jimmy unfolded himself. "Ellery, I went downtown this afternoon. The shop is a madhouse. Everybody's busy as little beavers denying rumors and believing every new one that comes in. I stopped on my way back to see if Mother and Father are maintaining their equilibrium and do you know what? I saw a Park Avenue doorman get hysterics. Brother, that's the end of the world." He swiped his nose back-handedly, glaring. "It's enough to make you cancel your membership in the human race. Come on, let's all get drunk."

"And the Cat?" Ellery asked his father.

"No news."

"Whithacker?"

"Cazalis and the psychiatrists have been working on him all day. Still are, far as I know. But they're not doing any backbends. And we didn't find a thing in his West 4th Street flop."

"Do I have to do it all by myself?" demanded Jimmy, pouring Scotch. "None for you, Celeste."

"Inspector, what's going to happen now?"

"I don't know," said the Inspector, "and what's more, Miss Phillips, I don't think I give an Irish damn." He got up. "Ellery, if Headquarters calls, I've gone to bed."

The old man shuffled out.

"Here's to the Cat," said Jimmy, lofting his glass. "May his giblets wither."

"If you're going to start toping, Jimmy," said Celeste, "I'm going home. I'm going home anyway."

"Right. To mine."

"Yours?"

"You can't stay up in that foul nest of underprivilege alone. And you may as well meet Father now and get it over with. Mother, of course, will be nightingale soup."

"It's sweet of you, Jimmy," Celeste was all olive-pink. "But just impossible."

"You can sleep in Queen's bed but you can't sleep in mine! What is this?"

She laughed, but she was angry. "It's been the ghastliest and most wonderful twenty-four hours of my life, darling. Don't spoil it."

"Spoil it! Why, you proletarian snob!"

"I can't let your parents think I'm some dead-end kid to be taken in off the streets."

"You are a snob."

"Jimmy." Ellery turned from the fireplace. "Is it the Cat you're worrying about?"

"Always. But this time the rabbits, too. It's a breed that bites."

"You can stop worrying about the Cat, at any rate. Celeste is safe."

Celeste looked bewildered.

Jimmy said, "The hell you say."

"For that matter, so are you." Ellery explained the diminishing-age pattern of the murders. When he had finished he packed a pipe and lit it, watching them, and all the time they stood peering at him as if he were performing a minor miracle.

"And nobody saw that," muttered Jimmy. "Nobody."

"But what does it mean?" Celeste cried.

"I don't know. But Stella Petrucchi was 22; and you and Jimmy being older than that, the Cat's passed your age groups by." Just relief, he thought, wondering why he was disappointed.

"May I print that, Ellery?" Jimmy's face fell. "I forgot. *Noblesse oblige.*"

"Well, I think," said Celeste defiantly, "that people ought to be told, Mr. Queen. Especially now, when they're so frightened."

Ellery stared at her. "Wait a minute."

He went into his study.

When he returned he said, "The Mayor agrees with you, Celeste. Things are very bad . . . I'm holding a press conference at 10 o'clock tonight and I'm

151

going on the air with the Mayor at 10:30. From City Hall. Jimmy, don't double-cross me."

"Thanks, pal. This descending-age business?"

"Yes. As Celeste says, it ought to quiet some fears."

"You don't sound hopeful."

"It's a question which can be more alarming," said Ellery, "danger to yourself or danger to your children."

"I see what you mean. I'll be right back, Ellery. Celeste, come on." He grabbed her arm.

"Just put me in a cab, Jimmy."

"Are you going to be pork-headed?"

"I'll be as safe on 102nd Street as on Park Avenue."

"How about compromising in a—I mean on a hotel?"

"Jimmy, you're wasting Mr. Queen's time."

"Wait for me, Ellery. I'll go downtown with you."

They went out, Jimmy still arguing.

Ellery shut the door after them carefully. Then he went back to the radio, turned it on, and sat down on the edge of the chair, like an audience.

But at the first blat of the newscaster he leaped, throttled the voice, and hurried to his bedroom.

It was afterward said that the press conference and radio talk of the Mayor's Special Investigator on that topsyturvy night of Friday, September 23, acted as a brake on the flight of New Yorkers from the City and in a matter of hours brought the panic phase of the case to a complete stop. Certainly the crisis was successfully passed that night and never again reached a peak. But what few realized who were following the complex psychology of the period was that something comparably undesirable replaced it.

As people straggled back to the City in the next day or so, it was remarked that they no longer seemed *interested* in the Cat case. The cataract of telephone calls and in-person inquiries which had kept City Hall, Police Headquarters, and precincts all over the

City swamped for almost four months ebbed to a trickle. Elected officials, who had been under continuous bombardment from their constituents, discovered that the siege had unaccountably lifted. For once, to their relief, ward politicians found their clubhouses deserted. *Vox populi,* which had kept the correspondence columns of the newspapers in an uproar, sank to a petty whisper.

An even more significant phenomenon was observed.

On Sunday, September 25, churches of all denominations throughout the City suffered a marked drop in attendance. While this fall from grace was deplored by the clergy, it was almost unanimously regarded by lay observers as an agreeable evil, considering "the recent past." (Already the panic had dwindled to the size of a footnote in the City's history, so dramatic was the change.) The unusually heavy church attendance during the summer, these observers said, had been inspired largely by Cat-generated fears and a panic flight to spiritual reassurance; the sudden wholesale defection could only mean that the panic was over, the pendulum had swung to the other extreme. Shortly, they predicted, church attendance would find itself back in the normal rhythm.

On all sides responsible people were congratulating one another and the City on "the return to sanity." It was recognized that the threat to the City's young people had to be guarded against, and special measures were planned, but everyone seemed to feel—in official quarters that the worst was over.

It was almost as if the Cat had been caught.

But there were contrary signs to be seen by those who were not blinded by sheer relief.

During the week beginning Saturday, September 24, *Variety* and Broadway columnists began to report an extraordinary increase in night club and theater attendance. The upswing could not be ascribed to seasonal change; it was too abrupt. Theaters which had not seen a full house all summer found themselves under the pleasant compulsion to rehire laidoff

153

ushers and hall out ropes and S.R.O. signs. Clubs which had been staggering along were regarding their jammed dance floors with amazement; the famous ones were haughtily turning people away again. Broadway bars and eating places sprang to jubliant life. Florist shops, candy shops, cigar stores were crowded. Liquor stores tripled their sales. Scalpers, barkers, and steerers began to smile again. Bookmakers rubbed their eyes at the flow of bets. Sports arenas and stadiums reported record receipts and new attendance marks. Pool room and bowling alleys put on extra employees. The shooting galleries on Broadway, 42nd Street, Sixth Avenue were mobbed.

Overnight, it seemed, show business and its feedline subsidiaries began to enjoy boomtime prosperity. Times Square from sundown to 3 A.M. was roaring and impassable. Taxi drivers were saying, "It's just like the war all over again."

The phenomenon was not restricted to midtown Manhattan. It was simultaneously experienced by the entertainment districts of downtown Brooklyn, Fordham Road in the Bronx, and other localities throughout the five boroughs.

That week, too, advertising agency executives were bewildered by advance reports from their radio-polling services. At a time when most major radio shows had returned to the air to begin the fall and winter broadcasting cycles and an appreciable rise in listener-response should have become apparent, the advance ratings unaccountably dropped in the metropolitan area. All networks were affected. The independent stations with local coverage had Pulse and BMB make hasty special surveys and discovered that the bottom had fallen out of their program-response and listener-circulation tables. The most significant of all—in all surveys—were those showing the percentage of sets-in-use. They were unprecedentedly small.

A parallel drop was noted in television surveys.

New Yorkers were not listening to the radio and watching the telecasts.

Account executives and broadcasting company vice-presidents were busy preparing explanations to their clients, chiefly masochistic. The truth seemed to have occurred to none of them, which was that radio and television sets could not be turned on in the home by people who were not there or why, if they were, were absent spiritually.

Police were puzzled by the abrupt rise in drunkenness and disorderly conduct cases. Routine raids on gambling houses bagged huge takes and a type of burgher clientele not ordinarily found throwing its money away. Marijuana and narcotics cases took a disturbing jump. The Vice Squad was compelled to put on a co-ordinated drive in an attempt to curb the sudden spread and acceleration of prostitution activities. Muggings, car thefts, holdups, common assaults, sex offenses increased sharply. The rise in juvenile delinquency was especially alarming.

And of peculiar interest was the reappearance all over the City of strangled alley cats.

It was evident to the thoughtful few that what had seemed a healthy loss of interest in the Cat case on the part of New Yorkers was not that at all. Fear had not died; the City was still in the mob mood and mob psychology was still at the panic stage; it had merely taken a new form and direction. People were now in flight from reality on a psychic rather than a physical level. But they were still fleeing.

On Sunday, October 2, an unsurprisingly large number of clergymen took as their texts Genesis XIX, 24-25. It was natural to cite Sodom and Gomorrah that day, and brimstone and fire were generously predicted. The ingredients of moral disintegration were all present in the melting pot, bubbling to the boil. The only trouble was that those whom the lesson would have profited were atoning for their wickedness in a less godly fashion, elsewhere.

By a sly irony the ninth life of the Cat proved the crucial one.

For the break in the case came with the ninth murder.

The body was found a few minutes after 1 A.M. on the night of September 29-30, exactly one week after the Cat Riots and less than two miles from the site of Stella Petrucchi's murder. It lay sprawled in deep shadows on the steps of the American Museum of Natural History, at 77th Street and Central Park West. A sharpeyed patrolman spotted it on his rounds.

Death was by strangulation. A cord had been employed, of tussah silk, dyed blue as in the cases of Archibald Dudley Abernethy and Rian O'Reilly.

According to a driver's license found in his untouched wallet, his name was Donald Katz, he was 21 years old, and he lived on West 81st Street. The address proved to be an apartment house between Central Park West and Columbus Avenue. His father was a dentist, with offices at Amsterdam Avenue and West 71st Street near Sherman Square. The family was of the Jewish faith. The victim had an elder sister, Mrs. Jeanne Immerson, who lived in the Bronx. Donald was enrolled in extension courses in radio and television engineering. He had been, it seemed, a bright quixotic boy given to quick enthusiasms and dislikes; he had had many acquaintances and few friends.

The father, Dr. Morvin Katz, officially identified the body.

It was from Dr. Katz that police learned about the girl his son had been out with that evening. She was Nadine Cuttler, 19, of Borough Park, Brooklyn, a student at the New York Art Students' League. Brooklyn detectives picked her up during the night and she was brought to Manhattan for questioning.

She fainted on viewing the body and it was some time before she could give a coherent story.

Nadine Cuttler said that she had known Donald Katz fror almost two years. "We met at a Palestine rally." They had had "an understanding" for the past year, during which period they had seen each other three or four times a week. "We had practically nothing in common. Donald was interested in science and technology, and I in art. He was politically unde-veloped; not even the war taught him anything. We didn't even agree about Palestine. I don't know why we fell in love."

The previous evening, Miss Cuttler stated, Donald Katz had met her at the Art Students' League after her classes and they had walked down Seventh Avenue from 57th Street, stopping in at Lum Fong's for a chow mein dinner. "We fought over the check. Donald had juvenile ideas about this being a man's world, and that women ought to stay home and have babies and smooth their husbands' brows when the men came home after an important day, and all that sort of thing. He got very angry with me because I pointed out to him it was my turn to pay. Finally, I let him pay the check just to avoid a scene in public."

Afterward, they had gone dancing in a little Russian night club on 52nd Street, The Yar, across from 21 and Leon and Eddie's.

"It was a place we liked very much and often went to. They knew us there and we called Maria and Lonya and Tina and the others by their first names. But last night it was crowded and after a while we left. Donald had had four vodkas and didn't touch any of the *zakuska,* so when we hit the air he got lightheaded. He wanted to go clubbing, but I said I wasn't in the mood and instead we strolled back uptown on Fifth Avenue. When we got to Fifth and 59th, Donald wanted to go into the Park. He was feeling very . . . gay; the drinks hadn't worn off. But it was so dark in there, and the Cat . . ."

At this point Nadine Cuttler broke down.

When she was able to continue, the girl said: "I found myself awfully nervous. I don't know why. We'd often talked about the Cat murders and neither of us ever felt a personal threat, I'm sure of it. We just couldn't seem to take it seriously, I mean really seriously. Donald used to say the Cat was anti-Semitic because in a City with the biggest Jewish population in the world he hadn't strangled a single Jew. Then he'd laugh and contradict himself and say the odds

157

were the Cat was Jewish because of that very fact. It was a sort of joke between us which I never thought very funny, but you couldn't take offense at anything Donald said, not really, he . . ."

She had to be recalled to her story.

"We didn't go into the Park. We walked crosstown on Central Park South, sticking to the side of the street where the buildings are. On the way Donald seemed to sober up a bit; we talked about the murder of the Petrucchi girl last week and the Cat Riots and the stampede out of the City, and we agreed it was a funny thing but it was usually the older people who lost their heads in a crisis while the young ones, who had most to lose, kept theirs . . . Then, when we got to Columbus Circle, we had another quarrel."

Donald had wanted to take her home, "even though we'd had an absolute compact for months that on weeknight dates I'd go back to Brooklyn by myself. I was really exasperated with him. His mother didn't like him to get in late; it was the only basis on which I allowed myself to see him so often. Why didn't I let him, why didn't I let him?"

Nadine Cuttler cried again and Dr. Katz quieted her, saying that she had nothing to condemn herself for, that if it was Donald's fate to become a victim of the Cat nothing would have changed the result. The girl clung to his hand.

There was little more to her story. She had refused to let the boy accompany her to Brooklyn and she had urged him to hop a cab and go right home, because "he was looking sick and besides I didn't like the idea of his being alone on the streets in that condition. That made him even madder. He didn't even . . . kiss me. The last I saw of him was when I was going down the subway steps. He was standing at the top talking to somebody, I think a taxi driver. That was about 10:30."

The taxi driver was found. Yes, he remembered the young couple's tiff. "When the girl sails off down the steps I open my door and say to this kid, 'Better luck next time, Casanova. Come on, I'll take you home.' But he was sore as a boil. 'You can take your cab and shove it,' he says to me. 'I'm walking home.' And he crossed the Circle and turns into Central Park West. Headed uptown. He was pretty rocky on his pins."

It seemed clear that Donald Katz had tried to carry out his intention, walking uptown along the west side of Central Park West from Columbus Circle for almost a mile to 77th Street, just four blocks short of his home. There seemed no question but that the Cat had followed him all the way. perhaps had followed the couple all evening, although nothing developed from inquiries made at Lum Fong's and The Yar, and the taxi driver could not recall having seen anyone acting suspiciously as Donald Katz left him. The Cat had undoubtedly bided his time, waiting for an opportunity to pounce. The opportunity had come at 77th Street. On the steps of the Museum, at the spot where Donald was found, there was a mess of regurgitated matter; some of it was on Donald's coat. Apparently as he was passing the Museum his intoxication reached the stage of nausea and Donald had sat down on the steps in a dark place and he had been ill.

And the Cat had approached him from the side and got behind him as he sat retching.

He had struggled violently.

Death occurred, said the Medical Examiner, between 11 P.M. and midnight.

No one heard screams or choked cries.

The most thorough examination of the body, the clothing, the strangling cord, and the scene turned up nothing of importance.

"As usual," said Inspector Queen at the dawn's early light, "the Cat's left not a clue."

But he had.

The fateful fact emerged obliquely during the morning of the 30th in the Katz apartment on West 81st Street.

Detectives were questioning the family, going through the familiar motions of trying to establish a connection between Donald Katz and the persons involved in the previous eight murders.

Present were the boy's mother and father; their daughter; the daughter's husband, Philbert Immerson. Mrs. Katz was a lean brown-eyed woman of bitter charm; her face was undressed by weeping. Mrs. Immerson, a chubby young woman without her mother's mettle, sobbed throughout the interview; Ellery gathered from something Mrs. Immerson said that she had not got along with her young brother. Dr. Katz sat by himself in a corner, as Zachary Richardson had sat on the other side of Central Park three and a half weeks before; he had lost his son, there would be no others. Donald's brother-in-law, a balding young man with a red mustache, wearing a sharp gray business suit, stood away from the others as if to avoid being noticed. He had freshly shaved; his stout cheeks were perspiring under the talcum.

Ellery was paying little attention to the automatic questions and the surcharged replies; he was dragging himself about these days and it had been a particularly depleting night. Nothing would come of this, he felt sure, as nothing had come of any of the others. A few slight alterations in the pattern—Jewish instead of Christian, seven days since the last one instead of seventeen, or eleven, or six—but the bulk features were the same: the strangling cord of tussah silk, blue for men, salmon-pink for women; the victim unmarried (Rian O'Reilly was still the baffling single exception); the victim listed in the telephone directory—Ellery had checked that immediately, and the ninth victim younger than the eighth who had been younger than the seventh who had been . . .

"—no, I'm positive he didn't know anybody of that name," Mrs. Katz was saying. Inspector Queen was being perversely insistent about Howard Whithacker, who had disappointed the psychiatrists. "Unless, of course, this Whithacker was somebody Donald met in training camp."

"You mean during the war?" asked the Inspector.

160

"Yes."

"Your son in the war, Mrs. Katz? Wasn't he too young?"

"No. He enlisted on his eighteenth birthday. The war was still on."

The Inspector looked surprised. "Germany surrendered in May, I think it was, of 1945—Japan in August or September. Wasn't Donald still 17 in 1945?"

"I ought to know my own son's age!"

"Pearl." Dr. Katz stirred in his corner. "It must be that driving license."

The Queens both made the slightest forward movement.

"Your son's license, Dr. Katz," said Inspector Queen, "gives his birth date as March 10, 1928."

"That's a mistake, Inspector Queen. My son made a mistake putting down the year on his application and never bothered to have it corrected."

"You mean," asked Ellery, and he found himself clearing his throat, "you mean Donald was *not* 21 years old, Dr. Katz?"

"Donald was 22. He was born on March 10, 1927."

"22," said Ellery.

"*22?*" The Inspector sounded froggy, too. "Ellery. Stella Petrucchi."

Abernethy, 44. Violette Smith, 42. Rian O'Reilly, 40. Monica McKell, 37. Simone Phillips, 35. Beatrice Willikins, 32. Lenore Richardson, 25. Stella Petrucchi, 22. Donald Katz . . . 22.

For the first time the diminishing-age sequence had been broken.

Or had it?

"It's true," Ellery said feverishly in the hall, "it's true that up to now the age drop's been in years. But if we found . . ."

"You mean this Katz boy might still be younger than Stella Petrucchi," mumbled his father.

"In terms of months. Suppose the Petrucchi girl

161

had been born in January of 1927. That would make Donald Katz two months younger."

"Suppose Stella Petrucchi was born in *May* of 1927. That would make Donald Katz two months *older*."

"I don't want to think about that. That would . . . What month *was* she born in?"

"I don't know!"

"I don't remember seeing her exact birth date on any report."

"Wait a minute!"

The Inspector went away.

Ellery found himself pulling a cigaret to pieces. It was monstrous. Fat with meaning. He knew it.

The secret lay here.

But what secret?

He tried to contain himself as he waited. From somewhere he heard the Inspector's voice, in tones of manhood. God bless the shade of Alexander Graham Bell. What secret?

Suppose it turned out that Donald Katz had been older than Stella Petrucchi. By so little as one day. Suppose. What could it mean? What *could* it mean?

"Ellery."

"Well!"

"March 10, 1927."

"What?"

"Father Petrucchi says his sister Stella was born on March 10, 1927."

"The same day?"

They glared at each other.

Later they agreed that what they did was reflexive; on its merits it promised nothing. Their inquiry was a sort of conditioned response, the detective organism reacting to the stimulus of another uncomprehended fact by calling into play the nerves of pure habit. The futility of any conscious consideration of the identical-natal day phenomenon was too painfully apparent. In lieu of explanation—even of reasonable hypothesis—the Queens went back to fundamentals. Never mind what the fact might mean; first, was it a fact?

Ellery said to his father, "Let's check that right now," and the Inspector nodded and they went down into West 81st Street and climbed into the Inspector's car and Sergeant Velie drove them to the Manhattan Bureau of Vital Records and Statistics of the Department of Health.

Neither man uttered a sound on the ride downtown.

Ellery's head hurt. A thousand gears were trying to mesh and failing to do so. It was maddening, because he could not rid himself of the feeling that it was all so very simple. He was sure there was a rhythmic affinity in the facts but they were not functioning through a silly, aggravating failure of his perceptive machinery.

Finally, he shut the power off and was borne blank-minded to their destination.

"The original birth certificates," said Inspector Queen to the Registrar of Records. "No, we don't have the certificate numbers. But the names are Stella Petrucchi, female, and Donald Katz, male, and the date of birth in each case is, according to our information, March 10, 1927. Here, I've written the names down."

"You're sure they were both born in Manhattan, Inspector?"

"Yes."

The Registrar came back looking interested. "I see they were not only born on the same day, but—"

"March 10, 1927? In both cases?"

"Yes."

"Wait, Dad. Not only born on the same day, but what?"

"But the same doctor delivered them."

Ellery blinked.

"The same . . . doctor delivered them," said his father.

"May I see those certificates, please?" Ellery's voice was cracked again.

163

They stared at the signatures. Same handwriting. Both certificates signed:

Edward Cazalis M.D.

"Now, son, let's take it easy," Inspector Queen was saying, his hand muffling the phone. "Let's not jump. We don't know a thing. We're just bumbling around. We've got to go slow."

"I'll go as I damn please. Where's that list?"

"I'm getting it. They're getting it for me—"

"Cazalis, Cazalis. Here it is! Edward Cazalis. I told you it was the same one!"

"He delivered babies? I thought—"

"Started his medical career in the practice of obstetrics and gynecology. I knew there was something queer about his professional history."

"1927. He was still doing O.B. work as late as 1927?"

"Later! Here. It says—"

"Yes, Charley!"

Ellery dropped the medical directory. His father began writing as he listened. He wrote and wrote. It seemed as if he would never stop writing.

Finally, he did.

"Got 'em all?"

"Ellery. It just isn't reasonable that *all* of them—"

"Would you please get the original birth certificates," Ellery said, handing the Inspector's paper to the Registrar, "of the people listed here?"

"Dates of birth . . ." The Registrar ran his eye down the list. "All Manhattan born?"

"Most of them. Maybe all of them. Yes," said Ellery. "I think all of them. I'm sure of it."

"How can you be 'sure' of it?" snarled his father. "What do you mean, 'sure'? We know about some of them, but—"

"I'm sure of it. All born in Manhattan. Every last one. See if I'm wrong."

The Registrar went away.

They kept walking around each other like two dogs.

The clock on the wall crept along.

Once the Inspector said in a mutter: "This could mean . . . You know this could mean . . ."

Ellery turned around, baring his teeth. "I don't want to know what this 'could' mean. I'm sick of thinking of 'possibilities.' First things first, that's my motto. I just invented it. One thing per time. Step by step. B follows A, C follows B. One and one make two, and that's the limit of my arithmetic until I have to add two more."

"Okay, son, okay," said the Inspector; after that he muttered to himself.

And then the Registrar came back.

He was looking baffled, inquisitive, and uneasy.

Ellery set his back against the office door. "Give it to me slowly, please. One at a time. Start with Abernethy. Abernethy, Archibald Dudley—"

"Born May 24, 1905," said the Registrar. Then he said. "Edward Cazalis, M.D."

"Interesting. Interesting!" said Ellery. "Smith. Violette Smith."

"Born February 13, 1907," said the Registrar. "Edward Cazalis, M.D."

"Rian O'Reilly. Is good old Rian O'Reilly there, too?"

"They're all here, Mr. Queen. I really . . . Born December 23, 1908. Edward Cazalis. M.D."

"And Monica McKell?"

"July 2, 1912. Edward Cazalis, M.D. Mr. Queen . . ."

"Simone Phillips."

"October 11, 1913. Cazalis."

"Just 'Cazalis'?"

"Well, of course not," snapped the Registrar. "Edward Cazalis, M.D. See here, I really don't see the point of going through this name by name, Inspector Queen. I said they're all here—"

"Give the boy his head," said the Inspector. "He's been reined in a long time."

"Beatrice Willikins," said Ellery. "I'm especially interested in Beatrice Willikins. I should have seen

165

it, though. Birth is the universal experience along with death; the two always played footsie under God's table. Why didn't I see that at once? Beatrice Willikins."

"April 7, 1917. The same doctor."

"The same doctor," nodded Ellery. He was smiling, a forbidding smile. "And that was a Negro baby, and it was the same doctor. A Hippocratic physician, Cazalis. The god of the maternity clinic, no doubt, on alternate Wednesdays. Come all ye pregnant, without regard for color or creed, fees adjusted according to the ability to pay. And Lenore Richardson?"

"January 29, 1924. Edward Cazalis, M. D."

"And that was the carriage trade. Thank you, sir, I believe that completes the roll. I take it these certificates are the untouchable trust of the Deparment of Health of the City of New York?"

"Yes."

"If anything happens to them," said Ellery, "I shall personally come down here with a derringer, sir, and shoot you dead. Meanwhile, no word of this is to get out. No whisper of a syllable. Do I make myself clear?"

"I don't mind telling you," said the Registrar stiffly, "that I don't like either your tone or your attitude, and—"

"Sir, you address the Mayor's Special Investigator. I beg your pardon," said Ellery, "I'm higher than the much-abused kite. May we use your office and your telephone for a few minutes—alone?"

The Registrar of Records went out with a bang.

But immediately the door opened and the Registrar stepped back into his office, shut the door with care, and said in a confidential tone, "A doctor who would go back to murder the people he himself brought into the world—why, gentlemen, he's nothing but a lunatic. How in hell did you let him weasel his way into your investigation?"

And the Registrar stamped out.

"This isn't," said the Inspector, "going to be easy."

"No."

"There's no evidence."

Ellery nibbled a thumbnail on the Registrar's desk.

"He'll have to be watched day and night. Twenty-four out of twenty-four. We've got to know what he's doing every minute of every hour of the day."

Ellery continued to nibble.

"There mustn't be a tenth," said the Inspector, as if he were explaining something abstruse, top-secret, and of global importance. Then he laughed. "That cartoonist on the *Extra* doesn't know it but he's run out of tails. Let me get to that phone, Ellery."

"Dad."

"What, son?"

"We've got to have the run of that apartment for a few hours." Ellery took out a cigaret.

"Without a warrant?"

"And tip him off?"

The Inspector frowned.

"Getting rid of the maid ought to present no problem. Pick her day off. No, this is Friday and the chances are she won't be off till the middle of next week. I can't wait that long. Does she sleep in?"

"I don't know."

"I want to get in there over the weekend, if possible. Do they go to church?"

"How should I know? That cigaret won't draw, Ellery, because you haven't lit it. Hand me the phone."

Ellery handed it to him. "Whom are you going to put on him?"

"Hesse. Mac. Goldberg."

"All right."

"Police Headquarters."

"But I'd like to keep this thing," said Ellery, putting the cigaret back into his pocket, "exclusive and as far away from Centre Street as you can manage it."

His father stared.

"We really don't know a thing . . . Dad."

167

"What?"

Ellery uncoiled from the desk. "Come right home, will you?"

"You going *home?*"

But Ellery was already closing the door.

Inspector Queen called from his foyer, "Son?"

"Yes."

"Well, it's all set—" he stopped.

Celeste and Jimmy were on the sofa.

"Hello," said the Inspector.

"We were waiting for you, Dad."

His father looked at him.

"No. I haven't told them yet."

"Told us what?" demanded Jimmy.

"We know about the Katz boy," began Celeste. "But—"

"Or has the Cat walked again?"

"No." Ellery scrutinized them. "I'm ready," he said. "How about you?"

"Ready for what?"

"To go to work, Celeste."

Jimmy got up.

"Sit down, Jimmy." Jimmy sat down. "This time it's the McCoy."

Celeste grew quite pale.

"We're on the trail of something," said Ellery. "Exactly what, we're still not sure. But I think I can say that for the first time since the Cat got going there's something encouraging to work on."

"What do I do?" asked Jimmy.

"Ellery," said the Inspector.

"No, Dad, it's safer this way. I've thought it over very carefully."

"What do I do?" asked Jimmy again.

"I want you to get me a complete dossier on Edward Cazalis."

"Cazalis?"

"Dr. Cazalis?" Celeste was bewildered. "You mean—"

Ellery looked at her.

"Sorry!"

"Dossier on Cazalis," said Jimmy. "And?"

"Don't jump to conclusions, please. As I said, we don't know where we are . . . Jimmy, what I want is an intimate sketch of his life. Trivial details solicited. This isn't just a *Who's Who* assignment. I could do that myself. As a working newspaperman you're in a perfect position to dig up what I want, and without arousing suspicion."

"Yes," said Jimmy.

"No hint to anyone about what you're working on. That goes in spades for your people at the *Extra*. When can you start?"

"Right away."

"How long will it take you?"

"I don't know. Not long."

"Do you suppose you could have a good swatch of it for me by . . . say . . . tomorrow night?"

"I can try." Jimmy rose.

"By the way. Don't go near Cazalis."

"No."

"Or anyone connected with him closely enough so that word might get back to him that somebody's asking questions about him."

"I understand." Jimmy lingered.

"Yes?" said Ellery.

"What about Celeste?"

Ellery smiled.

"Got you, got you," said Jimmy, flushing. "Well, folks . . ."

"Celeste has nothing to do yet, Jimmy. But I do want you to go home, Celeste, pack a bag or two, and come back here to live."

"What?" said the Inspector and Jimmy together.

"That is, Dad, if you have no objection."

"Er, no. None at all. Glad to have you, Miss Phillips. The only thing is," said the Inspector, "if I'm to get any rest I'd better stake out *my* bed right now. Ellery, if there's a call—anything at all—be sure and wake me." And he retreated to his bedroom rather hurriedly.

169

"Live *here,* you said," said Jimmy.

"Yes."

"Sounds tasty, but is it kosher?"

"Mr. Queen." Celeste hesitated.

"On second thought," said Jimmy, "this is a very delicate situation. It raises all sorts of possible conflicts."

"I'm going to need you, Celeste—when I do—on a moment's notice." Ellery frowned. "I can't predict when it will be. If it's late at night and you weren't at my fingertips—"

"No, sir," said Jimmy, "I can't say I'm wild about this development."

"Will you be quiet and let me think?" cried Celeste.

"I should tell you, too, that it may be quite dangerous."

"So taking it all in all," said Jimmy, "I don't think it's such a hot idea, darling. Do you?"

Celeste ignored him.

"I'll say it's dangerous! It's also downright immoral! What will people say?"

"Oh, muffle it, Jimmy," said Ellery. "Celeste, if my plans work out you're going to be right up there on the razor's edge. Now's the time for you to jump off. If you're going to do any jumping at all."

Celetes rose. "When do I move in?"

Ellery grinned. "Sunday night will do."

"I'll be here."

"You'll have my room. I'll bed down in the study."

"I hope," said Jimmy bitterly, "you'll both be very happy."

He watched Jimmy boost Celeste rudely into a taxi and then shamble angrily up the street.

Ellery began wandering about the living room.

He felt exhilarated. Jumpy.

Finally, he sat down in the armchair.

The hand that cut the cord.

Tightened it.

The end flows from the beginning.

The circular madness of paranoia.

God in the fingertips.

Was it possible?

Ellery had the feeling that he sat on the brink of a vast peace.

But he had to wait.

From some stronghold he had to summon the reserve to wait.

• 9

Inspector Queen phoned home a little after noon on Saturday to announce that everything was arranged for the following day.

"How long will we have?"

"Long enough."

"The maid?"

"She won't be there."

"How did you work it?"

"The Mayor," said Inspector Queen. "I got His Honor to invite the Cazalises for Sunday dinner."

Ellery shouted. "How much did you have to tell the Mayor?"

"Not very much. We communicated mostly by telepathy. But I think he's impressed with the necessity of not letting our friend go too soon after the brandy tomorrow. Dinner's called for 2:30 and there are going to be bigshot guests in afterward. Once Cazalis gets there, the Mayor says, he'll stay there."

"Brief me."

"We're to get a buzz the minute Cazalis sets foot in the Mayor's foyer." On that signal we shoot over to the apartment and get in through the service door by way of the basement and a back alley. Velie will have a duplicate key ready for us by tomorrow morning. The maid won't be back till late; she gets every other Sunday off and it happens tomorrow is her off-Sunday. The building help are being taken care of. We'll get in and out without being seen. Have you heard from Jimmy McKell?"

"He'll be up around ninish."

Jimmy showed up that night needing a shave, a clean shirt, and a drink, "but I can dispense with the first two items," he said, "providing Number 3 is produced forthwith," whereupon Ellery planted the decanter, a bottle of seltzer, and a glass at Jimmy's elbow and waited at least ten seconds before he made an encouraging sound in his throat.

"I'll bet the seismograph at Fordham is going crazy," said Jimmy. "Where do you sphinxes want it from?"

"Anywhere?"

"Well," said Jimmy, admiring his glass in the light, "the story of Edward Cazalis is kind of lopsided. I couldn't find out much about his family background and boyhood, just a few details. Seems he got away from home early—"

"Born in Ohio, wasn't he?" said the Inspector. He was measuring three fingers of Irish whiskey with care.

"Ironton, Ohio, 1882," nodded Jimmy McKell. "His father was a laborer of some sort—"

"Ironworker," said the Inspector.

"Whose report is this, anyway?" demanded Jimmy. "Or am I being checked up on?"

"I just happen to have a few facts, that's all," said the Inspector, holding his glass up to the light, too. "Go on, McKell."

"Anyway, Papa Cazalis was descended from a French soldier who settled in Ohio after the French and Indian War. About Mama I couldn't find out." Jimmy looked at the old gentleman belligerently, but when that worthy downed his whiskey without saying anything Jimmy continued. "Your hero was one of the youngest of fourteen ill-fed, ill-clothed, and ill-housed brats. A lot of them died off in childhood. The survivors and their descendants are strewn around the Middle West landscape. As far as I can tell, your Eddie's the only one who made anything of himself."

"Any criminals in the family?" asked Ellery.

"Sir, don't asperse the rank and file of our glorious heritage," said Jimmy, pouring another drink for himself. "Or are you taking a refresher course in sociology? I couldn't find anything special in that line." He said suddenly, "What are you digging for?"

"Keep going, Jimmy."

"Well, Edward seems to have been a very hep cookie. Not a prodigy, you understand. But precocious. And very ambitious. Poor but honest, he burned the midnight oil, worked his industrious little fingers to the bone, and got a southern Ohio hardware king all hopped up about him; in fact, he became this tycoon's protégé. A real Horatio Alger character. Up to a point, that is."

"What do you mean by that?"

"Well, in my book young Eduardo was something of a heelo. If there's anything worse than a rich snob, it's a poor one. The hardware hidalgo, whose name was William Waldemar Gaeckel, lifted the bloke clean out of his lousy environment, scrubbed him up, got him some decent clothes, and sent him away to a fancy prep school in Michigan . . . and there's no record that Cazalis ever went back to Ironton even on a visit. He ditched pa and ma, he ditched Tessie, Steve, and the other fifty thousand brothers and sisters, and after old Gaeckel sent him proudly to New York to study medicine he ditched Gaeckel, too—or maybe Mr. G. got wise to him; anyway, they had no further relations. Cazalis got his M.D. from Columbia in 1903."

"1903," murmured Ellery. "Aged 21. One of fourteen children, and he became interested in obstetrics."

"Very funny," grinned Jimmy.

"Not very." Ellery's voice was chill. "Any information on the obstetrical specialty?"

Jimmy McKell nodded, looking curious.

"Let's have it."

Jimmy referred to the back of a smudged envelope.

173

"Seems that back in those days medical schools weren't standardized. In some the courses were two years, in others four, and there weren't any obstetrical or gynecological internships or residencies . . . it says here. Very few men did obstetrics or gynecology exclusively, and those who did became specialists mostly by apprenticeship. When Cazalis graduated from Columbia—with honors, by the way—he hooked onto a New York medico named Larkland—"

"John F.," said the Inspector.

"John F.," nodded Jimmy. "East 20s somewhere. Dr. Larkland's practice was entirely O.B. and gyne but it was apparently enough to keep Cazalis with him about a year and a half. Then in 1905 Cazalis started his own specializing practice—"

"Just when in 1905?"

"February. Larkland died that month of cancer, and Cazalis took over his practice."

Then Archibald Dudley Abernethy's mother had been old Dr. Larkland's patient and young Cazalis had inherited her, thought Ellery. It soothed him. Clergymen's wives in 1905 were not attended by 23-year-old physicians except in extraordinary circumstances.

"Within a few years," continued Jimmy, "Cazalis was one of the leading specialists in the East. As I get the picture, he'd moved in on the ground floor and by 1911 or '12, when the speciality had become defined, he had one of the biggest practices in New York. He wasn't a money-grubber, I understand, although he made pots. He was always more interested in the creative side of his profession, pioneered a couple of new techniques, did a lot of clinic work, and so on. I've got lots of dope here on his scientific achievements—"

"Skip it. What else?"

"Well, there's his war record."

"World War I."

"Yes."

"When did he go in?"

"Summer of 1917."

174

"Interesting, Dad. Beatrice Willikins was born on April 7 that year, the day after Congress declared war on Germany. Must have been one of Cazalis's last deliveries before getting into uniform." The Inspector said nothing. "What about his war record?"

"Tops. He went into the Medical Corps as a captain and came out a full colonel. Surgery up front—"

"Ever wounded?"

"No, but he did spend a few months in a French rest area in '18, and in early '19 after the war ended. Under treatment for—I quote—'exhaustion and shell shock.'"

Ellery glanced at his father, but the Inspector was pouring his fourth, fifth, and sixth finger of whiskey.

"Apparently it wasn't anything serious." Jimmy glanced at his envelope. "He was sent home from France as good as new and when he was mustered out—"

"In 1919."

"—he went back to his specialty. By the end of 1920 he'd worked up his practice again and was going great guns."

"Still doing obstetrics and gynecology exclusively?"

"That's right. He was then in his late 30s, approaching his prime, and in the next five years or so he really hit the top." Jimmy hauled out another envelope. "Let's see . . . yes, 1926. In 1926 he met Mrs. Cazalis through her sister, Mrs. Richardson—and married her. She was one of the Merigrews of Bangor. Old New England family—blood transparent, blue, and souring, but I'm told she was a genetic sport, very pretty, if you went for Dresden china. Cazalis was 44 and his bride was only 19, but apparently he had Dresden china ideas; it seems to have been an epic romance. They had a fancy wedding in Maine and a long honeymoon. Paris, Vienna, and Rome.

"I find," said Jimmy McKell, "I find nothing to indicate that the Cazalises have been anything but happily married—in case you're interested. No whisper about him, in spite of all the ladies in his medical life, and for Mrs. Cazalis there's never been any man but her husband.

"They ran into hard luck, though. In 1927 Mrs. Cazalis had her first baby and early in 1930 her second—"

"And lost both in the delivery room," nodded Ellery. "Cazalis mentioned that the night I met him."

"He felt terrible about it, I'm told. He'd taken fanatical care of his wife during both pregnancies and he'd done the deliveries himself—what's the matter?"

"Cazalis was his wife's obstetrician?"

"Yes." Jimmy looked at them both. Inspector Queen was now at the window, pulling at his fingers behind his back.

"Isn't that unethical?" asked the Inspector casually. "A doctor delivering his own wife?"

"Hell, no. Most doctors don't do it because they're emotionally involved with the woman in labor. They doubt their ability to maintain—where's that note?—to maintain 'the necessary objective, detached professional attitude.' But many doctors do, and Dr. Edward Cazalis of the Tearing Twenties was one of them."

"After all," said the Inspector to Ellery, as if Ellery were arguing the point, "he was a big man in his field."

"The type man," said Jimmy, "so supremely egocentric he'd maybe become a psychiatrist. Hm?"

"I don't think that's quite fair to psychiatrists," laughed Ellery. "Any data on the two babies he lost?"

"All I know about it is that both babies were toughies and that after the second Mrs. Cazalis couldn't have any more children. I gathered that they were both breeches."

"Go on."

The Inspector came back and sat down with his bottle.

"In the year 1930, a few months after they lost

their second child, we find Cazalis having a break-down."

"Breakdown," said Ellery.

"Breakdown?" said the Inspector.

"Yes. He'd been driving himself, he was 48—his collapse was attributed to overwork. By this time he'd been practicing obstetrical and gynecological medicine for over twenty-five years, he was a wealthy man, so he gave up his practice and Mrs. Cazalis took him traveling. They went on a world cruise—you know the kind, through the Canal up to Seattle, then across the Pacific—and by the time they reached Europe Cazalis was practically well again. Only, he wasn't. While they were in Vienna—this was early in '31—he had a setback."

"Setback?" said Ellery sharply. "You mean another breakdown?"

" 'Setback' was the word. It was nerves again, or mental depression or something. Anyway, being in Vienna, he went to see Béla Seligmann and—"

"Who's Béla Seligmann?" demanded Inspector Queen.

"Who's Béla Seligmann, he says. Why, Béla Seligmann is—"

"There was Freud," said Ellery, "and there's Jung, and there's Seligmann. Like Jung, the old boy hangs on."

"Yes, he's still around. Seligmann got out of Austria just in time to observe *Anschluss* from an honored bleacher seat in London, but he went back to Vienna after the little cremation ceremony in the Berlin Chancellery and I believe he's still there. He's over 80 now, but in 1931 he was at the height of his powers. Well, it seems Seligmann took a great interest in Cazalis, because he snapped him out of whatever was wrong with him and aroused in the guy an ambition to become a psychiatrist."

"He studied with Seligmann?"

"For four years—one under par, I'm told. Cazalis spent some time in Zürich, too, and then in 1935 the Cazalises returned to the States. He put in over a year getting hospital experience and early in 1937—let's see, that would have made him 55—he set himself up in the practice of psychiatry in New York. The rest is history." Jimmy laced his flagging glass.

"That's all you got, Jimmy?"

"Yes. No." Jimmy referred hastily to his last envelope. "There's one other item of interest. About a year ago—last October—Cazalis broke down again."

"Broke down?"

"Now don't go asking me for clinical details. I don't have access to medical records. Maybe it was plain pooping out from overwork—he has a racehorse's energy and he's never spared himself. And, of course, he was 66. It wasn't much of a breakdown but it must have scared him, because he started to whittle down his practice. I understand he hasn't taken a new case in a year. He's polishing off the patients under treatment and transferring long-termers to other men when he can. I'm told that within a short time he'll be retiring." Jimmy tossed his collection of disreputable envelopes on the table. "End of report."

The envelopes lay there.

"Thanks, Jimmy," said Ellery in a curiously final voice.

"Is it what you wanted?"

"What I wanted?"

"Well, expected."

Ellery said carefully, "It's a very interesting report."

Jimmy set his glass down. "I take it you shamans want to be alone."

Neither man replied.

"Never let it be said," said Jimmy, picking up his hat, "that a McKell, couldn't recognize a brush."

"Fine job, McKell, just fine," said the Inspector. "Night."

"Keep in touch with me, Jimmy."

"Mind if I drift in with Celeste tomorrow night?"

"Not in the least."

"Thanks! Oh." Jimmy paused in the foyer. "There's one little thing."

"What's that?"

"Let me know when you clap him in irons, will you?"

When the door closed Ellery sprang to his feet.

His father poured another drink. "Here, have one."

But Ellery mumbled, "That touch of so-called shell shock in the first war. Those recurring breakdowns. And in the middle age the obvious attempt to compensate for something in that sudden, apparently unprepared-for interest in psychiatry. It fits, it fits."

"Drink it," said his father.

"Then there's the whole egocentric pattern. It's unusual for a man of 50 to begin studying psychiatry, to set up in practice at 55, and to make a success of it to boot. His drive must be gigantic.

"Look at his early history. A man who set out to prove something to—whom? himself? society? And who wouldn't let anything stand in his way. Who used every tool that came to hand and tossed it aside when it outlived its immediate usefulness. Professionally ethical always, but in the narrowest sense: I'm sure of it. And then marriage to a girl less than half his age—and not just any girl; it had to be a Merigrew of Maine.

"And those two tragic confinements, and . . . guilt. Guilt, decidedly: immediately that first breakdown. Overwork, yes; but not his body. His conscience."

"Aren't you doing an awful lot of guessing?" asked Inspector Queen.

"We're not dealing with clues you can put on a slide. I wish I knew more!"

"You're spilling it, son."

"The conflicts set in, and from then on it's a question of time. A gradual spreading of the warp. A sickening, a corruption of the whole psychic process—whatever the damned mechanism is. Somewhere along the line a personality that was merely paranoid in potential crossed over and became paranoid in fact. I wonder . . ."

"You wonder what?" asked his father when Ellery paused.

"I wonder if in either of those deliveries the infant died of strangulation."

"Of *what?*"

"Umbilical. The umbilical cord wound around its neck."

The old man stared.

Suddenly he bounced to his feet.

"Let's go to bed."

They found the white index card marked *Abernethy, Sarah-Ann* within twenty seconds of opening the file drawer labeled 1905-10. It was the eleventh card in the file. A blue card was clipped to it marked *Abernethy, Archibald Dudley, m., b. May 24, 1905, 10:26 A.M.*

There were two old-fashioned filing cabinets of walnut, each containing three drawers. Neither had locks or catches, but the storage closet in which they found the cabinets had to be unlocked, a feat Sergeant Velie performed without difficulty. It was a large cabinet filled with the memorabilia and bric-a-brackery of the Cazalis household; but on the side where the cabinets stood were also a glass case of obstetrical and surgical instruments and a worn medical bag.

The records of his psychiatric practice were housed in modern steel cabinets in his inner office. These cabinets were locked.

The Queens, however, spent all their time in the crowded musty-smelling closet.

Mrs. Abernethy's card recorded an ordinary case history of pregnancy. Archibald Dudley's recorded the data of birth and infant development. It was evident that Dr. Cazalis had provided the customary pediatric care of the period.

Ninety-eight cards later he ran across one marked *Smith, Eulalie* to which was clipped a pink card

180

marked *Smith, Violette, f., b. Feb. 13, 1907, 6:55 P.M.*

One hundred and sixty-four cards beyond the Smith cards they found the entries for *O'Reilly, Maura B.* and *O'Reilly, Rian, m., b. Dec. 23, 1908, 4:36 A.M.* Rian O'Reilly's card was blue.

In less than an hour they located the cards of all nine of the Cat's victims. There was no difficulty. They were arranged in chronological order in the drawers, each drawer was labeled with its year-sequence, and it was simply a matter of going through the drawers card by card.

Ellery sent Sergeant Velie for the Manhattan telephone directory. He spent some time with it.

"It's so damnably logical," complained Ellery, "once you have the key. We couldn't understand why the Cat's victims should be successively younger when there was no apparent connection among them. Obviously, Cazalis simply followed the chronology of his records. He went back to the beginning of his medical practice and systematically worked his way forward."

"In forty-four years a lot had changed," said the Inspector thoughtfully. "Patients had died off. Children he'd brought into the world had grown up and moved to other localities. And its nineteen years at a minimum since he had any medical contact with any of them. So most of these cards must be as obsolete as the dodo."

"Exactly. Unless he was willing or prepared to undertake a complicated search, he couldn't hope to make a clean sweep. So he'd tend to concentrate on the cards bearing names most easily traced. Since he'd had a Manhattan practice, the obvious reference was to the Manhattan phone book. Undoubtedly he began with the first card in his files. It's Sylvan Sacopy, a boy born to a Margaret Sacopy in March of 1905. Well, neither name is to be found in the current Manhattan directory. So he went on to the second card. Again no luck. I've checked every name on the first ten

181

listings and not one is to be found in the Manhattan book. Abernethy's the first card with a current listing. And Abernethy was the first victim. And while I haven't checked all the names on the ninety-seven cards between Abernethy and Violette Smith, I've taken enough of a sampling to indicate that Violette Smith became the Cat's second victim for exactly the same reason: despite the fact that her card is Number 109, she had the misfortune to be Number 2 in the phone book checkback. There's no doubt in my mind that the same thing is true of all the others."

"We'll check."

"Then there was the baffling business of the non-marital status of all but one of the victims. Now that we know how Cazalis picked them, the answer is childishly clear. Of the nine victims, six were women and three were men. Of the three men, one was married and two were not—but Donald Katz was a young-ster: it was a reasonable average. But of the six women not one was married. Why were the female victims consistently single? Because when a woman marries *her name changes!* The only women Cazalis could trace through the phone book were those whose names had remained the same as the names appearing on his case cards.

"And the curious color notes that ran through the crimes," continued Ellery. "That was the most obvious clue of all, damn it. Blue cords for males, salmon-pink for females. Maybe it was the salmony cast of the pink that threw me off. But salmon *is* a shade of pink, and pink and blue are the traditional colors for infants."

"It's a sentimental touch," muttered his father, "I could do without."

"Sentimental nothing—it's as significant as the color of hell. It indicates that deep in the chasm of his mind Cazalis regards his victims as infants still. When he strangled Abernethy with a blue cord he was really strangling a boy baby . . . using a cord to return him to limbo? The umbilical symbolism was there from the start. The murderous colors of childbirth."

182

From somewhere in the apartment came the peaceful sounds of drawers opening.

"Velie," said the Inspector. "God, if only some of these cords are here."

But Ellery said, "And that tantalizing gap between Victims 6 and 7—Beatrice Willikins to Lenore Richardson. Up to that point the age differential between successive victims was never more than three years. Suddenly, seven."

"The war—"

"But he was back in practice by 1919 or '20, and Lenore Richardson was born in '24."

"Maybe he couldn't locate one born during those years."

"Not true. Here's one, for instance, born in September 1921, Harold Marzupian. It's in the directory. Here's another, January 1922, Benjamin Treudlich. And he's in the directory. I found at least five others born before 1924, and there are undoubtedly more. Still, he bypassed them to strike at Lenore Richardson, 25. Why? Well, what happened between the murders of Beatrice Willikins and Lenore Richardson?"

"What?"

"It's going to sound stuffy, but the fact is that between those two homicides the Mayor appointed a Special Investigator to look into the Cat murders."

The Inspector raised his brows.

"No, think about it. There was an enormous splash of publicity. My name and mission were talked and written about sensationally. My appointment couldn't fail to have made an impression on the Cat. He must have asked himself what the sudden turn of events meant to his chances of continuing his murder spree with safety. The newspapers, you'll recall, spread out the whole hog. They rehashed old cases of mine, spectacular solutions—Superman stuff. Whether the Cat knew much about me before that, you may be sure he read everything that was printed and listened to everything that was broadcast afterwards."

183

"You mean he was scared of you?" grinned Inspector Queen.

"It's much more likely," Ellery retorted, "that he welcomed the prospect of a duel. Remember that we're dealing with a special kind of madman—a man trained in the science of the human mind and personality and at the same time a paranoiac in full flight, with systematized delusions of his own greatness. A man like that would likely consider my appearance in the investigation a challenge; and it's borne out by the seven-year jump from Willikins to Richardson."

"How so?"

"What's the outstanding fact about the Richardson girl in relation to Cazalis?"

"She was his wife's niece."

"So Cazalis deliberately skipped over any number of available victims to murder his own niece, knowing that this would draw him into the case naturally. Knowing he'd be bound to meet me on the scene. Knowing that under the circumstances it would be a simple matter to get himself drawn into the investigation as one of the investigators. Why did Mrs. Cazalis insist on her husband's offering his services? Because he'd often 'discussed' his 'theories' about the Cat with her! Cazalis had prepared the way carefully by playing on his wife's attachment to Lenore even before Lenore's murder. If Mrs. Cazalis hadn't brought the subject up, he would have volunteered. But she did, as he knew she would."

"And there he was," grunted the Inspector, "on the inside, in a position to know just what we were doing—"

"In a position to revel in his own power." Ellery shrugged. "I told you I was rusty. I was aware all along of the possibility of such a move on the Cat's part. Didn't I suspect Celeste and Jimmy of exactly that motive? Couldn't get it out of my mind. And all the while there was Cazalis—"

"No cords."

They jumped.

184

But it was only Sergeant Velie in the closet doorway.

"They ought to be here, Velie," snapped the Inspector. "How about those steel files in his office?"

"We'd have to get Bill Devander down to open them. I can't. Not without leaving traces."

"How much time do we have?" The Inspector pulled on his watch chain.

But Ellery was pinching his lip. "To do the job properly would take more time than we have today, Dad. I doubt that he keeps the cords here, anyway. Too much danger that his wife or the maid might find them."

"That's what I said," said Sergeant Velie heatedly. "I said to the Inspector—remember?—I said, Inspector, he's got 'em stashed in a public locker some place . . ."

"I know what you said, Velie, but they might also be right here in the apartment. We've got to have those cords, Ellery. The D.A. told me the other day that if we could connect a find of the same type of blue and pink cords with some individual, he'd be willing to go into court pretty nearly on that alone."

"We can give the D.A.," said Ellery suddenly, "a much better case."

"How?"

Ellery put his hand on one of the walnut filing cabinets.

"All we have to do is put ourselves in Cazalis's place. He's certainly not finished—the cards on Petrucchi and Katz took him only as far as March 10, 1927, and his obstetrical records extend over three years beyond that."

"I don't quite get it," complained the Sergeant.

But the Inspector was already at work on the drawer labeled *1927–30*.

The birth card following Donald Katz's was pink and it recorded the name "Rhutas, Roselle."

There was no Rhutas listed in the directory.

The next card was blue. "Finkleston, Zalmon."

There was no such name in the directory.

185

Pink. "Heggerwitt, Adelaide."

"Keep going, Dad."

The Inspector took out another card. "Collins, Barclay M."

"Plenty of Collinses . . . But no Barclay M."

"The mother's card gives her Christian name as—"

"It doesn't matter. All his victims have had personal listings in the phone book. I checked a few parents' names before, where the victim wasn't listed, and I found two in the book; there must be lots of others. But he passed those up, I imagine because it would have increased the amount of investigating he'd have to do and by that much increased the risk. So far at least he's taken only directly traceable cases. What's the next card?"

"Frawlins, Constance."

"No."

Fifty-nine cards later the Inspector read, "Soames, Marilyn."

"How do you spell that?"

"S-o-a-m-e-s."

"S-o-a . . . Soames. Here it is! Soames, Marilyn!"

"Let me see that!"

It was the only Soames listed. The address was 486 East 29th Street.

"Off First Avenue," muttered the Inspector. "Within spitting distance of Bellevue Hospital."

"What are the mother's and father's names? On the white card?"

"Edna L. and Frank P. Father's occupation given as 'postal employee.' "

"Could we get a quick check on Marilyn Soames and her family? While we're waiting here?"

"It's getting late . . . I'll ring the Mayor first, make sure he hangs on to Cazalis. Velie, where's the phone?"

"There's a couple in his office."

"No household phone?"

"In a phone closet off the foyer."

The Inspector went away.

When he returned, Ellery said, "They're not calling back here, are they?"

"What do you think I am, Ellery?" The Inspector was peevish. "We'd be in a fine mess if we answered a personal call! I'm calling them back in half an hour. Velie, if the phone rings out there don't answer it."

"What do you think *I* am!"

They waited.

Sergeant Velie kept tramping about the foyer.

The Inspector kept pulling out his watch.

Ellery picked up the pink card.

Soames, Marilyn, f., b. Jan. 2, 1928, 7:13 A.M.

Add to population of Manhattan one female. Vital statistics of a birth. Recorded by the hand of death.

Onset of labor	*Natural*
Position at delivery	*L.O.T.*
Duration of labor	*10 hrs.*
Normal	*Normal*
Anaesthesia	*Morphine-scopalamine*
Operative	*Forceps*
Crede—prophylaxis	*Crede*
Period gestation	*40 wks.*
Respiration	*Spontaneous*
Method of resuscitation	*None*
Injuries at birth	*None*
Congenital anomalies	*None*
Medication p-n.	*None*
Weight	*6 lbs. 9 oz.*
Length	*49 cm.*

And so on, unto the tenth day. *Behavior of Baby . . . Type of supplemental or complemental feeding . . . Disturbances noted: Digestive, Respiratory, Circulatory, Genito-urinary, Nervous system, Skin, Umbilicus . . .*

A conscientious physician. Death was always conscientious. Digestive. Circulatory. Umbilicus. Especially umbilicus. *The place where the extraembryonic structures are continuous with those of the body proper of the embryo,* anatomical and zoological definition. *To which is attached the umbilical cord connecting the fetus of the mammal with the placenta . . . Jelly of Wharton . . . Epiblastic epithelium . . .* No mention of tussah silk.

But that was to come twenty-one years later.

Meanwhile, pink cards for females, blue cards for males.

Systematized. The scientific mumbo jumbo of parturition.

It was all down here on a card in faded pen-marks. God's introductory remarks on another self-contained unit of moist, red, squirming life.

And even as the Lord giveth, He taketh away.

When the Inspector set the telephone down he was a little pale. "Mother's name Edna, nee Lafferty. Father's name Frank Pellman Soames, occupation post office clerk. Daughter Marilyn is public stenographer. Aged 21."

Tonight, tomorrow, next week, next month, Marilyn Soames, aged 21, occupation public stenographer, of 486 East 29th Street, Manhattan, would be plucked from the files of Dr. Edward Cazalis by the hand that had pulled her into the world and he would begin measuring her for a salmon-pink cord of tussah silk.

And he would set out on his quest, cord in hand, and later the cartoonist of the *New York Extra* would sharpen his pens and refashion his Cat to wave a tenth tail and an eleventh in the form of a question mark.

"Only this time we'll be waiting for him," Ellery said that night in the Queen living room. "We're going to catch him with a cord in his hands as close to the actual instant of attack as we can safely manage. It's the only way we can be sure of slapping the Cat label on him so that it sticks."

Celeste and Jimmy were both looking frightened.

From his armchair Inspector Queen kept watching the girl.

"Nothing's been left to chance," said Ellery. "Cazalis has been under twenty-four-hour observation since Friday, Marilyn Soames since late this afternoon. We're getting hourly reports on Cazalis's movements in a special office at Police Headquarters, where Sergeant Velie and another man are on continuous duty. These two officers are instructed to call us on our private line the moment a suspicious movement on Cazalis's part is phoned in.

"Marilyn Soames knows nothing of what's going on; no one in her family does. To let them in on it would only make them nervous and their actions might get Cazalis suspicious. Then we'd have the whole thing to do over again or it might scare him off permanently—or for a very long time. We can't afford to wait. We can't afford to miss.

"We're getting hourly reports on the girl, too. We're almost completely set."

"Almost?" said Jimmy.

The word hung among them in a peculiarly unpleasant way.

"Celeste, I've been holding you in reserve," said Ellery. "For the most important and certainly the riskiest job of all. As an alternate to Jimmy. If Cazalis's next available victim had turned out to be male, I had Jimmy. Female—you."

"What job would that be?" asked Jimmy cautiously.

"My original idea was to substitute one of you for the next victim indicated by Cazalis's files."

And there was McKell, out of the cubist tangle of his arms and legs and glaring down at Ellery. "The answer is no. You're not going to turn this woman into a slaughterhouse beef. I won't have it—me, McKell!"

"I told you we should have locked this character up as a public nuisance, Ellery." The Inspector snapped, "Sit down, McKell."

"I'll stand up and you'll like it!"

Ellery sighed.

"You're so cute, Jimmy," said Celeste. "But I'm

not going to run out no matter what Mr. Queen has in mind. Now won't you sit down and mind your own business like a lambie-pie?"

"No!" roared Jimmy. "Do you enjoy the prospect of getting your silly neck wrung? Even this vast intellect here can have his off-days. Besides, when was he ever human? I know all about *him*. Sits in this control tower of his and fiddles with little dials. Talk about delusions of grandeur! If he runs your neck into Cazalis's noose, what's the difference between him and Cazalis? They're both paranoiacs! Anyway, the whole idea is plain damn imbecility. How could you fool Cazalis into thinking you were somebody else? Who are you, Mata Hari?"

"You didn't let me finish. Jimmy," said Ellery patiently. "I said that was my original notion. But on second thought I've decided it's too dangerous."

"Oh," said Jimmy.

"Not for Celeste—she'd have been as well protected as Marilyn Soames is going to be—but for the sake of the trap. The Soames girl is going to be his objective; he's going to scout her, as he's scouted the others; it's safest to string along with her."

"I might have known even your reason for *not* making Cat bait out of her would be non-human!"

"Then what's my job, Mr. Queen?—Jimmy, shut up."

"As I said, we have every reason to believe Cazalis makes some sort of preliminary investigation of his victims. Well, we've got Marilyn covered every time she steps out of the Soames flat. But obviously with detectives we can only work from outside. That takes care of physical protection, but it doesn't give us a line on—for example—telephone calls.

"We could tap Cazalis's phones, on the chance that he'll try to contact Marilyn or her family from his home. But Cazalis is informed as well as shrewd, and the public's been made conscious of official wiretapping in the past year or two—the technique, what to listen for, have been well publicized; we can't chance Cazalis's getting suspicious. Besides, it's un-

190

thinkable that he'd be foolish enough to use his own phones for such a purpose; that he's cautious as well as daring is proved by his operations. So if he tries a phone approach it will undoubtedly be from a public booth somewhere, and that we can't prepare for.

"We could tap the Soames phone, but here again we can't run the risk of arousing the family's suspicions; too much depends on the Soameses behaving normally in the next few weeks.

"Or Cazalis may not phone at all. He may try a correspondence contact."

"It's true we've found no evidence of approaches by letter in previous cases," put in the Inspector, "but that doesn't mean there haven't been any; and even if he's never done it before, that's no guarantee he won't do it now."

"So a letter under an assumed name is possible," said Ellery. "And while we could intercept the United States mail . . ." Ellery shook his head. "Let's say it just wouldn't be practicable.

"In either event, our safest course is to plant somebody we can trust in the Soames household. Somebody who'll live with the family on a round-the-clock basis for the next two or three weeks."

"And that's me," said Celeste.

"Will somebody please tell me," came a choked voice from the sofa, "if this is or is not a nightmare concocted by Dali, Lombroso, and Sax Rohmer?"

But no one paid any attention to him. Celeste was frowning. "Wouldn't he recognize me, though, Mr. Queen? From the time when he—?"

"Scouted Simone?"

"And from those pictures of me in the papers afterward."

"I rather think he concentrated on Simone and didn't pay too much attention to you, Celeste. And I've checked the file on your newspaper photos and they're uniformly execrable. Still, it's possible he'd recognize you—yes. If he saw you, Celeste. But we'd make very sure," smiled Ellery, "that he didn't. This would be strictly an inside job and you'd never come out on the streets except under rigidly controlled conditions."

Ellery glanced at his father, and the Inspector got up.

"I don't mind telling you, Miss Phillips," began Inspector Queen, "that I've been dead set against this. This job calls for a trained operative."

"But," said Jimmy McKell bitterly.

"But two facts exist which made me let Ellery change my mind. One is that for years you nursed a paralyzed invalid. The other is that one of the younger children in the Soames family—there are four, with Marilyn—a boy of 7, broke his hip a month ago and he was brought home from the hospital only last week in a cast.

"We've had a medical report on this boy. He's got to stay in bed and he's going to need a lot of care for the next few weeks. A trained nurse isn't necessary, but a practical nurse is. We've already had an intermediary in touch with the family doctor, a Dr. Myron Ulberson, and it turns out that Dr. Ulberson had been trying to find a practical nurse for the child but so far hasn't had any luck." The Inspector shrugged. "The boy's accident could be a great break for us, Miss Phillips, if you felt qualified to act the part of a practical nurse in a broken hip case."

"Oh, yes!"

"Besides being fed, washed, and amused," said Ellery, "the boy will need massages, I understand, and care of that sort. Do you think you could handle it, Celeste?"

"I did exactly that kind of nursing for Simone, and Simone's doctor often told me I was better than a lot of trained nurses he knew."

The Queens looked at each other, and the Inspector waved.

"Tomorrow morning, Celeste," said Ellery crisply, "you'll be taken to see Dr. Ulberson. He knows you're not a working practical nurse and that your presence in the Soames household is required for a highly secret purpose not connected with the ostensible one. Dr.

192

Ulberson's been very tough—we had to get a high official of the City to give him personal reassurances that this is all in the interests of the Soames family. Just the same, he's going to test you unmercifully."

"I know how to move patients in bed, give hypos—I'll satisfy him, I know I will."

"Just turn on some of that charm," growled Jimmy. "The kind you befogged me with."

"I'll do it on merit, McKell!"

"I have a hunch you will," said Ellery. "By the way, you'd better not use your real name, even with Dr. Ulberson."

"How about McKell?" sneered McKell. "In fact, now about changing your name to McKell and to hell with this lady-dick opium dream?"

"One more crack out of you, McKell," snapped the Inspector, "and I'll personally escort you to the door on the end of my foot!"

"Okay, if you're going to be that selfish," muttered Jimmy; and he curled up on the sofa like an indignant sloth.

Celeste took his hand. "My real family name is Martin, pronounced the French way, but I could use it as just plain English-sounding Martin—"

"Perfect."

"—and then Mother Phillips used to call me Suzanne. It's my middle name. Even Simone called me Sue sometimes."

"Sue Martin. All right, use that. If you satisfy Dr. Ulberson, he'll recommend you to Mr. and Mrs. Soames as a live-in nurse and you can go right to work. You will charge, of course, the prevailing practical nurse fee, whatever it happens to be. We'll find that out for you."

"Yes, Mr. Queen."

"Stand up a minute, Miss Phillips," said Inspector Queen.

Celeste was surprised. "Yes?"

The Inspector looked her up and down.

Then he walked around her.

"At this point," said Jimmy, "they usually whistle."

"That's the trouble," rasped the Inspector. "Miss Phillips, I suggest you deglamorize yourself. Meaning no disrespect to the highly important profession of practical nursing, if you look like a practical nurse I look like Olivia de Havilland."

"Yes, Inspector," said Celeste, blushing.

"No makeup except a little lipstick. And not too vivid."

"Yes, sir."

"Simplify your hairdo. Take off your nail polish and clip your nails. And wear your plainest clothes. You've got to make yourself look older and more—more tired-looking."

"Yes, sir," said Celeste.

"Do you have a white uniform?"

"No—"

"We'll get you a couple. And some white stockings. How about low-heeled white shoes?"

"I have a pair that will do, Inspector."

"You'll also need a practical nurse's bag, equipped, which we'll provide."

"Yes, sir."

"How about a pearlhandled heater?" suggested Jimmy. "No eye-ette genuine without one."

But when they ignored him he got up and went to the Scotch decanter.

"Now as to this detective business," said Ellery. "Aside from nursing the Soames boy, you're to keep your eyes and ears open at all times. Marilyn Soames operates her stenographic business from home—she does manuscript typing and that sort of thing; that's why she has a phone in her name. Marilyn's working at home is another break; it will give you an opportunity to get friendly with her. She's only two years your junior and, from the little we've been able to learn so far, a nice, serious-minded girl."

"Gads," said Jimmy from the cellaret. "You have just described Operative 29-B." But he was beginning to sound proud.

"She seldom goes out socially, she's interested in books—very much your type, Celeste, even physically. Best of all, she's mad about her kid brother, the sick boy, so you'll have something in common right off."

"You're to pay particular attention to phone calls," said the Inspector.

"Yes, find out the substance of every conversation, especially if the caller is a stranger to the Soameses."

"And that goes whether the call is for Marilyn or anyone else."

"I understand, Inspector."

"You'll have to manage to read every letter Marilyn gets, too," Ellery said. "The whole family's mail, if possible. In general, you're to observe everything that happens in the household and to report it to us in detail. I want daily reports as a matter of routine."

"Do I report by phone? That might be hard."

"You're not to use the phone there except in an emergency. We'll arrange meeting places in the neighborhood of East 29th and First and Second Avenues. A different spot each night."

"Me, too," said Jimmy.

"At a certain time each night after Stanley's gone to sleep—you'll have to set the time for us after you get in and find out more about the setup—you'll go out for a walk. Establish the habit the very first night, so that the family comes to take your nightly absences as matter of course. If something should come up to prevent your leaving the house at the agreed time, we'll wait at the meeting place till you can get away, even if it means waiting all night."

"Me, too," said Jimmy.

"Any questions?"

Celeste pondered. "I can't think of any."

Ellery looked at her rather nakedly, Jimmy thought. "I can't stress too much how important you may be in this thing, Celeste. Of course, the break may come from outside and you won't be involved at all, which is what we're all hoping. But if it doesn't, you're our Trojan filly. Everything may then depend on you."

"I'll do my best," said Celeste in a smallish voice.

"By the way, how do you feel about this?"

"Just . . . fine."

"We'll go over all this again in greater detail after you've seen Dr. Ulberson tomorrow." Ellery put an arm around her. "You'll stay here tonight as we arranged."

And Jimmy McKell snarled, *"Me, too!"*

● 10

Celeste would have felt better about having to play female Janus in the Soames household if she had found Marilyn's father a burly lecher, Mrs. Soames a shrew, Marilyn a slut, and the youngsters a pack of street rats. But the Soameses turned out insidiously nice.

Frank Pellman Soames was a skinny, squeezed-dry-looking man with the softest, burriest voice. He was a senior clerk at the main post office on Eighth Avenue at 33rd Street and he took his postal responsibilities as solemnly as if he had been called to office by the President himself. Otherwise he was inclined to make little jokes. He invariably brought something home with him after work—a candy bar, a bag of salted peanuts, a few sticks of bubble gum—to be divided among the three younger children with Rhadamanthine exactitude. Occasionally he brought Marilyn a single rosebud done up in green tissue paper. One night he showed up with a giant charlotte russe, enshrined in a cardboard box, for his wife. Mrs. Soames was appalled at his extravagance and said she just wouldn't eat it, it would be too selfish, but her husband said something to her in a sly *sotto voce* and she blushed. Celeste saw her put the little carton carefully away in the ice chest. Marilyn said that in charlotte russe season her parents always got "whispery." Next morning, when Celeste went to the chest for milk for Stanley's breakfast, she noticed that the box was gone.

Marilyn's mother was one of those naturally powerful women whose strength drains off in middle age, leaving raw debility behind. She had led a back-breaking, penny-balancing life and she had not had time to spare herself; besides, she was going through a trying menopause. "I've got change of life, falling of the room rent, varicose veins, and bad feet," Mrs. Soames said to Celeste with grim humor, "but I'd like to see the Sutton Place lady who can bake a better berry pie," adding, "when there's money for berries." Often she had to lie down from weakness, but it was impossible to keep her in bed during the day for longer than a few minutes. "You know what Dr. Ulberson said, Edna," her husband would say anxiously. "Oh, you and your Dr. Ulberson," she would snort. "I've got the week's wash to do." Mrs. Soames was obsessive on the subject of her laundry. She would never let Marilyn touch it. "You girls these days expect soap to do your scrubbing for you," she would say scornfully. But to Celeste Mrs. Soames once said, "She'll have wash enough to do in her life." Mrs. Soames's single self-indulgence was the radio. There was only one machine in the house, a small table model which usually occupied the center of the catchall shelf above the kitchen range; this Mrs. Soames had placed with a sigh at little Stanley's bedside. When Celeste ruled that Stanley might listen to the radio for no more than two hours a day, at selected times—and selected those times which did not conflict with his mother's favorite programs—Mrs. Soames looked guiltily grateful. She never missed Arthur Godfrey, she told Celeste, or *Stella Dallas, Big Sister,* and *Double or Nothing.* And she confided that "when our ship comes in, Frank's going to get me a television set," adding dryly, "At least, that's what Frank says. He's that sure one of those Irish Sweepstakes tickets he's always buying will come through."

Stanley was the youngest child, a thin little boy with blazing eyes and an imagination which ran to mayhem and gore. In the very beginning he was suspicious of Celeste and she could get hardly a word out of him. But late that first day, when she was giving his bony body a massage, he suddenly said: "You a real nurse?" "Well, sort of," smiled Celeste, although her heart skipped a beat. "Nurses stick knives into you," Stanley said glumly. "Whoever told you a story like that?" "Yitzie Frances Ellis, that's my teacher." "Stanley, she didn't. And where did you get that awful nickname of 'Yitzie' for a perfectly nice lady teacher?" "The principal calls her that," said Stanley indignantly. "*Yitzie?*" "The principal calls Miss Ellis Yitzie-Bitzie when nobody's around." "Stanley Soames, I don't believe a single—" But Stanley had screwed his little head about, his eyes bugging with horror. "Lie still! What's the matter?" "You know something, Miss Martin?" whispered Stanley. Celeste heard herself whispering back, "What, Stanley, what?" "*I got green blood.*" After that, Celeste digested Master Stanley's remarks, revelations, and confidences with great quantities of salt. She often had to exercise judgment to distinguish fact from fancy.

Stanley was thoroughly familiar with the Cat. He told Celeste solemnly that he *was* the Cat.

Between her patient and Marilyn there were two other children: Eleanor, 9, and Billie, 13. Eleanor was a large calm child with an unhurried attitude toward life; her rather plain features were illuminated by a pair of remarkably direct eyes, and Celeste hastened to make friends with her. Billie was in junior high, a fact which he accepted philosophically. He was clever with his hands and the apartment was always turning up things he had built for his mother out of "nothing," as Mrs. Soames said. But his father seemed disappointed. "We'll never make a student out of Billie. His heart isn't in it. All he does is hang around garages after school learning about motors. He can't wait till he's old enough to get his working papers and learn some mechanical trade. The scholars in my family are the girls." Billie was in the weedy age, "a regular Ichabod Crane," as Mr. Soames put it. Frank Soames was something of a reader; he generally had his nose buried in some library book and he owned a prize shelf of decrepit volumes which he hoarded from young manhood—Scott, Irving, Cooper, Eliot, Thackeray—authors whom Billie characterized as "squares"; Billie's reading was restricted almost entirely to comic books, which he acquired in wholesale quantities by some complex barter-system incomprehensible to his father. Celeste liked Billie—his overgrown hands, his rather furtive voice.

And Marilyn was a darling; Celeste fell in love with her immediately. She was a tall girl, not pretty: her nose was a little broad and her cheekbones were pitched too steep; but her dark eyes and hair were lovely and she carried herself with a defiant swing. Celeste understood her secret sorrow: the necessity of earning a living to help her father carry the weight of the family's needs had kept her from going on from high school to the higher education she craved. But Marilyn was no complainer; outwardly she was even serene. Celeste gathered that she had another, independent life, a vicarious one: through her work she kept in touch with a sort of malformed, teasing shadow of the creative and intellectual world. "I'm not the best manuscript typist in the business," she told Celeste. "I get too blamed interested in what I'm typing." Nevertheless, she had built up a good clientele. Through a former high school teacher she had got in with a young playwrights' group whose art was, if nothing else, prolific; one of her accounts was a Columbia full professor who was engaged with writing a monumental work of scholarship, "a psychological outline of world history"; and her best client was a famous journalist author who, Mr. Soames said proudly, swore by her— "and sometimes at me," added Marilyn. Her earnings were capricious and the importance of maintaining them kept Marilyn a little on the grim side. For the sake of her father's self-esteem she preserved the fiction that her co-producing role in the family was a temporary one, "to tide us over the high prices." But Celeste knew that Marilyn knew there would be no escape for many years, if ever. The boys would grow up, marry, and move off; there was Eleanor's education to provide for—Marilyn was firm that Eleanor should go to college, "she's really a genius. You ought to read the poetry she writes right now, at 9"; Mrs. Soames was headed for invalidism; Frank Soames was not a well man. Marilyn knew her fate and was prepared for it. Because of this she discouraged the romantic advances of several men who were pursuing her, "at least one of them," Marilyn said with a laugh, "with honorable intentions." Her most persistent pursuer was the journalist author—"he's *not* the one. Every time I have to call for a new chapter—he writes in longhand—or deliver one I've typed, he chases me around his apartment with an African war club he picked up in his travels. It's supposed to be a gag, but it's gagging on the level. One of these days I'm going to stop running and poke him one. I'd have done it long ago if I hadn't needed his work." But Celeste suspected that one of these days Marilyn would stop running and not poke him one. She persuaded herself that the experience would do Marilyn good; Marilyn was a passionate girl who had kept herself, Celeste was sure of it, rigidly chaste. (It also occurred to the sophisticate that this was true of a certain Celeste Phillips as well; but at this point Miss Phillips dropped the whole subject out of her thoughts.)

The Soameses lived in a two-bedroom, five-room apartment in an ancient walkup; because they needed three sleeping rooms, the "front room" had been converted into a third bedroom, and this room served both as the girls' bedroom and Marilyn's workshop. "Marilyn ought to have her own room," sighed Mrs.

Soames, "but what can we do?" Billie had rigged up a partition—a drape on a long curtain pole—to cut off part of the room for Marilyn's "office"; here she had her work table, her typewriter, her stationery, her telephone; there was a modest illusion of separate quarters. The arrangement was also necessary because Marilyn often had to work at night and Eleanor went to bed early.

The location of the telephone prompted Celeste to make an ulterior suggestion. When she arrived to take up her duties she found Stanley occupying his own bed in the boys' room. On the plea that she could not very well share a bedroom with a boy as big as Billie—and obviously she had to be within call of her patient during the night—Celeste moved Stanley into the front bedroom, to Eleanor's bed, and Eleanor moved to the boys' room. "You're sure this won't interfere with you?" Celeste asked Marilyn anxiously; she was feeling wretched about the whole thing. But Marilyn said she had trained herself to work under impossible conditions: "With a boy like Stanley in the house you either learned how to turn your ears off or you cut your throat." Marilyn's easy reference to "throat" made Celeste sick; on her third day she became aware that she had been unconsciously avoiding that part of Marilyn's generous anatomy. It was a strong throat, and in the days that followed it became for Celeste a sort of symbol, a link between the lives of all of them and the death that waited outside. She trained herself to look at it.

The transfer of Eleanor to Stanley's bed created a problem and sharpened Celeste's feeling of guilt. Mrs. Soames said it was "not good" for brother and sister to share a bedroom at Eleanor's and Billie's ages. So Billie was sent to his parents' room and Mrs. Soames moved over to the boys' room to sleep with Eleanor. "I feel as if I've created a revolution," Celeste wailed, "upsetting your lives this way." And when Mrs. Soames said, "Why, Miss Martin, don't give a thought to us. We're so grateful you could come nurse our baby," Celeste felt like the most callous doubledealing spy. There was a small portion of consolation for her in the thought that the bed she had to sleep on in the front room, an antique cot borrowed from a neighbor, was as hard as the floor of a flagellant's cave. On this she did penance for her chicanery. She almost angrily rejected the family's offer of any one of their own beds in exchange.

"It's so mean," Celeste moaned to the Queens and Jimmy during their second-night rendezvous in a First Avenue areaway. "They're so sweet about everything I feel like a criminal."

"I told you she's too peasant-like for this job," jeered Jimmy; but in the dark he was nibbling her fingertips.

"Jimmy, they're the nicest people. And they're all so grateful to me. If they only knew!"

"They'd smother you with onions." said Jimmy. "Which reminds me . . ."

But Ellery said, "What's the mail situation, Celeste?"

"Marilyn goes downstairs for it first thing in the morning. Mr. Soames leaves the house before the first delivery—"

"We know that."

"She keeps her current correspondence in a wire basket on her desk. I won't have any trouble reading it," said Celeste in a trembly voice." Last night I managed to do it in the middle of the night, when Marilyn and Stanley were asleep. There are opportunities during the day, too. Sometimes Marilyn has to go out in connection with her work."

"We know that, too," said the Inspector grimly. Marilyn Soames's unpredictable excursions, sometimes in the evening, were keeping them all on the edge of ulcers.

"Even if she doesn't, she always eats lunch in the kitchen. I can even read her mail while Stanley's awake, because of the heavy curtain."

"Wonderful."

"I'm glad you think s-so!" And Celeste found herself irrigating Jimmy's dusty-blue tie.

But when she returned to the Soames flat she had color in her cheeks and she told Marilyn that the walk had done her oceans of good, really it had.

Their meeting time was set by Celeste at between 10 and 10:15. Stanley was not tucked in for the night much before 9. she said, and he rarely fell asleep until 9:30 or so. "Being in bed all the time he doesn't need so much sleep. I can't leave till I'm sure he's dropped off, and then too I've been helping with the supper dishes."

"You mustn't overdo that, Miss Phillips," said the Inspector. "They'll get suspicious. Practical nurses don't—"

"Practical nurses are human beings, aren't they?" sniffed Celeste. "Mrs. Soames is a sick woman who slaves all day and if I can save her some work by doing the supper things I'm going to do it. Would it put me out of the spy union if I told you I also pitch in to the housework? Don't worry, Inspector Queen, I shan't give anything away. I'm quite aware of what's at stake."

The Inspector said feebly that he just thought he'd mention it, that was all, and Jimmy reeled off some verse that he said he had made up but which sounded remarkably like one of the Elizabethan things.

So they met at 10 o'clock or a little later, each night in a different place by prearrangement the night before. For Celeste, at least, it took on the greenish cast of fantasy. For twenty-three and a half hours a day she worked, ate, spied, and slept among the Soameses; the half hour away was a flight to the moon. Only Jimmy's presence made it bearable; she had come to dread the taut, questioning faces of the Queens. She had to brace herself as she walked along the dark street to the appointed spot, waiting for the signal of Jimmy's soft wolf-whistle. Then she would join them in the doorway, or under the store awning, or just inside the alley—wherever the agreed rendezvous was—and she would report the increasingly pleasant monotonies of the past twenty-four hours and answer questions about the Soames mail and the telephone calls, all the while clinging to Jimmy's hand in the darkness; and then, feeling the pull of Jimmy's eyes, she would run back to what had come to signify for her the endearing sanity of the little Soames world.

She did not attempt to tell them how much the aroma of Mrs. Soames's rising bread reminded her of Mother Phillips or of how, by some witchery, Marilyn had become the best of remembered Simone.

And of how frightened, how icily frightened, she was during every moment of every waking hour, and beyond.

To tell any of them.

Especially Jimmy.

They speculated interminably. Beyond meeting Celeste each night, there was nothing else to do.

Over and over they came back to the reports on Cazalis. They were exasperating. He was acting exactly as if he were Dr. Edward Cazalis, Noted Psychiatrist, and not a cunning paranoiac bent on satiating his appetite for death. He was still working with his board on occasional private case histories sent in by psychiatric stragglers. He even attended a meeting called by the Mayor at which the Queens were present. At this meeting Cazalis was studied closely by men trained in the art of dissimulation; but it was a question who was the best actor present. The psychiatrist was affably discouraging; he said again that he and his board were wasting their time; they had cracked a few of their reluctant colleagues but the remainder were adamant and nothing was to be expected of them. (And Inspector Queen reported to the Mayor with a garmented face that in the trickle of suspects turned over by Dr. Cazalis and his co-workers there was exactly none who could be the Cat.) "Haven't you fellows made any progress at all on your end?" Cazalis asked the Inspector. When the Inspector shook his head, the big man smiled.

"It's probably someone from outside the metropolitan area."

Ellery thought it unworthy of him.

But he was looking poorly these days, and that was provocative; thinned out, fallen in, the ice of his hair crumbling. His heavy face was sludgy and cracked; he had developed twitches under both eyes; his large hands, when they were not drumming on the nearest object, kept drifting about his person as if seeking an anchorage. Mrs. Cazalis, who was in miserable attendance, said that the work her husband had done for the City had taken too much out of him, it was her fault for having pounded at him to continue investigating. The doctor patted his wife's hand. He was taking it easy, he said; what bothered him was that he had failed. A young man "rises above failure," he said, an old man "sinks under it." "Edward, I want you to go away." But he smiled. He was considering a long rest, he said. As soon as he tied off certain "loose ends" . . .

Was he mocking them?

The metaphor remained with them.

Or had he become suspicious and was uncertainty or the fear of detection strong enough to check the continuing impulse to kill?

He might have caught sight of one of his pursuers. The detectives were sure he had not.

Still, it was possible.

Or had they left a trace of their visit to his apartment? They had worked systematically, touching and moving nothing until they had fixed in their memories the exact position and condition of each object to be touched and moved. And afterward they had restored each object to its original place.

Still, again, he may have noticed something wrong. Suppose he had set a trap? He might have had a little signal for himself, a trivial thing, unnoticeable, in the storage closet or in one of the drawers. A psychotic of a certain type might have taken such a precaution. Elaborately. They were dealing with a man whose brilliance overlapped his psychosis. In certain flights he might be prescient.

It was possible.

Dr. Cazalis's movements were as innocent as those of a man walking across a field under the sunny sky. A patient or two a day in his office, chiefly women. An occasional consultation with other psychiatrists. Long nights when he did not step out of his apartment. Once a visit with Mrs. Cazalis to the Richardsons'. Once a concert at Carnegie, when he listened to the Franck symphony with open eyes and clenched hands; and then, curl-lipped and calm, listening with enjoyment to Bach and Mozart. Once a social evening with some professional friends and their wives.

At no time did he venture near East 29th Street and First Avenue.

It was possible.

That was the canker.

Anything was *possible*.

By the tenth day after the strangulation of Donald Katz, and in the sixth day of "Sue Martin's" practical-nursing career, they were sweating. They spent most of their time now in the report room at Police Headquarters. In silence. Or, when the silence became intolerable, snapping at one another with a querulousness that made silence a relief.

What was digging new hollows in Inspector Queen's face was the thought that Cazalis might be outwaiting them. Madmen had been known to exercise extraordinary patience. Sooner or later—Cazalis might be thinking—they would conclude that he had reached the end of his string . . . if only he did nothing long enough. Then they would call off their watchdogs. Sooner or later.

Was that what Cazalis was waiting for?

If, of course, he knew he was being watched.

Or, if he foresaw that this was one case in which the watchers would never be withdrawn, he might deliberately be waiting until he tired them into care-

206

lessness. And then . . . an opening. And he would slip into the clear.

With a tussah silk cord in his pocket.

Inspector Queen kept harrying his operatives until they hated him.

Ellery's brain performed more desperate acrobatics. Suppose Cazalis *had* set a trap in his storage closet. Suppose he *did* know someone had been looking through his old files. Then he knew they had exposed the heart of his secret. Then he knew they knew how he chose his victims.

In such case it would not be overcrediting Cazalis's acumen to say that he would also guess their plan. He had merely to do what Ellery was now doing: to put himself in the adversary's place.

Then Cazalis would know that they had gone beyond Donald Katz to Marilyn Soames, and that with Marilyn Soames they had baited a trap for him.

If I were Cazalis, said Ellery, what would I do then? I would give up all thought of snaring Marilyn Soames's card to the card of the next regularly indicated victim. Or, to play it even safer, I would skip the next regularly indicated victim to the one following on the chance that the enemy had taken out insurance as well. Which we haven't done . . .

Ellery writhed. He could not forgive himself. There was no excuse, he kept saying. To have failed to take the precaution of searching Cazalis's cards past Marilyn Soames to the next-indicated victim, and the next, and the next, and protecting them all—even if it meant going to the end of the file and having to guard a hundred young people all over the City . . .

If these premises were sound, Cazalis might even now be waiting for the detectives trailing him to relax their vigilance. And when they did, the Cat would slink out to strangle a tenth, unknown victim at his leisure, laughing all the while at the detectives he knew were guarding Marilyn Soames.

Ellery became quite masochistic about it.

"The best we can hope for," he groaned, "is that Cazalis makes a move toward Marilyn. The worst, that he's already moved against someone else. If that happens, we won't know about it till it's over. Unless we can keep Cazalis at the other end of the tail, Dad. We've got to hang on to him! How about assigning a few extra men ...?"

But the Inspector shook his head. The more men, the greater the chance of giving the game away. After all, there was no *reason* to believe that Cazalis suspected anything. The trouble was that they were getting too nervous.

"Who's nervous?"

"You are! And so am I!—though I wasn't till you started your old fancy mental gymnastics!"

"Tell me it couldn't happen that way, Dad."

"Then why not go after those records again?"

Well, muttered Ellery, they were better off stringing along with what they had. Let well enough alone. Watchful waiting. Time will tell.

"The master of the original phrase," snarled Jimmy McKell. "If you ask me, your morale is showing. Doesn't anybody give a slup in bloody borshch what happens to my girl?"

That reminded them that it was time to go uptown for the nightly meeting with Celeste.

They jostled one another getting through the door.

The night of Wednesday, October 19, was uncharitable. The three men huddled in the alley entrance between two buildings on the south side of East 29th Street, near Second Avenue. There was a cutting wet wind and they kept up a little dance as they waited.

10:15.

It was the first time Celeste had been late.

They kept yapping at one another. Swearing at the wind. Jimmy would poke his head out of the alley and say under his breath, "Come onnnnnn, Celeste!" as if she were a horse.

The lights of Bellevue over on First Avenue were no comfort.

208

The reports on Cazalis that day had been discouraging. He had not left his apartment. Two patients had called during the afternoon, both young women. Della and Zachary Richardson had shown up at 6:30 on foot; apparently for dinner, as by 9 P.M., the time of the last report the Queens had received before leaving Headquarters, they had still not come out.

"It's nothing, Jimmy," Ellery kept saying. "Cazalis is safe for the night. Can't mean a thing. She just couldn't get away—"

"Isn't that Celeste now?"

She was trying not to run and not succeeding. She would walk faster and faster, then break into a trot, then slow down suddenly, then run. Her black cloth coat kept flopping around her like birds.

It was 10:35.

"Something's up."

"What could be?"

"She's late. Naturally she'd hurry." Jimmy whistled the signal; it came back all dry and blowy. "Celeste—"

"Jimmy." She was gulping.

"What is it?" Ellery had her by both arms.

"He phoned."

The wind had dropped and her words shrilled through the alley. Jimmy shouldered Ellery aside, put his arms around her. She was trembling.

"There's nothing to be scared of. Stop shaking."

She began to cry.

They waited. Jimmy kept tumbling her hair.

Finally, she stopped.

Inspector Queen said instantly: "When?"

"A few minutes past 10. I was just leaving—out in the hall with my hand on the doorknob—when I heard the phone ring. Marilyn was in the dining room with Billie and Eleanor and their father and mother and I was nearest to the front room. I ran and got the phone first. It was . . . I know it was. I heard his voice over the radio the day he gave his press conference and talk. It's low and musical and at the same time sort of sharp."

"Cazalis," said the Inspector. "You mean this was

Dr. Edward Cazalis's voice, Miss Phillips?" He said it as if he did not believe it at all and as if it were of the greatest importance to corroborate his disbelief.

"I tell you it was!"

"Well, now," said the Inspector. "Just from hearing it on the radio." But he moved closer to Celeste.

"What did he say?" This was Ellery. "Word for word!"

"I said hello, and he said hello, and then he gave me the Soames phone number and asked if that was the number and I said yes. He said, 'Is this the public stenographer, Marilyn Soames, speaking?' It was his voice. I said no and he said, 'Is Miss Soames in —it is *Miss* Soames, isn't it, not Mrs.? I believe she's—the daughter of Edna and Frank Soames. I said yes. Then he said, 'I want to talk to her, please.' By that time Marilyn was in the room so I handed her the phone and hung around pretending I had to fix my slip."

"Checking up," muttered the Inspector. "Making sure."

"Go on, Celeste!"

"Give her a chance, will you!" growled Jimmy.

"I heard Marilyn say yes once or twice and then she said, 'Well, I am kind of piled up, but if it's that kind of deal I'll try to get it out for you by Monday, Mr.—What was your name again, sir?' When he told her, Marilyn said, 'I'm sorry, would you mind spelling that?' and she spelled it after him."

"The name."

"Paul Nostrum. N-o-s-t-r-u-m."

"Nostrum." Ellery laughed.

"Then Marilyn said yes, she could call for the manuscript tomorrow, and she asked him where she was to pick it up. He said something and Marilyn said, "I'm tall and dark and I have a mashed nose and I'll be wearing a cloth coat, big white and black checks, you can't miss it, and a beanie. How about you?' and after he answered she said, 'Well, then, maybe you'd better do all the looking, Mr. Nostrum. I'll be there. Good night,' and she hung up."

Ellery shook her. "Didn't you get the address, the time?"

Jimmy shook Ellery. "Give her a chance, I said!"

"Wait, wait." Inspector Queen pushed them both aside. "Did you get any other information, Miss Phillips?"

"Yes, Inspector. When Marilyn hung up I said as offhandedly as I could, 'New client, Marilyn?' and she said yes, she wondered how he knew about her, some writer she did work for must have recommended her. 'Nostrum' had said he was a writer in from Chicago with his new novel to see his publisher, that he'd have to revise his last few chapters and he needed them retyped in a hurry. He hadn't been able to get a hotel accommodation and he was staying with 'friends,' so he'd meet her tomorrow at 5:30 in the lobby of the Astor to give her his manuscript."

"Lobby of the Astor!" Ellery was incredulous. "He couldn't have picked a busier spot at a busier hour in the whole City of New York."

"You're sure it's the Astor, Miss Phillips."

"That's what Marilyn said."

They were silent.

Finally, Ellery shrugged. "No use beating our brains out—"

"No, indeed, for time will tell," said Jimmy. "Meanwhile what happens to our heroine? Does Celeste stay in that rat cage? Or does she show up at the Astor tomorrow in a checked coat, garnished with parsley?"

"Idiot," Celeste rested her head on his arm.

"Celeste stays where she is. This is just his opening move. We'll play along."

The Inspector nodded. "What time did you say he made that call?" he asked Celeste.

"It was just about five minutes past 10, Inspector Queen."

"You go back to the Soameses'."

Ellery squeezed her hand. "Stick to that phone,

Celeste. If there's a call tomorrow from 'Paul Nostrum'—or anyone else—changing the time and place of Marilyn's appointment, that's one of the emergencies I mentioned. Phone Police Headquarters immediately."

"All right."

"Ask for Extension 2-X," said the Inspector. "That's a code signal that will put you right through to us." The old man patted her arm awkwardly. "You're a good girl."

"Good, schmood," muttered Jimmy. "Give me a kiss."

They watched her walk down the windy street, not moving until she disappeared in the entrance of 486.

Then they ran toward Third Avenue, where the squad car was parked.

According to Sergeant Velie, Detective Goldberg's 10 P.M. report had stated that at 9:26 Mr. and Mrs. Richardson, accompanied by Dr. and Mrs. Cazalis, had left the Cazalis apartment house. The two couples had strolled up Park Avenue. According to Detective Young, Goldberg's partner, Cazalis had been in high spirits; he had laughed a great deal. The four had turned west on 84th Street, crossed Madison Avenue, and they stopped before the Park-Lester. Here the couples separated, the Cazalises walking back to Madison, turning north, and stopping in at a drugstore on the corner of 86th Street. They sat at the counter and were served hot chocolates. This was at two minutes of 10, and at 10 o'clock Goldberg had telephoned his hourly report from a coffee shop across the street.

Ellery glanced at the wall clock. "Ten after 11. What about the 11 o'clock report, Sergeant?"

"Wait," said Sergeant Velie. "Goldie called in again at 10:20. A special."

The Sergeant seemed to be expecting exclamations and excitement, for he paused dramatically.

But Ellery and Jimmy KcKell were doodling on

pads at opposite sides of the desk and all that the Inspector said was, "Yes?"

"Goldberg said he'd no sooner got off the phone in the coffee shop at 10 when Young signaled him from across the street and Goldie walked over and saw Mrs. Cazalis sitting at the soda counter—all by her lonesome. Goldie thought he was seeing things because he doesn't spot Cazalis any place and he says to Young, Where's our man, where's our man? Young points to the back of the drugstore and Goldie sees Cazalis in a booth back there, phoning. Young told Goldberg that right after Goldie left Cazalis looked at his watch like he'd all of a sudden remembered something. Young said it was a great big take and it looked phony to him, Cazalis putting on an act to fool his wife. He said a few words—like he was excusing himself—gets off the stool, and goes to the back. He looks up a number in one of the phone books on the rack, then he goes into the booth and makes a call. Time of entry into booth: 10:04."

"10:04," said Ellery. "10:04."

"That's what I said," said the Sergeant. "Cazalis is on the phone around ten minutes. Then he comes back to Mrs. Cazalis, drinks the rest of his hot chocolate, and they leave.

"They took a cab, Cazalis giving the hack his home address. Young tailed them in another cab and Goldie went into the drugstore. He'd noticed that the directory Young said Cazalis had looked a name up in was open on the stand, and he wanted a gander at it because nobody had used it after Cazalis. It turned out to be the Manhattan book, and it was open at the pages with . . ." Velie paused impressively, . . . "with the S-O names."

"The S-O names," said Inspector Queen. "Did you hear that, Ellery? The S-O names." His denture was showing.

"Would you think," said Jimmy, drawing a set of fangs, "that a kindly old gent like that could look so much like a Brontosaurus?"

But the Inspector said genially, "Go on, Velie, go on."

"There's nothing more," said the Sergeant Velie with dignity. "Goldberg said he thought that rated a hurry-up special report, so he phoned right in before leaving to go back to Park Avenue after Young."

"Goldberg was so right," said the Inspector. "And the 11 o'clock report?"

"The Cazalises went right home. At ten minutes to 11 their lights went out. Unless the doc is figuring on a sneak tonight, after his old woman is in dreamland—"

"Not tonight, Sergeant, not tonight," said Ellery, smiling; "5:30 tomorrow, at the Astor."

They saw him enter the Astor lobby through the 44th Street doorway. The time was 5:05 and they had already been there an hour. Detective Hesse was close on his tail.

Cazalis was dressed in a dark gray suit, a rather seedy dark topcoat, and a stained gray hat. He came in with several other people, as if he were one of their group, but well in the transverse corridor at the rear of the lobby he took himself off, bought a copy of the *New York Post* at the cigar counter, stood for a few moments glancing at the front page, and then began a strolling tour of the lobby. Moving a few feet at a time, with long pauses between.

"Making sure she hasn't come yet," said the Inspector.

They were on the balcony of the mezzanine, well hidden.

Cazalis kept circulating. The lobby was crowded and it was hard to keep him in sight. But Hesse had taken a central position; he had to move very little, and they knew he would not lose his man.

There were six other Headquarters men planted in the lobby.

When Cazalis had completed his tour, he edged alongside five people, men and women, who were

214

standing near the Broadway entrance talking and laughing. He held an unlighted cigaret.

On the steps outside they caught an occasional glimpse of the broad back and accented waistline of Detective Zilgitt. He was a Negro and one of the most valuable men at Headquarters; Inspector Queen had especially detailed him to work with Hesse for the day. Zilgitt, who was a modest dresser, had rigged himself out in sharp clothes for his assignment; he looked like a Broadway character waiting for a heavy date.

At 5:25 Marilyn Soames arrived.

She came hurrying into the lobby, out of breath. She paused by the florist's shop to look around. She wore a big-checked cloth coat and a little felt cap. She carried an old simulated-leather briefcase.

Detective Johnson walked in, passed her, and mingled with the crowd. But he kept within fifteen feet of her. Detective Piggott entered the florist's shop from Broadway; he took some time buying a carnation. He had a perfect view of both Marilyn and Cazalis through the glass walls of the shop. A little later he sauntered out into the lobby and stopped almost at the girl's elbow, looking around as if for a familiar face. She glanced at him doubtfully and seemed about to speak to him; but when his glance passed over her she bit her lip and looked elsewhere.

Cazalis had spotted her instantly.

He began to read his newspapers. Leaning against the wall, the cigaret between his fingers still unlighted.

From where the Queens stood watching they could see his glance fixed on her face above his paper.

Marilyn had begun scanning the area within her orbit from the side of the lobby opposite to which Cazalis stood. Her glance searched slowly. When it had all but completed its half-circle, just as it was about to reach him, Cazalis lowered his newspaper, murmured something to one of the men in the group by his side, and the man produced a packet of matches, struck a match, and held the flame to the tip of Cazalis's cigaret. For that moment Cazalis looked like one of the group.

Marilyn's glance passed him as if he were invisible.

He inched back. Now he stood with the group between them, studying her frankly.

The Soames girl remained where she was until 5:40. Then she moved off, walking around the lobby and searching among the men who were seated. A few smiled and one said something to her. But she frowned and walked on.

As she walked, Cazalis followed.

He made no attempt to get close to her.

At times he even stood still, his eyes taking up the hunt.

He seemed to be committing her to memory—her gait, the swing of her body, the plain strong profile.

He was flushed now, breathing heavily. As if he were tremendously excited.

By ten minutes to 6 she had gone completely around the lobby and returned to her original position near the florist's shop. Cazalis passed her. It was the closest he had come to her—he could have touched her, and Johnson and Piggott could have touched him. She actually studied his face. But this time his glance was elsewhere and he passed her briskly, as if he were going somewhere. Apparently he had given her a false description of himself, or no description at all.

He paused in the nearest doorway.

It was just inside the entrance where Detective Zilgitt waited. Zilgitt glanced at him casually and moved off the steps.

The girl's foot began tapping. She did not look behind her and Cazalis was able to study her without subterfuge.

At 6 o'clock Marilyn straightened up and with determination began to push toward the bell captain's desk.

Cazalis remained where he was.

A few moments later a bellboy began to call: "Mr. Nostrum. Mr. Paul Nostrum."

Immediately Cazalis went down the steps, crossed the sidewalk, and got into a taxicab. As the cab moved away from the curb into the Broadway traffic, Detective Hesse jumped into the next cab at the stand.

At 6:10 Marilyn Soames, looking very angry, left the Astor and walked with long strides down Broadway toward 42nd Street.

Johnson and Piggott were just behind her.

"Marilyn was fit to be tied," Celeste reported that night. "I almost kissed her when she got home, I was so relieved. But she was so mad at being stood up she didn't notice. Mr. Soames said writers were temperamental and she'd probably get a bouquet of flowers from him as an apology, but Marilyn snapped that she wasn't going to be blarneyed out of it, he was probably drunk in some bar and if he phoned again she'd meet him just so she could tell him where to get off." The Inspector was annoying his mustache. "Where on earth did he go from the Astor?"

"Home." Ellery seemed disturbed, too. "Where is Marilyn, Celeste? She hasn't gone out again, has she?"

"She was so mad she had supper and went right to bed."

"I'd better take a walk around and tell the boys to keep an extra eye out tonight," muttered the Inspector.

They watched him hurry down the street.

Finally Celeste pushed away from Jimmy. "Do you think he'll phone again, Mr. Queen?"

"I don't know."

"What was the idea today?"

"He's had to play this one differently. Marilyn doesn't go out to work, hasn't a predictable routine. He's probably too cagey to hang around here day after day hoping to catch a glimpse of her, so he had to use a trick to get a good look."

217

"That's . . . right, isn't it. He didn't know what Marilyn looked like."

"Not since he spanked her rosy bottom," said Jimmy. "Now can I have five minutes alone in this palatial hallway with my future wife? Before the bell tolls, Fairy Godfather, and I turn into a pumpkin."

But Celeste said, "When do you think he'll . . ."

"It won't be long." Ellery sounded remote. "Any night now, Celeste."

And they were quiet.

"Well," said Celeste at last.

Jimmy stirred.

"I'd better be getting back."

"Keep checking the phone calls. And pay particular attention to Marilyn's mail."

"Right."

"You've got to give me my five lousy minutes!" wailed Jimmy. Ellery stepped out into the street.

Inspector Queen came back before Jimmy and Celeste were finished in their hallway.

"Everything all right, Dad?"

"They're scratching fleas."

Afterwards, the three men went back to Headquarters. The latest word, delivered in Detective Goldberg's 11 P.M. report, was that the Cazalises were entertaining a large number of people who had arrived in chauffeur-driven limousines. The party, Goldberg had said, was gay. Once, prowling in the court, he heard the boom of Cazalis's laugh, accompanied by a chatter of crystal. "The doc," Goldberg had said, "sounded just like Santa Claus."

Friday. Saturday. Sunday.

And nothing.

The Queens were scarcely on speaking terms. Jimmy McKell found himself functioning as part peacemaker, part interpreter. He suffered the usual fate of middlemen; sometimes they both turned on him. He was beginning to wear a haunted look himself.

Even Sergeant Velie was antisocial. When he spoke at all it was in an animal growl.

Once an hour the telephone rang. Then they all leaped.

The messages varied, but their gist was the same.

Nothing.

They began to share a common loathing for the report room, which was only surpassed by their loathing for one another.

Then, on Monday, October 24, the Cat moved.

The announcement came from Detective MacGayn, who was Hesse's partner on the regular day trick. MacGayn called only a few minutes after his hourly report, in considerable excitement, to say that their man was taking a powder. Several suitcases had just been carried out of the Cazalis apartment by the doorman. Hesse had overheard him instruct a taxi driver to wait as he had "some people going to Penn Station to catch a train." Hesse was set to follow in another cab; MacGayn had run to phone in the news.

Inspector Queen instructed MacGayn to go immediately to Pennsylvania Station, locate Hesse and their man, and then wait at the 31st Street entrance nearest Seventh Avenue.

The squad car screamed uptown.

Once Ellery said angrily, "It isn't possible. I don't believe it. It's a trick."

Otherwise, there was no conversation.

On order, the driver cut his siren out at 23rd Street.

MacGayn was waiting for them. He had just found Hesse. Dr. and Mrs. Cazalis were standing in a crowd at the gate of a Florida train. They had been joined by Mr. and Mrs. Richardson. The gate was not yet open. Hesse was standing by.

They made their way cautiously into the station.

From the windows of the south waiting room MacGayn point out the Cazalis-Richardson group and, nearby, Hesse.

"Take Hesse's place," said Inspector Queen. "And send him here."

Hesse walked in briskly a few moments later.

Ellery kept his eyes on Cazalis.

"What's going on?" demanded the Inspector.

Hesse was worried. "I don't know, Inspector. There's something offbeat, but they're a little in the clear out there and I can't get close enough to listen in. His wife keeps arguing with him and he keeps smiling and shaking his head. The luggage has gone down. The Richardsons', too."

"Oh, so they're also going," said Ellery.

"Looks like it."

He was not wearing Thursday's disreputable top-coat. His coat looked new and fashionable, he wore a smart Homburg, a small 'mum in his lapel.

"If he ever wiggles out of this one," remarked Jimmy McKell. "he can always make himself a tidy zloty by posing as a Man of Distinction."

But Ellery muttered, "Florida."

The gate opened and the crowd began squeezing through.

Inspector Queen seized Hesse's arm. "Get down there after him and stick. Take MacGayn and if anything happens send him back up. We'll be waiting at the gate."

Hesse hurried away.

The gate had opened late; train-departure time, according to the figures posted above the gate, was only ten minutes off.

"It's all right, Ellery," said the Inspector. "They won't pull out on time." His tone was paternal.

Ellery looked wild.

They strolled out into the shed and mingled with the people gathering before a gate marked *Philadelphia Express: Newark-Trenton-Philadelphia.* The stairway to the Florida train was two gates away. They kept glancing from the gateway to the big clocks.

"I told you," said the Inspector.

"But why Florida? Suddenly!"

"He's called Operation Necktie off," said Jimmy.

"No."

"Don't you want him to?"

"Who says he's called it off?" Ellery scowled. "He's given up on the Soames girl, granted. Spotted something Thursday, maybe. Or figured she was too tough. Or this might be a trick to put us off guard, if he suspects something. After all, we don't know how much he knows. We don't know anything! . . . If he doesn't suspect, this mean he's gone on to somebody else—"

"Somebody who he found out is vacationing in Florida," nodded Inspector Queen.

Jimmy said, "New York papers please copy. Dateline Miami, Palm Beach, or Sarasota. *Cat Hits Florida.*"

"It could be," said Ellery. "But somehow I can't get myself to believe it. It's something else. Some other trick."

"What do you need, diagrams? I'll bet he's got those silk cords in his bags. What are you waiting for?"

"We can't chance it." Inspector Queen looked dour. "We just can't. If we have to we'll work through the Florida locals. We'll have him watched down there and set him up on his return to New York. It means doing the whole thing over again."

"The hell it does! Not with Celeste, Old Sleuth. I can't wait that long, see?"

And just then MacGayn came running out of the gateway making frantic signals. The trainman was looking at his watch.

"MacGayn—"

"Get back, he's coming back up!"

"What?"

"He's not going!"

They scuttled into the thick of the crowd.

Cazalis appeared.

Alone.

He was smiling.

He cut diagonally across the shed toward the corner marked *Taxicabs* with the happy stride of a man who has accomplished something.

Hesse shuffled after him studying a timetable.

As he walked he rubbed his left ear; and MacGayn wriggled through the crowd and began to saunter along behind.

When they got back to the report at Headquarters they found a message from MacGayn.

Their man had cabbed directly home.

Now they could look back on the four weeks just past and see what had undoubtedly happened. Cazalis had out-smarted himself. Ellery pointed out that in murdering his wife's niece and insinuating himself into the Cat case as a psychiatric consultant Cazalis had seriously hobbled himself. He had not foreseen the demands on his time; he had failed to take into account the white light in which he would have to operate. Before his murder of Lenore Richardson he had had only to deceive a submissive, trusting wife; is semi-retirement, he had moved very nearly at will and in satisfactory shadows. But now he was crippled. He had made himself accountable to officialdom. He was linked with a board of fellow-psychiatrists. Colleagues were communicating with him about their patients. His failing health was causing Mrs. Cazalis to take sharper notice of his activities. And there was the little family matter involving the Richardsons which he could scarcely ignore

"He strangled Stella Petrucchi and Donald Katz under difficulties," said Ellery. "Conditions were not as favorable to him in those two murders as in the previous ones. Undoubtedly he had to run bigger risks, invent more lies to account for his absences at least in the Katz case; how he managed it in the Petrucchi case, especially on the night of the murder itself, after the Cat Riot, I'd love to know. It's reasonable to suppose that his wife, the Richardsons, began to ask embarrassing questions.

"Significantly, it's those three who've gone to Florida.

"Hesse saw Mrs. Cazalis 'arguing' with Cazalis at the gate to the train. It's an argument that must have started days ago, when Cazalis first suggested

222

the Florida trip. Because it's a certainty Cazalis was the one who suggested it, or who saw to it that the suggestion was made.

"I'm inclined to think he worked it through his sister-in-law. Mrs. Richardson was his logical tool. In her Cazalis had an excellent argument for his wife, who must have been hard to persuade: Della could stand a rest and a change of scene after what had 'happened,' she leaned heavily on her sister, and so on.

"However Cazalis managed it, he got the Richardsons to leave town and his wife to accompany them. Unquestionably he explained his inability to go with them on the double ground of his remaining patients and his promise to the Mayor to clean up his end of the investigation.

"Anything to get his wife and in-laws out of the way.

"Anything to give himself freedom of movement."

Jimmy said. "There's still the maid."

"He's given her the week off," said the Inspector.

"And now they're all out of the way," nodded Ellery, "he has unlimited opportunity and mobility, and the Cat can really go to work on the delightful problem of Marilyn Soames."

And he did. Cazalis went to work on Marilyn Soames as if getting his noose around her throat was of the utmost importance to his peace of mind and he could no longer hold himself in.

He was so eager he was careless. He went back to his shabby topcoat and old felt hat; he added a motheaten gray wool muffler and scuffed shoes; but otherwise he neglected to alter his appearance and it was child's play to keep track of him.

And he went hunting in daylight.

It was evident that he felt completely sure.

He left his apartment early on Tuesday morning, just after Detectives Hesse and MacGayn took over from Goldberg and Young. He left by way of the service entrance, slipping out into the side street and walking rapidly toward Madison Avenue as if his destination lay westward. But at Madison he veered south and walked all the way down to 59th Street. On the southeast corner he looked casually around. Then he jumped into a parked taxicab.

The taxi headed east. Hesse and MacGayn followed in separate cabs to minimize the danger of losing him.

When Cazalis's cab turned south on Lexington Avenue the detectives tensed. It kept going south but as it did it worked its way farther eastward until it reached First Avenue.

It went straight down First Avenue to 28th Street.

Here Cazalis's taxi made a four corner turn and drew up before Bellevue Hospital.

Cazalis got out, paid his driver. Then, briskly, he began to stride toward the hospital entrance.

The cab drove off.

Immediately Cazalis stopped, looking after the cab. It turned a corner, heading west.

He retraced his steps and walked rapidly toward 29th Street. His muffler was high around his neck and he had pulled the snapbrim of his hat over his eyes as low as it would go without looking grotesque.

His hands were in the pockets of his topcoat.

At 29th he crossed over.

He walked past 486 slowly, looking the entrance over but without stopping or changing his pace.

Once he looked up. It was a four-story building of dirty tan brick.

Once he glanced back.

A postman was trudging into 490.

Cazalis continued to amble up the street. Without pausing he strolled around the corner to Second Avenue.

But then he reappeared, coming back at a fast clip, as if he had forgotten something. Hesse barely

224

had time to step into a doorway. MacGayn was watching from a hallway across the street, out of sight. They knew that at least one of the detectives assigned to guard Marilyn Soames was in 486, probably at the rear of the downstairs hall, in the gloom behind the staircase. Another was on MacGayn's side of the street somewhere.

There was no danger.

No danger at all.

Still, their palms were sweating.

Cazalis strode past the house, glancing in as he passed. The postman was now in the vestibule of 486, slipping mail into the letter boxes.

Cazalis stopped before 490, looking at the number inquiringly. He fumbled in an inner pocket and produced an envelope which he consulted elaborately, glancing from time to time at the house number above the entrance, like a collector of some sort.

The postman emerged from 486, shuffled up the street, turned into 482.

Cazalis walked directly into 486.

Detective Quigley in the hall saw him look over the letter boxes.

He studied Soames box briefly. The paper name plate bore the name *Soames* and the apartment number *3B*. There was mail in the box. He made no attempt to touch the box.

Quigley was having a bad time. The mail was delivered at the same time every morning and it was Marilyn Soames's habit to come downstairs for it within ten minutes of the regular delivery.

Quigley fingered his holster.

Suddenly Cazalis opened the inner door and walked into the hall.

The detective crouched in the blackest corner behind the stairs.

He heard the big man's step, saw the thick legs pass and disappear. He did not dare to make the slightest movement.

Cazalis walked up the hall, opened the back door. The door closed quietly.

Quigley shifted his position.

Hesse ran in and joined him under the stairs.

"In the court."

"Casing it." Then Hesse whispered, "Somebody coming down the stairs, Quig."

"The girl!"

She went into the vestibule, unlocked the Soames box.

Marilyn wore an old bathrobe; her hair was in curlers.

She took out the mail, stood there shuffling letters.

They heard the snick of the rear door.

Cazalis, and he saw her.

The men said afterward they expected the Cat case to be written off then and there. The setup was ideal: the victim in the vestibule in a bathrobe, bound to come back into the gloomy hall in a matter of seconds; no one about; the street outside almost deserted; the court for an emergency getaway.

They were disappointed. Hesse said, "Hell, he'd probably have tried to drag her behind the stairs, the way he did O'Reilly over in Chelsea. Where Quigley and I were parked. The crazy bastard must have had a premonition."

But Ellery shook his head. "Habit," he said. "And caution. He's a night worker. Probably didn't even have a cord along."

"I wish we had as standard equipment X-ray eyes," mumbled Inspector Queen.

Cazalis stood there at the end of the hall, pale eyes burning.

In the vestibule Marilyn was reading a letter. Her flattish nose, her cheekbones, chin, were tacked against the glass of the street door.

She stood there three minutes.

Cazalis did not move.

Finally, she opened the inner door and ran upstairs.

The old boards rattled.

Hesse and Quigley heard him let his breath go.

Then Cazalis walked down the hall.

Dejected. Furious. They could tell by the slope of his thick shoulders, the mauls of his fists.

He went out into the street.

He was back after dark, watching the entrance of 486 from a hallway across the street.

Until a quarter of 10.

Then he went home.

"Why didn't you jump him?" cried Jimmy McKell. "And end this Grand Guignol? You'd have found a cord in his pocket!"

"Maybe we would and maybe we wouldn't," said the Inspector. "He's trying to fix her habits. This may go on for a couple of weeks. She's a toughie for him."

"He'd certainly have one of those cords on him!"

"We can't be sure. We'll just have to wait. Anyway, an actual attack will put him away. A cord might slip. We can't risk anything." Jimmy heard Ellery's teeth grinding.

Cazalis prowled about the neighborhood all day Wednesday; with the night, he settled down in the doorway across the street again.

But at ten minutes to 10 he left.

"He must be wondering if she ever leaves the house," said the Inspector that night, when Celeste reported.

"I'm beginning to wonder myself," rapped Ellery. "Celeste, what the devil is Marilyn doing?"

"Working." Celeste sounded muffled. "On a rush job for one of her playwright customers. She says she won't be finished with it till Saturday or Sunday."

"He'll go nuts," said the McKell voice.

No one laughed, least of all the quipster.

Their nightly meetings in the dark had taken on the weightless flow of dreams. Nothing was real but

227

the unreality they watched. They were conscious only occasionally that the City ground and grumbled somewhere below. Life was buried under their feet; they marked time above it, a treadmill experience.

On Thursday he repeated himself. Only this time he gave up at two minutes past 10.

"Later each night."

Jimmy was fretful. "At this rate, Ellery, he'll be seeing Celeste leave the house. I won't have that."

"He's not after me, Jimmy." Celeste was sounding shrill.

"It's not that," said Ellery. "It's the regularity. If he spots Celeste coming out every night at the same time, he may get curious."

"We'd better change the time, son."

"Let's do it this way: Celeste, those third-floor windows are in the Soameses' front room, aren't they? The room where Stanley is?"

"Yes."

"From now on don't leave until 10:15, and then only under certain conditions. Is your wristwatch accurate?"

"It keeps very good time."

"Let's synchronize." Ellery struck a match. "I have 10:26 exactly."

"I'm about a minute and a half off."

He struck another match. "Fix it." When she did, he said, "From now on be at one of those front windows every night between 10:10 and 10:15. We'll meet you, starting tomorrow night, somewhere along First Avenue in the immediate neighborhood—tomorrow night let's make it in front of that empty store near the corner of 30th."

"We met there Sunday night."

"Yes. If between 10:10 and 10:15 you see a light flash three times from one of the doorways or alleys across from 486—we'll use a pocket pencil flash—that will mean Cazalis has left for the night and you can come down and make your report. If you see no signal, stay upstairs. It will mean he's still around. If he should leave between 10:10 and 10:25 you'll get the signal between 10:25 and 10:30. If there's no signal is those five minutes, he'll still be around; stay put. We'll operate on the same system till he leaves. Watch for a signal every fifteen minutes. All night if necessary."

By MacGayn's 5 P.M. report Friday Cazalis had still not left his apartment. It puzzled them. He did not leave until dusk. Friday night it was necessary to keep Celeste waiting until 11:15. Ellery flashed the signal himself and trailed her to the rendezvous.

"I thought that flash would never come." Celeste was white. "He's gone?"

"Gave up a few minutes ago."

"I tried to get a call in all afternoon and evening but Stanley was demanding and fidgety today—he's much better—and Marilyn stuck to her typewriter . . . He phoned a little after 1 P.M."

They pressed around her in the dark.

"Paul Nostrum again. Apologized for having stood her up at the Astor, said he was taken sick suddenly and that he's been laid up till today. He wanted her to meet him . . . tonight." Celeste was trying to sound steady. "I've been leaping."

"What did Marilyn say to him?"

"She refused. Said she was all tied up on a special piece of work and he'd have to get somebody else. Then he tried to date her."

"Go on!" Inspector Queen's voice was shaky.

"She just laughed and hung up."

Jimmy drew her away.

"He's getting impatient, Dad."

"That maid of his comes back Monday."

They milled a little.

"Celeste."

Celeste came back, Jimmy protesting.

"How much did she actually tell him about the work she's doing?"

"She said she couldn't possibly be finished before tomorrow night, probably Sunday, and then she'd have to deliver it—" Celeste caught her breath. Then she said in the queerest way, "Deliver it. She did say . . ."

"This weekend," said Ellery.

The Saturday sky was overcast; a glum rain fell intermittently on the City all day. It stopped at dusk and a fog settled over the streets.

The Inspector cursed and passed the word around: he did not consider an act of God sufficient for failure to keep their man covered. "If necessary, take chances. But stick with him." He added, gratuitously: "Or else."

It was a bad day.

The whole day was bad. During the morning Detective Hesse was seized with cramps. MacGayn put in a hurry call. "Hesse has to knock off. He's writhing. Step on it, he's all alone over there." By the time Hagstrom reached Park Avenue MacGayn was gone. "I don't know where," gasped Hesse. "Cazalis came out at 11:05 and walked off toward Madison, MacGayn covering him. Put me in a cab before I foul myself up." It took Hagstrom over an hour to locate MacGayn and his quarry. Cazalis had merely gone to a restaurant. He returned to his apartment immediately afterward.

But a little past 2 found Cazalis leaving in his working clothes, by way of the court. He headed for East 29th Street.

Then, shortly before 4 o'clock, Marilyn Soames walked out of 486. Celeste Phillips was with her.

The two girls hurried west on 29th Street.

The fog had not yet come down; it was still drizzling. But the sky was threatening to black out.

Visibility was poor.

Cazalis moved. He moved in a glide, very rapidly. His hands were in his pockets. He kept to the opposite side of the street. MacGayn, Hagstrom, Quigley, the Queens, Jimmy McKell followed. Singly, in pairs.

230

Jimmy kept mumbling. "Is Celeste out of her mind? The fool, the fool."

The Inspector was mumbling, too. A rather stronger characterization.

They could see Cazalis's rage. It told in his pace. He would lunge ahead, then walk, then trot, then come to a dead stop. As he followed the girls his head thrust itself forward.

"Like a cat," said Ellery. "There's the Cat."

"She's out of her mind," whispered Jimmy.

"She's out of her mind!" Inspector Queen was close to tears. "We set him up—we set him up all this time. His tongue is hanging out. He'd have tried it in this bad light sure. And she . . ."

The girls turned into Third Avenue and entered a stationery store. The man in the store began wrapping reams of paper, other articles.

It was growing quite dark.

Cazalis was beyond caution. He stood eagerly in the rain on one of the corners of Third Avenue and 29th Street before a drugstore window. The lights came on as he stood there, but he did not move.

The head was still thrust forward.

Ellery had to hang on to Jimmy's arm.

"He won't try anything while Celeste is with her. Too many people on the streets, Jimmy. Too much traffic. Take it easy."

The girls came out of the store. Marilyn carried a large package.

She was smiling.

They walked back the way they had come.

For a moment, fifty feet from the tenement, it looked as if Cazalis were going to take the plunge. The drizzle had thickened and the girls were running for the vestibule, laughing. Cazalis gathered himself, actually jumped into the gutter.

But a car drove up to the curb before 490 and three men got out. They stood on the opposite pavement, shouting to one another in the rain, arguing hotly about something.

Cazalis stepped back.

The girls disappeared into 486.

He walked heavily down the street, stepped into a hallway opposite the Soames building.

Goldberg and Young arrived to take over from MacGayn and Hagstrom.

They worked in close, for the fog had descended.

Cazalis lingered all evening, not moving except to change hallways when someone headed for the one he occupied.

Once he chose Young's, and the detective was within fifteen feet of him for over a half hour.

A few minutes after 11 o'clock he gave up. His bulky figure plunged along in the fog, chin on his breast. They saw him pass from their own observation post near Second Avenue and, a few seconds later, Goldberg and Young.

The three vanished going west.

With some grimness, Inspector Queen insisted on flashing the all-clear signal to Celeste himself.

The meeting place for the night was a dim-walled bar-and-grill on First Avenue between 30th and 31st Streets. They had used it once before; it was crowded, smoky, and mindful of the rights of man.

Celeste came in and sat down without waiting for anything she said, "I couldn't help it. When she ran out of onionskin second sheets and said she was walking over to Third Avenue for some, I almost died. I knew he wouldn't dare try anything if somebody was with her. Now give me ten demerits."

Jimmy glared. "Are you out of your everloving mind?"

"Did he follow us?" She was bloodless tonight, very nervous. Ellery idly noticed her hands. They were cracked and red; her nails were chewed-looking. There was something else about her, too, but it insisted on being elusive.

What was it?

"He followed you," said the Inspector. Then he

said, "Miss Phillips, nothing would have happened to her." He said, "Miss Phillips, this case has cost the City of New York I don't know how many tens of thousands of dollars and months of work. Today by acting like an irresponsible moron you undid every last bit of it. We may never get as good a chance again. It could mean not getting him at all. Today he was desperate. If she'd been alone, he'd have jumped. I can't tell you how put out I am with you. In fact, Miss Phillips, I'm not irreverent when I say I wish to God Almighty I'd never seen or heard of you."

Jimmy started to get up.

Celeste pulled him down, rested her cheeks on his shoulder. "Inspector, I just couldn't find the strength to let her walk out into that street alone. What do I do now?"

The old man raised his glass of beer with shaking hands and drained it.

"Celeste." What was it?

"Yes, Mr. Queen." Jimmy's clutch tightened and she smiled up at him.

"You're not to do that again."

"I can't promise that, Mr. Queen."

"You did promise it."

"I'm so sorry."

"We can't pull you out now. We can't disturb the status quo. He may try another trick tomorrow."

"I wouldn't leave. I couldn't."

"Won't you promise not to interfere?"

Jimmy touched her face.

"This may all be over by tomorrow night. He hasn't the remotest chance of hurting her. She's covered, so is he. Let him get that cord out, make one move toward her, and he'll be jumped by four armed men. Did Marilyn finish the play she's typing?"

"No, she was too exhausted tonight. She has a few more hours' work on it tomorrow. She says she's going to sleep late, so that means she won't have it done till late afternoon."

"She's to deliver it immediately?"

233

"The writer is waiting for it. It's overdue now."

"Where does he live?"

"The Village."

"Weather forecast for tomorrow is more rain. It will be dark or almost dark when she leaves the house. He'll make his pitch either on East 29th Street or in the Village. One day more, Celeste, and we can bury this with the rest of our bad dreams. Won't you let her go alone?"

"I'll try."

What *was* it?

Inspector Queen snarled, "Another beer!"

"You're making this awfully tough, Celeste. Did you leave Marilyn all right?"

"She's gone to bed. They all have. Mr. and Mrs. Soames and Billie and Eleanor are going to church early tomorrow."

"Good night." Ellery's chin angular. "I'd hate to think you let us down."

Jimmy said, "Cheese it. The aborigine."

The waiter slapped a beer down before the Inspector. He lisped, "What's for the lady?"

"Nothing," said Jimmy. "Remove yourself."

"Listen, pally, this is a going concern. She drinks, or you do your smooching someplace else."

Jimmy slowly uncoiled. "Listen yourself, no-brow—"

The Inspector barked, "On your way."

The waiter looked surprised and backed off.

"Go on back, baby," crooned Jimmy. "I would have a word or two with our associates here."

"Jimmy, kiss me?"

"Here?"

"I don't care."

He kissed her. The waiter glowered from afar.

Celeste ran.

The fog swallowed her.

Jimmy got up to lean over the Queens with a bitter expression. He opened his mouth.

But Ellery said, "Isn't that Young?" He was squinting through the murk.

They jerked about like rabbits.

The detective was in the open doorway. His glance darted along the bar, from booth to booth. There were deep yellowish lines around his mouth.

Ellery laid a bill on their table.

They got up.

Young spotted them. He was breathing through his mouth.

"Now listen, Inspector, listen." There was sweat on his upper lip. "It's this goddam fog, you can't see your hand in front of your face in this goddam fog. Goldberg and I were right on his tail when all of a sudden he doubled back on us. Back east. Back here. Like he got the urge again and decided to make a night of it. He looked crazy-mad. I don't know if he saw us or not. I don't think so." Young inhaled. "We lost him in the fog. Goldie's out there roaming around, looking for him. I've been looking for you."

"He headed back here and you lost him."

Inspector Queen's cheeks were damp and hardening plaster.

Now I remember.

"That checked coat," said Ellery mechanically.

"What?" said his father.

"She was so upset tonight she put it on instead of her own. *He's loose and Celeste is out there in Marilyn's coat.*"

They tumbled after Jimmy McKell into the fog.

• 11

They heard Celeste's shriek as they sprinted along First Avenue between 30th and 29th Streets.

A man was running toward them from the 29th Street corner waving them back wildly.

235

"Goldberg . . ."

Not on 29th Street, then. It was here, along First Avenue.

The scream gurgled. It gurgled again, like a song.

"That alley!" yelled Ellery.

It was a narrow opening between the 29th Street corner building and a block of stores. The alley was nearer to Goldberg but Jimmy McKell's praying mantis legs got him there first.

He vanished.

A radio-patrol car tore up, its headlights splashing against the fog. Inspector Queen shouted something and the car backed and lurched to train its brights and side light on the alley entrance.

As they dashed in, Johnson and Piggot skidded around the corner with drawn guns.

Sirens began sawing away on 29th, 30th, Second Avenue.

An ambulance shot diagonally across First Avenue from Bellevue.

In the boiling fog the girl and the two men were struggling casually. Staggered: Celeste, Cazalis, Jimmy; caught in the molecular path of a slow motion projection. Celeste faced them, arched; a bow in the arms of a bowman. The fingers of both hands were at her throat defending it; they had deliberately trapped themselves between her neck and the pinkish cord encircling it. Blood sparkled on her knuckles. Behind Celeste, gripping the ends of the noose, swayed Cazalis, bare head wrenched back by Jimmy McKell's stranglehold; the big man's tongue was between his teeth, eyes open to the sky in a calm expressionless glare. Jimmy's free hand was trying to claw Cazalis's clutch loose from the cord. Jimmy's lips were drawn back; he looked as if he were laughing.

Ellery reached them a half-step before the others.

He smashed Cazalis directly behind the left ear with his fist, inserted his arm between Jimmy and Cazalis and smacked Jimmy's chin with the heel of his hand.

"Let go, Jimmy, let go."

Cazalis slid to the wet concrete, his eyes still open in that curious glare. Goldberg, Young, Johnson, Piggott, one of the patrolmen, fell on him. Young kneed him; he doubled under them, screeching like a woman.

"That wasn't necessary," said Ellery. He kept nursing his right hand.

"I've got a trick knee," said Young apologetically. "In a case like this it goes pop! like that."

Inspector Queen said, "Open his fist. As if he were your mother. I want that cord smoking hot."

An intern in an overcoat was kneeling by Celeste. Her hair glittered in a puddle. Jimmy cried out, lunging. Ellery caught him by the collar with his other hand.

"But she's dead!"

"Fainted, Jimmy."

Inspector Queen was scrutinizing the pink cord with love. It was made of thick, tough silk. Tussah.

He said, "How's the girl, Doctor, hm?" as he eyed the noose dangling from his upheld hand.

"Neck's lacerated some, mostly at the sides and back," replied the ambulance doctor. "Her hands got the worst pressure. Smart little gal."

"She looks dead, I tell you."

"Shock. Pulse and respiration good. She'll live to tell this to her grandchildren till it's coming out of their ears." Celeste moaned. "She's on her way out of it now."

Jimmy sat down in the wet of the alley.

The Inspector was snaking the silk cord carefully into an envelope. Ellery heard him humming "My Wild Irish Rose."

They had Cazalis's hands manacled behind his back. He was lying on his soaked right side with his knees drawn up, staring through Young's big legs at an overturned trash can a few feet away. His face was dirty and gray, his eyes seemed all whites.

The Cat.

He lay in a cage whose bars were the legs of men, breathing ponderously.

The Cat.

They were taking it easy, waiting for the intern to get finished with Celeste Phillips; joking and laughing. Johnson, who disliked Goldberg, offered Goldberg a cigaret; Goldberg had lost his pack somewhere. Goldberg accepted it companionably and struck a match for Johnson, too, who said, "Thanks, Goldie." Piggott was telling about the time—it was during a train wreck—when he had been cuffed to a homicidal maniac for fourteen solid hours: "I was so jittery I smacked him on the jaw every ten minutes to keep him quiet." They guffawed.

Young was complaining to the patrolman, "Hell, I was on the Harlem run for six years. Up there you use your knee first and ask questions afterward. Shiv artists. The whole bastardly lot of 'em."

"I don't know," said the patrolman doubtfully. "I've known some that were white men. You take Zilgitt."

"What difference does it make?" Young glanced down at their prisoner. "He's squirrel bait, anyway. Where there's no sense there's no feeling."

The man lying at their feet had his mouth going a little, as if he was chewing on something.

"Hey," said Goldberg. "What's he doing that for?"

"Doing what?" Inspector Queen shouldered in, alarmed.

"Look at his mouth, Inspector!"

The Inspector dropped to the concrete and grasped Cazalis's jaw.

"Watch it, Inspector," someone laughed. "They bite."

The mouth opened docilely. Young flashed a light into it over Inspector Queen's shoulder.

"Nothing," said the Inspector. "He was chewing on his tongue."

Young said, "Maybe the Cat's got it," and most of them laughed again.

"Hurry it up, Doctor, will you?" said the Inspector.

"In a minute." The intern was wrapping Celeste in a blanket; her head kept lolling.

Jimmy was trying to fend off the other ambulance man. "Scatter, scatter," he said. "Can't you see McKell is in conference?"

"McKell, you've got blood all over your mouth and chin."

"I have?" Jimmy felt his chin, looked at his fingers with surprise.

"Mister, you bit halfway through your lower lip."

"Come onnnnn, Celeste," crooned Jimmy. Then he yelped. The ambulance man kept working on his mouth.

It had turned colder suddenly, but no one seemed to notice. The fog was thinning rapidly. There was a star or two.

Ellery was sitting on the trash can. "My Wild Irish Rose" was going patiently in his head, like a hurdy-gurdy. Several times he tried to turn it off but it kept going.

There was another star.

The back windows of the surrounding buildings were all bright and open; it was very cheerful. Crammed with heads and shoulders. Box seats. Arena, that was it. The pit. *It*. They couldn't possibly see *It*, but they could hope, couldn't they? In New York, hope dwells in every eye. A dwindling old building. A sidewalk excavation. An open manhole. A traffic accident. *What was it? What's happened? Who got hit? Is it gangsters? What are they doing down there?*

It didn't matter.

The Cat's in his Hell, all's right with the world.

New York papers please copy.

"Jimmy, come here."

"Not now."

"*Extra*," called Ellery, with significance. "Don't you want a bonus?"

Jimmy laughed. "Didn't I tell you? They fired me last week."

"Get to a phone. They'll make you editor."

"The hell with them."

"It's worth a million to them."

"I've got a million."

Ellery rocked on the trash can. The screwball was really a card. Swell kid, Jimmy. Ellery laughed again, wondering why his hand felt so queer.

The third floor windows at the rear of 486 East 29th were all filled, too.

They don't know. The name of Soames goes down in history and they're sitting up there wondering whose name they'll read in the papers.

"Here she is," announced the intern. "Greetings, Miss, and may I be the first to congratulate you?"

Her bandaged hands went to her throat.

Jimmy mumbled to the other one, "Will you get the devil off my lip? Baby, it's me. It's all over. *Fini.* Jimmy, baby. Remember me?"

"Jimmy."

"She recognizes me! All over, baby."

"That horrible . . ."

"It's all over."

My Wiiiiild Irish Rooooose . . .

"I was hurrying along First Avenue."

"Practically a grandmother. This iodine dispenser said so."

"He pulled me in as I passed. I saw his face and then it was dark. My neck."

"Save it, save your strength for a little later, Miss Phillips," said the Inspector genially.

"All over, baby."

"The Cat. Where is he? Jimmy, where is he?"

"Now stop shaking. Lying right over there. Just an alley cat. See? Look. Don't be afraid."

Celeste began to cry.

"It's all over, baby." Jimmy had his arms around her and they rocked together in a little puddle.

Wonder where they think Celeste is. Down here "helping out," probably. Clara Barton stuff . . . And is it not a battlefield? The Battle of First Avenue. After sending McKell's Marauders out on cavalry reconnaissance, General Queen feinted with Phillips's

Corps and engaged the enemy with his Centre Str ... Ellery thought he spied the dark head of Marilyn Soames among the other heads, but then he untwisted his neck and rubbed the back of it. *What was in that beer?*

"Okay, Doc, okay," the Inspector was saying. "Over here now."

The intern stooped over Cazalis, looked up. "Who did you say this is?" he asked sharply.

"He got a hard one in the groin. I don't want to move him till you say it's all right."

"This man is Dr. Edward Cazalis, the psychiatrist!"

Everybody laughed.

"Thanks, Doc," said Detective Young, winking at the others. "We're beholden to you."

They laughed again.

The intern flushed. After a while he got to his feet. "Hold him up and he'll make it. Nothing serious."

"Upsadaisy!"

"Say, I'll bet he was pulling a fakeroo all the time."

"Young, you better practice up that knee action."

"Watch him, watch him."

He was making a strong effort to move his legs, mincing along half on his toes like a student ballet dancer, his knees not quite supporting him.

"Don't look," Jimmy said. "It's not the least bit important."

"It is. I want to. I promised my—" But then Celeste shuddered and looked away.

"Keep that street out there cleared." The Inspector looked around. "Hold it." The procession stopped and Cazalis seemed grateful. "Where's Ellery?"

"Over there, Inspector."

"Hey."

"What's the matter with him?"

My Wiiiiild Ir ...

The trash can clattered and rolled a few feet.

"He's hurt."

"Doctor!"

The intern said, "He passed out. His hand is fractured. Easy . . ."

Easy. Easy does it, a mere five months' worth of sniff and dig and hunt and plot—twenty-one weeks of it; to be exact, twenty-one weeks and one day, one hundred and forty-eight days from a soft rap on the door of an East 19th Street apartment to a hard smash to a man's head in a First Avenue alley; from Abernethy, Archibald Dudley to Phillips, Celeste, alias Sue Martin, Girl Spy; from Friday, June 3, to Saturday, October 29; point four-o-four per cent of a single year in the life of the City of New York, during which period one of the City's numerous hatchetmen cut down the population of the Borough of Manhattan by nine lives although, to be sure, there was that little matter of the Metropol Hall panic and the rioting that followed; in the sum, however, statistical chicken feed lost in Bunyan's barnyard, and what was all the excitement about?

Easy does it.

Easy does it, for the Cat sat in a hard chair under photographic light and he was not the tails-lashing chimera of the broken metropolitan dream but a tumbledown old man with shaking hands and an anxious look, as if he wanted to please but not quite sure what was required of him. They had found a second salmon-pink cord of tussah silk on his person and at the rear of one of the locked filing cabinets in his Park Avenue office a cache of two dozen others of which more than half were dyed the remembered blue; he had instructed them where to look and he had picked out the right key for them from the assortment in his key case. He said he had had the cords for many years; since late in 1930, when he was on a tour around the world after retiring from his obstetrical practice. In India a native had sold him the cords, representing them to be old strangling cords of thuggee origin. Later, before putting them away, he had dyed them blue and pink. Why had he saved them all these years? He looked bewildered. No, his wife had never known about them; he had been alone when he purchased them in the bazaar and he had kept them hidden afterward . . . His head slanted readily to their questions and he answered in a courteous way, although there were stretches when he became uncommunicative or slightly erratic. But the rambling episodes were few; for the most part he caught the pertinent past in brilliant focus, sounding quite like the Dr. Cazalis they had known.

His eyes, however, remained unchanged, staring, lenslike.

Ellery, who had come there directly from Bellevue Hospital with Celeste Phillips and Jimmy McKell, sat to one side, his right hand in a splint, listening and saying nothing. He had not yet run down; he still had a feeling of unreality. The Police Commissioner and the District Attorney were also present; and at a little past 4:30 A.M. the Mayor hurried in, paler than the prisoner.

But the grimy old man in the chair seemed not to see any of them. It was a deliberate avoidance, they all felt, dictated by a kind of tact. They knew how plausible such madmen could be.

In the main, his account of the nine murders was remarkable for its detail. Barring his few lapses from clarity, which might well have resulted from pain, confusion, emotional and physical exhaustion—had they not known what he really was—his confession was excellent.

His least satisfactory reply came in response to Ellery's only contribution to the night's inquisition.

When the prisoner had nearly concluded, Ellery leaned forward and asked: "Dr. Cazalis, you've admitted that you hadn't seen any of these people since their infancy. As individuals, therefore, they couldn't possibly have meant anything to you. Yet obviously you had something against them. What was it? Why did you feel you had to kill them?"

Because the conduct of the psychotic appears unmotivated only when judged in the perspective of

243

reality—that is, by more or less healthy minds viewing the world as it is . . .

Said Dr. Cazalis.

The prisoner twisted in his chair and looked directly at the source of Ellery's voice, although because of the lights beating on his bruised face it was plain that he could not see beyond them.

"Is that Mr. Queen?" he asked.

"Yes."

"Mr. Queen," said the prisoner in a friendly, almost indulgent tone, "I doubt that you're scientifically equipped to understand."

Sunday's morning was full-grown when they got away from the reporters. Jimmy McKell sprawled in a corner of the taxi with Celeste in his arms and in the other corner Ellery pampered his immobilized hand, looking out the window on his side not for reasons of delicacy but because he wanted to see through it.

The City looked different this morning.

Felt, smelled, sounded different.

New.

The air had a tune in it. Maybe it was the church-bells. Churches were bellowing their wares downtown and up, East Side to west. *Adeste fideles!* Come and get it!

In the residential sections delicatessens, bakeries, newsstands, drugstores were busy opening.

An El train went bucketing by somewhere.

A newsboy, bluepawed.

Occasionally an early riser appeared, rubbing his hands together, walking smartly.

At taxi stands cabs stood parked. Bootleg radios going. Drivers intent.

People began collecting around them.

New York was stretching.

Waking up.

New York awoke and for a week or two the ugly vision tarried. Had radio's celebrated planetary invasion of Earth been real, people would have stood in long lines afterward to view the Martian remains and wonder at their gullibility. Now that the monster was localized in a cage, where it could be seen, heard, pinched, reported, read about, even pitied, New York queued up. The clarity of hindsight engagd the facts of postmortem and out of it came citywide conversation pieces in shame, a safe and even enjoyable exercise for all. The Cat was merely a demented old man; and what was one lunatic against a city? File and forget; Thanksgiving was coming.

New York laughed.

Still, like his British cousin from Cheshire, the Cat lingered in his grin atfer the rest of him had vanished. It was not the grin of the old man in the cell; that old man did not grin. It was the grin of the dream monster. And there were the children, with shorter memories but fresher senses. Parents had still to contend with nightmares. Not excluding their own.

Then, on the morning after Armistice Day, the body of a young girl later identified as Reva Xavinzky, of Flushing, was found in various places about Jamaica Bay. She had been ravished, mutilated, dismembered, and decapitated. The familiar horrors of this case, its recognizably atrocious details, instantly diverted public attention; and by the time the murderer, an ex-Army deserter with a typical history of the sexual psychopath, was caught, the diversion—at least insofar as adults were concerned—was complete. Thereafter the word "cat" raised no grislier image in the mind's eye of the average New Yorker than that of a small domestic animal characterized by cleanliness, independence, and a useful appetite for mice. (That the case of Reva Xavinzky, performed a like service for younger New York may be questioned; but most parents seemed to feel that with Thansgiving and Christmas hovering, the Cat would be supplanted in their children's dreams by turkey and Santa Claus. And perhaps they were right.)

There was a minority with special interests, however, who hung on. For some—certain City officials, reporters, psychiatrists, the families of the Cat's victims—this was a matter of duty, or specific assignment, or professional or personal implication. For others—the sociologists, the psychologists, the philosophers—the capture of the nine-times murderer signalized the opportunity to launch a socio-scientific investigation of the City's behavior since early June. The second groups were wholly unconcerned with Edward Cazalis; the first were concerned with no one else.

The prisoner had retreated to a sullen phase. He refused to talk, he refused to exercise, for a time he refused to eat; he appeared to exist only for the visits of his wife, for whom he called constantly. Mrs. Cazalis, accompanied by her sister and brother-in-law, had flown back from Florida on October 30. She had refused to believe the reports of her husband's arrest as the Cat, protesting to reporters in Miami and New York that "there's some mistake. It can't be. My husband is innocent." But that was before her first meeting with him. She emerged from it deathly pale, shaking her head to the press, going directly to the home of her sister. She was there for four hours; then she returned to her own apartment.

It was noted in those first excited days after the monster's capture that it was his mate who took the full impact of the City's animus. She was pointed out, jeered at, followed. Her sister and brother-in-law vanished; no one could or would say where they had gone. Her maid deserted her and she was unable to engage another. She was asked to vacate her apartment by a management that made it frantically clear they would use every means within their power to evict her if she resisted. She did not resist; she placed her household furnishings in storage and moved to a small downtown hotel; and when the hotel management discovered who she was the next morning, she was asked to leave. This time she found quarters in a lugubrious rooming house on Horatio Street in the Village; and it was here that her eldest brother, Roger Braham Merigrew of Bangor, Maine, located her.

Merigrew's visit to his sister did not outlast the night. He had come accompanied by a shadlike man carrying a briefcase; when the two emerged from the Horatio Street building at 3:45 in the morning and found the reporters waiting, it was Merigrew's companion who covered his factor's escape and gave the statement which appeared in the newspapers later that day. "As Mr. Merigrew's attorney I am authorized to state the following: Mr. Merigrew has attempted for several days to persuade his sister, Mrs. Cazalis, to rejoin her kin in Maine. Mrs. Cazalis refused. So Mr. Merigrew flew down to renew his appeal in person. Mrs. Cazalis still refuses. There is nothing further Mr. Merigrew can do, therefore he is returning home. That's all there is to this." Asked by reporters why Mr. Merigrew did not remain by his sister's side in New York, the Maine attorney snapped, "You'll have to ask Mr. Merigrew that." Later, a Bangor paper managed to get a few words from Merigrew. He said, "My sister's husband is insane. Ther's no cause to stand by a murdering lunatic. It's not fair to us, the publicity and so on. Any further statement will have to come from my sister." The Merigrews owned large conservative business interests throughout New England.

So Mrs. Cazalis faced her ordeal alone, living in a squalid Village room, dogged by reporters, visiting her husband, and growing daily wilder-eyed and more silent.

She engaged the famous attorney, Darrell Irons, to defend her husband. Irons was uncommunicative, but it was rumored that he was having his hands full. Cazalis, it was said, "refused" to be defended and would not co-operate with the psychiatrists Irons sent endlessly to his cell. Stories began to circulate of maniacal rages, attempted physical violence, incoherent ravings on the part of the prisoner; those who knew Darrell Irons stated that he had inspired them and that most likely, therefore, they were not true. It was clear what Irons's defense would be, for the District Attorney seemed determined to prosecute Cazalis as a man who knew the nature and quality of his acts, who had demonstrated in his daily life even during the period of his crimes his capacity to act rationally and who therefore, under legal definition, must be considered "sane," no matter what he may have been under the medical definition. The District Attorney set considerable store, it was said, by the prisoner's conversations with the Mayor's Special Investigator and Inspector Richard Queen of Police Headquarters on the night of the Lenore Richardson investigation, when he had outlined his "theory" of the Cat case as pointing to a psychotic pure and simple. This had been the calculated act of a calculating murderer, the D.A. was said to hold, purposely turning the investigation into a channel of "gibbering idiocy" the more effectually to divert attention from the responsible mentality behind the stranglings.

A dramatic trial was forecast.

Ellery's interest in the case flagged early. He had lived with it far too long at too steep a pitch to experience anything but exhaustion after the events of the night of October 29–30. He found himself trying not merely to forget the past but to dodge the present. The present, at least, would not to be evaded; it insisted on applying pomp to circumstance. There were Athenian honors, press and radio-television interviews, a hundred invitations to address civic groups and write articles and investigate unsolved crimes. He managed to back away from most of these with approximate grace. The few he could not avoid left him irritable and profane. "What's the matter with you?" demanded his father. "Let's say," snapped Ellery, "that success has gone to my head." The Inspector puckered; he was no stranger to migraine, either. "Well," he said cheerfully, "at least this time it's not caused by failure."

Ellery continued to fling himself from chair to chair.

One day he decided he had located the infection. It was the boil of pressure. But not of the past or the present; of the future. He was not finished. On the morning of January 2, in one of the larger courtrooms under the gray dome of the Supreme Court building in Foley Square, a Mr. Justice-Somebody would make his blackrobed entrance from chambers and one Edward Cazalis, alias the Cat, would go on trial charged with murder. And in this trial one Ellery Queen, Special Investigator to the Mayor, would be a major witness for the people. There would be no release for him until that ordeal was passed. Then he could go about his business purged of the whole corrupting mess.

Why the trial should cause him such twinges Ellery did not attempt to diagnose. Having discovered—as he thought—the source of his malady, he adjusted his psychic screws to the inevitable and turned to other matters. By this time Reva Xavinzky had been collated and the spotlight probed elsewhere. He was able almost to relax. Even to think about getting back to writing. The novel he had neglected since August 25 lay in its lonely grave. He exhumed it and was surprised to find it as alien as any tax roll papyrus dug out of the Nile delta after three thousand years. Once, long ago, he had labored greatly on this, and now it had the historic smell of shards. *Look on my Works, ye Mighty, and despair!* Despairing, Ellery dropped the primitive effort of his pre-Cat days into the fire.

And sat him down to compose a newer wonder.

But before he could settle his feet on the bottom drawer, there was an agreeable interruption.

Jimmy McKell and Celeste Phillips were being wed and it seemed that Mr. Queen, in his single person, was to constitute the wedding party.

"Exclusive," grinned Jimmy, "by McKell."

"Jimmy means," signed Celeste, "that his father hit the roof and won't come."

"He's biting the Chippendale," said Jimmy, "because his hitherto invincible weapon—disownery? disownment?—has turned to womanish water in his hand, now that I'm buckled into Grandfather's millions. And Mother'd no sooner got over sopping up the tears than she started planning a twenty-thousand guest wedding. So I said the hell with it—"

"And we got our license, we've taken our Wasser-manns—"

"Successfully," added Jimmy, "so would you hand my bride over to me in City Hall at 10:30 tomorrow morning, Mr. Q?"

They were married between the Arthur Jackson Beals of Harlem and the Gary G. Cohens-to-be of Brownsville, Brooklyn; the City Clerk did them distinguished honor by going no more than half so rapidly as usual; Mr. Queen bussed the bride with a fervent "At last!"; and afterward there were only eighteen reporters and cameramen waiting for them in the hall. Mrs. James Guymer McKell exclaimed that she couldn't imagine how in the world they had all known, because she and Jimmy hadn't breathed a word to anyone but Ellery . . . and her groom growled an invitation to his ex-fellow-journalists to hoist a few on him, whereupon the augmented party set out for La Guardia Airport and the wedding luncheon was imbibed in a cocktail lounge, with Parlay Phil Gonachy of the *Extra* crying the square dance which somehow followed. At the climax of the thunderous quadrille the Airport police appeared, causing certain strict constitutionalists among the working guests to defend with camera, bottle, and bar stool the sacred freedom of the press and enabling the happy couple to slip away with their sponsor.

"Whither do you fly with your unravished bride?" inquired Mr. Queen in a slightly wobbly tone. "Or is said question none of my olfactory business?"

"It is entirely *comme il faut*," replied Mr. McKell with the grandeur of one who has also given generous lip service to the sacraments of Reims and Epernay, "since we fly no-whither," and he steered his bride gallantly exitward.

"Then why La Guardia?"

"A ruse to mislead those roistering anteaters. Equerry!"

"We're spending our honeymoon at the Half-Moon Hotel," confided the bride with a blush as a cab rushed up. "You're positively the only one who knows *that*."

"Mrs. McKell, I shall guard your secret with my honor."

"Mrs. McKell," murmured Mrs. McKell.

"All my life," said her husband in a whisper that shot heads around twenty feet away, "I have yearned for a winter's honeymoon among the frolicking Polar Bears of Coney Island." And Mr. McKell yelled to the apprehensive hack, "Okay, White Fang. Mush!"

Ellery observed their exhaust fondly as they rode off into the smog.

After that he found it joy to settle down to work. Ideas for a new mystery novel flowed like the wedding party's champagne; the only problem was to keep a sober judgment.

One morning Ellery looked around to find Father Christmas breathing down his neck. And he saw with some astonishment that New York's Yule was to be white; overnight, 87th Street sparkled. A Samoyed rolling in the snow across the street made him think of the arctic huskies; and thus he was reminded of the James McKells and their Coney Island honeymoon among the curious tribe of New Yorkers who called

251

themselves the Polar Bears. Ellery grinned, wondering why he had not heard from Jimmy and Celeste. Then it occurred to him that he had, and he began looking through his deserted mail, an accumulation of several weeks.

He found Jimmy's note in the middle of the heap.

We like it Ellery. We *like* it.

If you have a mind to crack a friendly jeroboam for auld lang syne, the McKells are receiving in the back room of Kelly's Bar on East 39th at 2 P.M. tomorrow for all of the tribe of Jurgen. We still haven't found an apartment and are bedding down with various disreputable characters. I *won't* take my *wife* to a hotel.

JAMES

P.S. If you don't show, we'll see you at the Assizes.
P.P.S. Mrs. McK. sends love.   J.

The postmark was ten days old

The McKells and, Chrismas . . . This called for heroism.

A half hour later Ellery was up to his armpits in lists, and a half hour after that he was sallying forth in galoshes.

Fifth Avenue was already a speckled swamp. The plows were still working in the side streets but along the Avenue they had toiled all night like beetles rolling dung and the brown-spattered snowplows challenged the agility of jaywalkers and squeezed motor traffic into an impossible bottleneck.

A white Christmas, everybody was saying, shuffling through the slush, sneezing and coughing.

At Rockefeller Center Noel was being caroled and in the Plaza, dwarfed by a hundred-foot tree raped from some Long Island estate, the skaters were whizzing along to a determined version of "Jingle Bells."

Santas in wrinkled red suits clanged at almost every corner, shivering. Shop windows were faery glimpses into the magic wood of advertising. And everywhere people slipped and sloshed, and Ellery slipped and sloshed with them, wearing the glazed frown by which

252

you may know all New Yorkers, in the last week before Christmas.

He dodged in and out of great stores, trampling on little children, pushing and being pushed, clawing at merchandise, shouting his name and address, writing out checks—until, in midafternoon, his master list was reduced to a single uncrossed-off name.

But beside that name stood a large, repulsive question mark.

The McKells were the nice problem. Ellery had not sent them a wedding gift in view of the uncertainty surrounding their future habitat. At the time he had thought that by Christmas they would surely be settled, whereupon he could combine the nuptial gift with the seasonal; and here was the annual Miracle and neither the problem of the McKells' residence nor the nature of his gifts to them had been solved. He had kept an eye alerted for inspiration all day. Silver? Glass? Silk?—no, not silk, definitely not silk. Ceramic? He saw a glossy Bubastis and shuddered. Native wood carving, something primitive? An antique? Nothing came, nothing at all.

Until, in late afternoon, Ellery found himself on 42nd Street between Fifth and Sixth Avenues. Before Stern's a Salvation Army lass, a strapping soldier of charity, sang hymns accompanied by a bluing comrade at a portable organ set down in the slush.

The organ made tinkly sounds in the treble and for a moment sounded like a musicbox.

Musicbox.

Musicbox!

They were originally a fad of French exquisites, dispensing snuff to little metallic tunes, but centuries of delight had made them currency in the realm of childhood and their pure elfishness purchased smiles from lovers.

Ellery dropped a dollar in the tambourine and considered his idea excitedly. Something special . . . featuring the Wedding March . . . yes, that was a must . . . inlays of precious woods, mother-of-pearl, cunning stonework . . . a big one, artfully made. An import, of course. The most delicate pieces came from central Europe . . . Swiss. A Swiss musicbox of the most elaborate craftsmanship would be expensive, but hang the expense. It would become a household treasure, a little chest of golden sentiment unawed by the McKell millions, to be kept at their bedside until they were eigh—

Swiss.

Swiss?

Switzerland!

ZÜRICH!

In a twinkling musicboxes, Wedding Marches, Christmas itself were forgotten.

Ellery waded wildly across 42nd Street and dashed through the side entrance into the New York Public Library.

For a point in his plot-in-progress had been bothering him for days. It concerned phobias. Ellery was postulating a significant relationship (of such is the kingdom of mystery writers) among morbid fear of crowds, of darkness, and of failure. Just how he had come to juxtapose these three phobias plotwise he did not know; it was his impression that he had read about their interrelationship, or heard about it, somewhere. But research had failed to turn up the source. It was holding him up.

And now Zürich. Zürich on the Limmat, Athens of Switzerland.

Zürich rang that bell!

For now Ellery remembered having either read or been told that in Zürich, at some recent international meeting of psychoanalysis, precisely such a phobic relationship had been the subject of a paper.

Search in the foreign periodical section of the Library rewarded him in less than an hour.

The source was a *Züricher* scientific journal, one of a pile Ellery was leafing through as he exercised his stiffened German. The entire issue was given over to the proceedings of the convention, which had lasted ten days, and all scientific papers read before it were reprinted in full. The paper he was interested in bore the alarming title of *Ochlophobia, Nyctophobia, and Ponophobia;* but when he glanced through it he found it to contain exactly what he was looking for.

He was about to go back to the beginning to start rereading carefully when an italic note at the end of the article caught his eye.

A familiar name.

—Paper read by Dr. Edward Cazalis of the United States . . .

Of course! It was Cazalis who had been responsible for the birth of the idea. Ellery recalled it all now. It had come up during that September night in the Richardson apartment, in the first hours of the on-scene investigation of Lenore's murder. There had been a lull and Ellery found himself in conversation with the psychiatrist. They had talked about Ellery's fiction and Dr. Cazalis had remarked with a smile that the field of phobias offered Ellery's craft rich stores of material. On being pressed, Cazalis had mentioned work he himself had done on "ochlophobia and nyctophobia" in relation to the development of "ponophobia"; in fact, Ellery remembered his saying, he had read a paper on the subject at a convention in Zürich. And Cazalis had talked for a little about his findings, until they were interrupted by the Inspector and recalled to the sorry business of the night.

Ellery made a face. The brief conversation had sunk into his unconscious under the weight of events, to emerge two months later under pressure, its source forgotten. *Sic semper* the "original" idea.

It was an irony of coincidence that Cazalis should prove responsible for it.

Smiling, Ellery glanced at the footnote again.

—Paper read by Dr. Edward Cazalis of the United States at the night session of 3rd June. This paper was

*originally scheduled for presentation at 10 P.M. However,
the preceding speaker, Dr. Naardvoessler of Denmark, ex-
ceeded his allotted time and did not conclude the reading
of his paper until 11:52 P.M. A motion to adjourn was
withdrawn when President Dr. Jurasse of France, Chairman of the Convention, asserted that Dr. Cazalis had attended all the sessions patiently awaiting the Convention's
pleasure and that, notwithstanding the lateness of the
hour, in view of the fact that this was the concluding session of the Convention, the distinguished Members present
should extend the adjournment hour to enable Dr. Cazalis
to present his paper. This was done* viva voce, *Dr. Cazalis
presented his paper, concluding at 2:03 A.M., and the Convention was adjourned for the year by President Dr.
Jurasse as of 2:24 A.M. 4th June.*

Still smiling, Ellery flipped the journal to the front
cover and glanced at the year of issue.

Now he did not smile. Now he sat staring
at the last digit of the date as it grew rapidly larger,
or as he himself rapidly shrank.

"Drink Me."

He felt—if it could be called feeling—like Alice.

The *Zürcher* rabbit-hole.

And the Looking-Glass.

How did you get out?

At last Ellery got up from the table and
made his way to the information desk outside the
main reading rooms.

He crouched over copies of *Who's Who* and the
latest annual roster of the American Psychiatric Association.

Who's Who . . . Cazalis, Edward.

The national roster of the American Psychiatric
Association . . . Cazalis, Edward.

In each case a single Cazalis, Edward.

In each case the same Cazalis, Edward.

It was really not to be borne.

Ellery returned to his Zürich journal.
He turned the pages slowly.
Calmly.

Anyone watching me is saying: There's a man who's sure of himself. He turns pages calmly. Knows just what's what."

There it was.

> Dr. Fulvio Castorizo, Italy
> Dr. John Sloughby Cavell, Great Britain
> Dr. Edward Cazalis, United States

Of course he'd be listed.
And that old man? Had he been present?
Ellery turned the page.

> Dr. Walther Schoenzweig, Germany
> Dr. Andrés Selborán, Spain
> Dr. Béla Seligmann, Austria

Someone tapped Ellery on the shoulder.
"Closing time, sir."
The room was empty.
Why hadn't they caught it?
He trudged into the hall. A guard directed him to the staircase when he made the wrong turn.
The District Attorney knows his business. His office is topnotch. They're old hands.
He supposed they had backtracked from Katz, Donald, to Petrucchi, Stella, past Richardson, Lenore, to Willikins, Beatrice, the way growing fainter as they retreated in time until, at the five-months-ago mark, it had disappeared to become impassable. But that wouldn't have stopped them. They probably had one or two or even three others they hadn't been able to fix. It would actually not seem necessary to fix each one. Not in so many murders. Not over such a long period in such a peculiar case where the identity of the victim was a detail hardly meriting notice. Six, say, would do the District Attorney nicely. Plus

257

the caught-in-the-act attempt on Celeste-Phillips-thinking-she-was-Marilyn-Soames and the minute-to-minute evidence of his Soames stalk in the days preceding the attempt.

Ellery walked uncertainly up Fifth Avenue. The weather had turned very cold and the slush had frozen in serrated little icehills of dirty gray, rutted and pocked, a relief map of nowhere on which he teetered along.

This will have to be done from home . . . I've got to have a place where I can sit and feel safe.

When the ax falls.

Executions brought to your door.

At no extra charge.

He stopped at a shop window through which a faceless angel with a needlethin torch was trying to fly, and he looked at his watch.

In Vienna it's the middle of the night.

Then I can't go home.

Not yet.

Not till it's time.

He drew back from the thought of facing his father like a turtle rapped on the nose.

Ellery let himself in at a quarter of 4 in the morning.

On the tips of his toes.

The apartment was dark except for a night light in the majolica lamp on the living room table.

He felt refrigerated. The mercury had dropped to five above in the streets and the apartment was only a little less icy.

His father was snoring. Ellery went to the bedroom door and shut it, thievishly.

Then he stole into his study and turned the key. He did not remove his overcoat. Switching on the desk light, he sat down and drew the telephone to him.

He dialed the operator and asked for the Overseas Operator.

There were difficulties.

It was almost 6 o'clock. The steam had just begun to rattle the radiators and he kept his eye apprehensively on the door.

The Inspector was a 6 o'clock riser.

Finally, he got through.

Ellery prayed that his father oversleep as he waited for the Vienna operator to settle matters at her end.

"Here is your party, sir."

"Professor Seligmann?"

"Ja?"

It was an old, old voice. Its bass cracked and a little peevish.

"My name is Ellery Queen," said Ellery in German. "You do not know me, Herr Professor—"

"Incorrect," said the aged voice in English, Oxonian English with a Viennese accent. "You are an author of *romans policiers*, and out of guilt feelings for the many crimes you commit on paper you also pursue malefactors in life. You may speak English, Mr. Queen. What do you want?"

"I hope I haven't caught you at an inopportune moment—"

"At my age, Mr. Queen, all moments are inopportune except those devoted to speculations about the nature of God. Yes?"

"Professor Seligmann, I believe you are acquainted with the American psychiatrist, Edward Cazalis."

"Cazalis? He was my pupil. Yes?" There was nothing in the voice, nothing at all.

Is it possible he doesn't know?

"Have you seen Dr. Cazalis in recent years?"

"I saw him in Zürich earlier this year. Why do you ask?"

"On which occasion, Herr Professor?"

"At an international convention of psychoanalysis. But you do not tell me why, *mein Herr.*"

"You don't know the trouble Dr. Cazalis is in?"

"Trouble? No. What is this trouble?"

"I can't explain now, Professor Seligmann. But

it's of the greatest importance that you give me exact information."

The line wheezed and keened and for a moment Ellery thought: *Let us pray.*

But it was only the mysterious defects of the transoceanic process coming up through Professor Seligmann's silence.

He heard the old voice again.

Growling this time.

"Are you Cazalis's friend?"

Am I?

"Yes, I'm Cazalis's friend," said Ellery.

"You hesitate. I do not like this."

"I hesitated, Professor Seligmann," said Ellery carefully, "because friendship is a word I weigh."

He thought he had lost, but there was a faint chuckle in his ear and the old man said: "I attended the last few days of the Zürich meeting. Cazalis was present, I heard him read his paper on the night of the last session and I kept him up until long past dawn afterward in my hotel room telling him how absurd I thought it was. Are you answered, Mr. Queen?"

"You have an excellent memory, Herr Profesor."

"You question it."

"Forgive me."

"I am reversing the usual process of senescence. My memory is apparently the last to go." The old voice sharpened. "You may rely on the accuracy of the information."

"Professor Seligmann—"

There was a word, but it was swallowed up by such a howl of atmospheric expletive that Ellery snatched the receiver from his ear.

"Herr Professor Seligmann?"

"Yes. Yes. Are you—?" But then he faded, bolting into space.

Ellery cursed. Suddenly the line was clear.

"Herr Queen! Yes?"

"I must see you, Professor Seligmann."

"About Cazalis?"

"About Cazalis. If I fly to Vienna at once, will you see me?"

"You would be coming to Europe for this alone?"

"Yes."

"Come."

"Danke schön. Auf Wiedersehen."

But the old man had already broken the connection.

Ellery hung up.

He's so damned old. I hope he lasts.

His European flight was a bother from beginning to end. There was trouble about his visa, long talks with the State Department, much questioning and headshaking and form-filling. And passage seemed an impossibility; everyone was flying to Europe, and everyone who flew was a person of terrestial importance. Ellery began to realize what a very small tuber he was in the vast potato patch of world affairs.

He spent Christmas in New York after all.

The Inspector was magnificent. Not once in those days of pacing did he question the purpose of Ellery's trip. They merely discussed ways and means and the impediments.

But the Inspector's mustache grew noticeably ragged.

On Christmas Day Ellery cabled Professor Seligmann that he was being delayed by transportation and other nuisances but that he expected clearance at any hour.

The hour arrived late on December 28, in time to save the crumbs of Ellery's sanity.

Exactly how his father managed it Ellery never learned, but at dawn on December 29 he found himself on a conspicuously special plane in the company of persons of obvious distinction, all of whom were unmistakably bound on missions of global gravity. He had no idea where the plane was going or when it was scheduled to arrive. He heard murmurs of "London," "Paris," and such, but he could detect no Strauss

261

waltzes, and to judge from the pursed blankness that met his worried inquiries the *Wiener Wald* was something in Moscow.

Neither his nails nor his stomach survived the Atlantic crossing.

When they did touch soil, it was fog-choked and British. Here a mysterious delay occurred. Three and a half hours later they took off again and Ellery sank into a doze. When he awoke it was to no thunder of motors. He sat in a great hush. As far as he could make out through his window, they had landed on an Arctic ice field; his very corpuscles were frozen. He nudged his companion, a U.S. Army officer. "Tell me, Colonel. Is our destination Fridtjof Nansen Land?"

"This is France. Where you going?"

"Vienna."

The colonel pushed out his lips and shook his head.

Ellery doggedly began to work his glaciated toes. Just as the first motor exploded, the co-pilot tapped his shoulder.

"Sorry, sir. Your space is required."

"What!"

"Orders, sir. Three diplomats."

"They must be very thin," said Ellery bitterly, getting up. "What happens to the bum?"

"You'll be put up at the field, sir, till they can find space for you on another ship."

"Can't I stand? I promise not to sit on anybody's lap and I'll gladly drop off over the Ringstrasse by parachute."

"Your bag's already off, sir. If you don't mind . . ."

Ellery spent thirty-one hours in a whistling billet, surrounded by the invisible Republic of France.

When he did reach Vienna, it was by way of Rome. It seemed impossible, but here he was on a frozen railway station with his bag and a little Italian priest who had unaccountably clung to him all the way from Rome and a sign somewhere that said *West-*

bahnhof, which was certainly in Vienna, so he was in Vienna.

On New Year's Day.

Where was Professor Seligmann?

Ellery began to worry about the Viennese fuel situation. He had a frostbitten recollection of engine trouble, a forced landing after tumbling over and over among the stars like a passenger on a space ship out of control, and a miserable railway train; but his chief memory was of the cold. As far as Ellery could make out, Europe was in the Second Ice Age; and he fully expected to locate Professor Seligmann imbedded in the heart of a glacier, like a Siberian mastodon, in a perfect state of preservation. He had telephoned Seligmann from Rome, giving the old man such information as he had had about his Italian plane's scheduled arrival. But he had not foreseen the journey through outer space and the groaning aftermath of the miserable train. Seligmann was probably getting pneumonia at . . . which airfield had that been?

The hell with it.

Two figures approached, crunching the icy platform. But one was a saber-toothed porter and the other a *Schwester* of some Austrian Roman Catholic order and neither satisfied Ellery's conception of a world-famous psychoanalyst.

The *Schwester* hurried the little Italian priest away and the saber-toothed porter came dashing up, full of colloquialisms and bad breath. Ellery found himself engaged in a battle of unconquerable tongues. Finally he left his bag in the fellow's charge, although not with confidence; the porter looked exactly like Heinrich Himmler. And he went sleuthing for a telephone. An excited female voice answered. "Herr Kavine? But is not Herr Professor with you? *Ach,* he will die in the cold! He must meet you. You are to wait, Herr Kavine, to wait where you are. *Westbahnhof?* Herr Professor will find you. He said it!"

"*Bitte schön,*" muttered Herr Kavine, feeling like Landru; and he returned to the platform and the glacial epoch. And waited again, stamping, blowing on his fingers, and catching only every fifth word of the porter's. Probably the coldest winter Austria's had in seventy-nine years, he thought. It always is. Where was the *Föhn*, that lecherous Lurleian breeze from the Austrian Alps which reputedly caressed the jeweled hair of Danube's Queen? Gone, gone with all the winds of myth and fantasy. Gone with *Wiener Blut, leichtes Blut,* now a sullen mass of crimson icicles; gone with the *Frühlingsstimmen,* the spring voices, stilled by the throttling winter and the shrilling of boys crying the postwar *Morgenblätter,* such as they were; gone with the *Geschichten aus dem Wiener Wald,* now tales imprisoned in an antique musicbox which was forever broken . . . Ellery shivered, stamped, and blew as the disguised Himmler whined to him about *die guten, alten Zeiten.*

In the gas chambers, Ellery thought unreasonably. Tell it to Hitler, he thought.

An der schönen, blauen Donau . . .

Ellery kept his refrigerated feet pumping and blew *pfuis* on the whole postwar European world.

Professor Seligmann came along at a little after 10 o'clock. The mere sight of that huge body, made huger by the black sheeplined greatcoat collared with Persian lamb and topped with a Russian-style *bashlyk,* was thawing; and when he took one of Ellery's disembodied members in his great, dry, warm hands Ellery melted to the inner man. It was like wandering lost over the earth and coming unexpectedly upon the grandfather of your tribe. The place did not matter; where the patriarch was, there was home. Ellery was struck by Seligmann's eyes particularly. In the lava of that massive face they were eternal fumaroles.

He barely noticed the changes in the Karlsplatz and on the Mariahilferstrasse as they rode in the psychoanalyst's ancient Fiat, driven by a scholarly looking chauffeur, into the Inner City through toppling streets toward the Universität district where the old man lived. He was too agreeably occupied in warming himself at his host.

"You find Vienna not as you expected?" asked Professor Seligmann suddenly.

Ellery started; he had been trying to ignore the shattered city. "It's been so many years since I was here last, Herr Professor. Since long before the War—"

"And the Peace," said the old man with a smile. "We must not overlook the Peace, Mr. Queen. Those difficult Russians, *nyet?* Not to mention those difficult English, those difficult French, and—*bitte schön*—those difficult Americans. Still, with our traditional *Schlamperei,* we manage to drag along. After the first War there was a song popular in Vienna which went, *'Es war einmal ein Walzer; es war einmal ein Wien.'* And we survived. Now we are singing it again, when we do not sing *'Stille Nacht, heilige Nacht.'* Everywhere in Vienna people are speaking of *die guten, alten Zeiten.* How do you say this? 'The good old days.' We Viennese swim in nostalgia, which has a high saline content; that is how we remain afloat. Tell me about New York, Herr Queen. I have not visited your great city since 1927."

Ellery, who had flown an ocean and crisscrossed half a continent to talk about something else, found himself giving a Times Square sightseeing busman's description of postwar Manhattan. And as he talked his sense of time, numbed by his hyperborean flight, began to revive and tick away; and he experienced the shock of recognition, as if this—now—were something very old insisting in a flash on being re-experienced. Tomorrow the trial of Edward Cazalis began and here he was, gossiping with a very old man over four thousand miles away by any route. A pulse began to clamor, and Ellery fell silent as the car drew up before a shellpocked apartment building on some broad *Strasse* whose name he had not even bothered to watch for.

Frau Bauer, Professor Seligmann's housekeeper, greeted her aged employer with aspirin, tea, a hot-water bag, and imprecation—and Ellery with a reminiscent frigidity; but the old man brushed her aside with a smiling *"Ruhe!"* and led Ellery by the hand, like a child, into the land of *Gemütlichkeit.*

Here, in Seligmann's study, were the best of the grace and charming intelligence of *Alt Wien.* The décor was twinkly with wit; it had animation, a leisurely joyousness, and it was a little sly in a friendly way. Here the self-conscious new did not intrude; there was nothing of Prussian precision; things had a patina, they were fine and they glowed.

Like the fire. Oh, the fire. Ellery sat in the lap of a motherly chair and he felt life. And when Frau Bauer served a starving man's breakfast, complete to melting, wonderful *Kaffee-kuchen* and pots of rich and aromatic coffee, he knew he was dreaming.

"The best coffee in the world," Ellery said to his host, raising his second cup. "One of the few national advertising claims with the merit of exact truth."

"The coffee, like almost everything else Elsa has served you, comes to me from friends in the United States." At Ellery's blush Seligmann chuckled. "Forgive me, Herr Queen, I am an old *Schuft,* as we say, a scoundrel. You have not crossed an ocean to indulge in my bad manners." He said evenly, "What is this now about my Edward Cazalis?"

So here it was.

Ellery left the motherly chair to stand before the fire like a man.

He said: "You saw Cazalis in Zürich in June, Professor Seligmann. Have you heard from him since?"

"No."

"Then you don't know what's been going on in New York this summer and fall?"

"Life. And death."

"I beg pardon?"

The old man smiled. "I assume it, Mr. Queen. Has it not always? I do not read newspapers since the war begins. That is for people who like to suffer. I, I do not like to suffer. I have surrendered myself to eternity. For me there is today this room, tomorrow

266

cremation, unless the authorities cannot agree to allow it, in which case they may stuff me and place me in the clock tower of the *Rathaus* and I shall keep reminding them of the time. Why do you ask?"

"Herr Professor, I've just made a discovery."

"And what is that?"

Ellery laughed. "You know all about it."

The old man shook silently. He didn't when I phoned him from New York, thought Ellery, but he's done some catching up since.

"You do, don't you?"

"I have made some inquiries since, yes. Was it so evident? Sit down, Mr. Queen, sit down, we are not enemies. Your city has been terrorized by a paranoid murderer who strangled nine people, and now Edward Cazalis has been arrested for the crimes."

"You don't know the details."

"No."

Ellery sat down and related the story, beginning with the discovery of Archibald Dudley Abernethy's body and ending with the capture of Cazalis in the First Avenue alley. Then he briefly indicated the subsequent conduct of the prisoner.

"Tomorrow, Professor Seligmann, Cazalis's trial begins in New York, and I'm in Vienna—"

"To what purpose?" The old man regarded Ellery through the reek of his meerschaum. "I treated Cazalis as a patient when he came first to Vienna with his wife eighteen years ago, he studied under me subsequently, he left—I believe in 1935—to return to America, and since that time I have seen him once. This summer. What is it you want of me, Herr Queen?"

"Help."

"Mine? But the case is concluded. What more can there be? I do not understand. And if there is more, in which way could I be of assistance?"

"Yes." Ellery fingered his cup. "It must be confusing. Especially since the evidence against Cazalis is so damning. He was captured in the act of attempting a tenth murder. He directed the police to the hiding place of a stock of strangling cords and they found

267

where he said they would be, in the locked medical files in his office. And he confessed to the previous nine murders in considerable detail." Ellery set his cup down with care. "Professor Seligmann, I know nothing of your science beyond, let's say, some intelligent layman's understanding of the differences among neurotic behavior, neurosis, and psychosis. But in spite of—or perhaps because of—my lack of knowledge in your field I've been experiencing my own brand of tension, arising from a rather curious fact."

"And that is?"

"Cazalis never explained his . . . forgive me for hesitating . . . his motive. If he's psychotic, his motives proceed from false views of reality which can have only clinical interest. But if he's not . . . Herr Professor, before I'm satisfied, I've got to know what drove Cazalis to those murders."

"And you believe I can tell you, Herr Queen?"

"Yes."

"How so?" The old man puffed.

"You treated him. Moreover, he studied under you. To become a psychiatrist he had himself to be analyzed, a mandatory procedure—"

But Seligmann was shaking his great head. "In the case of a man so old as Cazalis was when he began to study with me, Mr. Queen, analysis is not a mandatory procedure. It is a most questionable procedure, Mr. Queen. Very few have been successfully analyzed at the age of 49, which is how old he was in 1931. Indeed, the entire project was questionable because of his age. I attempted it in Cazalis's case only because he interested me, he had a medical background, and I wished to experiment. As it happened, we were successful. Forgive me for interrupting—"

"At any rate, you analyzed him."

"I analyzed him, yes."

Ellery hitched forward. "What was wrong with him?"

Seligmann murmured: "What is wrong with any of us?"

"That's no answer."

"It is one answer, Mr. Queen. We all exhibit neurotic behavior. All, without exception."

"Now you're indulging your *Schufterei*, if that's the word." The old man laughed delightedly. "I ask you again, Herr Professor: What was the underlying cause of Cazalis's emotional upset?"

Seligmann kept puffing.

"It's the question that's brought me here. Because I know none of the essential facts, only the inconclusive superficial ones. Cazalis came from a poverty-laden background. He was one of fourteen children. He abandoned his parents and his brothers and sisters when a wealthy man befriended and educated him. And then he abandoned his benefactor. Everything about his career seems to me to point to an abnormal ambition, a compulsive overdrive to success—including his marriage. While his professional ethics remained high, his personal history is characterized by calculation and tremendous energy. And then, suddenly, at the apex of his career, in his prime—a breakdown. Suggestive."

The old man said nothing.

"He'd been treated for a mild case of what they called 'shell shock' in the first war. Was there a connection? I don't know. Was there, Herr Professor?"

But Seligmann remained silent.

"And what follows this breakdown? He abandons his practice, one of the most lucrative in New York. He allows his wife to take him on a world cruise, apparently recovers . . . but in Vienna, world's capital of psychoanalysis, another breakdown. The first collapse had been ascribed to overwork. But to what was the second collapse, after a leisurely cruise, ascribable? Suggestive! Professor Seligmann, you treated him. What caused Cazalis's breakdowns?"

Seligmann took the pipe from his mouth. "You ask me to disclose information, Mr. Queen, of which I came into possession in my professional capacity."

"A nice point, Herr Professor. But what are the ethics of silence when silence itself is immoral?"

The old man did not seem offended. He set the pipe down. "Herr Queen. It is evident to me that you have come not for information so much as for confirmation of conclusions which you have already reached on the basis of insufficient data. Tell me your conclusions. Perhaps we shall find a way of resolving my dilemma."

"All right!" Ellery jumped up. But then he sat down again, forcing himself to speak calmly. "At the age of 44 Cazalis married a girl of 19 after a busy life devoid of personal relationships with women although in his work all his relationships were with women. During the first four years of their married life Mrs. Cazalis gave birth to two children. Dr. Cazalis not only cared for his wife personally during her pregnancies but performed both deliveries. Neither infant survived the delivery room. A few months after the second fatality in childbirth, Cazalis broke down—and retired from obstetrics and gynecology, never to go back to them.

"It seems to me, Professor Seligmann," said Ellery, "that whatever was wrong with Cazalis reached its climax in that delivery room."

"Why," murmured the old man, "do you say this?"

"Because . . . Professor Seligmann, I can't speak in terms of libido and mortido, Ego and Id. But I have some knowledge of human beings, and the sum of whatever observations I've been able to make of human behavior, and of my own and others' experience of life, impels me to the conclusion.

"I observe the fact: Cazalis turns his back with cold purpose on his childhood. Why? I speculate. His childhood was predominated by a mother who was always either carrying a child or having a child, by a laborer-father who was always begetting them, and by a horde of other children who were always getting in the way of his wishes. I speculate. Did

270

Cazalis hate his mother? Did he hate his brothers and sisters? Did he feel guilt because he hated them?

"And I observe the career he sets for himself, and I say: Is there a significant connection between his hate for maternity and his specialization—as it were—in maternity? Is there a nexus between his hate for the numerous progeny of his parents and his determination to make himself an expert in the science of bringing more children into the world?

"Hate and guilt—and the defenses against them. I've put two and two together. Is this permitted, Herr Professor? Is this valid?"

Seligmann said, "One tends to oversimplify in your sort of mathematics, *mein Herr*. But go on."

"Then I say to myself: Cazalis's tensions lie deep. His guilts are profound. His defenses against the unconscious becoming conscious—if that's a fundamental identification of neurotic behavior—are elaborate.

"Now I observe his marriage. Immediately, it seems to me, new tensions—or extensions of old ones—set in. Even a so-called normal man of 44 would find a first marriage, after a life of overwork and little socializing—would find such a marriage, to a 19-year-old girl, unsettling and conflicting. In this case the young bride was from a thinblooded New England strain. She was emotionally of delicate balance, rather rarefied, on the frigid side, and almost certainly inexperienced. And Cazalis was as he was. I speculate.

"I say: It seems to me Cazalis must at once have found himself involved in serious sexual dissatisfactions, frustrations, and disagreeable conflicts. I say: There must have been recurrent episodes of impotence. Or his wife was unresponsive, unawakened, or actually repelled. He began to feel an erosive inadequacy, perhaps? Yes, and a resentment. It wouldn't be unnatural. He, the highly successful entrepreneur of the biological process, can't master the technique of his own marriage. Also, he loves his wife. She is an intelligent woman, she has a fragile charm, reserve, breeding; even today, at 42, she's handsome; at 19 she must have been extremely attractive. Cazalis loves her as only a man can love who is old enough to be the father of the highly desirable object of his affections. And he's inadequate.

"So I say: A fear is born. Undoubtedly this fear arises from altogether different causes, but it expresses itself in a disguised form: he becomes afraid he will lose his young wife to another man."

Ellery drank some coffee and Seligmann waited. The ormolu clock on the mantelpiece kept a sort of truce between them.

"The fear is nourished," continued Ellery, "by the great difference in their ages, temperaments, backgrounds, interests. By the demands of his practice, his long hours at the hospital assisting other men's wives to bring other men's children into the world, by his enforced professional absences from Mrs. Cazalis—frequently at night.

"The fear spreads like cancer. It gets out of control. Cazalis becomes violently suspicious of his wife's relationships with other men, no matter how slight. no matter how innocent—especially of her relationships with younger men.

"And soon this fear grows into an obsession.

"Professor Seligmann." Ellery eyed the old Viennese. "Was Edward Cazalis obsessively jealous of his wife during the first four years of their marriage?"

Seligmann picked up his pipe and rather deliberately set about knocking it out. "Your method, Mr. Queen, is one unknown to science," he said with a smile. "But this of great interest to me. Continue." He stuck the empty pipe in his mouth.

"Then Mrs. Cazalis becomes pregnant." Ellery frowned. "One could imagine at this point Cazalis's fears would recede. But no, he's passed the point of reasonableness. Her very pregnancy feeds his jealousy and becomes suspect. Isn't this a confirmation of his suspicions? he asks himself. And he insists—he insists—on taking care of his wife himself. He is undoubtedly excessively devoted, solicitous, and watchful. Gestation unfortunately takes nine months. Nine months in which to watch a fetus grow. Nine months in which to torture himself with a question which at last bursts forth in the full deformity of obsession: Is this child mine? Is it?

"Oh, he fights it. He fights an endless battle. But the enemy is discouraging. Kill it in one place and it springs up, viciously lively as ever, in another. Does he ever tell his wife of his suspicions? Accuse her outright of infidelity? Are there scenes, tears, hysterical denials? If so, they only serve to strengthen his suspicions. If not, if he keeps his raging fears bottled up, then it's even worse.

"Mrs. Cazalis comes to term, goes through labor.

"And there she lies.

"In the delivery room.

"Under his hands.

"And the baby dies.

"Professor Seligmann, do you see how far I've traveled?"

The old man merely waggled the pipe in his jaws.

"Mrs. Cazalis becomes pregnant a second time. The process of suspicion, jealousy, self-torment, and uncertainty-certainty repeats itself. Again Cazalis insists on seeing his wife through her pregnancy. Again he insists on performing the delivery.

"And again his baby dies in the delivery room.

"His second child, dead like the first.

"*Under his hands.*

"Under those powerful, delicately nerved, practiced surgeon's hands.

"Professor Seligmann." Ellery loomed over the old man. "You're the only being on the face of the earth in a position to tell me the truth. Isn't it fact that when Edward Cazalis came to you eighteen years ago for psychiatric treatment he had broken down under a dreadful load of guilt—*the guilt of having murdered his own two children in the act of delivery?*"

After a moment old Seligmann took the empty pipe from his lip. He said carefully, "For a physician to murder his own unborn children under the delusion that they were another's—this would be psychosis,

273

Herr Queen, no? You could not expect him to follow his subsequent brilliant, stable career, most particularly in the field of psychiatry. And my position, what would that have been? Still, you believe this, Herr Queen?"

Ellery laughed angrily. "Would it make my meaning clear if I amended my question to conclude: 'the guilt of *fearing* he had murdered his own two children'?"

The old man looked pleased.

"Because it was the logical development of his neurosis, wasn't it? He had excessive feelings of guilt about his hates and a great need for punishment. He, the eminent obstetrician, had brought thousands of other men's children into the world alive, but under his hands his own children had died. *Did I kill them?* he agonized. *Did my obsessive jealousy and suspicions make my hands fail? Did I want them to be born dead and my hands saw to it that they were? I did want them to be born dead. And they were born dead. Therefore I killed them.* The terrible illogic of neurosis.

"His common sense told him they had been breech births; his neurosis told him he had performed countless other breeches successfully. His common sense told him that his wife, let's say, was not ideally constructed for motherhood; his neurosis told him her babies were fathered by other men. His common sense told him he had done his efficient best; his neurosis told him that he had not, that he might have done this or that, or not done that or this, or that had he not insisted on performing the deliveries himself but placed his wife in the hands of another obstetrician, his children would have survived. And so on.

"Because he had an overwhelming compulsion to believe it, within a short time Cazalis had convinced himself that he'd murdered both babies. A little of this mental *Schrecklichkeit* and he broke. When his wife took him traveling and he came to Vienna—odd coincidence, wouldn't you say, Professor?—lo, he collapsed again. And went to you. And you, Professor

Seligmann, you probed and analyzed and treated and . . . you cured him?"

When the old psychoanalyst spoke, his rumbling voice held a growl. "It is too many years and I know nothing of his emotional problems since. Even at the time there was a menopausal complication. If in the past few years he has been pushing himself too hard—at the present stage of his life . . . Often in the middle age people are unable to defend themselves by means of neurotic symptoms and they break down completely into a psychosis. We find, for example, that paranoid schizophrenia is frequently a disease of late middle age. Still, I am surprised and troubled. I do not know. I should have to see him."

"He still has guilt feelings. He must have. It's the only explanation for what he's done, Professor."

"What he has done? You mean, Mr. Queen, murdering nine persons?"

"No."

"He has done something else?"

"Yes."

"In addition to the nine murders?"

"To the exclusion," said Ellery, "of the nine murders."

Seligmann rapped the bowl of his meerschaum on the arm of the chair.

"Come, *mein Herr*. You speak in riddles. Precisely what is it that you do mean?"

"I mean," said Ellery, "that Cazalis is innocent of the charge for which he is going to trial in New York tomorrow morning."

"Innocent?"

"I mean, Professor Seligmann, that Cazalis did not kill those nine people. Cazalis is not—and never was —the Cat."

• 13

Seligmann said, "Let us expose Fate, whose other name is Bauer." He bellowed, "Elsa!"

Frau Bauer appeared, pure jinni.

"Elsa—" began the old man.

But Frau Bauer interrupted, stumbling from a secure "Herr Professor" into uncertain English so that Ellery knew her remarks were intended for his ears also. "You have breakfast eaten when it is already lunch. Lunch you have not eaten. Now comes your time to rest." Fists on bony hips, Frau Bauer glared challenge to the non-Viennese world.

"I'm so very sorry, Professor—"

"For what, Mr. Queen? Elsa." The old man spoke gently, in German. "You've listened at the door. You've insulted my guest. Now you wish to rob me of my few remaining hours of consciousness. Must I hypnotize you?"

Frau Bauer whitened. She fled.

"It is my only weapon against her," chuckled the old man. "I threaten to put her under hypnosis and send her into the Soviet zone to serve as the plaything of Moscow. It is not a matter of morals with Elsa; it is sheer horror. She would as soon get in bed with the Antichrist. You were telling me, Mr. Queen, that Cazalis is innocent after all?"

"Yes."

The old man sat back, smiling. "Do you arrive at this conclusion by way of your unique scientifically unknown method of analysis, or is it based upon fact? Such fact as would, for example, satisfy your courts of law."

"It's based on a fact which would satisfy anyone above the mental age of five, Professor Seligmann," Ellery retorted. "Its very simplicity, I think, has obscured it. Its simplicity and the fact that the murders have been so numerous and have dragged on for so long. Too, it's been the kind of case in which the individuality of the victims has tended to blur and blend as the murders multiplied, until at the end one looked back on a homogeneous pile of carcasses, so many head of cattle passed through the slaughter pen. The same sort of reaction one got looking at the official pictures of the corpses of Belsen, Buchenwald, Oswiecim, and Maidanek. No particularity. Just death."

"But the fact, Mr. Queen." With a flick of impatience, and something else. And suddenly Ellery recalled that Béla Seligmann's only daughter, married to a Polish Jewish doctor, had died at Treblinka. Love particularizes death, Ellery thought. And little else.

"Oh, the fact," he said. "Why, it's a mere matter of beginners' physics, Professor. You attended the Zürich convention earlier this year, you told me. Exactly when this year?"

The white brows met. "The end of May, was it not?"

"The meeting lasted ten days and the concluding session was held on the night of June 3. On the night of June 3 Dr. Edward Cazalis of the United States read a paper entitled *Ochlophobia, Nyctophobia, and Ponophobia* in the convention hall before a large audience. As reported in a *Zürcher* scientific journal, the speaker scheduled to precede Cazalis, a Dane, ran far over his allotted time, to virtually the adjournment hour. Out of courtesy to Dr. Cazalis, however, who had attended all the sessions—according to a footnote in the journal—the American was permitted to deliver his paper. Cazalis began reading around midnight and finished at a few minutes past 2 o'clock in the morning. The convention was then adjourned for the year. The official adjournment time was 2:24 A.M. 4th June."

Ellery shrugged. "The time difference between Zürich and New York being six hours, midnight of

June 3 in Zürich, which is when Cazalis began reading his paper to the convention, was 6 P.M. June 3 in New York; 2 A.M. June 4 in Zürich, which is about when Cazalis finished reading his paper there, was 8 P.M. June 3 in New York. Assuming the absurd—that Cazalis whisked himself from the convention hall immediately on adjournment or even as he stepped off the platform at the conclusion of his talk, that he had already checked out of his hotel and had his luggage waiting, that the slight matter of his visa had been taken care of, that there was a plane ready to take off for the United States at the Zürich airport the instant he reached there (for which specific plane Cazalis had a ticket, notwithstanding Dr. Naardvoessler's windiness, the unusual hour, or the impossibility of having foreseen the delay), that this plane flew to New York nonstop, that at Newark Airport or La Guardia Cazalis found a police motorcycle escort waiting to conduct his taxi through traffic at the highest possible speed—assuming all this nonsense, Herr Professor, at which hour could Edward Cazalis have reached midtown Manhattan, would you say? The earliest conceivable hour?"

"I have a poor acquaintance with the progress—if that is the word—of aeronautics."

"Could the entire leap through space—from a platform in Zürich to a street in Manhattan—have been accomplished in three and a half to four hours, Professor Seligmann?"

"Obviously not."

"So I telephoned to you. Whereupon it came out that Edward Cazalis did not go from the convention hall to an airfield that night. Came out not as speculation but as fact. For you told me you had kept Cazalis up talking in your hotel room in Zürich all through that night until 'long past dawn.' Surely that would mean, at the very earliest, 6 A.M.? Let's say 6 A.M., Professor, to please me; it must have been, of course, even later. 6 A.M. in Zürich on the 4th of June would be midnight in New York on June 3. Do you recall my giving you the date of the first Cat murder? The murder of the man named Abernethy?"

"Dates are a nuisance. And there were so many."

"Exactly. There were so many, and it was so long ago. Well, according to our Medical Examiner's report, Abernethy was strangled *'around midnight'* of June 3. As I said, a matter of simple physics. Cazalis has demonstrated many talents, but the ability to be in two places thousands of miles apart at the same moment is not one of them."

The old man exclaimed, "But, as you say, this is so basic! And your police, your prosecutors, have not perceived this physical impossibility?"

"There were nine murders and an attempted tenth. The time-stretch was almost exactly five months. Cazalis's old obstetrical files, the strangling cords hidden in his psychiatric case history files, the circumstances of his capture, his detailed and voluntary confession—all these have created an over-whelming presumption of his guilt. The authorities may have slipped through overconfidence, or carelessness, or because they found that in the majority of the murders Cazalis could physically have committed the crimes. Remember, there is no direct evidence linking Cazalis with any of the murders; the people's entire case must rest on that tenth attempt. Here the evidence is direct enough. Cazalis was captured while he was in the act of tightening the noose about the throat of the girl who was wearing Marilyn Soames's borrowed coat. The noose of tussah silk. The Cat's noose. *Ergo,* he's the Cat. Why think of alibis?

"On the other hand, one would expect the defense attorneys to check everything. If they haven't turned up Cazalis's alibi, it's because of the defendant himself; when I left New York, he was being extremely difficult. After attempting to get along without legal help altogether. And then there's no reason why a lawyer, merely because he is a lawyer for the defense, should be immune to the general atmosphere of conviction about his client's guilt.

"I suspect, however, a more insidious reason for

279

the alibi's remaining undiscovered, one that goes to the roots of the psychology which has operated in this case virtually from its outset. There has been a neurotic anxiety of epidemic proportions to catch the Cat, drive a stake through his heart, and forget the whole dreadful mass incubus. It's infected the authorities, too. The Cat was a *Doppelgänger*, his nature so tenuously drawn that when the authorities actually laid their hands on a creature of flesh and blood who fitted the specifications . . ."

"If you instruct me whom to address, Mr. Queen," rumbled old Seligmann, "I shall cable New York of my having detained Cazalis all night until past dawn of the 4th June in Zürich."

"We'll arrange for you to make a formal deposition. That, plus the evidence of Dr. Cazalis's attendance throughout the Zürich convention and of his return passage to the United States, which can't have begun earlier than June 4, will clear him."

"They will be satisfied that, having been unable physically to murder the first one, Cazalis did not murder the others?"

"To argue the contrary would be infantile, Professor Seligmann. The crimes were characterized and accepted as the work of the same individual almost from the beginning. And with abundant reason. The source of the supply of victims' names alone confirms it. The method used in selecting the specific victims from the source of supply confirms it. The identical technique of the strangulations confirms it. And so on. The strongest point of all is the use in all nine murders of the strangling cords of tussah silk—cords of East Indian origin, exotic, unusual, not readily procurable, and obviously from the same source."

"And, of course, in a sequence of acts of violence of a psychotic nature showing common characteristics—"

"Yes. Multiple homicides of this kind are invariably what we call 'lone wolf' operations, acts of a single disturbed person. There won't be any trouble on that score . . . Are you sure you wouldn't like to rest now, Professor Seligmann? Frau Bauer said—"

The old man dismissed Frau Bauer with a scowl as he reached for a tobacco jar. "I begin to glimpse your destination, *mein Herr*. Nevertheless, take me by the hand. You have resolved one difficulty only to be confronted by another.

"Cazalis is not the Cat.

"Then who is?"

"The next question," nodded Ellery.

He was silent for a moment.

"I answered it between heaven and earth, Professor," he said at last with a smile, "in a state of all but suspended animation, so you'll forgive me if I go slowly.

"To arrive at the answer we must examine Cazalis's known acts in the light of what we've built up about his neurosis.

"Just what was it Cazalis *did?* His known activities in the Cat cases begin with the tenth victim. His very choice of 21-year-old Marilyn Soames as the tenth victim must have arisen from his application of the same selective technique employed by the Cat in hunting through Cazalis's old obstetrical case cards—I used the technique myself and arrived at the same victim. Anyone of reasonable intelligence could have done it, then, who had access to both the facts of the preceding nine crimes and the files.

"Having employed the Cat's method in selecting the next victim in the series, what did Cazalis then proceed to do?

"As it happened, Marilyn Soames works at home, she was extemely busy, and she didn't regularly come out into the streets. The Cat's first problem in each case must have been to become familiar with the face and figure of the victim he had marked for destruction. Had the real Cat, then, been working on Marilyn Soames he would have attempted to lure her from her home in order to be able to study her appearance. This was precisely what Cazalis did. By a subterfuge, he lured Marilyn Soames to a crowded public place where he could 'study' her in 'safety.'

"For days and nights Cazalis scouted the girl's neighborhood and reconnoitered the building where she lives. Just as the Cat would have done. Just as the Cat must have done in the previous cases.

"While he was apparently on the prowl, Cazalis exhibited eagerness, cunning, disappointment of an extravagant nature at temporary frustrations. The kind of behavior one would have expected the unbalanced Cat to evince.

"Finally, on that climactic, October night, Cazalis waylaid a girl who resembled Marilyn Soames in height and figure and who was accidentally wearing Marilyn Soames's coat, dragged this girl into an alley, and *began* to strangle her with one of the tussah silk cords associated with the Cat's previous homicidal activities.

"And when we captured him Cazalis 'confessed' to being the Cat and reconstructed his 'activities' in the nine previous murders . . . including an account of the murder of Abernethy, committed when Cazalis was in Switzerland!

"Why?

"Why did Cazalis imitate the Cat?

"Why did he confess to the Cat's crimes?"

The old man was listening intently.

"This was patently not the case of a deluded man's identifying himself with the violent acts of another by merely claiming, as many psychotics did in those five months—every sensational crime brings people forward—to have committed the Cat's crimes of record. No. Cazalis *proved* he was the Cat by thought, plan, and action; by creating a new and typical Cat crime based upon exact knowledge and a clearly painstaking study of the Cat's habits, methods, and technique. This was not even imitation; it was a brilliant interpretation, consisting of omissions as well as of commissions. For example, on the morning when Cazalis actually entered the Soames apartment house, while he was out in the court, Marilyn Soames came downstairs to the vestibule and stood there for several minutes looking over her mail. At this moment Cazalis re-entered the hall. No one was apparently about except Cazalis and his victim; it was early morning, the street beyond was deserted. Nevertheless, at that time Cazalis made no move to attack the girl. Why? Because to have done so would have broken the consistent pattern of the Cat's murders; those had been committed, to the last one, after dark—and this broad daylight. Such scrupulous attention to detail could not conceivably have come out of an ordinary psychotic identification. Not to mention the self-restraint exhibited.

"No, Cazalis was rational and his deliberate assumption of the Cat's role in all its creative vigor was therefore rationally motivated."

"It is your conclusion, then," asked Seligmann, "that Cazalis had no intention of strangling the girl to death in the alley? That he merely made the pretense?"

"Yes."

"But this would presuppose that he knew he was being followed by the police and that he would be captured in the act."

"Of course he knew, Professor. The very fact that he, a rational man, set out to prove he was the Cat when he was not raises the logical question: Prove it to whom? His proof did not consist merely of a confession, as I've pointed out. It consisted of elaborate activities stretching over a period of many days; of facial expressions as well as of visits to the Soames neighborhood. A deception presupposes that there is someone watching to be deceived. Yes, Cazalis knew he was being followed by the police; he knew that each move he made, each twist of his lips, was being noted and recorded by trained operatives.

"And when he slipped the silk cord around Celeste Phillips's neck—the girl he mistook for his victim —Cazalis was playing the final scene for his audience. It's significant that the tenth case was the only case in which the intended victim was able to cry out loudly enough to be heard. And while Cazalis tightened the cord sufficiently to leave realistic marks on the girl's neck, it's also significant that he permitted her to get her hands between the noose and her throat, that he did not knock her unconscious as the Cat had done in at least two of his assaults, and that Celeste Phillip' was able within a short time of the attack to speak and act normally; what slight and temporary damage she sustained was chiefly the result of her own struggles and her terror. What Cazalis would have done had we not run into the alley to 'stop' him is conjectural; probably he would have permitted the girl to scream long enough without fatal injury to insure interference from some outside source. He could be certain detectives weren't far away in the fog, and it was a congested section of the City.

"He wanted to be caught in the act of a Cat murder-attempt, he planned to be caught in the act of a Cat murder-attempt, and he was successful in being caught in the act of a Cat murder-attempt."

"Whereupon it becomes evident," murmured the old man, "that we approach our destination."

"Yes. For a rational man to assume another's guilt and to be willing to suffer another's punishment, the rational mind can find only one justification: the one is shielding the other.

"Cazalis was concealing the Cat's identity.

"Cazalis was protecting the Cat from detection, exposure, and punishment.

"And in doing so Cazalis was punishing himself out of deeply buried feelings of his own guilts as they centered about the Cat and his emotional involvement with the Cat.

"Do you agree, Professor Seligmann?"

But the old man said in a curious way: "I am only an observer along this road you travel, Mr. Queen. I neither agree nor disagree; I listen."

Ellery laughed. "What did I now know about the Cat?

"That the Cat was someone with whom Cazalis

284

was emotionally involved. With whom he was therefore in a close relationship.

"That the Cat was someone whom Cazalis had an overpowering wish to protect and whose criminal guilt is tied in Cazalis's mind to his own neurotic guilts.

"That the Cat was a psychotic with a determinable psychotic reason for seeking out and murdering people who a generation and more before had been brought into the world by Cazalis the obstetrician.

"That, finally, the Cat was someone who has had equal access with Cazalis to his old obstetrical records, which have been stored in a locked closet in his home."

Seligmann paused in the act of putting the meerschaum back into his mouth.

"Is there such a person, I asked myself? To my certain knowledge?

"There is. To my certain knowledge," said Ellery. "Just one.

"Mrs. Cazalis."

"For Mrs. Cazalis," said Ellery, "is the only living person who fits the specifications I have just drawn.

"Mrs. Cazalis is the only living person with whom Cazalis is emotionally involved in a close relationship; in his closest relationship.

"Mrs. Cazalis is the only living person whom Cazalis would have a compulsion to protect and for whose guilt Cazalis would feel intensely responsible . . . whose criminal guilt would be tied in his mind to his own neurotic guilt feelings.

"Mrs. Cazalis has a determinable—the only determinable—psychotic reason for seeking out and murdering people her husband had brought into the world.

"And that Mrs. Cazalis has had equal access with her husband to his obstetrical records is self-evident."

Seligmann did not change expression. He seemed neither surprised nor impressed. "I am chiefly interested in pursuing your third point. What you have called Mrs. Cazalis's 'determinable psychotic reason' for murdering. How do you demonstrate this?"

"By another extension of that method of mine you've characterized as unknown to science, Herr Professor. I knew that Mrs. Cazalis had lost two children in giving birth. I knew, from something Cazalis told me, that after the second delivery she was no longer able to bear children. I knew that she had thereafter become extremely attached to her sister's only child, Lenore Richardson, to the point where her niece was more her daughter than her sister's. I knew, or I had convinced myself, that Cazalis had proved inadequate to his sexual function as a husband. Certainly during the long period of his breakdowns and subsequent treatment he must have been a source of continual frustration to his wife. And she was only 19 when they married.

"From the age of 19, then," said Ellery, "I saw Mrs. Cazalis as leading an unnatural, tense existence, complicated by strong maternal desires which were thwarted by the deaths of her two infants, her inability to have another child, and what could only have been a highly unsatisfactory and unsettling transference of her thwarted feelings to her niece. She knew that Lenore could never really be hers; Lenore's mother is neurotic, jealous, possessive, infantile, and interfering—a source of unending trouble. Mrs. Cazalis is not an outgoing individual and apparently she never was. Her frustrations, then, grew inward; she contained them . . . for a long time.

"Until, in fact, she was past 40.

"Then she cracked.

"I say, Professor Seligmann, that one day Mrs. Cazalis told herself something that thenceforward became her only reason for living.

"Once she believed that, she was lost. Lost in the distorted world of psychosis.

"Because, Professor, I believe the oddest thing occurred. Mrs. Cazalis did not have to know that her husband thought he had murdered their children at birth; in fact, she undoubtedly did not know it—in her rational life—or their marriage would hardly have survived the knowledge for so many years. *But I think she arrived at approximately the same point in her psychosis.*

"I think she finally told herself: *My husband gave thousands of living babies to other women, but when I was to have my own babies he gave me dead ones. So my husband killed them. He won't let me have my children, so I won't let them have their children. He killed mine; I'll kill theirs.*" And Ellery said, "Would it be possible for me to have more of that wonderful non-Viennese coffee, Professor Seligmann?"

"Ach." Seligmann reached over and tugged at a bellpull. Frau Bauer appeared. "Elsa, are we barbarians? More coffee."

"It's all ready," snapped Frau Bauer in German. And as she returned with two fat, steaming pots and fresh cups and saucers, she said, "I know you, you old *Schuft.* You are in one of your suicidal moods." And she flounced out, banging the door.

"This is my life," said the old man. He was regarding Ellery with bright eyes. "Do you know, Herr Queen, this is extraordinary. I can only sit and admire."

"Yes?" said Ellery, not quite following but grateful for the gift of the jinni.

"For you have arrived, by an uncharted route, at the true destination.

"The trained eye looks upon your Mrs. Cazalis and one says: Here is a quiet, submissive type of woman. She is withdrawn, seclusive, asocial, frigid, slightly suspicious and hypercritical—I speak, of course, of the time when I knew her. Her husband is handsome, successful, and in his work—his obstetrical work—he is constantly in contact with other women, but in their married life her husband and she have disturbing conflicts and tensions. She has managed nevertheless to make an adjustment to life; in—as it were—a limping fashion.

"She has done nothing to warrant special notice.

In fact, she has always been overshadowed by her husband and dominated by him.

"Then, in her 40s, something occurs. For years, secretly, she has been jealous of her husband's rapport with younger women, his psychiatric patients—for it is interesting to note that in recent years, as Cazalis told me in Zürich, he has had an almost totally female clientele. She has not required 'proof,' for she has always been of a schizoid tendency; besides, there was probably nothing to 'prove.' No matter. Mrs. Cazalis's schizoid tendency bursts forth in a delusional state.

"A frank paranoid psychosis.

"She develops the delusion that her own babies were killed by her husband. In order to deprive her of them. She may even think that he is the father of some of the children whose successful deliveries he performed. With or without the idea that her husband is their father, she sets out to kill them in retaliation.

"Her psychosis is controlled in her inner life. It is not expressed to the world except in her crimes.

"This is how the psychiatrist might describe the murderer you have delineated.

"As you see, Mr. Queen, the destination is the same."

"Except that mine," said Ellery, his smile slightly bitter, "seems to have been approached poetically. I recall the artist who kept depicting the stranger as a cat and I warm to his remarkable intuition. Doesn't a tigress—that grandmother of cats—go 'mad' with rage when she is robbed of her cubs? Then, Professor, there's the old saying, *A woman hath nine lives like a cat*. Mrs. Cazalis has nine lives to her debit, too. She killed and she killed until . . ."

"Yes?"

"Until one day Cazalis entertained a ghastly visitor."

"The truth."

Ellery nodded. "It could have come about in one of a number of ways. He might have stumbled on the hiding place of her stock of silk cords and recalled their visit to India years before and her purchase—not his—of the cords. Or perhaps it was one or two of the victims' names striking a chord of memory; then it would require merely a few minutes with his old files to open his eyes. Or he may have noticed his wife acting oddly, followed her, and was too late to avert a tragedy but in quite sufficient time to grasp its sickening significance. He would go back in his mind to the recent past and discover that on the night of each murder he could not vouch for her whereabouts. Also, Cazalis suffers from chronic insomnia and he takes sleeping pills regularly; this, he would realize, had given her unlimited opportunities. And for purposes of slipping in and out of the building at night unobserved by the apartment house employees, there was always Cazalis's office door, giving access directly to the street. As for the daytimes, a woman's daytime excursions are rarely examined by her husband; in our American culture, in all strata, 'shopping' is the magic word, explaining everything . . . Cazalis may even have seen how, in the cunning of her paranoia, his wife had skipped over numerous eligibles on the list in order to strike at her niece—the most terrible of her murders, the murder of the unsatisfying substitute for her dead children—in order that she might maneuver Cazalis into the investigation and through him keep informed as to everything the police and I knew and planned.

"In any event, as a psychiatrist Cazalis would immediately grasp the umbilical symbolism in her choice of cords to strangle—as it were—babies; certainly the infantile significance of her consistent use of blue cords for male victims and pink cords for females could not have escaped him. He could trace her psychosis, then, to the traumatic source upon which her delusion had seized. It could only be the delivery room in which she had lost her own two children. Under ordinary circumstances this would have been a merely clinical, if personally agonizing, observation, and Cazalis would either have taken the medical and legal steps usual in such cases or, if the prospect of revealing the truth to the world involved too much pain, mortification, and obloquy, he would at the least have put her where she could do no more harm.

"But the circumstances were not ordinary. There were his own old feelings of guilt which had expressed themselves through and revolved about that same delivery room. Perhaps it was the shock of realizing what lay behind his wife's mental illness that revived the guilt feelings he had thought were dissolved. However it came about, Cazalis must have found himself in the clutch of his old neurosis, its tenacity increased a thousandfold by the shock of the discovery that had brought it alive again. Soon he was persuaded by his neurosis that it was all his fault; that had he not 'murdered' their two babies she would not have erupted into psychosis. The sin, then, was his; he alone was 'responsible,' therefore he alone must suffer the punishment.

"So he sent his wife south in the care of her sister and brother-in-law, he took the remaining silk cords from his wife's hiding place and stored them in a place indentifiable with him alone, and he set about proving to the authorities that he, Edward Cazalis, was the monster the City of New York had been hunting frantically for five months. His subsequent 'confession' in detail was the easiest part of it by far; he was fully informed through his affiliation with the case of all the facts known to the police, and upon a foundation of these facts he was able to build a plausible, convincing structure. How much of his behavior at this point and since has been playacting and how much actual disturbance I can't, of course, venture to say.

"And that, Professor Seligmann, is my story," said Ellery in a tightened voice, "and if you have any information that controverts in, this is the time to speak out."

He found that he was shivering and he blamed it on the fire, which was low. It was hissing a little, as if to call attention to its plight.

Old Seligmann raised himself and devoted a few minutes to the Promethean chore of bringing warmth back to the room.

Ellery waited.

Suddenly, without turning, the old man grumbled: "Perhaps it would be wisdom, Herr Queen, to send that cable now."

Ellery sighed.

"May I telephone instead? You can't say much in a cable, and if I can talk to my father a great deal of time will have been saved."

"I shall place the call for you." The old man shuffled to his desk. As he took the telephone, he added with a twitch of humor, "My German—at least on the European side, Mr. Queen—will undoubtedly prove less expensive than yours."

They might have been calling one of the more distant planets. They sat in silence sipping their coffee, attuned to a ring which did not come.

The day was running out and the study began to blur and lose its character.

Once Frau Bauer stormed in. Her bristling entrance startled them. But their unnatural silence and the twilight they sat in startled her. She tiptoed about, switching on lamps. Then, like a mouse, she skittered out.

Once Ellery laughed, and the old man raised his head.

"I've just thought of something absurd, Professor Seligmann. In the four months since I first laid eyes on her, I've never called her or thought of her or referred to her as anything but 'Mrs. Cazalis.'"

"And what should you call her," said the old man grumpily, "Ophelia?"

"I never did learn her Christian name. I don't know it at this moment. Just Mrs. Cazalis . . . the great man's shadow. Yet from the night she murdered her niece she was always there. On the edges. A face in the background. Putting in an occasional—but very important—word. Making idiots of us all, including

291

her husband. It makes one wonder, Herr Professor, what the advantages are of so-called sanity."

He laughed again to indicate that this was pleasantry, a sociable introduction to conversation; he was feeling uneasy.

But the old man merely grunted.

After that, they resumed their silences.

Until the telephone rang.

The line was miraculously clear.

"Ellery!" Inspector Queen's shout spurned the terrestrial sea. "You all right? What are you still doing in Vienna? Why haven't I heard from you? Not even a cable."

"Dad, I've got news for you."

"News?"

"The Cat is Mrs. Cazalis."

Ellery grinned. He felt sadistically petty.

It was very satisfactory, his father's reaction. "Mrs. Cazalis. *Mrs.* Cazalis?"

Still, there was something peculiar about the way the Inspector said it.

"I know it's a blow, and I can't explain now, but—"

"Son, I have news for *you.*"

"News for me?"

"Mrs. Cazalis is dead. She took poison this morning."

Ellery heard himself saying to Professor Seligmann: "Mrs. Cazalis is dead. She took poison. This morning."

"Ellery, who are you talking to?"

"Béla Seligmann. I'm at his home." Ellery took hold of himself. For some reason it was a shock. "Maybe it's just as well. It certainly solves a painful problem for Cazalis—"

"Yes," said his father in a very peculiar tone indeed.

"—because, Dad, Cazalis is innocent. But I'll give you the details when I get home. Meanwhile, you'd better start the ball rolling with the District Attorney.

I know we can't keep the trial from getting under way tomorrow morning, but—"

"Ellery."

"What?"

"Cazalis is dead, too. He also took poison this morning."

Cazalis is dead, too. He also took poison this morning. Ellery thought he was thinking it, but when he saw the look on Seligmann's face he realized with astonishment that he had repeated these words of his father's aloud, too.

"We have reason to believe it was Cazalis who planned it, told her just where to get the stuff, what to do. She's been in something of a fog for some time. They weren't alone in his cell more than a minute or so when it happened. She brought him the poison and they both swallowed a lethal dose at the same time. It was a quick-acting poison; before the cell door could be unlocked they were writhing, and they died within six minutes. It happened so blasted fast Cazalis's lawyer, who was standing . . ."

His father's voice dribbled off into the blue. Or seemed to. Ellery felt himself straining to catch remote accents. Not really straining to catch anything. Except a misty, hard-cored something—something he had never realized was part of him—and now that he was conscious of it it was dwindling away with the speed of light and he was powerless to hold on to it.

"Herr Queen. Mr. Queen!"

Good old Seligmann. He understands. That's why he sounds so excited.

"Ellery, you still there? Can't you hear me? I can't get a thing out of this goddam—"

A voice said, "I'll be home soon, goodbye," and somebody dropped the phone. Ellery found everything calmly confusing. There was a great deal of noise, and Frau Bauer was in it somewhere and then she wasn't, and a man was sniveling like a fool close by while his face was hit by a blockbuster and burning lava tore down his gullet; and then Ellery opened his eyes to find himself lying on a black leather couch

293

and Professor Seligmann hovering over him like the spirit of all grandfathers with a bottle of cognac in one hand and a handkerchief in the other with which he was gently wiping Ellery's face.

"It is nothing, nothing," the old man was saying in a wonderfully soothing voice. "The long and physically depleting journey, the lack of sleep, the nervous excitements of our talk—the shock of your father's news. Relax, Mr. Queen. Lean back. Do not think. Close your eyes."

Ellery leaned back, and he did not think, and he closed his eyes, but then he opened them and said, "No."

"There is more? Perhaps you would like to tell me."

He had such a fantastically strong, safe voice, this old man.

"I'm too late again," Ellery heard himself saying in the most ridiculously emotional voice. "I've killed Cazalis the way I killed Howard Van Horn. If I'd checked Cazalis against all nine murders immediately instead of resting on my shiny little laurels Cazalis would be alive today. Alive instead of dead, Professor Seligmann. Do you see? I'm too late again."

The grandfatherly voice said, "Who is being neurotic now, *mein Herr?*" and now it was not gentle, it was juridical. But it was still safe.

"I swore after the Van Horn business I'd never gamble with human lives again. And then I broke the vow. I must have been really bitched up when I did that, Professor. My bitchery must be organic. I broke the vow and here I sit, over the grave of my second victim. What's the man saying? How do I know how many other poor innocents have gone to a decenter reward because of my exquisite bitchery? I had a long and honorable career indulging my paranoia. Talk about delusions of grandeur! I've given pronunciamentos on law to lawyers, on chemistry to chemists, on ballistics to ballistic experts, on fingerprints of men who've made the study of fingerprints their lifework. I've issued my imperial decrees on criminal investigation methods to police officers with thirty years' training, delivered definitive psychiatric analyses for the benefit of qualified psychiatrists. I've made Napoleon look like a men's room attendant. And all the while I've been running amok among the innocent like Gabriel on a bender."

"This in itself," came the voice, "this that you say now is a delusion."

"Proves my point, doesn't it?" And Ellery heard himself laughing in a really revolting way. "My philosophy has been as flexible and as rational as the Queen's in *Alice*. You know *Alice*, Herr Professor? Surely you or somebody's psychoanalyzed it. A great work of humblification, encompassing all the wisdom of man since he learned to laugh at himself. In it you'll find everything, even me. The Queen had only one way of settling all difficulties, great or small, you'll remember. 'Off with his head!' "

And the fellow was standing. He had actually jumped off the couch as if Seligmann had given him the hotfoot and there he was, waving his arms at the famous old man threateningly.

"All right! All right! I'm really through this time. I'll turn my bitchery into less lethal channels. I'm finished, Herr Professor Seligmann. A glorious career of *Schlamperei* masquerading as exact and omnipotent science has just been packed away forever without benefit of mothballs. Do I convey meaning? Have I made myself utterly clear?"

He felt himself seized, and held, by the eyes.

"Sit down, *mein Herr*. It is a strain on my back to be forced to look up at you in this way."

Ellery heard the fellow mutter an apology and the next thing he knew he was in the chair, staring at the corpses of innumerable cups of coffee.

"I do not know this Van Horn that you mention, Mr. Queen, but it is apparent that his death has upset you so deeply that you find yourself unable to make the simple adjustment to the death of Cazalis which is all that the facts of the case require.

"You are not thinking with the clarity of which you are capable, *mein Herr*.

"There is no rational justification," the deliberate voice went on, "for your overemotional reaction to the news of Cazalis's suicide. Nothing that you could have done would have prevented it. This I say out of a greater knowledge of such matters than you possess."

Ellery began to assemble a face somewhere before him. It was reassuring and he sat still, dutifully.

"Had you discovered the truth within ten minutes of the moment when you first engaged to investigate the murders, the result for Cazalis would have been, I am afraid, identical. Let us say that you were enabled to demonstrate at once that Mrs. Cazalis was the psychotic murderer of so many innocent persons. She would have been arrested, tried, convicted, and disposed of according to whether your laws admitted of her psychosis or held that she was mentally responsible within the legal definition, which is often absurd. You would have done your work successfully and you would have had no reason to reproach yourself; the truth is the truth and a dangerous person would have been removed from the society which she had so greatly injured.

"I ask you now to consider: Would Cazalis have felt less responsible, would his feelings of guilt have been less pronounced, if his wife had been apprehended and disposed of?

"No. Cazalis's guilt feelings would have been equally active, and in the end he would have taken his own life as he has done. Suicide is one of the extremes of aggressive expression and it is sought out at one of the extremes of self-hate. Do not burden yourself, young man, with a responsibility which has not been yours at any time and which you personally, under any circumstances, could not have controlled. So far as your power to have altered events is concerned, the principal difference between what has happened and what might have happened is that Cazalis

296

died in a prison cell rather than on the excellently carpeted floor of his Park Avenue office."

Professor Seligmann was a whole man now, very clear and close.

"No matter what you say, Professor, or how you say it, the fact remains that I was taken in by Cazalis's deception until it was too late to do more than hold a verbal post-mortem with you here in Vienna. I did fail, Professor Seligmann."

"In that sense—yes, Mr. Queen, you failed." The old man leaned forward suddenly and he took one of Ellery's hands in his own. And at his touch Ellery knew that he had come to the end of a road which he would never again have to traverse. "You have failed before, you will fail again. This is the nature and the role of man.

"The work you have chosen to do is a sublimation, of great social value.

"You must continue.

"I will tell you something else: This is as vital to you as it is to society.

"But while you are doing this important and rewarding work, Mr. Queen, I ask you to keep in mind always a great and true lesson. A truer lesson than the one you believe this experience has taught you."

"And which lesson is that, Professor Seligmann?" Ellery was very attentive.

"The lesson, *mein Herr*," said the old man, patting Ellery's hand, "that is written in the Book of Mark. *There is one God; and there is none other but he.*"

A NOTE ON NAMES

If one of the functions of fiction is to hold a mirror up to life, its characters and places must be identified as in life; that is, through names. The names in this story have had to be numerous. For verisimilitude they are common as well as uncommon. In either category, they are inventions; that is to say, they are names deriving from no real person or place known to the Author. Consequently if any real person finds a name in this story identical with or similar to his or her own, or if any place in this story has a nominal counterpart in life, it is wholly through coincidence.

The story has also required the introduction of certain official- and employee-characters of New York City. Where names have been given to characters in this category, if such inventions should prove identical with or similar to the names of real officials and employees of New York City, again the resemblance is coincidental and the Author states in the most positive terms that no real official or employee of New York City has been drawn on in any way. Where names have not been used, only official titles, the same assurance is given. A special point should be made in the case of the characters of the Mayor ("Jack") and the Police Commissioner ("Barney"). Neither the present Mayor and Police Commissioner of the City of New York, nor any past Mayor or Police Commissioner, living or dead, has been drawn on in any way whatsoever.

The list of person- and name-places invented follows. If any occur in the text which do not appear on the list, it is through failure of a weary proofreading eye and the reader should assume its inclusion.

Abernethy, Archibald Dudley
Abernethy, Mrs. Sarah-Ann
Abernethy, Rev.

Bascalone, Mrs. Teresa
Bauer, Frau Elsa, *Austria*
Beal, Arthur Jackson

Castorizo, Dr. Fulvio, *Italy*
Caton, Dr. Lawrence
Cavell, Dr. John Sloughby,
 Great Britain
Cazalis, Dr. Edward
Cazalis, Mrs. Edward
Chorumkowski, Stephen
Cohen, Cary G.
Collins, Barclay M.
Cuttler, Nadine

Devander, Bill

Ellis, Frances

Ferriquancchi, Ignazio
Finkleston, Zalmon
Frankburner, Jerome K.
Frawlins, Constance

Gaeckel, William Waldemar
Goldberg (Detective)
Gonachy, Phil

Hagstrom (Detective)
Heggerwitt, Adelaide
Hesse (Detective)

Immerson, Mrs. Jeanne
Immerson, Philbert
Irons, Darrell

Jackson, Lal Dhyana
Johnson (Detective)
Jones, Evarts
Jurasse, Dr., *France*

Katz, Donald
Katz, Dr. Morvin
Katz, Mrs. Pearl
Kelly's Bar

Kollodny, Gerald Ellis

Larkland, Dr. John F.
"Leggitt, Jimmy"
Legontz, Mrs. Maybelle

MacGayn (Detective)
"Martin, Sue"
Marzupian, Harold
Mayor of New York City
 ("Jack")
McKell, James Guymer
McKell, Monica
Merigrew, Roger Braham
Metropol Hall
Miller, William

Naardvoessler, Dr., *Denmark*
"Nostrum, Paul"

O'Reilly, Mrs. Maura B.
O'Reilly, Rian
O'Reilly, Mrs. Rian

Park-Lester Apartments
Petrucchi, Father
Petrucchi, Mr. and Mrs.
 George
Petrucchi, Stella
Phillips, Celeste
Phillips, Simone
Piggott (Detective)
Police Commissioner of New
 York City ("Barney")
Pompo, Frank

Quigley (Detective)

Registrar of Records, Man-
 hattan Bureau of Vital Rec-
 ords and Statistics of the
 Department of Health
Rhutas, Roselle
Richardson, Mrs. Della
Richardson, Leeper & Com-
 pany
Richardson, Lenore
Richardson, Zachary

Sacopy, Mrs. Margaret
Sacopy, Sylvan
Schoenzweig, Dr. Walther,
   Germany
Selborán, Dr. Andrés, *Spain*
Seligmann, Dr. Béla, *Austria*
Smith, Mrs. Eulalie
Smith, Violette
Soames, Billie
Soames, Mrs. Edna Lafferty
Soames, Eleanor
Soames, Frank Pellman
Soames, Marilyn
Soames, Stanley
Stone, Max
Szebo, Count "Snooky"

Treudlich, Benjamin

Ulberson, Dr. Myron

Velie, Barbara-Ann

Whithacker, Duggin
Whithacker, Howard
Willikins, Beatrice
Willikins, Frederick

Xavinzky, Reva

Young (Detective)

Zilgitt (Detective)